Raven's Blood

Also by Deborah Cannon:

The Raven's Pool
White Raven
Ravenstone
The Pirate Vortex

Raven's Blood

DEBORAH CANNON

Order this book online at www.trafford.com
or email orders@trafford.com

Most Trafford titles are also available at major online book retailers.

Printed in the United States of America.

ISBN: 978-1-4669-1559-6 (sc)
ISBN: 978-1-4669-1560-2 (hc)
ISBN: 978-1-4669-1561-9 (e)

Library of Congress Control Number: 2012902710

Trafford rev. 02/08/2012

 www.trafford.com

North America & international
toll-free: 1 888 232 4444 (USA & Canada)
phone: 250 383 6864 ♦ fax: 812 355 4082

For Anonymous

CHAPTER ONE

September 23, 2010
Hilazon Tachtit, Northern Israel

Jake Lalonde groaned, massaging a pain in his neck that had awakened him. He had slept badly. He had spent the night on the edge between sleep and wakefulness, leaving him questioning if he had slept at all. The camp was up and the crew were fixing breakfast. Some were packing their belongings, preparing for their ascent up the mountain. Jake discarded the jagged rock he was lying on and shrugged off the pain. Then he stuffed his backpack with his things.

He watched the expedition leader give orders to make haste. She wanted to reach the cave by tomorrow afternoon. Her body swayed as she moved, directing preparations. She was fluid, almost ethereal about her movements. There was something odd about Sophia Saveriano, something that drew him to her. It was not anything sexual or emotional, or even intellectual . . . nor anything as simple as curiosity. It was more powerful than that. Like something touched him deeply, lowered him to the very basis of his core. The lowest primitive feeling that existed, the level of pure sensation. He felt solid in her presence. That was the only way he could describe it.

"We must leave now!" she shouted. "Anyone who is not ready will have to catch up on their own."

The expedition started off, cheerfully, along an old goat track peppered with dried dung. The younger members of the crew laughed and told jokes to kill the time. The local guides, surly but polite smiled under their kerchiefs smug in their knowledge of the terrain's peculiar dangers. The hours passed, and single file they climbed rock and scree, mostly silent now. The sun arced into the sky, the light filtered by a grey mist. The trek was difficult. Jake's feet flung dust onto the back of his jeans, while dark splotches of sweat soaked the armpits of his shirt.

Hours later when they stopped, Jake pushed past the grumbling hikers to learn the cause, and saw that two objects poked sharply from the hard earth. The object nearest was the tip of some large bird's wing and beside it lay a severed foot. The bird might have been an eagle, a hawk or a raven, but the foot was human, rotted away to clean bone, whitened by the sun.

"*Witch*," the peasant boy standing beside him spat.

Dust flaked off Jake's lips as he eased his camera bag to the ground. "Why do you think the bones belong to a witch?"

The boy went silent.

"We'll make camp here," Saveriano said.

The sky was red, the grey mist had settled on the outer rim of the valley. Jake dropped his pack and settled his camera bag to the ground, walked to the ridge of the hillside and surveyed the landscape. The air was warm and reeked with the roasted scent of animal waste. Downwind breathing was easier, and he gazed across the hills to rusty pockets of land, speckled with sparse, green scrub and raw, white stone.

When he turned back some sort of stew made of goat meat was ready for dinner. Its piquant aroma evaporated into his nostrils, the flavour strong and exotic. After they ate it was dark, and most of the crew turned in. Jake was restless. He took a flashlight and walked back to where they had seen the bones. He sensed eyes on his back, and he half-hoped Saveriano planned to join him. She was strangely uncommunicative and he had questions for her, many questions. But it seemed the time was never right, and she kept her distance. It was the boy who watched him.

Jake lifted a stick and casually dragged it over the ground. He stopped when he caught sight of one of the crew hunched over the bones in the moonlight. The young man rose, smiled sheepishly. "Weird, eh? But then the locals *are* pretty superstitious.

Well, guess I'll turn in." He shoved his fist into the pocket of his cargo pants and left. Jake squatted to get a closer look. A star was scored into the earth around the bones where no such marking had existed earlier. It resembled the Star of David or Satan's star, but it was neither. He had seen this symbol before. The spicules of each point, radiating from a perfect circle, showed the acute angles of an arrow.

He glanced around. *Hmmm, that was odd.* The boy had disappeared and the young man who had just left was zipping something into a plastic bag.

Jake dropped his gaze to the ground, felt a sudden need to touch base with Vincent. He had agreed to see the mountain caves of Hilazon Tachtit with him, but where was he? Vincent had left word that they should meet in town, but when he failed to show up the expedition had left without him. Was he already at the caves? Jake sent a text, then lifted his lightweight digital videocam, and aimed it downward. He raised his eyes over the camera toward the camp and saw Saveriano staring at him; he switched his attention to the star, and then to the bones that lay in its centre. He pried out a toe bone and examined it. Surely, the bones were archaeological?

But their presence was chilling. The ankle had been cleanly axed.

Before turning in, he checked his cell phone for messages.

Nothing.

He went back to the camp and stopped in front of the expedition leader who had watched his approach.

"Vincent never told you where he was going before he was due to join you here?"

"No," she said. "He did not. I assume something came up."

"Shouldn't he have left a message with someone? He asked me specifically to join him."

"Then that is *his* problem, and *yours*. Not mine. Vincent and I are simply colleagues who happen to be interested in the same thing—at the moment. We agreed that whoever reached the cave first would take possession of its prize. It is not my concern that he has forfeited the race."

"I was unaware there was a race."

"A figure of speech Dr. Lalonde. A figure of speech."

That night Jake tossed and turned. It wasn't the lumpy ground that had him awake. He'd slept on worse. No, it wasn't the ground. It was the dream.

Half awake, half asleep; whispered words, surreal visions; a high-pitched whine in his head. What was happening to him? It was as though he were dreaming someone else's dream, like the dream had been transposed from a stranger's mind into his own.

A dark taste persisted on his tongue. The smell of mould lingered, cupped in the cavities of his sinuses. Was he hallucinating? Or were the sensations the after effects of a rather noxious goat stew? An aura, a scintillating stream waxed out of the shadows of the mountainside, and flowed in a multi-coloured chaos around his ankles. Jake almost shot out of his sleeping bag. But he knew he was asleep, his muscles paralysed, eyes deeply shut, only his thoughts had any life.

This is it then. I must follow her to the sleep of death.

Jake felt himself in the dream, a dream where his eyes and mouth were wide open and his body separated from his mind, and he had no will but to lie back and watch.

The shimmering circled his throat. His hands flew up to stop it, but there was no quitting now. It swelled and sucked and surged, lifting a jagged piece of sculpture into the air. He saw the familiar symbols, recognized the frieze—the slim fragment he had stolen from the cave. It plunged like a living knife toward him.

Heart hammering against his ribs, sweat pouring like hot oil down his neck to his spine, the aura pulsated around him. His vision was dimming, his hearing gone. Arms numb, tongue thick, legs useless as butchered meat. Only his brain remained

clear, a severed link to the reality that was somewhere out there.
Nausea began to rise and a pain exploded in his gut. Shock and
horror, understanding struck him at last. She had lied. Lied!
He was not the one. He was going to die, and that was all. He
fell over backwards, hands raised, his final thought:
"Whatever you do, do not listen to her . . . . To the lies."

Jake sat up in a cold sweat.

It was unlike any dream he had had before.

The next day, around noon, they reached a plateau, flanked
by sheer walls dotted with caves. Jake let his gritty eyes take in
the tumultuous landscape of the red valley where the surrounding
hills sloped to belts of white, arid land. There was no campsite, no
evidence of human activity.

Saveriano moved to the opening of the nearest cave. "I will
go in," she said.

She instructed everyone to make camp on the plateau and
motioned for Jake to take his camera into the cave.

He blinked at the daylight that lit the first few feet of the
interior. He took a flashlight from his backpack and directed it
to the rear. What he saw made his jaw quiver. A mammoth stone
figure stood half interred at the extreme of the walled cavern.
Around the perimeter the ruined wall punctured the earth, and
pale grey shards lay askew on the floor from natural erosion.

What struck him most was not the statue itself—or the
masonry around it. True, this was nothing short of a shrine, and
the statue was obviously female with large breasts, a protruding
belly and swollen hips. But what was curious about the statue
were its accoutrements.

The following morning the archaeologists went to work,
and Jake documented their progress. By the end of the week,
the sculpture was delivered from its vertical tomb, the scrub
on the hillside had dwindled to brown, and the sky was
smoke-coloured.

It was day four of backbreaking physical labour. Quarrying
the crumbling earth and stone was the easy part. The hard part

was persuading the crane up the mountainside to hoist the statue from the cave to the road where it could be transported by truck. Saveriano was pleased when it finally came to rest on a bed of straw inside a monstrous wooden crate and sealed with a fitted lid. When all was secure, she motioned the workmen to load it.

But a bone-splitting human screech exploded from inside the truck. A student bulleted out baggy shorts and hair flying, sweatered arms flapping like a lunatic as though she'd seen a ghost. After listening to an incoherent explanation, Saveriano motioned at the crane to wait, and for Jake to follow her. She put one foot onto the loading ramp, and Jake heaved himself into the truck, rocking the platform, effectively stopping her from entering first. The stench inside the cargo hold punched them both in the lungs. With his shirtsleeve over his nose to filter the smell, he rolled onto his knees. On the bare platform a body lay on its back.

Dread filled his mind; his stomach went cold.

The skin and muscles of the face were desiccated, the head turned to the right. And what he saw in the mouth made him gag. He removed his jacket and covered the head, noticing beneath it a stain of dried blood. Dead, he thought. No doubt about that. But the hands—the hands were something else.

CHAPTER TWO

October 13, 2010
The University of Washington, Seattle, WA

Voices burbled over the shuffle of leaves as students crossed the campus to change classes outside the office window. Angeline Lisbon sat at the desk and glared through splashes of sunshine at the journalist seated opposite her. Cristine Kletter's eyelids batted in sympathy, blue-fingernailed hands folded on her lap, which a few minutes before were tinkering with a Blackberry.

"I'm sorry Angeline. I'm pissed off, too. I spent weeks researching and structuring Jake's interviews for my article. Turns out, his story isn't provocative enough. The boss wants pizzazz, a piece that'll have everyone talking. Something that might have 'documentary' written all over it—something like what Vincent's been doing. It's all about buzz, you know. Sales. Thanks to the Internet subscriptions are down. Everyone is focusing on maximizing sales."

"I understand why your editor would be drawn to Vincent's research. But nothing's conclusive. Everything he's done to date has been pure speculation."

"The boss is fascinated by Vincent's theory. The archaeology of religion and myth is all the rage right now."

"But that's what Jake is doing."

"He's not exactly doing that, Angeline. Look, like I said, I'm sorry. I really am. And I probably shouldn't be talking to you about this, but since Jake hasn't returned from his trip yet, it's better if it comes from you than from an email. Personally, I think his theories are brilliant. But he's been touting the same fairytale

7

for years and he doesn't have any more evidence now than he did when he first made the discovery. If he could give me concrete proof, then yeah, I'd say we'd do a piece on him. Jump all over it, in fact. Even feature him on the cover." Her eyes gleamed with a mixture of sadism and pathos. "The competition's tough. The magazine's going with Vincent's story of a Persian origin of a female Raven cult, that spawned the Mithraic Mysteries."

Angeline leaned over the desk. "Are you serious?"

Vincent had hinted at a major discovery that was going to turn the world on its head. He had kept Cristine in suspense for half a year. She was meeting with him this afternoon; they had made the appointment weeks ago. He was taking a redeye from Rome back to the U.S. and should be in his office at three fifteen.

Angeline sighed. It wouldn't have hit so hard except that the magazine was *the* most prestigious one in the field. And not only that, but it had the widest popular readership in the world. A feature article on Jake's research would have given his career the jump it needed. She settled herself in the swivel chair as the phone rang. The journalist got up to leave, but stopped wrestling with her raincoat when Angeline grabbed her sleeve. A few seconds later, the person with whom Angeline was speaking appeared at the door. He snapped his cell phone shut and smiled as Angeline set the handset down to greet him.

He was clad in navy blue suit, yellow tie and beige trench coat. "The Anthropology Office pointed me your way. Is this Dr. Lalonde's office?" he asked.

Angeline nodded, and released the journalist's arm.

She wiped a hand through her long black hair, irritably aware that she was dressed very inofficiously in a skinny red sweater and tight jeans.

"Thomas Chancellor, Interpol," the agent said, clamping strong fingers around hers.

"Angeline Lisbon," she replied. "I'm afraid Dr. Lalonde isn't here at the moment."

A slim, blue-fingernailed hand cut across her face. "Cristine Kletter. I'm a journalist with *Archaeology Magazine.*"

He returned her grip, flashing a handsome smile. "I know your magazine."

The charm got results and she coloured, did the flirtatious hair thing, and Angeline winced. "I'm here to interview one of Dr. Lalonde's colleagues, Vincent Carpello," Cristine said. "His research is being featured in our summer issue."

"Oh?" Chancellor's eyes narrowed slightly. "And you are in Dr. Lalonde's office instead of Dr. Carpello's because . . . ?"

Her head dipped faintly as she shifted a quick glance at Angeline. "I'm the one to tell him that his story for my magazine will be superseded by Dr. Carpello's. But he isn't here."

"In other words, to use the journalistic jargon, they 'killed' his story?"

She nodded.

Chancellor took a notebook computer out of a nylon satchel that was slung over his shoulder and camped it on the desk. He flipped up the monitor and turned it on. "You don't mind, do you? Since you were both professionally involved with Dr. Carpello, there is something I want you to see."

The computer was a MacBook and it chimed into action almost instantly. Chancellor selected a file and waited the three seconds for it to upload. It was a photograph of a man lying on his back. "I'm afraid he was discovered much too late for help. The body was shipped to Rome by request of the family and will remain there pending investigation."

"The body?" Cristine said.

Angeline's voice came as a gasp. "That's Vincent? He's dead?"

He peered at her curiously. "I'm afraid so."

"What's he doing with his hands?" Cristine asked.

"Rigor mortis."

The lighting was odd in the photograph, late evening sun shooting straight onto the body. A fine mist hovered to one side, red and yellow fading to white. And if this hadn't been a still photo, Angeline would have sworn that the mist was waxing and waning, assuming a female form. The more she stared at the digital image the less she liked what she saw. When she got over the bizarre sight and dismissed the strange-looking mist, she focused on Vincent's fingers. They were curled in an unnatural position, arched as though he were mimicking something specific. But what? Angeline widened the screen to the edge of the image where the shadows hit the wall of wherever it was the body had been discovered. The black shapes cut against the metallic, pale grey surface. This was the interior of a cargo truck, isn't that what the Interpol agent was saying? Why was Vincent making shadow puppets inside a locked freight truck?

A quick intake of breath from Cristine made Angeline realize the journalist had noticed it, too. The shadow cast against the side panel of the truck was eerily familiar.

At one of the bookcases, Cristine lifted a volume and took it back to the desk. She opened it to a page where several Haida raven rattles were pictured.

The shape was identical. Vincent's hands were miming the form of a raven rattle, and the Raven image was pitched acutely against the anaemic wall for everyone to see—a black oblong head with a straight and powerful beak formed by his right fist and first two fingers, while the body of the bird sloped away from the beaked head, fashioned by his left hand.

"This means something to you," the Interpol agent said, breaking into her thoughts.

As if he didn't know. He was a cop; he must have done his homework. Everyone knew that Jake studied the Raven in all its iconic forms. Oh my God. Had Jake gone to Israel instead of Rome? Why would he keep something like this from her?

"Who do I see about getting a key to Dr. Carpello's office?" Chancellor asked.

Angeline snapped out of her shock. She was doing some research for Vincent. She had a key. She was about to answer when she heard the pounding of footsteps outside the door and a student came rushing into the office. His face was flushed, eyes bright with excitement. He started talking as soon as their eyes met, even before he crossed the threshold and saw that she had company. He had terrible news. Someone had broken into Vincent's lab. He stopped his nervous jabber when he realized that Angeline was just staring at him in stunned silence. The others were in the shade of the bookcase, slightly hidden by the door.

Angeline swallowed, turned. "Mr. Chancellor, this is one of Vincent Carpello's students, Adam McIntyre."

"Adam," he said, stepping forward. "Thomas Chancellor from Interpol. I'm investigating Dr. Carpello's death. I am going to have to ask you some questions about the murder. You say his lab was broken into? I'll need you to take me there after I'm finished here."

Murder! Angeline gaped at him. This was the first time he had called the accident 'murder.' When she spoke, her voice cracked and scarcely a sound came out. Then it was like a valve had released and she was talking nonstop. Vincent was dead. Someone had killed him. Why would anyone do that? Questions rattled out one after the other. Vincent might have had his quirks, and she could think of a student or five that wouldn't mind seeing him take early retirement, but kill him?

Chancellor watched her twist a lock of her hair around her middle finger.

He reiterated the circumstances of Vincent Carpello's death. The body was found in the cargo area of a freight truck. Preliminary tests showed that he was killed en route from Italy to Israel. At present, jurisdiction was undetermined. Meanwhile it was the job of the International Police to find out why an Italo-American archaeologist was killed on an archaeological site. "I think that's where you might be able to help us," Chancellor concluded. "What was he working on, Ms. Lisbon?"

Angeline nibbled her lower lip, told him that Vincent was working on an ancient text. The words were in Latin, which was fairly easy to translate, but there were also symbols. The young professor was on the verge of deciphering the symbols. She

11

paused before elaborating. The text depicted a repetitive sequence that was found on numerous friezes in several sites that he had excavated over the years. He dug up mithraea—the shrines of the ancient god Mithras, a religion that was adopted by the Roman military. Most of the temples were in Rome, but other shrines had been discovered in England, Bosnia, France, Germany and even North Africa.

"And the symbols?" Chancellor's tone rose oddly.

"A bird, a cup, a staff, a torch, a diadem and a lamp."

"Mr. Chancellor," Cristine interrupted. "If you don't mind. How exactly does any of this pertain to Vincent's death?"

The Interpol agent had neglected to describe the suspected cause of death. "He was asphyxiated. At least that's the consensus at the moment. We'll know more, when all of the tests have been completed. A sharp segment of a frieze was found lodged in the victim's throat. There was blood under his head which meant he fell and cut it. The results of all of the tests have not been confirmed yet, but it's a good guess that he was overcome by lack of oxygen and suffocated to death."

"And the frieze?" Angeline asked, voice hoarse. "Was there anything special about it?"

"Only if you can tell me the significance of a bird, a cup, a staff, a torch, a diadem and a lamp."

Those symbols were engraved on the frieze.

"By the way, what exactly *is* a diadem?"

"It's a crown or band that holds a veil in place." She quickly added. "Like a wedding veil."

She flushed, as she saw the journalist's smirk of pity. Yes, Jake had issues with setting a wedding date and talking about it made them both uncomfortable, it being the source of some of their most spectacular arguments. Why couldn't he make the commitment? Well, it might have something to do with the fact that marriage didn't quite make sense to him. They loved each other. He was totally committed to her. He had proven that by asking her to marry him and giving her a ring. They had melded their lives together, but as far as he was concerned the deed was done. Curse Cristine's accusatory eyes. Did she need their love to be sanctioned by the law? Did she trust him that little? What was his was hers, and what was hers was hers. And he was fine with that. Was it because her father was a lawyer? Was that why she needed a piece of paper stamped by the government or some mumbo jumbo spewed by a religious figurehead to prove that he was devoted to their relationship? Maybe, maybe, maybe, and maybe. Jake had witnessed marriage ceremonies from wedding potlatches to Justice of the Peace pronouncements to elaborate, pocketbook-destroying, religious fabrications. As far as he was concerned religion and ritual had no bearing on a marriage. Of course, he might be biased since he was the product of an unlikely summer fling. But did any of that justify his denying *her* a wedding?

Chancellor's next comment was barbed. "Ms. Lisbon, I've been told by the dean of your faculty that Dr. Lalonde is up for promotion, but he was not awarded a research grant last year."

"He has reapplied. He might get it *this* year." Angeline frowned. How did Jake's career have anything to do with what had happened to Vincent?

"And the bird among the symbols. A raven, perhaps?"

What was he getting at? Why would it be a raven? She shook her head, eyes widening in sudden understanding. Oh, no. He couldn't possibly think that. The room started to swim before her eyes. She struggled to focus on Chancellor's next words.

"Did you know that he was among the expedition that discovered the crime scene?"

CHAPTER THREE

"I did not know that," Angeline whispered.

Chancellor nodded and turned to Adam, the student. "So, Dr. Carpello's lab was broken into." He withdrew a small notebook from his shirt pocket. Adam gulped and Chancellor said, "Ransacked huh? Lock forced and door left swinging wide? And you just discovered this before coming here?"

"Just before I came up here," Adam repeated like a parrot.

"Was anything missing?"

"I don't know. I'm pretty sure I *wouldn't* know. I was just hired to help with some data entry."

"Why did you go to Dr. Carpello's lab just then?"

Adam hesitated. "I was wondering if he had returned."

"Was he planning to return?"

"Yes."

"When?"

"Today."

"When was the last time you saw him?"

"About five weeks ago. Before he left for Israel."

"And had you been in touch with him since he left?"

"No."

Chancellor nodded and took out his cell phone. He called for a team of forensics specialists to scour Vincent's office. He had the support of the local precinct while he was in Seattle. As he waited for their arrival, he questioned Cristine Kletter, dismissed her. She wanted to stay, but the officious Interpol agent made it clear that her hanging around to observe wasn't an option.

At his request, Adam led Chancellor into Vincent's lab when the team arrived. Angeline hauled Cristine aside, then down the corridor a ways and whispered into her ear. Before Cristine left she wanted her to return to Jake's office. She handed her a memory key. When Adam appeared so unexpectedly it had thrown Chancellor off and he had left his computer on Jake's desk. Angeline wanted that picture.

"I can't, Angeline. That's a felony. He's Interpol. And that photograph is evidence."

Evidence? Evidence of what? It was a picture of a crime scene, a murder, sure. But it was only a picture, not the murder weapon.

"What if I get caught?"

"You won't get caught. Every single one of those self-important technicians is inside Vincent's lab right now, and no one will see you." Cristine hesitated, fingered the memory key like it burned while Angeline demanded, "Do you think Jake did it?"

"Of course not."

"Well, that cop's not so sure."

"Oh, for heaven's sake. Jake's not a suspect." She raised her hand to drop the key into Angeline's, but instead of accepting it, Angeline cupped the journalist's hand into a fist with her own.

"You're a reporter, Cristine. You're always getting into trouble. You do this for me and I owe you big time. I promise." With her hand clamped between Angeline's, any more objections the journalist might have had ended in a squeak.

Angeline turned as Chancellor came to the door. "Ms. Lisbon, we're waiting. And you Ms. Kletter, was there something you forgot to tell me?"

Cristine shook her head, whipped her fist out from under Angeline's grasp, tucked both hands into her jacket pockets, and made her way to the elevator. Angeline exhaled and followed Chancellor into the lab. "Perhaps you could look to see if anything is missing," the Interpol agent said.

Angeline went to the far end of the lab. Until she knew how Jake was involved in this, she was not saying another word.

She suddenly choked on a gasp. Chancellor's back was to her and he didn't see her expression. She frantically sorted through the artifact boxes stacked on the countertop, swung to her left and unlocked a map drawer.

It was gone. The text that Vincent was working on was gone. The writing and its accompaniment of cryptic symbols were drawn on a piece of 2nd century parchment found in a mithraeum beneath the current Basilica of San Clemente in Rome. It had been preserved because the underground shrine in which it was buried was airtight, protecting it from the damaging effects of moisture, light and oxygen. Vincent normally kept it in a self-contained, digitized, environmentally-controlled container. But the box was gone. Who could have taken it? No one had access to this lab except the secretaries, who had a spare key—and Security.

And me, she thought.

"Angeline," Adam said. "Is something wrong? You found something missing?"

She looked up at Adam suspiciously, dismissed the idea. Adam didn't even know it existed. She shook her head. Chancellor's back was still turned and she sent Adam to occupy him.

Chancellor already thought Jake had something to do with this. And if she told Chancellor the parchment was missing, he'd assume that she was a culprit as well. But she didn't steal the parchment *and* she didn't kill Vincent.

She tossed a sharp glance in Chancellor's direction where he was busy directing his people, collecting samples of hair and skin cells, and dusting for fingerprints. A woman scanned the images into a handheld computer. Why were they doing that? Vincent wasn't killed here. They were only going to find *her* fingerprints, and probably Jake's, too, amidst a host of student prints. All sorts of people had visited this lab.

"Oh, great," Angeline mumbled as Thomas Chancellor approached her. "He's coming to talk to me."

"Are you finished your inventory, Ms Lisbon?"

"Yes . . . and I . . . didn't find anything missing." She forced her eyes to remain steady.

"Nothing at all? What about the text?"

She sucked in a short breath, tried not to blink. "He took it with him."

Chancellor's stare went dark, and Angeline could see now that the man's irises were a bottomless, molten brown, almost black when he frowned. "You're sure of this?"

She swallowed. "Quite sure."

"Just one more question, Ms. Lisbon. As Dr. Carpello's research assistant, how often were you and he in touch?"

"Not often. When he went into the field I wouldn't hear from him in months."

"And Dr. Lalonde. How often are you in touch while he's away?"

Angeline hesitated. For a few weeks Jake's cell phone had been out of range. That was curious but not out of character. He had left the number of the hostel where he would be staying in Rome, but so far she hadn't called it because she'd had no real reason to. "He usually calls just before he plans to come home."

"And when will that be?"

"I'm not sure."

Chancellor gave her a dubious look. "Would you mind calling him right now?"

"He's in Italy. It's night time there."

He snapped his notebook closed. "All right then. We're finished here for now." He told her not to leave town and that he would have more questions for her later, then he handed her a card with his name and cell number on it.

"So, am I a suspect?" she demanded.

"Not exactly."

That answer was loaded, and she couldn't wait for him to leave. When he did, she returned to the mess in the lab. She hated lying and couldn't believe she had boldfaced lied to a cop, but that man was out for blood, and she was pretty sure whose blood he wanted. Jake had a lot of explaining to do. She started to put things away. She wasn't told not to touch anything since Vincent's lab wasn't technically a crime scene, at least not as far as the police knew.

The only clue she had was that the killer probably stole the text with the undeciphered symbols. What was Vincent working on that could be so important that someone was willing to kill him for it? She rubbed her forehead, squashing her frustration. That was a question she should be asking Jake. Hell, just what was going on with him? What was he doing in Israel?

Angeline raced out of Vincent's lab and up the stairs to Jake's office. She went to his computer, which was on and resting at an oblique angle on his desk. The Interpol agent's laptop sat on his desk as well, and on the other side of the monitor was the memory key she'd given to Cristine. Angeline was tempted to access the photo of Vincent's gruesome death on Chancellor's laptop, but decided to see if the journalist had been successful in downloading it onto the key. She thrust it into one of the computer's USB ports and searched for the file. What would she have called it? The only file that wasn't previously on this key was one that read 'Roadkill.' Did she think that was funny?

As Angeline started the download a knock came at the open door.

"Mr. Chancellor," she said, heart racing.

He entered the room and his eyes dropped to the laptop.

She yanked the key from the port and tucked it in her palm. The Interpol agent looked at her and noticed that his laptop was on even though the monitor showed only a 'desktop' image of flying birds.

Chancellor slapped down the lid to his laptop, one-handed it under his arm and extended a hand to Angeline. She pretended to cough into her cupped right hand, and swivelled on one heel to grab a tissue from a Kleenex box behind her before transferring the memory key to the tissue and dropping it into the garbage. For a second Chancellor's eye followed.

"Allergies," she said, and bent to gather the plastic together as perspiration beaded on her forehead.

Chancellor gave her a sympathetic smile and nodded as he turned away. Angeline lifted a limp hand as a gesture of farewell, as he shut the door behind him. She stooped over the garbage can, wrinkling her nose and prodded its contents, then rose holding the crumpled-up tissue.

The memory key fell out and she thrust it into the USB port, and pulled up the pertinent file. The picture of Vincent appeared on the screen. The scene would have seemed more gruesome if it didn't look so theatrical—like it was staged. A weird sound left her lips as she zoomed in on the hands, expanding the image to include the shadow that was cast by the oddly positioned fingers. The raven shape sent winter into her veins. Was Vincent sending some kind of message to Jake? Vincent was one of the few people who knew about Jake's inherited memories and his belief that the myth of the Haida Raven was inspired by a man, a man who was a prehistoric shaman—*and* Jake's ancestor.

This was a touchy subject between them. She was afraid of his shamanic heritage. She didn't want him to delve into it, but he did. And he mostly did it on the sly.

The only person that could help him to understand his strange visions was gone. His Haida father was dead. Jake didn't have an affinity with the natural world, animals didn't like him, and he'd made one too many faux pas when he tried to participate in traditional ceremonies. Those with the 'gift' had the 'vision,' but it seemed he had the 'vision' without the 'gift.'

Angeline angled the computer to emphasize the shadow cast by Vincent's hands. She glanced up from watching the screen to see Chancellor watching her.

CHAPTER FOUR

The muscles in Jake's neck ached from holding them so tense. What a foul, soul-sucking, wearying day. He was reeling from the shock of Vincent's death.

At the tourist hostel where he was staying in Rome, Jake slumped down on the cot in front of the window. That sight of Vincent, his hands frozen in the shape of the Raven: what did it mean? Just, exactly, what had happened to him between Rome and Israel?

A year ago Vincent had discovered the statue. He had said very little about it, swore Jake to secrecy, even begged him not to mention it to Angeline. At the time, Jake had no interest in it, so it was an easy promise to keep. After a yearlong wait for funding, he hired a local crew. They were supposed to make the hazardous trek up the mountains of Hilazon Tachtit together. Jake churned over the events of the last few months. The only clues Vincent had given were that his latest discovery had something to do with life and death. And God.

So, what did the Raven have to do with it?

When Jake was ten years old he lived with a set of foster parents in a downtown Seattle high-rise. The apartment building rose twenty stories into the sky and although he was warned to stay off the balconies, he had a habit of climbing the rails where he would perch to view a pair of ravens nesting in a tall tree. The species was unheard of in Seattle, and here were two that had found their way to his neighbourhood. He was fascinated at how the pair bonded to each other, returning yearly to mate and raise their brood. A biology teacher told him that ravens mated for life. The female laid eggs and, with this particular duo, not until there were five did she incubate them. From that time on she never left the nest and sometimes she would cry like a hatchling until her mate returned with food, while at other times the male would nudge her beak, encouraging her to eat when she was finicky.

A day came when no one was home, and Jake stepped out onto the balcony and climbed the rain-slick rail to see whether the male had returned to his mate. He had left her five days earlier and Jake was worried. Had the male been hit by a car, attacked by a raccoon or a coyote? Was he dead? Jake settled one foot onto the rail and hauled the other sneakered foot beside it, but when he couldn't see the raven's nest clearly, he flattened one hand against the apartment wall, the other seeking the balcony ceiling, and stretched himself upright. At that moment he got the shock of his life—the male had not returned and the female was eating her own eggs. At the sight of the slimy yolk on her beak, he lost his grip on the balcony rail, and crashed six stories to the ground.

He lay on the grass, blackness folding his vision, but he could still see. The strange thing was it wasn't the grey light of a Seattle morning he discerned, but the pale luminosity of a cave. *Drink this*, a voice said to him. *You'll feel better.* The voice came from the shadows and its figure cast a silhouette shaped like a giant bird. Jake shuddered, but knew if he failed to obey, he would never get out of here. His arms and legs were confined somehow, and he couldn't move. The shadow drew nearer, urging him. *Drink . . . . Only if you drink can you leave this place.* The proffered brew came in a stone bowl that glittered, the odour rising from it smelling of the Death Cap. Drums beat in the background and fires twisted in the distance.

He couldn't remember what happened next except that he awoke in the hospital with a bitter taste in his mouth, the scent of mushroom in his nostrils, his eyes swimming. As the nurses went about their business, an aura seemed to follow their every move. His arms and legs were locked in casts, and the doctors said he would never walk again.

They were wrong.

Jake set his laptop down on the crumpled sheets and searched under the cot. He had been debating whether to experiment with entheogens for a while now, and had hidden the stash inside his rubber boot. Snatching up the paper bag, he dumped the contents onto the mattress, glanced about furtively. His door was closed. No voices outside in the corridor or the lobby. If he was going to do this, he'd better hurry.

The mushrooms were dried by now, smelled musty, and maybe even mouldy. He selected a curled up, whitish specimen, pinched off a piece from the cap and placed it on his tongue, while the excess was swept from the laminate countertop into the bag.

Nothing happened. He pinched off another piece, swallowed it and waited.

The mushroom remaining in his hand began to feel heavy like it was growing in size. He closed his fist around it, jolting forward when everything went black.

His head felt heavy like lead, like the mushroom in his hand, only heavier. His heart palpitated and his breath came unsteadily as flashes of heat consumed his torso, washing toward his face. Sweat broke out on his forehead, and the palms of his hands felt icy. The palpitations lasted a minute and were replaced by a sensation of utter calm, he breathed easier, widening his eyes against the blackness. Where was he? Some kind of shaft? A pick struck rock, pinging in his ears, and overhead, a massive hole in the ceiling sent twilight below. Through the fog of his drugged mind, familiarity tingled in his senses. How could that be? He had never seen such a sight before. The bleakness in front of him eroded into shimmering light and a labyrinth of tunnels lacerated out before his vision, the passages deep and empty.

He started to walk, arms outstretched, mocking a child's game of Blind Man's Bluff. The walls felt rough and cold to his trembling fingers, and a sense of foreboding assailed him. Instinct told him that this was not a place he had visited before, but a place he would see in the future. He struggled to stay clued to his senses as his heart pulsed and his tongue flicked around his dry mouth. A tomb. He was inside a maze of tombs, honeycombed with crypts. Deep in one of the caverns, pale light flared over a painted fresco. The colours had faded, but the scene showed a man leading a pilgrimage. Beside the fresco was an epigraph in Latin.

Follow me to the sleep of death.

Jake paused to muse over its meaning, then moved on to another opening where a shimmering stirred. Through the entrance, over the dirt floor, he went to where a light burned to the far right over a row of skulls protruding from the wall. Jake felt a scream well inside him. Adjacent to the skulls, ceramic tiles formed a pattern on the wall, decorated with symbols. He recognized one of them—the Raven.

The shimmering he had been following now ebbed and flowed assembling into a human form.

Its sudden appearance startled him and he jerked up his head to see a face just as a hand floated out of the gloom to tap his shoulder. The concierge of the hostel shook him out of his daze, and as soon as he was conscious of his surroundings, he crushed the remains of the hallucinogenic fungus in his fist. How much time had passed? It seemed like hours and he felt weak, his mouth numb. Three words churned in his mind. Life. Death. And God.

"*Scusi*, Signor Lalonde. But you did not answer. I knew you were in here. I could hear you walking around, bumping into things. Are you alright?" A look of alarm crossed her peasant features as she studied his face. "Do you need a doctor?"

A doctor? No. Why? Jake managed to push his fist into the brown paper bag, and dropped the now powdered fungus into it. "I'm fine," he said. "Sorry I disturbed you."

She looked at him sharply. He caught a glimpse of his puffy face and dilated pupils in the cracked mirror on the wall, and blinked hard as though that would return his pupils to normal. He crunched the paper bag containing the mushrooms into a ball, and dropped it on top of some fruit peelings in the garbage can beside the bed. The concierge stared at the mess, then watched him zip up his duffle bag and shove his locked, black pelican case beside it.

"There is a telephone call for you. Long distance."

Jake realized his cell phone had not been recharged, so anyone trying that number would be unable to reach him. He thanked her and followed her to the lobby.

"You were there!" Angeline accused him when he lifted the receiver.

"Wait a minute, sweetie. What are you talking about?"

"Why didn't you tell me about Vincent? And why is your cell phone off?"

"It wasn't off. I forgot to charge it. As for Vincent: you mean you know already? It just happened a few days ago. I just got back to Rome."

"And that's another thing. Why didn't you tell me you were going to Israel? I thought you were meeting Vincent in Rome!"

"I did go to Rome."

"And then you went to Israel!"

He cupped his hand over the phone like he thought the concierge could hear. "Vincent asked me to see something he'd found."

"What was it?"

"A giant fertility goddess."

"That's hardly your area of expertise. What's it got to do with you?"

Jake shook his head. "That's just it. I never got to see him. I went to the rendezvous spot, but he never showed up, so I assumed he had changed his plans and meant to meet me at the cave site. I joined the expedition and went with them, but he never showed up."

"Weren't you worried? Suspicious? Didn't you think something might have happened to him?"

"Well, no. Not really. Archaeologists do stuff like that all the time. You know that." Hadn't *he* just done the same? Not told her where he was? "I got so intrigued with the find that I stayed for the excavation. Most of the statue was still encrusted with dirt and we won't know what the final thing looks like until its been cleaned up."

There was silence at the end of the line before Angeline said, "Did you take it? Did you take the text?"

"What text?"

"The one Vincent was working on. Surely he showed it to you?"

Jake frowned. Yes, he had, but again, he hadn't given it much thought.

"I'd better report the theft to Chancellor," Angeline said.

"Who's Chancellor?"

"He's the Interpol agent that's on your ass. Jake, you're in big trouble. You'd better come home and clear yourself of this mess. Tell Chancellor everything you've told me."

"Interpol's involved? The local authorities interviewed the crew and then let us go. No one said anything about Interpol. He doesn't know where I am, does he?"

"How could he? *I* didn't even know where you were!"

"Angeline, I didn't know at the time that the body was Vincent. I had my suspicions but I didn't say anything, because I had no proof it was him. He'd been dead for at least three weeks. He was unrecognizable. I think that's why they didn't detain us. There was nothing to connect any of us to his death."

"But now there is. I saw the picture of the crime scene. Did you notice his hands?"

"Yes. Like he was making the shape of a raven."

"But why a raven, Jake?"

"That's what I have to find out. I want to see that statue again. And it's in Rome. And I have to find that archaeologist, Sophia Saveriano. She headed up the expedition in Vincent's absence. Then when they let us go, she disappeared. If anyone knows anything about Vincent's research, it will be her. She excavated his site. At the time I thought they were co-investigators. Now I'm not so sure."

"I'm coming to join you," Angeline said.

"No. I don't want you involved.'"

"I'm already involved. And if you don't come home to be questioned, they'll think you killed Vincent."

Jake exhaled. It wasn't just about Vincent anymore. Angeline knew nothing of his childhood fall from that sixth floor balcony, the strange episode with the ravens, and the dream just before he awoke in the hospital. He had never told anyone, had assumed the taste in his mouth and the smell of mushroom in his nostrils had been something the nurses had fed him. But right this second, he wasn't so sure. The taste, the smell—he had it now. How that experience was related to his latest escapade—his fungus-induced junket into the realm of the metaphysical—he didn't know. But he did know one thing. That vision wasn't a coincidence.

Angeline knew about his inherited memories. He wasn't sure if what he had experienced was one of those, but she would likely think so. He had no choice. Vincent, those tunnels and the Raven were somehow connected. He omitted the part on how he had triggered the vision, and described for her the maze of tunnels and the Raven engraved on a tile inside the crypt of skulls.

*   *   *

Angeline paced their apartment, went to Jake's desk, noticing the mess of books and papers he had left, and started to straighten them for something to do. After Chancellor had caught her with the stolen digital photo, he had not reprimanded her. All he said was that he would come to her home that evening. He had something important to discuss.

What? Jake's arrest?

One of the books was opened to a chapter on shamanism. Chills swept her spine. Although that vision he had described and this had something to do with each other, how could any of it have to do with Vincent's murder? Jake seemed to think there was a connection, but no matter what convolutions and permutations she conjured up to wend the two together, she produced nothing. Jake was obsessed by the idea that he was descended from a 10,000-year-old shaman. What did *that* have to do with Vincent?

She leaned over the book to read a few lines: fascinating magical and religious elements appeared in the raven myths of the Old World and the New, and specific relationships existed between the raven figure and the practices of shamanism. Shamanic powers were inherited. In fact, a highly sensitive individual sometimes felt a calling, and to become a shaman you had to die and be visited by spirits, have your body transformed and then be reborn.

No wonder, Jake hadn't received a research grant yet. Shamanism wasn't considered archaeology—it wasn't provable—and he was supposed to be one of the preeminent archaeologists of North America.

One of the sheets of paper on his desk had writing on it, a list of psychoactive plants that shamans formerly used to put themselves into an altered state by which they could fly into the world of the spirits. There was also a strange list of mushrooms . . . .

A buzz from the intercom jolted her out of her thoughts and the voice of Thomas Chancellor came over the intercom. "Ms. Lisbon," he said. "I'm coming up."

She buzzed him into the building and he was at her door in a matter of minutes, dangling a black briefcase at his hip. She let him inside their apartment, stared at him expectantly. He had the latest lab report on Dr. Carpello's autopsy, which was faxed to him late that afternoon, but instead of explaining the details, his quick eye went to Jake's desk—to the books opened to the sections on magic mushrooms.

"When do you expect Dr. Lalonde?" he asked, returning his attention to her.

"I don't know." That was true. He hadn't said.

The sharp glance returned to the mycological volumes. How long had Jake been interested in the properties of psychoactive mushrooms? Angeline went to Chancellor's side and slammed the books closed. So what if he had those books. What made him think Jake was interested in the properties of poison mushrooms?

27

He was studying shamanism, and shamans often induced a hallucinatory state to help them experience the Spirit World.

Chancellor glanced down at the report he had retrieved from a file folder in his briefcase while Angeline stood awkwardly waiting. She refused to invite him into the living room to sit down. Was he ever going to say anything about the fact that she had stolen evidence? He had caught her red-handed, smiled as though a suspicion were confirmed, and left without a word.

"We wondered how Vincent Carpello was overcome and forced into the position in which he was found dead when there wasn't any obvious struggle," Chancellor said.

"I thought you said there was a blow to his head."

"That happened when he fell. That wasn't how he was overcome. He was made helpless through a drug." His next words rendered her speechless. The blow to the head was too minor to kill him, and although it looked like a lot of blood, it really didn't amount to enough to even cause the loss of consciousness. No one could force a piece of a sculpture down someone's throat without a huge struggle ensuing, but signs of resistance were absent. The conclusion? It must have occurred post-mortem. Other than the cut on the base of the head that the Medical Examiner determined was caused by the fall, no further violence to the body was evident. He paused from explaining, his eyes fixed on her expression, before elucidating.

"The cause of death was mycetism. Mushroom poisoning. One bite of the Destroying Angel can be lethal if not treated immediately. Diluted, the fungus can be made into a powerful hallucinogenic. Apparently Dr. Carpello ingested a lethal dose."

Angeline stared.

Chancellor nodded at her silence. "I know you're trying to protect him, but it would be better for your husband if he cooperated and helped us with this investigation rather than hindering it by hiding."

"He is not hiding. And I am not trying to protect him. No one had gone after him. There are no police hunting him down, are there? So, he hasn't done anything wrong. And while we're on the subject, Jake is not my husband. Well, not yet anyway. We're engaged, not married."

She scowled, unable to mask her true feelings. They had been living together for the last year, and he liked to call her his wife and wanted everyone else to call her his wife, too, hoping that *that* would be enough. "He's got cold feet," she said, her voice shaking with emotion. She mentally muzzled herself, embarrassed that she had just confided in a complete stranger. "He doesn't want to set a wedding date." Her diamond engagement ring flashed briefly as she fidgeted and babbled, breaking her resolution for silence, unable to squash the need to qualify her feelings. The Interpol agent had gone quiet. Okay, she didn't know why she'd said any of that—except that it was true—and one year later, after he'd asked her to marry him, he still refused to commit.

Chancellor's face was blank and an awkward silence stretched between them. He was obviously uncomfortable and maybe that was good, because at least now, he was off the subject of Jake as a murder suspect.

"So . . . how long has he been interested in the shamanistic use of psychoactive plants?"

"I guess he started to research shamanism more actively this past year. He's—" She couldn't bring herself to reveal what Jake perceived himself to be. It would make him look nuts.

"Can we sit down, Angeline? You don't mind if I call you Angeline? You can call me Tom."

She nodded, but it was unlikely she'd feel comfortable calling him Tom.

"All right then. I know I came off sounding a bit alarmist and accusatory, but your husban—Excuse me, your fiancé—"

"Jake," she corrected him. "It's okay. Just call him Jake."

"Right. Jake might be involved in something bigger than just the murder of one individual." He went to the sofa in front of their flat screen TV. "Okay if I sit down?" He sat as she nodded, but she remained standing. His voice had become softer, less aggressive, and she almost preferred the cold, indifferent and inimical Chancellor.

"I think you should sit down, Angeline. I think we can help each other."

She perched on the edge of the chair opposite him, but didn't let down her guard. She did not trust him.

If he didn't dress so conservatively, he'd be quite good-looking. He was wearing a grey suit now, but with the same yellow tie and trench coat that he had worn earlier. His hair was thick and wavy, a light brown colour that went well with his dark brown eyes. He had high cheekbones, a chiselled jawline, and looked like he might have stepped off the pages of *Gentleman's Quarterly*. Tarzan in office duds. She smirked. But whatever it was he wanted to tell her was serious because every muscle in his face was tight with tension.

"You probably know that Interpol is involved in antiquities thefts. A very large, primitive Venus statue was en route to Rome when it was snatched. I know you're wondering what the connection between Vincent Carpello's death and this statue is, but I can only tell you that the statue was removed from the excavation site in Israel at the same time that his body was discovered. What's more, the archaeologist in charge of the expedition is missing."

She was having a hard time keeping her expression blank. Jake was involved in stolen artifacts? That was a laugh.

"Dr. Sophia Saveriano is a renowned Italian feminist archaeologist. Maybe you know her?"

She hesitated. Jake had mentioned her, and she *had* heard of her. She was one of the foremost feminist archaeologists in Biblical archaeology until her last discovery a few years ago when she announced to the world that God had a wife and her name was Asherah. Apparently, she had thousands of Venus figurines excavated from hundreds of Middle Eastern sites—which she thought were absolute proof that ancient Hebrew men and women worshipped a female goddess alongside the one true God, Yahweh—before she was laughed out of the academic community.

"Saveriano has disappeared. We need to find her."

Angeline thrust her chin out. "Well then, I think you have your killer."

"It's not as simple as that."

"Why not?"

Just because Jake was researching shamanism didn't mean he had anything to do with Vincent's poisoning. Maybe Vincent was experimenting with magic mushrooms himself, and accidentally took an overdose. People were known to do that. Academics were a strange and troubled breed. Much as she hated to admit it, their exceptional intelligence sometimes made them do stupid things. They were known to adopt vices. Maybe concocting cocktails with *Amanita* was one of Vincent's. She told Chancellor this, but all he had to say was, "So you know the species?"

It was a variety called *Amanita bisporigera*, commonly known as the Destroying Angel.

If Vincent Carpello was using psychoactive mushrooms as a recreational drug he wouldn't have chosen to experiment with the Destroying Angel, Chancellor informed her. Not if he knew anything about mushrooms at all. He was a professor of archaeology with an additional degree in ethnobotany, so he would know the difference between a deadly poisonous species and a recreational hallucinogen. "I think this feminist archaeologist is after Lalonde. Do you know what her current research is about?" Chancellor asked.

Sophia Saveriano had dropped out of the archaeology loop after her disgrace among the world's foremost experts in religious archaeology. There had not been a mention of her, or a paper published by her, or an appearance at the SAA's or the AIA's, or any of the other prominent world archaeology conferences in a very long time.

Until now.

Why had she taken over Vincent's expedition?

"Jake Lalonde is the foremost expert in Raven mythology, origins and migrations, is he not?" Chancellor asked.

She nodded, shifting her position on the chair.

"Sophia Saveriano is currently researching a mithraeum in the tunnels beneath the Basilica of San Clemente in Rome

31

which points to an ancient Raven cult. The Mithraic Mysteries generally prohibit women, but she has found evidence of a female subcult that worshipped a raven. I've been following her activities for years. Ever since she made that claim that God has a wife, I think she's been searching for Her."

Angeline squeezed her eyes shut. *Her?* What was he talking about? Saveriano was searching for God's wife? The sneer that threatened to break out on her face got lost in the gravity of Chancellor's voice. There had been mysterious disappearances surrounding her for the past five or six years, young men, many of them graduate students, research assistants or colleagues, always between the ages of twenty-five and thirty-eight. The bodies were never found, but neither were the young men.

So what? What exactly was he implying? Academics travelled all the time; they didn't account for their every move. Grad students and research assistants came and went. Angeline could honestly say that she had no idea where her own classmates were today. She met the Interpol agent's cool stare and said nothing.

"Lalonde was there, Angeline. There, in Israel with Saveriano. She'll be looking to reconnect with him, now that she knows her research intertwines with his."

"There's no intertwining," she objected adamantly. "Lots of people study the Raven and Raven lore." Jake happened to be fascinated by the widespread occurrence of the Raven myths and their symbols that were scattered throughout the world. Besides, she failed to see the connection between fertility goddesses and raven iconography. She put her hands to the sides of her face, moved her fingers to cover her mouth, then suddenly dropped her hands and looked up. "So, you *don't* think Jake killed him?"

"I'm not making any claims right now. I don't know what Jake knows about the Carpello murder or what his relationship is with Saveriano."

"There is no relationship. He only just met her—" Angeline clapped a hand over her mouth, exhaled. "If he's in danger I have to find him."

"I was hoping you would say that."

She glared at Chancellor. "Just tell me. How dangerous do you think she is?"

"She is as slippery as an eel. We have never been able to make anything stick. I can't accuse her of murdering these young men because I can't find their bodies. But if they were alive, why does no one know where they are? They have not contacted their families or friends."

"How many?"

"At least fifty that we know of."

She whistled. How could fifty guys go missing and leave no trace of their whereabouts? She thought about it for a long minute, asked, "What would a scholar like her want with those men? Why would she kill them?"

"That is my dilemma, Angeline," he said, saccharinely. "Will you help me?"

She rubbed a hand to her creased brow. That may be *his* dilemma, but *hers* was more complex. Did she trust him? Why did an Interpol agent know so much about magic mushrooms, cult mysteries and Old World archaeology in general? *Who are you, really, Mr. Chancellor?*

He wasn't giving her too much time to decide. Under his obsequious gaze, she realized he was aware that she hadn't told him everything she knew—the missing text, for example.

The parchment was found in the same shrine beneath the Basilica of San Clemente, in Rome, where Chancellor had said Sophia Saveriano worked. That meant Vincent *was*, in fact, working on the same site as her, and she very possibly was in possession of the missing text.

A bird, a cup, a staff, a torch, a diadem and a lamp. Those were the symbols that Vincent was about to decipher when the text went missing, and they were also the symbols engraved on the piece of frieze that was rammed down Vincent's throat. Angeline winced. It was certainly a message but who was it meant for and what did it mean? Although she was not the expert in ancient cults that Vincent was, she knew something about art motifs, and if she looked at these symbols from an art standpoint, she recognized where they came from. Vincent had shown her some of the art from the Roman mithraea that he had excavated.

She snapped her eyes shut. What did she know about the seven ranks of initiation in the Mithraic Mysteries? Of one thing, she was sure. The actual symbols were not the mystery. Vincent knew what those symbols represented as well as she did. No, the mystery was not the meaning of the symbols themselves, but the juxtaposition of them.

Suddenly aware that the Interpol agent was watching her, she opened her eyes. *I don't trust you, Mr. Chancellor.* But going it alone might not be so smart.

She got off the armchair and went to the bedroom while he followed.

"Where are you going?"

She gave him one sharp look. "Go home and get packed. I take it where I go, you'll follow—whether I like it or not. So pack your things. We're going to Rome."

CHAPTER FIVE

The engines of the jet droned in Angeline's ears until she couldn't stand it anymore. For an hour she had pretended to sleep, knowing he was watching her. Through slit eyes, she was aware of his presence—the wavy hair and dark scrutiny. He had finally chucked his jacket, slouching beside her in shirtsleeves and skewed tie. Was he even human? Except for the slightly more breezy state of his apparel, his appearance was as perfect this morning as it was before he went to sleep last night. A wisp of lemon, cedar and musk found their way to her nostrils as he switched on the TV at the back of the seat ahead of him: a sublime scent. Soap, shampoo, or what?

She squinted annoyed that she was even giving him that much thought. She opened her eyes fully.

He smiled. "Sleep okay?"

She shrugged, shucking her irritation. "I can never sleep on a plane."

Angeline grazed Chancellor's elbow as she doubled up her blanket. He didn't pull away and instead seemed amused by her touch. She tucked the blanket behind her and rose to use the bathroom, while he stepped into the aisle to let her pass.

The first lavatory she came to was free, and she went inside and locked the door to wash her face and brush her teeth, fluff out her hair and apply fresh makeup. She paid attention to her lips with cherry-flavoured gloss. Then calm and composed, and satisfied with her appearance, she adjusted her low-riding black pants beneath a skin-tight sweater, and opened the door to make her entrance. Chancellor fiddled with some paperwork in his seat, not even looking.

A sheet of paper was in his hand as she approached, and he snapped it into the elasticized pocket on the seat in front of him. Disgusted by her self-consciousness, she made an effort to hide it, but whenever you decide to hide anything, that's when people are likely to notice. He shuffled the papers on his lap into a leather briefcase, and glanced up with a cynical smile. When he rose to let her into the window seat, their hips briefly touched.

A flight attendant appeared in the aisle to serve breakfast. Chancellor put away his briefcase, and as Angeline ate her omelette, she watched the view. The sky was clear and below was blue water. They were over the Azores and would soon fly over Rome.

Seven had been Rome's legendary number since ancient times: 7 hills on which the city was founded; 7 kings; 7 septemviri, the territorial magistrates; 7 epulones, priests at the banquets in honour of Jupiter; 7 cohorts of the wardens; 7 collossues of the gods on the hill. If only she believed in lucky numbers—because she was going to need all the help she could get to convince Jake to talk to Chancellor.

He leaned over his breakfast tray to the pocket on the seat in front of him. One-handed, he removed the sheet of paper he had placed there earlier, passing it over to her.

She had barely extended her hand before he let go and the computer printout went sailing onto the floor. She leaned forward aware of exposing the skin above her low-riders, scowling before looking up with the sheet in her hand.

"That's a photo of the piece of the frieze they found in Vincent's throat?"

"You recognize it?" he asked.

Most fragments of statuary looked the same when out of context, and she wasn't sure she'd tell him anything even if it *did* look familiar. "Never saw it in my life," she said crisply.

At her snippy tone, Chancellor slammed down his empty coffee cup, and since the cup was made of Styrofoam it made no sound. But the action spoke for itself. He shoved at his breakfast tray, rattling the plastic dishes just to push home his point. Fifty men were missing, presumed dead. And now her friend and colleague Vincent Carpello had been added to the list. Wasn't she the least bit concerned over what he had told her about Saveriano? Lalonde could be next. Just what was she hiding?

Angeline stabbed a piece of kiwi from the fruit medley on her plate. Who the hell was he to accuse her of anything? "Look, *Tom*." Her voice sounded waspish even to herself. "I don't appreciate you assuming that Jake is guilty of some heinous crime, so let's just stop this dancing around. I don't know what your game is, whether you're in earnest about helping Jake or whether you just want to trap him. But I'm telling you right now that I'm not helping you to trap him."

She tore into the cold bread roll that remained of her breakfast, and it crumbled to paste in her mouth. Jake was unaware that she was on her way to Rome. And that she was bringing Interpol with her. They had spoken last night. She hadn't time to call again and inform him of Saveriano. She wasn't sure what she thought. Was Chancellor telling the truth? Or was it just a ploy to get her to lead him to Jake? She slumped into her seat, resting her hands on her stomach, squashing the tears that formed behind her lids. What had Jake gotten himself into by refusing to come home?

* * *

The Grande Raccordo Anulare encircled Rome and channelled traffic into various destinations inside the city. He had clearly driven this route before, and although it looked to Angeline like chaos, there was a method to the madness of ring roads. All one had to do was plot a course and be prepared to enter the city on the right route.

The smells of the city greeted them. Gasoline and car exhaust, dust and old food smells. This was the 'Eternal City.' Chancellor pointed out the Tiber River. On the horizon rose the elliptical bowl of the Colosseum, partially crumbled away. Traffic was bad, jammed at every intersection, and forty minutes elapsed before they passed the amphitheatre. He thumbed toward the

Roman Forum to their left. Several stops and kilometers farther, they curved past the grand pillars of the Pantheon, and made a sharp right to the Piazza di Trevi, site of the multi-statued Trevi fountain.

They left the borders of Ancient Rome and cruised at a gondola's pace along the Via Sistina to the famed Spanish Steps, which were filled to brimming with brilliant azaleas. Odd for this time of year, but then the weather was eerily warm.

He pointed with his chin. "Over there is the Vatican City and the Sistine Chapel. Are you religious, Angeline?"

She had no intention of visiting the Vatican. She was here for one purpose—to find Jake.

"It's going to be hard to find a hotel," Chancellor said. "The city is inundated with delegates from the WCOPS."

"What's that?"

"The World Congress on Paranormal Sightings."

And how would you know that? She dismissed the thought as she realized how right he was. There were no rooms at the first few good hotels they tried.

The traffic crawled, and the noise and congestion and smog were beginning to get to her while a dull aching throb began on the sides of her head. The sounds of the city were too loud, all the honking and yelling; Italians were a lively, vital people.

"Tell you what," Chancellor said, returning to the rented Fiat convertible after the fifth try at getting a decent room. "Let's go to Saveriano's villa. I've got the address. I have a sneaking suspicion we'll learn something about the missing professor's whereabouts there."

"If you thought that," Angeline said, slamming the Fiat's door as she got into the passenger seat. "Why didn't you check out her villa in the first place? I'm assuming you must have done some preliminary queries in Rome before coming to Seattle to harass me."

"I thought I stood a better chance with you at my side." He winked and pulled into the stream of traffic. As he honked his horn aggressively, several drivers looked their way, recognized them as foreigners, and slowed their vehicles. He nodded, shouted a robust *grazie*, and catapulted his car through a gap in the bottleneck.

In twenty minutes they were on a level expressway heading into the countryside. Thirty minutes more and they approached a long winding drive bordered by grass, colourful wildflowers and slender pine trees. He wheeled up the drive, steering past marble fountains and statues, flowerbeds and cypress trees until he reached the villa. She stared at the three-storied pillared palace, its exterior ochre-coloured with iron railed terraces on the top and middle levels.

Chancellor parked and stepped out of the car. The architecture he told her was 17th century Palladian, neo-classical. Sophia Saveriano's ancestors had built it. He went around to the passenger side and held the car door wide, and waited for her to get out. She gathered up her handbag and followed him.

Her stomach suddenly went cold. She had that eerie feeling of walking into the unknown as she looked up at the house. A curtain moved from a top window. But no face appeared. A thin mist seemed to surround the roof even though it was perfectly sunny out. Angeline shivered. What was the matter with her? Had her style been short, every hair on her nape would be standing on end.

"What's the matter, Angeline? You look pale as a ghost."

Angeline swallowed, rubbed her cold hands together, flashed a smile she didn't feel and said, "So what's our story? What are we going to say to her if she's here?"

"You're an archaeologist, right? Wing it. Think of a reason why you'd want to meet a renowned scholar like Saveriano. Flatter her. We have to find out if she's gotten in touch with Lalonde."

The front door opened, and the odour of cigarettes greeted them. Chancellor beamed at a young woman in grey slacks and a short-sleeved white blouse. Big brown eyes stared out from an oval face framed by sleek, black hair. Her red lips parted.

"I am Dr. Saveriano's assistant. The professor is not home. Who may I say is calling?" She puffed on a cigarette, then tossed the butt out onto the veranda.

Chancellor gave his name, and added, "This is Angeline Lisbon. She's an archaeologist from the University of Washington and I'm a historian from the same. We tried to find her at the museum, but she wasn't there. I emailed her to tell her to expect us. When will she return?"

Angeline frowned at the lies, which didn't faze Chancellor in the least, and returned her attention to the assistant, noting the opulence in the lobby behind her. The floor was polished black and white marble, a crystal chandelier plunged from the high ceiling, and white statues and columns were tucked into numerous niches ringing the oval foyer.

"I don't know her plans," the assistant replied in French-accented English. "She has not been home for days and only tells me what she wants me to know."

There was something familiar about the way the assistant was watching them, something unnerving. A cold change in the air brought Angeline's hands to her shoulders, and she hugged herself.

"Chilly?" Chancellor asked. "It's hot enough to wilt lettuce."

She gave him a withered look, and dragged her attention to the assistant. "I was wondering . . . we just came from a long drive . . . Could I possibly use the bathroom?"

The assistant looked down her nose at her, shrugged. "Not at all. Go up the stairs then turn to your left. The powder room, *la toilette, il bagno*, is there."

Saveriano's assistant obviously spoke Italian as well as French. With inexplicable nervousness, Angeline walked past her, hurried up the marble staircase and found the bathroom door. Inside the opulent bath were travertine marble floors, a gleaming white porcelain tub with gold-clawed feet, and wine-coloured bath sheets on gold towel racks. Angeline closed the door and walked down the hall until she came to another opened door. Something was familiar about that assistant. Why? She stepped into what turned out to be a bedroom and fished out her cell phone. Her hands still felt icy as she punched in Jake's number and listened to the phone ring. Then a mechanical voice came on and told her that the party she wished to reach was unavailable.

She walked farther into the room over plush carpeting to a large bed, and noted an armoire and two armchairs opposite it. The wardrobe in the corner was partly opened, exposing the corner of a black canvas bag, and the walls were hung with gaudy tapestries and religious oil paintings. A window on the far side opened out onto a terrace overlooking a river, and if she didn't know better, she would say that it was July rather than October because the sun glared down on a scene of lazy riverboats. She returned her attention to the room. A cell phone sat on one of the armchairs near the window, and she reached out to pick it up, but withdrew her arm when the odour of tobacco reached her.

A voice behind her said, "A lovely view, no?"

Angeline whirled to face Sophia Saveriano's beautiful assistant.

CHAPTER SIX

The Basilica of San Clemente was a bold, white, three-tiered edifice on the Piazza San Clemente, Via Labicana. Jake had entered by way of a side entrance, noting that the original entrance was through an axial peristyle flanked by arcades, which now served as a cloister. Splendid mosaics stippled the ceiling and floor. He emulated some tourists through to the rear to see Fontana's chaste facade braced on antique columns. The basilica church in back of it had three naves broken by arcades on early marble columns with inlaid paving. Here he stopped to consult his map. Where was the mithraeum?

Down a short passage, and he was in an unused portion of the church. It was quiet and unlit except for a row of small arched windows near the ceiling. Some buckets and shovels lay littered about, and when his eyes adjusted to the lower light level he could see that the floor was dug up and there was a neat, square pit at the rear. Why he had been led to this particular church wasn't clear to him, but he had obeyed his instinct. After that drug-induced vision he recently experienced, he felt a strange pull of familiarity every time he passed this church. The church was across the street from the hostel where he was staying.

Jake manoeuvred to the pit and looked down. A ladder led into the darkness. Should he? He glanced around. No one was nearby. The place was as dead as a tomb. Mithraea were always underground so maybe this would lead to one. He lowered himself into the cold, silent shaft. *Holy Mother of God.* It did feel like he had entered a tomb. He touched the walls, fumbling for balance, recognizing the feel of mortared tile and marble slabs. He caught his breath as he gazed at his surroundings. He *was* in a tomb, standing on a gravestone.

"Don't worry. There is no one under that stone."

Jake jumped at the sound of the voice, jerked his head to see a woman, partially shadowed, leaning against one of the walls, one leg casually braced behind the other. She looked quite natural in the semi-lit shaft like she belonged there. She stepped forward, and the tube of light struck her fingers, which combed through her dark hair, tinged with strangely attractive streaks of grey. When he didn't speak, both of her hands went to the pockets of her khaki shorts, and she shifted her hips to settle her weight on the opposite foot.

It was cool down here, but under her gaze he sweated. She tossed a glance at a large crypt to their left. "You are afraid. Why? These are Christian burials—martyrs, saints. Their spirits will not harm you . . . unless you mean harm to them."

"Sophia," he said, swallowing his awkwardness. "I've been looking for you."

She rubbed a smudge of dirt from her chin on the white collar of her open-necked shirt. Her brows pinched together. "You know me? Who *are* you? What are you doing here?"

"It's me, Jake Lalonde." He frowned. Why was she acting so strange? "I was on your expedition to Hilazon Tachtit. I video-recorded the excavation of the fertility goddess—" He stopped at her disturbing expression.

"Yes, of course. We worked together at Hilazon Tachtit. I didn't recognize you in the dark. How did you find my excavation? It is currently closed to the public. I am on sabbatical and no one knows where I am. I like to keep it that way."

Her words were stilted, her voice cold.

"You have a reason for hiding?" he asked.

"Hiding? I am not hiding. I am working. I do not like to be disturbed. When I am on research leave I feel no need to account for my whereabouts."

"Not even to the police?"

"Excuse me? Police? I was not aware that the police were looking for me. I said all I had to say to the local authorities in Jerusalem."

"They have learned the identity of the dead man that we found."

She gave him a quizzical look and said nothing. Did she really not know? It was hard to tell by her attitude. Vincent's body had not been identified until after she and the expedition members had parted ways. A shiver travelled up Jake's arm as she took him by the hand, and his first reaction was to jerk it away. The three weeks he had worked with her in Hilazon Tachtit, she was friendly but professional. He was a colleague, not a man. And now as she laced her fingers through his, she was acting like he was the most attractive man in the world. He didn't like her presumptuousness and yet the sensation was magnetic.

A single, bare lightbulb swung from a wire over their heads, and in Saveriano's left hand was a flashlight. Jake stared at her, confused. She jolted him alert, beckoning him into a tunnel, their shadows dancing on the wall ahead. "The tunnels opened to the public have lights, but after hours most are turned out. In case we go astray, I have a torch. Stay close . . . ."

Jake had not moved. He had come to look for her. He had found her. So what was his deal? His feet seemed frozen in place.

His deal was that she refused to answer his questions.

"What's wrong, Dr. Lalonde? I thought you came here for a tour? Are you coming?"

Jake followed until she stopped in front of a crypt with a frescoed arch, not knowing why. She smiled at him and started lecturing as though he were a student. That, she informed him pointing to an arcosolium, was a burial chamber for an entire family which used to be sealed by a marble slab. She stroked a polished stone resting against the wall. She moved on past the chamber and through another tunnel that branched into several smaller rooms. Cubicula, she explained, waving her hand as she moved close to him, and he felt her thigh graze his leg as she whisked past, pointing to the floor. Those were the forma, human tombs dug into the ground. He quickly walked into another of the rooms. This one held a stone sarcophagus in the centre of the floor, adorned with sculptured reliefs and inscriptions, and beyond it, in the walls, were the vertical tiles marking more loculi, which reminded him of a morgue. If the tiles had contained sliding drawers behind them, that was exactly what this chamber would have mimicked.

A dull hammering echoed from the depths of one of the tunnels, and she glanced at her watch before starting toward the chamber's exit.

"It smells like death in here," Jake said, his voice reverberating into the silence.

"It should." She gestured to him to watch his footing. There were dark shafts and open pits hidden by the shadows.

"Wait. You haven't answered my questions."

"You really have not asked me any," Saveriano replied.

The tunnel they traversed was empty, the earth and tufa walls coarse and primitive. Inside one of the caverns Jake stopped to have a peek and saw a lone lightbulb waning over a painted fresco. He stood with his jaw hanging open as he stared. The colours were faded, but it was the same fresco he had seen in his vision of a man leading a pilgrimage. Beside it was the epigraph.

Follow me to the sleep of death.

Jake shuddered, turned. Now where was she? He had to hurry to catch up. She was farther up the tunnel at another opening where a smoky glow illuminated the path. Through the entrance, over the dirt floor, more light burned to the far right, and straight ahead, a row of grinning skulls stood out from the wall.

Kitty-corner to the skulls, a pattern of tiles, the loculi, the vertical burials of the Christians were dug into the earth on the right side of the crypt. Engraved into one of the tiles was the likeness of a fish. Most of the tiles were decorated with symbols: the Dove holding an olive branch, symbolic of the soul in divine peace; the Alpha and Omega, the first and last letters of the Greek alphabet, alluding to Christ as the beginning and end of all things; the Phoenix, the mythical Arabian bird, exemplifying the resurrection of the body. And the Raven.

A shot of adrenalin pierced Jake like a lightening bolt. He twisted to find his guide but she had disappeared. *Sophia? Dr. Saveriano, where are you!*

He had no voice, though his mouth was open and he thought he was shouting. The shouts echoed inside his head but not outside his ears. A strange dizziness assailed him; his breath shortened, and he stretched his eyes to see a terrifying figure in a Raven mask circling a ring of burning stones. Jake moved and it moved, came toward him offering a stone cup filled with a malodorous liquid. Jake's hands went to grasp the figure—it was a shaman—but his body passed through the vision and he hit the wall. He tottered, fell to his knees and crawled like a baby. *Come back! I need to talk to you!* Silence. Illusions. He was seeing things, and now he wasn't sure if he was even awake as he followed the edge of the wall toward a white glow in the distance. There was something burning at the end of this tunnel. Jake lowered his arms, shot forward and emerged into a crypt that seemed to burst with light. He looked around startled when the row of grinning skulls reappeared on the wall in front of him.

Scuffmarks patterned the dirt floor, and he squatted to examine the tread, which led to some tiles mounted on the opposite wall. The tiles, decorated with symbols, were arranged in a checkerboard pattern, and on one of them was an engraved fish.

On another was the Raven.

This was the same crypt where he had seen the shadow of the shaman. And those were his own tread marks.

Still dizzy, he slumped to his knees behind a marble tomb and let his eyes dart about. There was no movement, no sound. He waited a few seconds, got to his feet. He had to see the shaman again. He pinched his eyes shut. There was too much light in here. Shamans liked it dark. A flash went off in his brain, then the lightbulb accenting the skulls on the walls shattered, and everything went black.

A voice sliced through the darkness. "Dr. Lalonde, are you in here? Where have you disappeared to?"

The beam of a flashlight erupted into his eyes and Saveriano emerged from the shadows.

Jake was speechless, mortified that he had experienced a vision as he pointed to the shattered tile and the splinters of glass on the floor. "What happened there?" she asked.

He shook his head, perplexed, still unable to speak. But he remembered blacking out just as that happened. Saveriano frowned and a strange expression came over her face. "Tell me what you were doing just before it broke."

He hesitated, coughed to find his voice, then gave a version of what he thought he saw and felt. One thing he was sure of. He never touched that lightbulb. It spontaneously exploded.

She stared at him, nodded, and studied his face and body, the tenseness of his muscles beneath his black T-shirt and jeans. His shadow cast an eerie image against the earthen wall. For a second, he thought he glimpsed the wings of a giant raven.

"You're wrong, Dr. Lalonde. You *did* break that bulb."

"I wasn't anywhere near it."

"You didn't have to be. You did it with your thoughts. You have powers that you don't even know about."

Was this woman insane? "What are you jabbering about? Who the hell *are* you?"

"I am exactly who you think I am. My name is Dr. Sophia Saveriano. I permitted you to accompany my expedition to the caves of Hilazon Tachtit."

"I know that," Jake said, frustrated. Why did she constantly repeat herself? "What I meant was . . . . Wait a minute. *Your* caves?" His voice faded. Powers? What kind of powers?

He *had* heard of her prior to meeting her in Israel. But he hadn't been interested in her research until now. She was the scholar who was laughed off the stage when she made the inane assertion that God had a wife. He muffled a snicker as a blanket of humiliation swamped his scepticism almost as quickly as it had surfaced. Who was he to judge her theories? His peers mocked his own regarding the Raven. He postulated that the mythical icon of the Raven, so prominent in Northwest Coast indigenous art was originally a man, a hybrid of a priest and a healer—a real historical person whose deeds earned him notoriety as the legendary bird figure that represented him today. Was that any less preposterous than what Saveriano proposed? Why couldn't God have had a wife? Venus figurines were an archaeological staple in the Holy Land.

He had shadowed her around this underground maze for what must be over an hour, his thoughts and senses so clouded that he hadn't thought to mention the real reason why he was here in Rome. Saveriano and Vincent were colleagues.

"Don't you understand?" he asked. "The body we discovered in the cargo truck was Vincent Carpello's. Someone murdered him."

The flashlight flickered, illuminating Saveriano's face—a perfect slate of blankness—before she shrugged. "Yes. I read it in the papers."

"Interpol is involved. They're looking to interrogate us."

A smile played on her lips. "Is that why you came to look for me? To turn me in?"

She and Vincent worked in many of the same regions like Italy and Israel. The police would think their mutual interests highly suspicious.

"I am not his keeper," she said. "I haven't seen Dr. Carpello in over a year."

You're lying, Jake thought. "Aren't you the least bit concerned that whoever did this to him might come after you next?"

"And why would they do that?"

"Your research overlaps with Vincent's: *You* study fertility goddesses, *he* studies fertility goddesses. *He* was interested in the Mithras Mysteries and here I find *you*—"

"You find me where, Dr. Lalonde? Where do you think we are?"

Well, this was clearly some kind of catacomb, but his purpose in coming here was to find the shrine of Mithras. Even the tourist brochures—he whipped the documents out of his back pocket to double-check—said that there was a Roman pagan temple dedicated to Mithras somewhere beneath the foundations of the basilica.

The smile returned and she snapped her lids shut for a second.

"So, you *don't* deny it," Jake pressed. "You and Vincent were on to something."

"I don't know what Vincent planned to do with his findings."

"Well, for starters, *Archaeology Magazine* plans to do a feature on his theory of a Persian origin of a female Raven cult as part of the Mithras Mysteries."

Her laughter rang throughout the cavern.

She seriously couldn't persist in arguing that there was no conflict between their research interests when it was a well-known fact.

"All right. So, Vincent and I were in a tight little competition, but that doesn't mean I had anything to do with his death. Besides, I came up with the idea first."

"Ideas can't be copyrighted or patented. You know that. Not in academia anyway."

"Well, lucky for me, then, that he's out of the picture."

The gloat in her voice worried him. Was she admitting that she had something to do with his murder?

"I haven't seen the man in over a year; I swear, Jake." She looked up with determined eyes. "I would like to call you Jake, and please, call me Sophia. After all, we are hardly strangers. Do you plan to turn me in as a suspect? Because if you do, you will never see the evidence for the Raven's supremacy in the Mithras cult."

Was she baiting him? The Raven was his obsession. How did she know that?

"There are many things I know about you, *Nankilslas*."

How did she know his Haida name, He-Whose-Voice-Is-Obeyed?

"I know many things about you. I know that you are sometimes called *Yehlh*."

"I was never called *Yehlh*." *Yehlh* was the name of the ancient shaman who possessed his dreams. *Yehlh* was the name of the Raven, an old and mythical figure who only existed in his nightmares.

CHAPTER SEVEN

"Thank God, you came when you did," Angeline said, sending a nervous glance over her shoulder at the rear traffic as she climbed inside Chancellor's rented Fiat. "I thought that scary Frenchwoman was going to eat me."

"Strange lady," Chancellor said. "What did you say to her? She *looked* like she was going to eat you."

"I don't know, but one thing I *do* know, she gives me the creeps."

"Do you know her?"

"What do you mean? I've never seen her before—until today."

"She said she was Saveriano's assistant. That means she's probably also some kind of archaeologist."

"Maybe. But I'm sure I've never met her before. I would remember that face."

"She seemed like she knew *you*."

He drove them back into town so that she could freshen up at a hotel. They finally found one that had available rooms, an old facility that didn't have the greatest plumbing, but at this stage Angeline didn't care as long as it had hot running water, a toilet, and a bed. Alone in her room now while Chancellor went to his, she showered and changed into sundress and sandals just purchased from the boutique next door. There was only one other time she could remember an October being this warm. Those unseasonable temperatures hadn't lasted and by month's end it had turned bone-chillingly cold.

She was too hopped up to take a nap or even to eat despite the jetlag and, in fact, she was so overtired she *couldn't* sleep. She was jumpy like someone was standing behind her breathing cold air down her neck. And as she dressed alone in her room, she caught flickering movements out of the corner of her eye. I'm getting paranoid, she thought, and shook herself like a dog.

She tried to call Jake's cell phone again, but there was no answer. He wasn't at the hostel either. She finally left her room and went onto the street to flag a taxi.

A cab pulled up and now was her chance to escape Chancellor. She flashed a look behind her before getting in. She had no idea how to start looking for Jake.

Rome was huge and there were so many places he could be, but from the way he had described his vision, she knew it had to be in one of the underground tangles of tunnels leading to a Mithraic temple. Many were located beneath present-day churches, and Vincent had several of them on his list. The parchment with the strange configuration of symbols had been found in the same one where Chancellor had said Sophia Saveriano worked. So that was where she was going.

"*Basilica di San Clemente, per favore,*" she said, to the driver.

The taxi dropped her off in front of a church with a white steeple, and she entered the front doors and saw that a service was in full swing. This church was small, not what she expected, and did not match the description of the basilica in her tourist book.

If a mithraeum existed here, where would it be? She left quietly and walked around to the rear of the church. There were no signs of an excavation or a door that could lead to a subterranean passage. All mithraea were located underground, unless they had been excavated and brought to the surface for display. She couldn't return inside the church to search for a basement passageway without disturbing the sermon. Retracing her footsteps, she wandered to the front of the church and saw a sign off to the side that said, BASILICA DI SAN CLEMENS.

No wonder she couldn't find it. This was the wrong church. She stood on the pavement and looked around. The city was crawling with people and cars, and this was also the wrong street. Where was the Via Labicana? To her right she glimpsed the elliptical bowl of the Colosseum. The tourist brochures had said that the Basilica of San Clemente was behind the Colosseum, so it must be nearby. Well, if all else failed, she might get a view from there because that was one monument a taxi driver would know.

Checking out every church in the vicinity proved impossible, so Angeline headed for the most famous of Rome's ancient monuments where she paid the entrance fee and followed some tourists under a stone archway. Looking up at the massive structure, she estimated the surrounding walls to be as high as a 15-story building. Under the vaulting arches ancient Roman gladiators fought in the elliptical arena, and in the three tiers of seating overhead 50,000 watchers ogled the spectacle while beneath the tiers underground rooms and corridors crisscrossed the floor. That was where the gladiators and lions waited for their turn on the stage.

Angeline wandered behind some noisy tourists, forcing herself to stick to the public paths. Most of the archways leading to the upper tiers were blocked off by NO PUBLIC ACCESS warnings, but one of the stairways lacked a sign. She glanced sideways, extracting herself from the clot of tourists and dipped under an archway.

She had to find Jake before Chancellor did. Where else might he have gone other than the mithraeum beneath the Basilica of San Clemente? There were so many churches, basilicas and cathedrals, and her feet had just about had it. If she climbed the stairs and reached the next level, she could see the city from an aerial perspective and possibly locate the three-levelled structure with vaulted windows and short spires.

The stone steps were in good shape and she climbed to the second level to stare down at the arena. When she looked up again, her sight happened to land on a dark figure in an archway. A security guard come to scold her? She angled her gaze so that she was peering through a veil of her own hair and saw that the man who was heading straight for her was Chancellor.

"How did you find me?" she demanded as they met.

"I followed you. What do you think? And what the devil are you doing up here?" He paused, obviously not expecting an answer.

Dressed in a tennis shirt and casual slacks instead of his usual shirt, tie, and trench coat, Chancellor touched the crisp cotton strap at her shoulder. "This new?"

The sensation of his fingers on her skin was like being zapped by static shock, and she jerked away, while his eyebrows rose, amused.

"I was looking to see where the Basilica of San Clemente is. It's supposed to be somewhere behind the Colosseum," she said coldly.

"Is that where you think Lalonde is?" He paused. "So, just how serious *are* you and Lalonde?"

"*Very.* I have every intention of marrying him."

"I see. Can I ask you a personal question?"

"No."

"I'm going to ask it anyway . . . . Why do you think Lalonde doesn't want to get married?"

The arrogance! she thought. "What's that got to do with Vincent's murder?"

"Maybe nothing, maybe everything. Just answer the question."

She was tempted to say nothing. "Who said Jake doesn't want to get married? He gave me this, didn't he?" She flashed the diamond in his face.

"That doesn't mean he wants to get married. You said yourself he won't agree to a wedding date. All that ring means is that he doesn't want *you* to marry anyone else."

"Why are you so concerned with our relationship?"

"I'm not concerned with your relationship. I'm interested in Lalonde's character, his motives. How gullible do you think he is?" His emphasis was on the word 'gullible.'

Angeline glared, wanted to wallop him good. "He is *not* gullible. Why are you saying that?"

He caught her arm. "Don't get melodramatic on me. I'm just asking questions."

"These are hardly routine questions pertinent to a murder case."

Releasing her, he looked across the arena at the next level, and Angeline's eyes followed. Above the third tier was an attic story with Corinthian pilasters and a series of small square windows in alternate bays. Up there were brackets and sockets that formerly held the masts of the velarium, a kind of canopy for shade. "The view must be spectacular from there. Bet you can see through the broken wall over the city. I'm going up. Don't follow me," she said.

"You do that," he warned. "And I'll get Security to bring you down."

She marched into the nearest passage while Chancellor left in the opposite direction. Through the opening under the arch she sighted a staircase, and on either side of her the path continued with more arches and vaults and steps, some leading to nowhere. Parts of the amphitheatre were falling down; other parts were under restoration. There were loose blocks, crumbling tufa and unstable piers. She put a hand to the wall to steady herself, and when she felt calmer, she withdrew her hand, causing crumbs of mortar to fall away from the stone blocks.

The amphitheatre was designed for excellent acoustics and her footsteps echoed across the smooth, worn marble. She could hear the roar of the tourists below as she stepped over some rubble, avoiding a large section of fallen masonry to her right. She went to the stairs and tested the first one with her foot. It rocked slightly, but seemed sturdy. She began her climb.

As she neared the top, her breath came in short, rapid gulps. What was she doing? This was insane, but Chancellor seemed to bring out the worst in her. She would rather do something stupid like climb to someplace off-limits than accompany him back to the tourist grotto. Too late now. She was on the third tier and looking out of one of the window arches to the street below. The city was alive. Cars and buses were parked in the plaza and vendors were closing up. The air was rife with traffic exhaust and the musty odour of stone. She ventured across the worn floor to the side facing the arena, and from there she could see where the broken wall opened out to an amazing vista.

Leaning over the balustrade, she felt her pulse quicken as she realized how high up she was. A loud drilling sound blasted her ears and her head shot up. In the attic story above her, workmen were chiselling away, hidden behind some heavy blocks of stone.

She strained her neck to see as far as she could. Many buildings had spires. She glanced down at the tourist brochure in her hand to study the photo of the Basilica of San Clemente.

A loud sound like thunder brought her head up just as something huge fell from above, striking the ledge she was resting on, followed by a tumble of small rocks, broken concrete, and fill. Squatting as the barrier beside her collapsed, she twisted to avoid the avalanching rubble, arms curled over her head. From the arena below she could hear shouting and the clatter of trampling feet on the walkway. As she crawled to the edge on her elbows and saw Chancellor under an arch, he turned, stared up, than bolted for the stairs with two security guards at his rear. By the time everyone reached the third tier, the workmen above had lowered a ladder and were already down.

The dust was settling, and Angeline scrambled to her knees as the workmen jabbered to the approaching Chancellor in Italian. The tumble of masonry had missed her, crashing to her side, a huge bite gone from the balustrade and debris strewn everywhere.

Chancellor reached down. "You little fool. I told you not to come up here."

Dust fell from her hair; dirt smeared her cheeks, her arms and legs were powdered white but there was no blood. Shaking herself loose from his grasp, she felt mortified by her escape. The two guards approached and called out in stilted English, voices charged with emotion. The first guard clenched his teeth and asked, "*Signorina*, what are you doing up here? This area is off limits to tourists. The supporting columns and walls of these old monuments are shaky. Are you hurt?"

She flexed her arms and massaged a bruised knee, apologizing profusely for her idiocy. She was thoroughly embarrassed for having done such a dangerous thing. *This is not me*, she desperately wanted to explain. *I was ticked off at Chancellor; he was such a jerk and I wanted to get away from him.* Lame, lame, lame. What did it matter? She had already done the stupid thing of ignoring the warning signage and entering a prohibited area.

The first guard ordered everyone back to work, then firmly led her to the stairway clear of the workmen who had begun to clean up while Chancellor followed.

*   *   *

On the return trip to their hotel, Chancellor was quiet. No interrogation, no reprimands. She already felt bad enough, and he knew it was because of him. Besides, it would do no good. Angeline did not trust him. And why should she? He had told her nothing but half-truths and a good measure of fabrication. One thing was obvious, however, and that was simply that she had no idea where Lalonde was. Her escape to the Colosseum was no elaborate ruse to put him off her boyfriend's track. She honestly did not know where he was.

He left her at her room so that she could get cleaned up, then reappeared an hour later and found her in T-shirt and jeans when she opened the door.

"How about dinner?" he asked, wanting to make up for the upsetting escapade. "I made reservations."

"You could have saved yourself the trouble. I'm not hungry."

"I already got us a table. Besides, you have to eat."

She looked like she wanted to rip into him, but instead sighed, noticed his suit and tie, and shrugged. "Fine. Come back in fifteen minutes. I need to change."

Prime seating on the rooftop patio of *Parisella's Ristorante* usually had to be booked weeks in advance, but Chancellor lucked out and got them a table. Angeline was dressed in black and white silk with her hair twisted above her nape when he returned to get her for dinner. Draped over her arm was a black wrap. No sign of her earlier mishap was visible except for a bruise on her elbow. She hung her wrap on the spine of her chair and went to sit down, a firm set to her jaw.

The maitre d' pushed in her chair. The waiters were polite and unobtrusive, and knew better than to chatter or to explain the chef's specialties before the customer had been offered an aperitif. Chancellor perused the menu, trying to think how he could convince Angeline to go home. Things had not gone well today and he now suspected he might be putting her in danger. He had requested a background check on Saveriano's assistant, and when the report arrived via email from HQ in Lyons, France, it had disturbed him.

He often ate at the same restaurants when in Rome. Tonight he had no appetite, and shifted his eyes from the menu to lean over the balustrade and observed the rooftops below.

In a city the size of Rome, the rich mixed with the poor, though the rich seemed to have an invisible force field shielding them. Here and there, the looping lines of laundry strung between buildings crosshatched his view. A harried mother strained out of a narrow window onto the steel fire escape to hang out one more faded T-shirt, while behind her a child cried. Nightfall had come to the Eternal City; the lights of the urban core blazed below; traffic crawled. When the weather was mild like it was now, the streets were never empty and the beggars, gypsies and youths loitering on the pavement gave Rome its colour and interest. Although tourist season was waning, the cafes and bars were busy, the churches open. Where, among all of this, was Lalonde hiding? Was he so fixated on his crusade that he'd neglect his woman?

Chancellor turned back to Angeline. "You must be hungry by now. If you like seafood, this *ristorante* specializes in fresh catches. They're famous for their *insalata di frutti di mare*. It's made with squid, lobster, octopus and shrimp."

She shrugged and looked away at the terrace toward the soft lamps perched at intervals along the stone balustrade and a plethora of elegant white lilies. On the tables more lilies garnished the crystal and silver settings.

"Let's have a drink first," he suggested.

"I'm not thirsty either."

"In Italy, one doesn't drink because one is thirsty." He summoned a waiter, and ordered two Campari and sodas.

When the drinks arrived, Angeline inspected her drink, which was served in a short glass with a slice of lemon and cracked ice. She took a sip, but when she set the glass down her agitation showed, and she accidentally knocked over the saltshaker.

"What's the matter?" he asked. "I promise I'll behave myself. It's only dinner. Besides, I want to talk to you about what happened at the Colosseum today."

"I don't think that was an accident," she said.

He screwed up his eyes. "So what was it?"

"I felt something. Saw something. It's been happening ever since we left Sophia Saveriano's villa."

"What did you see?"

"It's not exactly what I saw. It's more a feeling. Like I'm being watched."

He studied her expression, frowned. "Let's get out of here," he said, rising.

"You want to leave? But we just got our drinks. What will the waiters think?"

"We'll take the drinks with us."

An aroma of garlic, tomatoes and basil drifted toward them as he led her inside, past the startled wait staff, down the stairs and out the door. On the street, his rental was parked nearby, but he led her past it, down the pavement toward the city lights. Chancellor sucked back his Campari and soda, clinking the ice as it sloshed forward, and emptied the lemon peel into the gutter. He dropped the glass into his jacket pocket, and when Angeline finished her drink he dumped out the ice and shoved her glass into the other. At the intersection, he grabbed her wrist, yanking her to a halt as the lights changed, then he steered her toward the street where they shot across four lanes of traffic, heedless of the honking horns, menacing fenders and suffocating exhaust. On the other side four gypsies were waiting, hands outspread, and one of them, a grubby little girl clad in a droopy purple wrapping of cheap cloth, reached for Angeline's wrap. Chancellor cuffed the gypsy girl until she backed off.

"There's no need for that," Angeline said. "Here, let me give them something." She rummaged in her handbag for some euros.

"If you do that, they'll never leave you alone."

"I don't have any cash, only credit cards. Do you have any change, Tom?" The gypsies were becoming insistent now, aggressive. Their hands were grasping at her arms, her skirt, her handbag, and although she tried to shrug them off, they swarmed about like tourists in front of Michelangelo's statue of David. She was agitated now, verging on panic. The congregation of four had turned into six, and now ten. Finally, she had to elbow a particularly persistent young woman who was trying to slide her wrap off her shoulders.

Chancellor grabbed the gypsy woman by the arm and pushed her aside, revealing beneath her ratty shawl the grubby little girl in the purple sari grinning at Angeline. He checked the girl's hands but they were empty, and as the horde pressed closer, he shouted harshly in Italian and they dispersed. He gave Angeline a sardonic smile. "Better check for your wallet."

Her wallet and credit cards were intact.

"Next time, maybe you'll listen to me. Those gypsies know what they're doing."

She scowled and turned toward an ostentatious structure of sculpted stone, rising from a pool of water where a number of noisy tourists gathered. In contrast to the white sculpture, the water in the Trevi Fountain was a rich aquamarine.

How to do this? he thought, and waited a few seconds for Angeline to calm down before he spoke. "You'll probably find this hard to believe, but fifty years ago this piazza was nearly always deserted." He was stalling. "There's been a lot of restoration in the last few decades. This fountain is supplied by water from the Acqua Vergine aqueduct and was designed in the Baroque style by Nicolo Salvi. It was completed in 1762 after his death, but it wasn't until Hollywood made it famous in the 1950s film *Three Coins in the Fountain* that it was restored."

"You know an awful lot about history for a cop," she said suspiciously.

True. He stared at the fountain's main focus where a statue, guiding a shell chariot drawn by winged steeds flanked by a pair of tritons, was illuminated by submerged floodlights. "That's Neptune. The two figures on either side are Health and Fertility."

He had stalled long enough. "That gypsy girl was up to no good. And that assistant of Saveriano's has a suspicious background. I had HQ in Lyons check her out. She has no history before she came to work for Saveriano a year ago. I can't find one damn thing about her: where she was born, who her parents are, where she went to school, employment records, medical and dental records. Nada. As far as the world is concerned she didn't exist pre June 2009. That can only mean one thing. Her name's a phony. Angeline, are you sure you don't know her? Because I saw the way she looked at you. And it wasn't a girl-on-girl crush. You said you felt like you were being watched all day? I think you're right. And I think it's her."

Angeline bit on her lower lip, rubbed her temples and snapped her eyes shut briefly.

Clearly, she thought the same thing.

CHAPTER EIGHT

Next morning Chancellor awoke before the sun broke through the curtains of his hotel room. He decided to let Angeline have the day to herself. The best way for him to find Lalonde was to let her explore on her own.

He sat in the lobby reading a newspaper until he saw her leave the elevator and head for the front doors. Then he got up and noticed another figure in the shade of a potted palm. He waited a few minutes to see if the figure was watching Angeline. She was. He followed her outside to a silver Volkswagen beetle. She put on a pair of dark glasses, lowered her head and started the car. Then she waited.

Chancellor got into his own car and drove through the city making various twists and turns before finally leaving the convertible on the street. He headed southwest on foot, across the plaza, kitty corner to the Trevi Fountain where he and Angeline had stood last night. As he looked back, he saw the Volkswagen stop a block behind his Fiat and the woman exit the vehicle.

Chancellor leaned against the stone wall of an old church, holding the door wide as the woman ambled up. He motioned her inside. She stepped forward to a battery of fluttering bats that had been roosting beneath the bell-tower.

Under the arch into a vestibule, she clenched her short leather jacket to her chest, eyes rigid like he held a gun on her. He urged her through a set of panelled doors where rows of engraved wooden pews lined the chapel. The pulpit was of solid lumber, draped in a tapestry of religious icons. Lit candles in pewter sconces flickered from the walls, and in front of the pulpit, on either side, votive candles glowed on tiered tables. A plaque of stained glass hung above. No service was in progress and only a shrouded woman occupied the room. Having lighted a candle and crossed herself, she slipped to her knees, hands laced in prayer.

Chancellor led the way over a patchy rug to an arch, which opened into a corridor of natural maple with carvings on the beams. At the end of the hall was a gallery of mortared stone. The room was windowless and at adjacent corners candles dripped from pewter holders, sending wax down the wooden stands.

He raised a candle. Now that their eyes were adjusting to the lesser light, she tried to identify some wrapped packages enclosed in glass cases. Shadows flickered on her face, deforming her features.

"We're inside a church," Chancellor replied to her questing eyes.

She waved her hands about taking in the odd furnishings. "Obviously, but what's this room? What *are* those behind the glass?"

She squatted to face an object coiled in cloth bandages. The fabric was old and threadbare, threatening to come unwound. Suddenly, she rose with a startled step backwards, and bumped into Chancellor.

Wax splashed to the floor. The tower bell chimed, ringing through the building, making her jump again. The room was not noise proof. Wide gaps in the mortar allowed traffic sounds inside, and they heard the screech of a car cutting a corner too sharp. Wind whistled through the walls, and the flame snuffed out.

"Those are embalmed organs. Holy remains."

"Remains of who?" she demanded. Chancellor smiled as her voice croaked. "The priests? The popes?"

"Who do you think? Of course, the popes."

He laughed and instead of bringing a heart to her, he struck a match from a box he'd found left behind by the keeper of this hall of horrors.

"All right, Cristine," he said as he relit the candle. "Why are you here? You were supposed to stick with Angeline."

"If you're going to yell at me, I'm not going to say anything."

"If you want an exclusive on this story, you'll do as you're told."

The journalist hesitated while Chancellor scowled, then he lowered the flame to her face. "Well?"

"This place sucks. Can we go somewhere else to talk?" Her hands were gripping her jacket, her eyes darting everywhere. "Why are you so interested in creepy stuff like this anyway?"

He put the candle on top of one of the glass cases, and gestured for her to follow. The brighter chapel with its pews and ornate pulpit was empty, and he indicated for Cristine to sit at the front row while he went to the votive candles. Taking a match from a glass bowl, he lit a few and rejoined her. "That's not much for light, but it'll have to do. Now, tell me what you've got."

"Hold on a second," she said, flapping a hand at the exit. "Just exactly what was that back there? I didn't appreciate the scare tactics."

"And *I* don't appreciate your indiscretion. Now talk."

A laptop appeared from out of her carryall and she turned it on, hit a key on the type-pad to reveal a screen listing shamanic attributes from around the world.

You can run, he thought, *but how long can you hide? Are you what you purport to be?*

Words leaped off the screen, a single line grabbing his eye. *Shamanic powers were usually inherited, but to become a shaman a person must 'die,' be visited by spirits, and be 'reborn.'* Was Lalonde willing to do that? A shaman experienced a trance state before he could enter the Spirit World—a place which was either in the sky or underground, and which was where he obtained knowledge and power from spirits and learned the language of animals. Chancellor chuckled softly, ignoring Cristine's arched brow. He'd like to hear Lalonde caw like a raven.

A shaman communicated with two types of spirits: one that appeared in animal form and one that was the soul of a dead shaman.

Significant?

Maybe.

A shaman had the gift of precognition and clairvoyance.

Now *that* was significant.

The shaman's costume was some kind of animal with the three chief types being the bird, the reindeer and the bear—but especially the bird.

Yes, they were getting somewhere.

As he looked up from the laptop he caught Cristine's self-satisfied smile. "So, this stuff means something to you."

It certainly did, but he wasn't letting her in on his suspicions. He sucked in his cheeks, pursing his lips. All of these characteristics ascribed to shamans fit perfectly. Ritual. Trance. Entrance into the Spirit World: a Spirit World that was in the sky or underground. *Underground*, like the subterranean temples of Mithras. Furthermore, a shaman communicated with two types of spirits: one that appeared in animal form and one that was the soul of a dead shaman. He knew Lalonde's late father was a Haida artist. Was he possibly a shaman, too?

"Look at this—" the journalist pointed to a spot on the screen, number four on the list of shamanic traits. "A shaman has the gift of precognition and clairvoyance. Did you know that Lalonde claims to have inherited memories?"

His face was purposefully vacant. "Explain. What do you mean by inherited memories?"

"Didn't Angeline tell you?"

Angeline had told him a number of things, but not that. He urged her to be specific, and she told him about the skeleton in the pool on the San Juan islands and how Jake believed the bones belonged to a 10,000-year-old shaman who was his ancestor, a man he was linked to through genetic memories.

Chancellor was careful not to react. He would confront Angeline with this bit of info but for now he filed it away. He glanced back at the screen, nodding silently.

Number 5 on the list was obvious. The shaman's costume was some kind of animal, and the three main types were the bird, the reindeer and the bear.

The Raven was Lalonde's family crest. He was obsessed with the mythical avian figure, proving its origins, following the global migrations of its motifs and symbols. The way Vincent Carpello died was definitely a message—the shadow of his hands formed the shape of a raven rattle. Shamans used Raven rattles. As he cogitated over this idea, something else struck him. Didn't Sophia Saveriano also have an interest in ravens?

"Can I see this for a second?" Chancellor pulled the laptop onto his lap and accessed the meaning of the Raven in mythology. The definition confirmed what he had already guessed. The belief, that the raven was the wisest of animals and the oldest of animals stemmed from his divinity or sacredness. In the late Middle Ages the raven became an icon of evil, but this trait also pointed to his deification. Many devils were originally gods, and the Latin word *sacer* meant both 'holy' and 'evil.'

"What do you know about the raven in the Mithraic Mysteries?" he asked.

"Not much, only that the raven was the messenger of the god Mithras." She thought for a bit. "There *was* something interesting that Vincent told me in one of our correspondences before he died. He said that primitive cultures had animal gods and civilized cultures had anthropomorphic gods, and that in Egyptian culture you can see the transition. Egyptian gods have human bodies and animal heads. But what I thought was really interesting is this—When a god is anthropomorphized, the animal figure doesn't always disappear, but may remain as a symbol, a pet, or a messenger of the god."

The revelation hit like a bullet—as in *the* Mithraic cult! So, the raven might have once been a god himself, but appeared later as a *messenger* of Mithras—

She plucked the computer off Chancellor's lap and slapped the top down. "So, where does that leave us? What does it all mean? Why this interest in Jake, shamanism and his affiliation with the Raven? And how does Sophia Saveriano, Vincent Carpello's murder and the cult of Mithras come into it?"

"That leaves *us* nowhere; exactly where we were before. I want Lalonde. I want you to stick with Angeline, but don't be too obvious. In the next few days make contact with her. Think up a reason why you're in Rome without making her suspicious. Get to be her best friend."

"I don't think that will be necessary," Cristine said with a smile. "If you hadn't been such a jerk earlier, I would have already told you why I was following you. I know where Jake is."

CHAPTER NINE

Despite the spooky weather, chills chased up Angeline's spine. Why couldn't she shake this feeling? No one was behind her, it was broad daylight, and if anyone followed she would see. Chancellor was feeding her scraps of her own fear. She should never have told him that she suspected the Frenchwoman of anything. Not once had she seen the assistant outside of Sophia Saveriano's villa. Angeline stared at the poster on the door of the National Museum of Rome. The *bastard*, she thought. He had lied to her. The woman was not missing. The poster read:

SUBTERRANEAN:
The Black Goddess and the Mysteries of Mithras
Lecture and Exhibition
Dr. Sophia Saveriano
November 1ˢᵗ
8:00 P.M.
Gala Reception

She looked both ways before she opened the doors of the museum and walked in. She wouldn't be surprised to find the elusive professor in her lab. Why had Chancellor lied to her?

She was at the Baths of Diocletian, the headquarters of The National Museum. She had assumed that this was where Saveriano's office would be, but now she wasn't sure if she was right. The museum housed its archaeological collections in three different facilities. The building of the Baths included numerous rooms with a *natatio* or *frigidarium*, which was a large open-air swimming pool, meeting rooms, libraries, nymphiums, dressing rooms, concert rooms and rooms for physical exercise. The place was a maze and seemingly deserted. She went through an exhibition of funerary materials that housed sarcophagi, statues and urns. The Masterpiece Rooms were now the Epigraphical Department and contained 10,000 inscriptions, most of which were not on display. In the Michelangelo cloister, there was an exhibition on the protohistory of Rome.

She meandered for a while, but couldn't find a single person who seemed to work here to ask about the notorious scholar.

In the Octagonal Hall, which stood at the southwest corner of the complex, she walked past the Lyceum Apollo and the Aphrodite of Cyrene. When she emerged through a doorway, she found herself in an exhibition gallery with a single statue in the centre of the floor. It was being prepared for display, but at the moment, no one was around. Angeline moved closer to the statue. At first glance, it looked like an ordinary Venus figurine except that it was ten to twelve feet tall. It was female, with large breasts, a protruding belly and swollen hips. But there was something odd about this statue.

"Excuse me," someone said in a heavy Italian accent. "This gallery is not intended for the public."

She looked up to see a man standing behind her. "I'm sorry. The door was opened, so I just wandered in."

"We don't get too many guests here as we are undergoing restoration, so Security is a little lax."

He made to lead her to the exit, but she hesitated. "My name is Angeline Lisbon. I'm an archaeologist from Seattle, Washington. I'd love it if you'd let me stay and study this statue."

He frowned for a second at her obvious youth. "You're a professor?"

"Uh, no. I'm a PhD candidate. And you are?"

"Dr. Leo Nunzo. I'm the head curator. Well, I suppose it couldn't hurt for you to stay. Just no picture-taking. Are you studying Neolithic religion?"

She nodded, conscious that her response was only a partial lie. "This is a very unusual piece," she said, indicating the Venus statue.

"Yes." He led her around to the side and she gasped. "Yes," he repeated. "She is called the Black Goddess. She is part of the triple goddess phenomenon: The Nymph, the Mother, the Crone. You are looking at the Mother facade. She represents fertility."

Angeline could now see that the statue was made up of three images. On the other two sides were the Nymph and the Crone. The Nymph was a slimmer, more delicate version of the Mother, but without the diadem or the torch. Instead she wore a skirtlike garment around her hips.

The Crone was the most frightening side. This facet of the goddess was ugly, withered and stooped. "The creator and destroyer of all life," the curator said.

"Why is she called the Black Goddess?"

"Because she is at the heart of all creative process. She is also wisdom and death. Look at the Crone aspect of the figure. Is not she the image of evil?"

Angeline shuddered at the horrific rendition of female aging.

"This image espouses the belief that a woman who has outlived her husband has somehow used up his life force."

"That's horrible."

The curator shrugged. "Are you coming to Dr. Saveriano's lecture and unveiling of the goddess? You'll learn much more about the rites and mythology surrounding the Black Goddess from her."

"Actually, I came here looking for her. Is she around?"

"To be honest, I haven't seen her in weeks. Ever since that nasty business with that American archaeologist in Israel where the statue was found."

"She must have been devastated. I understand he was a colleague of hers."

"That's right. So she was . . . . And now if you'll excuse me, I have work to do. Please stay as long as you like, but don't touch anything. When you leave, I'd appreciate it if you would close the door. I don't want anyone else wandering loose in here."

She frowned at his abrupt departure. Everything surrounding Saveriano seemed odd. He obviously had conflicted feelings concerning her. She almost called him back for an explanation, but decided against it and returned to the statue.

It was too bad Vincent hadn't told her what the symbols on the missing text meant. Knowing its secrets would have answered a lot of questions. Angeline traced the Black Goddess's triple forms with her eyes.

You have something to do with the missing text, don't you? What does a bird, a cup, a staff, a torch, a diadem and a lamp have to do with you?

The statue wasn't answering.

Angeline wandered around the statue, in awe of its size and symbolism, then faced the Mother aspect of the triple goddess. *Do you have a name?* Black Goddess seemed so dark, and the motherly version of her was hardly sinister. The diadem on her head was puzzling as was the torch and the lamp in her hands. Angeline was itching to caress the rough, pitted stone, but knowing how the oils from human hands would damage the statue, she refrained and ran her fingers along the base of the plinth. She followed until the sculpture ended in a sharp edge, then gazed up at the Crone's expression of exquisite pain.

Or was it a face of agonized pleasure?

A burst of frosty air swirled around her, the stone of the statue burned to the touch. She tucked her hands under her armpits. Was she losing her mind?

She rubbed her fingers together, then fumbled in her handbag for her cell phone, rested her index finger on the keypad, mind numb.

Jake's number was absent from her Contacts.

A gentle pressure cupped her hand, like a human touch. She watched her hand as though it belonged to someone else, as though some invisible force was lifting her index finger and placing it on specific keys until a single word appeared in the search bar.

C-R-O-N-E

Fingertips icy, she snatched her hand to her chest and squashed a shiver.

The next moment, the pressure on her hand was gone. Her digital thesaurus appeared and a list of synonyms emerged bright on the screen:

Hag
Witch
Shrew
Virago
Termagant
Harridan
Hellion
Scold
Nag
Xanthippe

Was she imagining things? She rubbed her hands together to generate some heat and get the blood flowing. What was wrong with her? It wasn't cold; at least it wasn't a minute ago. Her eyes dropped to the display on her cell phone. Was this her subconscious playing games with her? She had not powered this search.

Most of the terms suggested that older women had some sort of evil power. Unpleasant descriptors for an elderly woman, the word 'Witch,' in particular, jumped out at her. The last time she'd heard this term tossed around, the accused had turned out to be more a bitch than a witch. The woman had caught on fire, and was horribly maimed, as though she *had* been one. Oh my god, Angeline moaned. *A ghost just walked over my grave.* For one frightening, irrational, inarticulate instant, the aphorism made sense to her.

But that episode in Tonga was ancient history, and a very unpleasant memory.

Her fingernails scratched some paper, making a scraping sound. She traced the brow of the plinth. Her action was intentional, though mindless, and not at all like that freaky incident with her cell phone. She looked down to see a draft of the text below her fingertips, describing the Crone side of the sculpture.

She picked up the printout and slipped it into her handbag, remembering that she had seen a room with office machines when she was wandering through the museum's galleries. Maybe she could get it photocopied. As she went to withdraw her hand, something didn't seem quite right. She fished frantically inside the bag. Panicking, she inverted her purse onto the floor.

Her heart did a triple flip as she realized what had happened.

CHAPTER TEN

She might not be able to go home, but there *was* somewhere she could go. She flagged a taxi and made a B-line to the hotel. Mr. Chancellor had a lot of explaining to do. Not only was Saveriano *not* missing, the statue was never stolen.

His door was ajar. Was the maid in there? She listened but heard no whirring of a vacuum cleaner or the thumping of someone lifting objects to dust. She knocked again, and again she heard silence. She turned the knob and pushed the door open, looked in. It was almost noon and the light from the corridor arrowed across the hotel room onto the bed like artificial sunshine; otherwise all was dark. The curtains were drawn to a crack and, although the sheets were tousled, the bed was empty. On the floor was Chancellor's opened luggage, his clothes tossed any old way.

Angeline walked in, barely able to discern the outline of his furniture in the ribbons of light, moved to the windows intending to pull apart the drapes, but stopped at the sounds of movement. "Tom?"

A rivulet of steam bled from the base of the bathroom door and a light flashed from the crack, turning the steam into a nebulous multicoloured lightshow before it dispersed. She gaped, stunned by the strange apparition. Then a sensation of otherworldliness circled her, fogging her mind. A bubble of fear curled around her neck, sending adrenalin straight into her heart. Clear, second thoughts came fast and thick. *What was that? What am I doing?* She shouldn't even be here. She turned, ran for the hallway but before she could reach it something knocked her to the floor. She gasped, kicking, straining to see her attacker even as her blows struck air. Gagging, she spun to her knees, rolled onto her hips to leap to her feet. Whatever had hit her wasn't getting a second chance to make her tryst with the hotel's dingy carpet permanent, and for a painful second she stopped as she waltzed into a wall of cold . . . .

She raced to the door, looked left, then right. The hall was empty. A finger poked her shoulder and she nearly jumped out of her shoes. When she turned to look, Chancellor was there and the expression on his face was hostile.

"What did you think you were doing? Now you've scared her away."

Angeline choked trying to catch a breath, her heartrate already ratcheted up from her encounter in the museum. She swallowed, glanced to either side of her. "Scared who away? I didn't see anyone."

He led her into his room and went to the window to draw back the drapes. Sunlight flooded the hotel room, revealing clothing and paper and equipment in disarray.

Aggravated, Angeline pulled herself together, voice hoarse from shock. "What in blazes happened in here? Where *were* you?"

"Waiting for someone."

"Is that so? Who? Were you waiting to ambush them in the dark? Good grief, Tom, is everyone crazy around here? Why were you hiding in the dark? And what was all that steam coming out of the bathroom?" He was dry, and fully clothed, once again in suit and tie and trench coat. She recognized his favourite yellow necktie, and tugged at it. He obviously wasn't having a shower.

He refused to react and she threw her hands up like a drama queen. "All right, don't answer me." She thumped the dust off her clothes and stared at him. "You lied to me. Sophia Saveriano is *not* missing."

Chancellor made no denial and Angeline's line of vision went straight past him to the dresser beyond. She barged by and spread her hands, palms up. Some strange equipment sprawled on the dresser top and she poked at them with a finger—night vision goggles, an infrared and thermal camera, an electromagnetic field meter, a K2 meter, a Geiger counter, digital and analog audio recording gadgets and several other gizmos that she couldn't identify. Chancellor stuck his head over her shoulder, gripping her wrist. "Don't touch."

"What were you doing in the dark? And why was your door open if you were in the bathroom? Anyone from off the street could have come inside and robbed you. And again, I want to know what *was* that with all the multicoloured steam?" She held up a small triangular plastic object with a digital reader and buttons with various icons labelling them. "What is this? What were you measuring?"

Chancellor snatched the device from her and shoved it into a dresser drawer.

"I think it's time you stopped the charade. Tell me who you really are or else I'm calling the police." She made to dig out her cell phone from her purse, froze as she remembered what had happened with it earlier.

"If you'll just stop talking for a minute and stop touching my stuff, I'll tell you. That's delicate equipment by the way. Mishandling of it can upset the calibration."

She went to sit on the bed while he paced the floor.

"I'll make it easy for you. You aren't with Interpol, are you?"

"That's one thing that I told you that *wasn't* a lie. I *am* with Interpol. Only I'm a consultant in paranormal cult activities. I deal in antiquities with unusual attributes and the cults they're associated with."

Her laugh sounded hysterical in her own ears. "You're some kind of quack psychic cop?"

He said nothing and went to the dresser to check on his equipment as Angeline fell silent. Oh, my God, he's serious, she thought. Was that a ghost that had knocked her down? She shivered before mentally slapping herself and snorting at her own delusions.

"You can't stay here, Angeline. You should catch the next flight to Seattle." He let out a long breath, met her eyes. "I left the door open because I was expecting someone."

"So you were going to tackle them onto the floor? Then what?"

"I wasn't planning to tackle them at all. Not physically, anyway." Her skin crawled at the tone of his voice. Then, *what* way? She stared at the gadgets on the dresser, the K2 meter he had in his hand. What was he going to do with that?

"It's a communication device."

"No kidding. I've seen *Ghost Hunters* on TV. They use that thing to communicate with the 'other' world." She made air quotes with her fingers and mimed the theme song from the *Twilight Zone* but despite her mockery of him, she was ready to believe anything.

"Okay, I told you what I'm about. Now I want you to go home."

Her brows narrowed suspiciously. He was being awfully insistent. *Just what are you hiding, Mr. Chancellor?* She had a sudden 'aha!' moment. "You know where Jake is! You lied about that, too!"

"No. I just found out where he is an hour ago. I don't need you anymore. Go home."

He touched her shoulder, his expression soft, looking her straight in the eye. She touched her tongue to her dry lips, jerked away from his grip and lifted one of the cameras. This she recognized. It was an infrared camera. What was he planning to do with it?

"I don't have to tell you anything."

"Where's Jake?"

"Go back to Seattle, Angeline. Or to Toronto. Or wherever it is you prefer to be. That's the best place for you now."

How did he know she was Canadian, and that her divorced father lived in Toronto? What kind of a background check had he done on her? She frowned. So, he was hunting for ghosts. Whose ghost? And how did this involve Vincent? *How does it involve Jake?* If Chancellor was a crackpot—and God help her because he was filling her head with similar thoughts—then she had to warn Jake.

"I haven't lost it, Angeline. And I can't read minds either. I *can* interpret faces though and I know exactly what's spinning around on those cogs of yours. Lalonde believes he's the incarnation of a 10,000-year-old shaman, and Saveriano thinks likewise. Do you believe your fiancé is nuts? Because if you don't, then what I'm hunting is not in the domain of crazy either."

"Just, exactly, what *are* you hunting, Tom?"

"I'm not at liberty to say. I'm sorry I had to use you to find Lalonde, but now that I've found him, I don't need you anymore. I've used you as far as I'm willing to use you. Now go home."

"Can't."

Angeline twirled her handbag with her forefinger, flipped it inside out, dumping everything she normally carried onto his bed. Wallet, comb, lipstick, eyeliner, compact, cell phone, keys sprawled over the twisted covers.

"You got it right, Tom. That gypsy girl was up to no good. She stole my passport."

CHAPTER ELEVEN

He didn't have to tell her where Jake was. Alarms sounded in her head. Jake was with Sophia Saveriano. But where was the elusive scholar? She could not forget what she had read beneath the plinth supporting the Black Goddess in her Crone phase:

> *When a culture has no word for 'wise elder woman,' the feminine becomes feared as the triple goddess transforms from Nymph to Mother to Crone. The fear for women is annihilation, to be nonexistent. To be a woman becomes negative. The Crone is seen as the one who brings death to the old way of being and becomes the image of Evil.*

Angeline left Chancellor and went to her room to pack, then lugged her bags down the hall. The man was a lunatic and she wasn't staying one minute longer in this hotel with him than she had to. She stepped out of the elevator and checked her bags with the concierge, then headed straight for the taxi rank outside the hotel. *I'm going back to the villa*, she decided. And have it out with that black-haired, red-lipped French harpy—if she was still there.

The assistant opened the door when she arrived and didn't deny that Jake was staying at the villa. Angeline had no use for the woman and her coquettish drama, and ran up the marble staircase to the very room she had been in before. Had he been here all along? Of course, they hadn't exactly asked for him the first time around—they had asked for the villa's owner—but she had a sneaking suspicion that Frenchie was quite aware of Jake's relationship status.

She reached the landing and turned to her right, saw that the door was open. As she walked in, an arm reached out and grabbed her wrist, swinging her into the room.

"Thank God, you're okay, Jake."

"Of course, I'm okay. What are you doing here? How did you find me? I told you not to come."

"Is that all I get after weeks of separation? No hug? No 'how are you? I missed you?' And what is with the strong-arm tactics?" She pried his hand off her arm and stepped aside. "You could've broken something."

"Sorry," he mumbled.

What was the matter with him? He seemed spaced out, like he barely realized that she was there. His hands were cold, his pupils dilated. Angeline tried to break her gaze with him, couldn't. He was breathing hard. Then he drew her to him, his heart pounding into her ribs, and his mouth came down hard on hers. This was crazy. They hadn't seen each other in weeks and all he wanted to do was have sex? He owed her an explanation! She shoved him back, but his hand went to the base of her head, tugging her hair, forcing her lips to his until she could hardly breathe.

"You can't walk around me garbed like that and not have the fireworks go off," he growled.

She was dressed in a denim miniskirt, which showed off her legs, and her top was a turquoise fitted sleeveless shirt, buttoned low so that a glimpse of her black bra showed. Her hands flew to her sternum to fasten the incriminating button, her thoughts a scrambled stew of questions. That kind of comment was uncharacteristic of him.

"I've been busy, Angel. I've got so much to tell you. But, I need you right now."

Why? Because that French harpy downstairs was trying to seduce you? She'd seen the way the assistant's expression intensified when she mentioned his name. She tried to restrain him; he was never like this, so forceful. Something was weird about his face and it wasn't just the pupils. A peculiar smell surrounded him.

His mouth fought its way to hers again, and then to her ear, and she felt a shiver as his lips took her lobe, then he ran his tongue down her throat to her chest. He hesitated for a second, and began to unbutton her shirt, lifted her and brought her to a queen-sized bed, and removed his pants. There, he pressed her down on her back in full view of a horrible painting depicting Hell. Was it a warning, an omen? She paid no attention because he was already on top of her.

*   *   *

It was obvious he didn't know what to say. He was standing at the dresser, bare-chested, his unbelted jeans zipped, observing her reflection in the mirror. Oh, hell, she thought. It had never been like this before. Like two animals rutting. Neither of them voiced what they felt. What had happened to him? He seemed different.

She had to speak because if she didn't, if she just let it go, they would never talk about this strangeness between them.

"Well? Is this just slam bam, thank you ma'am?" she asked, jokingly. She had to keep it light or she would cry.

She saw him swallow in the mirror's reflection, but he refused to turn around. He tugged his shirt on, not saying a word. She buttoned her shirt and let the first thing she could think of roll off her tongue.

"Are you upset because *Archaeology Magazine* dumped your story?"

He dropped the comb that he was using to tidy his hair onto the dresser.

"What?"

"Your feature. Cristine Kletter came to see me. She actually wanted to tell you in person. I assume she sent an email?"

His head lowered. "No."

"Then, what's wrong? You seem very distracted. Disturbed."

Jake swung to face her, eyes darting briefly to the bed, face flushed. He came and took her by the shoulders. "You shouldn't have come. There's something I have to do and I don't want you to get hurt."

"I already hurt, Jake. What's going on with you? I came here to tell you that Tom Chancellor is in Rome. He's not going to arrest you. It's Sophia Saveriano that he's after. I think he believes she's some kind of spirit seeker."

"Keep him away from her."

"Why?"

"Sophia knows things. She's told me things about my heritage that even I didn't know, and if she's involved in Vincent's murder, I want Chancellor kept away from her until I find out the truth."

About what? What was going on that he thought could hurt her?

"Have you ever heard of the Black Goddess?" he asked.

"Yes. I just saw an ad for a lecture that Saveriano is giving at the National Museum of Rome. I actually saw the statue."

His eyes grew huge. "You did? She wouldn't let me see it again, said I had to learn what the statue meant before I could see it."

The look on Jake's face puzzled her. Since when did he need anyone's permission to do anything? Air suddenly caught in her throat as she recalled Interpol's warning. "You have to stay away from that woman."

She wasn't sure how much she trusted Chancellor, but if they got out of Rome, it wouldn't matter. "That woman is dangerous. Chancellor told me that she's involved in some kind of a cult, that young men associated with her have gone missing. Come to my hotel with me now." She tugged on his arm, realizing in the same instant that she no longer had a hotel room and that she had paid the bill and checked out. Well, they could find another.

His eyes reached out to her through hooded lids. "It's too late, Angeline. I'm in it too deep. I have to find out what I'm capable of."

She let her hand fall away from his arm. She could hardly believe her ears. What was he babbling about? What was he capable of? She inhaled. "What's that smell? It's sort of musty smelling, like earth. Like fresh earth."

He sniffed the air. "I don't smell anything."

She moved up close to him. *He* smelled like it.

"I smell bad?" he asked as she sniffed him. "Maybe I should take a shower."

She shook her head. No. It wasn't a bad smell. It was kind of a nice smell, but it wasn't what he usually smelled like. "Never mind. Get packed, I want you to leave with me."

She had lost her passport, but if they went to the embassy, she was certain she could get a replacement fast-tracked. Her father knew people. Being a hotshot lawyer in Canada had its advantages when some of your best clients were high-level politicians.

"No," he said.

No? Well, if he was staying then she was staying, too. "I'm moving in with you."

She knitted her brows at him as he opposed her. Was he having an affair with Saveriano? She regretted the thought almost as soon as it entered her mind. Jake may have had a reputation as a ladies' man year's back, but that was before they had met. Still . . . sometimes she suspected that his reputation preceded him.

He was silent and she didn't break it. He was not himself and now was not the time to accuse him of anything.

She left him, still objecting to her plan, and backtracked by taxi to the hotel to collect her luggage from Reception where they were holding it. Dr. Saveriano was getting an extra houseguest whether she liked it or not, even if Angeline had to stand below Jake's bedroom windows and holler to be let in. She left the hotel hoping that she wouldn't run into Chancellor in the lobby or on the street. She was pretty sure he wouldn't condone her plan.

CHAPTER TWELVE

His name was Lucas Holland. He had been recruited into this important research two years ago. He had the calling. He knew he did. When she first approached him, he had felt her presence even before he saw her, knew he was a good candidate, an initiate.

Mithraism was an order, passed from initiate to initiate. It was not based on a body of scripture, so almost nothing in the way of documents existed. No scripts or first-hand accounts of its secret rituals survived with the exception of a 4th century papyrus—a text.

He moved in the dark, set the bowl down on the floor, no longer sure where he was. He had drunk the potion for months now. Its effects were fully engaged. Numbed into euphoria, he only knew that he was in the temple and the only way out was through the tunnels. The room he lived in was a dark cave, windowless and subterranean. The *spelaeum* had raised benches along the side walls for the ritual meal, and its sanctuary at the far end contained the pedestalled altar recessed into the wall. It had been many, many weeks since he had seen another individual, months since he had eaten with another human being. His company were bats and vermin.

He stared at the ceiling, at its ordered cosmos, an image of the universe. Mithraic iconography stemmed from the concept that the "running" of the sun from solstice to solstice reflected the movement of the soul through the universe, from pre-existence, into the body, and then beyond the physical body into an afterlife.

He was ready for that afterlife.

He was promised it.

He had already passed through the first rank of the initiation process. All members were expected to progress through the first four ranks, while only a few would proceed to the three higher ranks. The first four ranks represented spiritual progress and he had proven true. The new initiate became the *Corax*, the Raven, while the *Leo*, the lion was an adept. Why was she holding him back? He was not worthy to be the *Nymphus*, she said, the Bridegroom. But perhaps he could be the *Miles*, the soldier.

You are the soldier. Her voice whispered in his ear. She was *deus invictus*, the invincible one. The Black Goddess. Every follower must enrol in her service. *Take the oath and enter into my ranks.*

Holland slung the kitbag over his brown military tunic, removed the helmet from his head and laid down his lance. He squeezed his eyes shut as a burning sensation tore into his skin. The smell of frying flesh filled his nostrils, but he squashed the urge to scream. Minutes later, a tingling replaced the burning, and he knew that she had seared the brand of the *Miles* on his forehead.

You represent the element of Earth. You are now under the patronage of the god of war.

Holland could not see her. He could only hear her in his head. *Soldier*, she repeated. *Take this sword. Fall in battle. Become worthy.*

He went to the altar and lifted the sword from its bed. The ancient blade gleamed, its hilt crusted with an unearthly patina. He planted his foot on the pedestal. The sword twirled into the air—and landed with a shriek of pain on his shin, just above his right foot.

*　*　*

The foot was found in a drainage ditch outside the Basilica of San Clemente. Interpol agent Thomas Chancellor stared at the bloody appendage that sat on the gurney at the City of Rome

Morgue. The cut was so perfect it could have been done with a bone saw.

"No body?" he asked the Medical Examiner.

"No," he said.

The investigating officer of the Crime Scene Investigation Unit shrugged. "A young couple stumbled on this, on their way to a wedding."

Chancellor grimaced. "Sort of puts a damper on the nuptials. Let me know if you find the body or any clues as to who this foot belongs to."

The policeman nodded. Chancellor left for his hotel. Trudy, the forensics anthropologist in Lyons had left a message for him to contact her as soon as possible.

After he entered his hotel room he went to his computer and engaged it, turning the speaker up as Trudy's voice emerged. She transmitted an image to his screen, followed by data ascertaining that the toe bone—the human remains retrieved from the midway point on the mountain—was not archaeological. Radiocarbon tests provided an unquestionable contemporary date range, and further tests provided estimates of death for the individual at less than ten years, which put the victim squarely in the range of Chancellor's investigation.

She was getting away with serial murders and there was nothing he could do about it. Every move she made, every step she took, he had her watched. So far, she hadn't slipped, not even when the body was discovered in the cargo truck at Hilazon Tachtit. He had no grounds on which to act. One of his operatives had been with her the entire time, disguised as a local, and had witnessed the removal of the Venus statue. Never once was she out of his sight, so how could she have killed, and then stashed the body in that freight truck without being observed?

The foot bone was a right distal phalanx from a male between the ages of 25 and 40. Chancellor wished the entire severed foot had been retrieved, but they would have to make do with this toe sample until a drop team could relocate and salvage the remaining bones.

He replayed a recording from his operative's trip up the mountain.

"Witch" the boy had mumbled under his breath. The village lad was hired to help guide the expedition to the cave. The crew were halfway up, having struggled by foot over scrub, rock and debris following a goat track when the human convoy stopped. The boy had pointed to the ground, to the severed human foot. The flesh was eaten away, showing the sharp edge of the long bones above the ankle cleanly axed.

Why had the boy thought the remains belonged to a witch? His head shot up in sudden comprehension. The boy was not referring to the bones. The toe bone was modern, belonging to a male—and a few more tests would verify who the victim was.

CHAPTER THIRTEEN

Angeline's return to the villa was strangely uncontested. The assistant put her in a separate bedroom from Jake, claiming house rules. Clearly, he had not told his host that Angeline was his fiancée, because even when she flaunted the diamond engagement ring, the assistant shrugged. "You are not husband and wife. The least you can do is respect Dr. Saveriano's feelings while you're in her house," she said, and paused for drama. "You *are* in her house without her knowledge."

Angeline shrugged. She decided not to kick up more trouble, and accepted the conditions. Her room was down the hall from Jake's and very similar, with the same kind of paintings on the wall—horrible depictions of Hell.

Alone now, she removed her day clothes, tossed her shoes aside. Great. Apparently, they dressed for dinner in this house, or so the French harpy had stipulated before retiring from her presence. *Formal attire, huh?* Just how would Jake respond to that?

She had nothing but the same black and white dress she had worn for dinner with Chancellor the other night. No way was she going to spend a bunch of money to buy clothes just so she could stay in the mansion. Her fingertips felt as cold as steel as she tapped them over the lipstick she'd applied to give her an aura of being dressed up. This seemed so fake, a farce. When all she wanted to do was take Jake home. He was not himself and if she'd had any doubt before, that look of mindlessness in his eyes this afternoon confirmed it.

"Angeline?"

Jake's voice outside her door. He rapped lightly, and she glanced at the alarm clock by the bed and composed her face. Wiping her fingers on a tissue, she smoothed back her pinned up hair—another effort at looking dressed up—and went to the door.

"You look nice," he said.

"Thanks." But not as nice as him.

He was incongruously dressed in a suit and tie. Had Saveriano bought the getup for him? Left to his own devices, Jake would never fork out the cash for fancy clothes. Angeline decided not to comment even though he looked outrageously handsome.

He kissed her on the cheek and took her hand. "You like the duds," he said.

"I'm a little surprised you have anything like that. You sure didn't bring that from home."

He nodded. "When in Rome . . ." he said, and laughed.

Yeah, literally. She frowned. "I wish I'd known. I would have brought some opera clothes."

"You're being sarcastic," he said.

"Yeah, duh. Isn't it supposed to be the other way around? I'm the uptown girl and you're the downtown guy. Since when do you dress like a gigolo?"

He smiled. His hands were warm and his eyes soft. Whatever was wrong with him before had passed.

They strolled down the plush carpet without further sartorial commentary. Jake led her down the marble staircase under the chandelier, and crossed the foyer to the dining hall.

Everything in the dining room was dark wood. Another chandelier glittered over the rectangular table above a floral centrepiece. There were elegant white candles in slim silver holders, rose-coloured table linens and napkins, and the china was eggshell trimmed with gold.

Around the table two faces lifted to greet her.

"Sophia," Jake said. "This is Angeline Lisbon."

No one had told her that the owner of the villa had returned, and her eyes took in Sophia Saveriano's elegance, an indisputable attractiveness despite her fifty plus years. She didn't rise at the introduction but gazed at Angeline, smiling warmly. "I'm glad to meet you. Jake has told me of you."

"Good things I hope. I guess your assistant informed you that I was here earlier . . . ."

Before she could finish explaining, Jake turned to someone seated opposite their host and she realized with a jolt that it was Chancellor, who had somehow managed to finagle an invite. He rose and dipped toward her, took her hand, calm and cool, while something in his eyes warned her to leave the lies to him.

How did you explain your presence here? she wanted to ask, for surely the assistant had reported their earlier intrusion.

"You know Chancellor, of course," Jake said. "He popped up a few minutes ago at the door."

"Yes. And Dr. Saveriano was kind enough to invite me to dinner. When I explained that I was investigating Vincent Carpello's death, she graciously forgave my earlier indiscretion and agreed to cooperate."

Angeline reddened at the smooth talk and Jake motioned for her to sit next to the Interpol agent while he himself took a place at the head of the table by their host. As she went over, Chancellor pulled out her chair, grazing her arm with his knuckles, the touch annoyingly intentional.

"I apologize for being the last one down to dinner. Unfortunately I had a bit of a scare at the Colosseum the other day and I'm still a bit stiff from the fall. A boulder slipped from the attic story and landed quite near me, and I fell trying to avoid getting hit."

Saveriano's eyes jerked wide, Chancellor frowned like he'd wanted her to keep this quiet, and Angeline glanced sideways at Jake.

"Why didn't you tell me?" He looked nervous, maybe a little scared, and she felt her pulse quicken.

It was an accident and she wasn't hurt, but she still had a niggling feeling that something wasn't quite right. She looked to see if there was any reaction among the faces around her. The assistant stood near the doorway smirking, then disappeared into the kitchen. Angeline studied the worry on Jake's face, the frown on Chancellor's and the puzzled expression on Saveriano's.

"Would you prefer to have a plate brought to your room?" Saveriano asked.

She shook her head, smiled, ignoring Chancellor, who had placed his foot against her sandaled toes, urging her to accept the suggestion. Why? *So that you can get me out of your way? Forget it. Whatever plans you have for Jake will have to go past me.*

When she glanced at his face, his expression was totally blank, and she kicked him before tucking her foot under her chair.

Saveriano turned to Chancellor and asked him how she could help with his investigation.

"I'd like to know where you've been this past week."

"I've been at my excavation beneath the Basilica of San Clemente."

"You haven't shown up at the Museum. When I asked for you there, no one seemed to know where you were."

"As I said, Mr. Chancellor, I was at my excavation. Dr. Lalonde can vouch for that. He found me there."

Eyes flashing, she waited for Jake to answer. His jaw stiffened and a muscle in his cheek twitched. Saveriano's lips stretched indulgently as she reached across the table and gently touched his hand, which was resting near his wine glass as though he were a small boy nursing a glass of milk. "It's all right, Jake. Mr. Chancellor only wants to know where I've been. Tell him."

Angeline's eyes flitted from one to the other. Why did Jake look that way? Before he could answer, Saveriano's assistant entered the dining room laden with a silver tray of fresh baked bread. Behind her a middle-aged man pushed a cart holding an ornate soup terrine. She stopped in front of Jake and set down the tray. The aroma of the bread was mouth-watering and the smell spiralling up from the soup delectable—mushrooms in cream.

"*Grazie*, Susanne," Saveriano said. "Please serve our guests first."

So her name was Susanne.

A filled dish was placed in front of Jake, Susanne moved down to the other side of Angeline to where Chancellor sat. Was this what she had meant when she'd said she was an assistant? She was the maid?

Angeline caught Susanne's eye and her expression changed from a look of pleasure to one of pure spite. She dipped low so that her cleavage hung at Chancellor's eye level as she shoved a white china soup dish ladled with a creamy white broth flecked with brown under his chin. Chancellor failed to notice her physical endowments because he was examining the soup.

He snapped his head up sharply.

"There is the matter of the foot."

"Foot?" Angeline said.

"I think Dr. Saveriano knows what I'm talking about as the severed foot was found in a ditch outside her basilica."

"The Basilica di San Clemente does not belong to me."

"But you are excavating the tunnels beneath the buildings. Are you telling me you're unaware of the gruesome discovery?"

"What foot?" Jake interrupted. "Who does the foot belong to?"

"Well, that is the question of the hour, Dr. Lalonde," Chancellor said.

Saveriano frowned. "Coincidence. It could have happened anywhere."

"What could have happened anywhere?" Jake demanded.

The question seemed to stump her for the moment. Surely severed feet weren't routinely discovered outside of churches in Rome. Saveriano glanced down at her soup.

"Perhaps the timing for your question could have been better, Mr. Chancellor. I was about to taste my soup."

Angeline studiously examined her own steaming dish. The little brown slices of exotic mushroom with the soft stems still intact resembled small feet floating in a snowy broth.

CHAPTER FOURTEEN

Angeline woke up to a screaming inside her head. Scarcely awake she tore at her eyes, squinted, and laid still, vision unfocused. The weight of Jake's arm lay across her chest and she could feel his fingers laced with hers, his body hard against her hip. *What is that horrible noise?* Groggy with sleep, she sent a glance at the phone on the nightstand next to her pillow, unable to reach it for the strength of Jake's embrace.

"Let go, sweetie," she murmured, feeling his torso glued against her rapidly chilling skin. "Have to answer that."

She bent her other hand to unlatch his from hers, but his fingers were unrelenting, hurting. She groped for the nightstand and found the receiver, raising it to her ear.

"Hello?" she croaked.

Silence. The crackle of static. She sat up when the sound escalated into an unbearable, screeching, electronic tone. Wide awake, she slapped the receiver down, knocking the set over the nightstand, but now the whine seemed to be inside her head, increasing to a torturous, high-pitched intensity that had her silently screaming. She clapped her hands to her ears, and a few minutes passed before the shrilling began to ebb and she could fumble for the phone that was dangling by its cord over the nightstand.

She turned to the bed. "Jake, can you hear that? Jake . . . ."

Her heart stopped. He wasn't there. She was alone under the covers. Her eyes darted everywhere; she realized with a start that he was *never* there. She had dreamt it.

Angeline flicked a dry tongue onto her cracked lips. But she could swear she had felt his arm, his fingers intertwined with hers.

He was squeezing so tight that when she rolled over to answer the phone, he had not let go.

A shiver like silver pricked her spine, her hands felt lifeless like dead meat. He *must* have been here. He must have been! Pulse palpitating she grappled her way out of bed. She was freezing and hugged a thin robe—the only thing she had—over her satin nightgown. She was so shaky that the slippery sash refused to knot.

I must be going stark raving crazy.

"Jake," she whispered hoarsely, as she banged on his door in desperation. "Please, let me in!"

She knocked louder, but still no response. She opened the door, fumbled for the light switch, turned it on. The bed was empty, unslept in, and a black Pelican case lay on the floor.

The marble staircase clicked to her padded satin slippers, skating like fingernails on stone when she finally raced downstairs. Moonlight filtered in through the vaulted windows over the front doors. *Where are you?* She had to find him, had to know that he had been with her tonight. Otherwise, who was it that was lying next to her? Who was holding her hand? She could see her way through the foyer, past the dining room and into a hallway. Her fingers fumbled along the walls, tracing the textured wood, the sound of squeaking hinges alerting her to a door. She backstepped, hit a wall, and fell into an alcove. A marble statue broke her fall, its stone muscles jutting between her shoulder blades. Swallowing a cry of pain, she reeled in her robe's sash as the door opened.

Light scooted across the floor, a man backed out and she crowded herself into the tight space. Facing the man was Saveriano's assistant dressed for bed in a short, cotton eyelet nightgown, feet bare. The light was soft and her view of his face obscured, but whoever had spent the evening there was good because Susanne was flushed, bright-eyed. The two spoke in muted whispers and the man nuzzled her throat, raised his head expecting a response. As she gave it to him in a kiss, wrapping a bare leg around his trousered knee, Angeline almost puked. When she looked back the door snicked shut, the hallway vanished into blackness, and a hint of movement suggested that Susanne's visitor was headed for the front foyer.

Angeline waited until she was sure he was gone, slipped out of the alcove and down the hall into a dark room. This was the library, empty. She blinked at the silver streaming through the oblong windows. Ribbons of light flowed between the partially drawn drapes, and she wrapped her sash about her waist, staring at the branches swaying outside. She was so cold, blood roared in her ears. The memory of the man with Susanne chilled her.

A low tone bonged from a grandfather clock. Hundreds of books made up this library. A majestic desk sat in front of one of the windows with a fringed lamp perched at the corner, and in the room's centre, leather chairs and a matching sofa circled an elaborately carved coffee table. On top of it were some photographs. Angeline bent to inspect them and choked.

In her fist was a picture of Jake wearing a strange costume. On his shoulders were feathered wings and in his hands a Haida Raven mask.

She sank onto the leather sofa, spidering her fingers to steady herself, then replaced the photograph and went to the desk.

The swivel chair behind the desk rolled back as she bent forward to switch on the lamp. Light bloomed over a buttery soft leather pad with a blotter overtop. Beside the blotter was a pamphlet advertising Sophia Saveriano's forthcoming talk:

SUBTERRANEAN: *The Black Goddess and the Mysteries of Mithras*

One of the desk's drawers was ajar, and she dropped the pamphlet when she saw a letter with a familiar signature—Jake's.

"*Alors*. Angeline, is it not?"

The voice sent her heart into her throat, and she dropped the letter into the drawer and bumped it closed. She looked up at Saveriano's assistant who was clad in her nightgown, standing in the doorway, a sneer on her face.

Susanne sauntered across the room to thump the top drawer, the one that Angeline had just shut. "Did you find what you were looking for?"

When she got no answer, Susanne pursed her mouth with lips that looked crimson even at bedtime, before the familiar hateful smile returned.

Angeline couldn't stop shaking, but she summoned all of her courage to meet her accuser's stare.

"Is there something in particular you were looking for?" she repeated.

Their eyes simultaneously went to the pamphlet on the blotter, and Susanne lifted it and passed it over. "You're tired, Angeline. Go back to your bed."

"No, not until I've had this out with you. Leave Jake alone. He's not himself."

"Whatever are you babbling about *chère amie?*"

"I saw him leave your room. He's engaged to *me.*" She raised her left hand to flaunt the diamond on her third finger.

Susanne's brows arced higher and she laughed. "If you say so."

"I say so."

Angeline turned, made a swift exit and went upstairs to her room. She dropped the pamphlet onto her mattress, the image of the Frenchwoman's smug smile etched in her memory.

Listen you bitch, this isn't over.

Jake was *not* himself. His behaviour was erratic, and she had to get to the bottom of this, but how, if he wouldn't talk about it?

On the dressing table in her room a candle sat in a burnished pewter holder. She lit the wick with a match she found in a garnet-encrusted box in front of the mirror. Every so often the power failed because old villas had complicated wiring, but tonight the power was operating fine.

She raised the candle—she had no flashlight, so the candle would have to do—and carried it to the lamp, which she switched off. Then she walked carefully across the carpet to the door.

At the other end of the hallway near the staircase, the row of bedroom doors was shut and beneath the doors, no light showed except one. Near the landing a shadow crossed the carpet under Jake's door. Angeline stepped into the hall and rubbed her icy hands together. She wanted to tell him about the horrible experience she'd had in her bed. She needed reassurance that it was he who had been lying beside her, he who was squeezing her hand so hard she could feel his bones.

The light in Jake's room went out and he moved toward the landing. She bolstered herself to meet him, slunk back into her doorway.

> *He'll think I'm crazy.*
> *I'll think I'm crazy.*

She waited tortured by indecision until he was out of sight. She stared at the staircase where he had disappeared, then walked along the corridor in the direction of his room, clasping the candle in one hand and her sash in the other. Every step she took made her conscious of the rustling of her nightclothes. The door to his bedroom was not quite closed, and with a finger she pushed it wide. It was silent inside and dark, and she quickly slipped in, and even more quickly elbowed the door to a sliver.

The bed stood in a large chamber, larger than hers. The room had a distinct masculine air about it. The furniture wasn't any less ornate, but it was bulkier. The quilted coverings were bolder and in the light of her candle she could see the horrific tapestries on the wall.

She set the candle on the edge of the dressing table where it reflected light from the mirror. She began to search his room. Books and strange objects littered the top of the dresser; artifacts lay on the chairs and the bed—shaman's objects. He had been busy since she last peeked in here. A raven rattle, a drum decorated with an eagle, a pestle and mortar. What was he using this stuff for? In the middle of the floor lay the black Pelican case, only now it was empty.

A laptop sat on a small table between the two armchairs and Angeline knelt on the floor to get her eyes level with the screen. She turned the computer on. Jake had been working on something these last few weeks. What was it?

Psychoactive mushrooms. *Psilocybin* mushrooms (also called *psilocybian* mushrooms or *teonanacati*). Recipes for entheogens to help the shaman on his spiritual journey to the Netherworld.

A noise came from the hallway. Angeline shut the screen. She crept to the crack at the door.

This room was at the top of the hall where the window above the staircase sent moonlight onto the carpet. Someone had stopped outside. The figure looked down for a second, squatted, then stood up. A strong earthy scent rose with it, the same smell that surrounded Jake. The satin of Angeline's robe felt more inadequately thin than ever, and a chill swept up her spine and down her chest, raising the gooseflesh. Why was he standing there? She braced herself to confront him, but just as he was about to enter, he changed his mind and moved to the landing and down the stairs. She waited another moment, looked behind her. The candle dripped down the side of the dresser. She rushed over, blew it out, and wondered if the flame had been visible through the crack in the door. The candle had been set out of sight; the passageway was dark. She could have been staring right into his eyes.

Angeline lifted the holder and fumbled her way back to the door to listen. Pushing it as wide as she dared, she gazed toward the staircase. The grandfather clock moaned in the distance. She held the unlit candle steady, wildly groping for the loose sash with her free hand. Where was it? She stepped over the threshold, and there by her feet was her satin sash, bright in the moonlight like a silver snake.

Snatching it up, she turned to run for her room, and slammed into someone, hard. Oh God, how was she going to explain why she was snooping around the house in the dead of night? While she mentally rehearsed an excuse, a scintillating, nebulous rainbow materialized into a human form, and vanished before her incredulous eyes.

Her ears began to ring, that nerve-grating high-pitched, electronic whine.

She clapped her hands over her head, tears streaming down her face, jaw gaping but unable to speak. Then she saw Chancellor's face. "Tom! Did you see that? That thing in the air shaped like a woman! It was behind you!"

Chancellor had almost knocked her off of her feet, and was now helping her to regain her balance. She stared into the dense air where the apparition had disappeared, along with the irksome mind-bending ringing.

"What did you see?"

Angeline started to answer but then the absurdity of her whole night's adventure locked into place.

CHAPTER FIFTEEN

At the end of the labyrinth of tunnels beneath the Basilica of San Clemente was a mithraeum, which was a small rectangular subterranean chamber, maybe seventy-five feet long by thirty feet wide. The ceiling was vaulted. An aisle ran lengthwise down the center of the temple with a stone bench on either side three feet high. A mithraeum could hold thirty people, but this night he was alone. Sophia had left him directions and told him to meet her here after everyone had gone to bed. He walked down the aisle to the rear of the cavern where a carved, painted relief of the Tauroctony hung above a pedestalled altar. The god Mithras was pictured in the act of slaying a bull with the icons of a dog, a snake, a raven and a scorpion.

Sophia's voice came huskily from behind the altar. She stepped out in full view and smiled. "You like the sculpture?"

"It's very well preserved," Jake said.

"I restored it myself."

"What does the god Mithras have to do with me? I see there is a raven in the relief, but other than that I don't see why this should interest me."

She waved her hands to take in the cavernous chamber and the beautiful sculptures and paintings that decorated it.

"Did you know that Vincent Carpello thought the Tauroctony was a pictorial representation of a Persian—or if you prefer modern terms—a representation of an Iranian myth?"

"Yes, but he thought that women were somehow involved in the mysteries."

"Maybe so, but he was wrong about its origins. The Tauroctony was not an Iranian myth but an astronomical star map. Every

100

figure in the standard Tauroctony has a parallel among a group of constellations located along a continuous band in the sky. The bull is paralleled by Taurus, the dog by Canis Minor, the snake by Hydra, the raven by Corvus, and the scorpion by Scorpio."

He nodded. "So what?"

"Don't you see, Jake? The cave which is depicted in the Tauroctony and which the underground Mithraic temples were designed to mimic was intended to be an image of the Cosmos."

"That's one theory."

"No, that's the *truth*. I have proof, concrete proof."

"Where?"

"Not here."

"Sophia, you said if I came, you'd help me to understand my shamanic heritage. So far, I see no connection. I've just been getting blistering headaches and blurred vision. I can't concentrate and I feel this inexplicable urge—" he cut himself off. It was too embarrassing to explain what he'd done with Angeline. But he felt like that almost all the time.

"It's all right, Jake," she said. "Soon, you'll understand. It's part of the initiation. But I have to prep you for it first. Come with me."

She led him behind the altar, under the overhanging wall where the Tauroctony was displayed. They were in a shaft now and the only light they had was the flashlight in her hand. They came to an arched doorway where a huge slab rested against the wall.

"That slab used to cover the entrance to the mithraeum," she said. "I had it moved."

She would have needed a crane to move that rock. How the devil did she do that?

Above the arch something was inscribed on the flat rock that protruded through the earth.

MITHRAEVM

Jake grabbed a deep breath, steadied himself, as a wave of vertigo consumed him. For a second his eyes had read MYTH RAVEN. Raven Myth.

"You're beginning to see," Sophia said.

I don't see anything. He didn't voice his apprehension aloud. He needed to go through with this, had to find out what she knew.

"You are the messenger of Mithras. Are you willing to find out where that journey will take you?"

"The Haida Raven and the Raven messenger of Mithras are not connected," he argued. "Even I know that. And I've been known to stretch a theory for as far as it will go."

This cavern was smaller than the outer one, and inside it were stone blocks that served as tables. On the tables, were between thirty and fifty tall candles that Sophia now lit until the chamber glowed like a pagan temple. She gestured him over to where she had removed some dried fungus from a ceramic jar, ground it in a pottery bowl with a clay pestle, then mixed the powdered results with water that she was boiling in a stainless steel pot over a portable propane hotplate.

When the brew was ready, she strained it through a sheet of cheesecloth into a stone bowl to remove any residue. Jake recognized this bowl. It was the same plain bowl that he had seen in that vision just before he passed out in the crypt of skulls when he first met her.

"I thought so," she said. "You've seen this bowl before."

"It could be any bowl," he argued.

"But it's not."

Sophia passed him the bowl. "Drink."

He hesitated. Everything she had been feeding him lately was making him feel strange, and this hadn't started until she invited him to stay at her house. Susanne was the cook and Susanne had a penchant for wild mushrooms. He had never eaten so much fungus in his life. He hadn't mentioned this to anyone; he didn't want to complain. And since everyone was eating the same thing, including Susanne, how could he complain? But something was going on. He knew his body and his mind—and something had changed.

He hadn't accused her of spiking his food because he had no proof, but he was feeling hotter and hornier than he had ever felt in his life, almost to the point where he couldn't control himself. That was why he was keeping his distance from Angeline; that was why he couldn't tell her what was wrong with him. He had no proof.

"What's in it?" he asked, suspiciously.

"Only something to help you see what you want to learn." Sophia lowered the bowl to her waist level. "A shaman needs help to achieve spiritual enlightenment."

"The Haida don't do it this way. They use drums, music, dance and costumes."

"And how did that work for you?"

It didn't. It hadn't. The last time he had tried to reach a state of euphoria to seek the spirit guidance, he'd come away dizzy but unchanged.

"This won't hurt you, Jake. Look, I'll taste it myself." She put the bowl to her lips and swallowed lustily.

He still didn't move to take the bowl from her.

"Remember the lightbulb in the crypt?" she asked.

He nodded.

"Remember how you crushed out its light?"

"I didn't do that."

"You did, Jake. Don't you want to know what more you're capable of?"

Yes, he did. But how could he trust her without hurting Angeline? Angeline wouldn't want him to do this. And yet, he knew no matter how he objected, he was going to do it anyway.

"How did I do that? Tell me," he demanded. "I want to be able to do it again. I want proof."

"I don't need to tell you how. Just will it. Turn out the lights!"

Jake clenched his fists, grit his teeth. There was no draft in here. The candles barely flickered. The air was stale. But there *was* air or the candles wouldn't be burning.

All right. Turn out the lights!

He snapped his eyes shut, opened them. All fifty candles went out.

Shit, he thought. *Holy shit and a half. Did I do that?*

"Yes, you did, Jake." Sophia's voice came out of the gloaming. Faint light appeared to be filtering from somewhere. Among all of her other talents, it seemed Sophia could also read his thoughts. "Now do you believe? You can do anything if you set your mind to it. But you can do better. I can take you into that past world that you crave so much. But you have to trust me. And you have to leave Angeline out of it. She can't know a thing about this. If you tell her anything, then the promise is broken. A shaman's journey is a solitary journey. His power is a solitary power. You have to choose, but you can't involve her in your decision or the promise becomes null and void."

"Sophia, can you tell me how my inherited memories work? Can you tell me what they mean?" They were still conversing in the dark, and he didn't know why he trusted her to have the answers, but he did.

She moved to where she had left her flashlight upended on a stone table, and raised it. A splash of light struck Jake full in the face, causing him to flap his eyelids. She placed the bowl with the strange brew onto the same stone table and moved around the cavern, relighting the candles until the chamber burst into brilliance like a bonfire.

"When was the last time you had one of these dreams?"

"How did you know the memories came to me in dreams?"

"How else?" Sophia asked.

"It was a few days ago. While I was still staying at the hostel."

"What did you see in this dream?"

"Well, that was what was so strange. I saw the tunnels leading to this mithraeum. I was inside one of the passages and I saw that crypt of skulls." Jake suddenly paused. "Come to think of it, that wasn't the last time it happened. I lapsed into a dream state the day I met you *inside* the same crypt of skulls. I saw a Haida shaman in a Raven mask and—" He glanced at the stone bowl where it now sat on one of the tables. Come to think of it, neither of those experiences had occurred while he was asleep. They were not dreams, but more like premonitions.

He rubbed his aching head. "I take it all back," he said. "It seems the memories are no longer coming to me in dreams. I can induce them through psychoactive substances or through fear." He proceeded to describe his experiences with the hallucinogenic mushroom that he'd sampled back at the hostel and the absolute terror he had felt the first time he was in that labyrinth of tunnels.

Sophia smiled sagely. "You must drink this brew. It's the only way to find the meaning of your visions. It's the only way to control them. You do want to be in control of them, don't you? Until now, I think that *they* have been controlling *you*. If you don't go on this spiritual journey, you and Angeline will never be happy. You have to find out if you were meant to be with her or if you were meant for something else. After all, there is a reason why you won't set a wedding date."

How did she know?

Jake exhaled, closed his eyes for a second. Sophia was right. She was right about everything. PNR. Angeline was always sending him emails marked PNR whenever he was about to make an impulsive decision. Think, she'd say, before you pass the Point of No Return. So many times she'd saved him. And so many times when she couldn't.

The problems they were having now had nothing to do with her, and everything to do with him. Life with him was a tortuous, unpredictable, roller coaster ride, and she didn't deserve that.

Sophia returned to the stone table that held the bowl and held it out to him. "The moment of truth."

Jake took the bowl. One sip and he will have passed the point of no return.

CHAPTER SIXTEEN

"A ghost?" Chancellor said.

Angeline gave him a dark scowl. "Don't look at me like that, as though I'm hallucinating or something. You're the ghost chaser. I saw what I saw." The scepticism on his face stayed firm and she sighed. She closed her eyes to recall the sight of the female apparition, opened them to stare evenly at the Interpol cop. "All right. You want it plain and clean. You're telling me that I only *think* I saw something."

Chancellor shook his head. "I'm not saying I doubt you. I'm serious about what I do. The paranormal exists. But so do overactive imaginations triggered by stress and fear. Visions can also be brought on by artificial means, you know."

The rustle of Angeline's satin robe punctuated her frustration and she twirled the sash around her finger in an agitated spiral. "You mean like the consumption of psychoactive drugs? We all ate the same thing at dinner. So if those were magic mushrooms we had, then you should be seeing things, too."

The moon slid lower in the sky, angling light directly into Chancellor's face. It gave him a ghostly, wolfish countenance. "Okay," she said. "Forget what I saw. Maybe I didn't see anything; maybe I was just so spooked I thought I saw an ethereal, vapour-like image of a woman. But she vanished."

"Was she bright?" he asked.

"What do you mean?"

"Was the specter bright, like a halo cloud or a lightening sprite?"

"What is that?"

"They are electrical phenomena caused by physical and chemical changes in the air. They shimmer."

"Yes, that's it. She was shimmering." And a high-pitched whine had accompanied her.

"And you're positive it was a female form you saw?"

Angeline nodded into the dark.

Chancellor nodded in return. "Which room is Lalonde's?"

She was just about to tell him when it occurred to her that he shouldn't even be here. She had glanced at the alarm clock beside her bed when awakened by the ringing in her ears. It was 1:00 A.M. By now it must be almost three in the morning. What was he doing snooping around in the villa? How had he gotten back inside? They had said their goodnights around ten o'clock. Everyone had turned in by eleven P.M. He was not invited to stay overnight. "What are you doing here, Tom? I thought you went back to the hotel." Then another thought occurred to her. That was *him* outside Jake's bedroom door.

"I meant to go back," he said. "But I was invited by Susanne to stay for a nightcap."

Angeline didn't dare express her feelings. So, the man she had caught exiting Susanne's boudoir wasn't Jake. She was simply paranoid, and the silhouette of the man with his tongue down Frenchie's throat had seemed familiar, so she had assumed it was Jake. It never dawned on her that Mister Tall Dark And Gorgeous could be Chancellor. Still it wasn't a happy thought, but it was also none of her business. He was free to hook up with whomever he chose. She sniffed the air around him. Why did he smell like earth, like Jake? Where had he been?

"It saved me having to break into the house later on when everyone was asleep and risk exposure," Chancellor explained. "I wanted to follow Saveriano."

Angeline was pretty sure the Interpol agent had exposed everything there was to expose to Susanne. "Where did you go after you left her? You smell strange. You have the same smell that Jake had when I saw him earlier this afternoon. What *is* that smell?"

"What smell?" He sniffed himself. "I don't smell anything."

She decided to change tactics. "Where do you think Saveriano went so late at night?"

He glanced up at the decorative window above the landing to the stairwell, his face lighting up in silver and green. "Hunter's moon," he murmured.

Her eyes followed to the huge orb glowing in the sky. Clearly that comment was not meant to answer her question. The moon was unusually huge and bright, and a dog howled in the distance.

"You know what they say in this country? When a dog howls at the full moon, something bad is about to happen."

"You think something bad is going to happen to Jake?"

Chancellor returned Angeline's penetrating stare without addressing her query. Instead, he asked, "Which room is his? I've been wandering down this hallway trying to locate it."

Her forehead knotted suspiciously, but she pointed to the one at the top of the staircase, and followed him as he made his way by moonlight to the aforementioned door. Everything was as she had left it: the bed was still unslept in, the horrific paintings and tapestries still on the wall. Books and strange objects littered the top of the dresser and artifacts lay on the chairs and the bed. The shaman's objects—the raven rattle, the drum decorated with the eagle, the pestle and mortar, and in the middle of the floor the empty black Pelican case.

She set the candle holder that she had been hugging all this time onto the dresser between two books, found a small pewter box holding matches and struck one to light the candle. Chancellor had a penlight on him and flicked it on to examine the pestle and mortar. There was a powdery residue in the bowl of the ceramic mortar, and he tasted it.

"What is it?" she asked, her heart starting to palpitate. "Is Jake doing drugs?"

He raised the mortar to Angeline's nose and she sniffed. "That smells like cedar."

"Why would he be grinding cedar?"

Haida shamans sometimes used cedar to create an altered state when they wanted to visit the Spirit World, and some varieties of cedar, mixed in specific concentrations with certain species of psychoactive plants, could create that kind of effect. The look on Chancellor's face had a kind of 'I told you so' gloat to it when she informed him of the practice. "Fine," she said. "I told you he was obsessed with his Haida heritage. I didn't realize that he'd gone this far."

He went to the books that sat on the dresser and opened one that was book-marked as she shuddered, realizing that somewhere within this shamanistic riddle, Sophia Saveriano played a strong role.

The volume was all about psychoactive substances. What were the effects of psychedelic mushrooms? Were they arbitrary? Did they vary among users? What were the effects on an apprehensive, hyper-imaginative, overwrought individual? The mind altering effects lasted anywhere from three to eight hours depending on dosage, preparation method and personal metabolism, and, could even seem to last longer because one of the mushrooms' unique effects was to alter time perception. Physical symptoms were loss of appetite, coldness in extremities, increase in heartrate, numbness of the mouth and cheeks, elevated blood pressure, weakness in limbs, muscle relaxation, swollen features, and pupil dilation. Jake certainly had exhibited some of these symptoms.

Changes to the audio, visual and tactile senses occurred ten minutes to one hour after ingestion. Some of these included enhancement of colour, strange light phenomena such as auras or haloes around light sources or people, increased visual acuity, surfaces seeming to ripple, shimmer or breathe, objects appearing to warp, morph or change colour. A sense of melting into the environment and wakes behind moving bodies . . . . Jake claimed his hearing was more acute, that his senses were sharper. *Synesthesia* whereby the user perceived a visualization of colour on hearing a particular sound . . . . Had Jake described this? The experience was dependent on setting and emotional state: a negative environment induced a bad trip—paranoia; a positive environment induced a good trip—a sense of euphoria and wellbeing. His recent behaviour suddenly made sense. If Jake was experimenting with hallucinogens, it accounted for his disturbing mood swings.

Angeline looked up at Chancellor, frowned. "Do you think she was feeding us magic mushrooms? Some of those symptoms describe exactly what I was feeling tonight. Because honestly, Tom. I *don't* believe in ghosts."

Chancellor met Angeline's eyes. "Yeah? Well, *I* do. And I haven't seen any tonight. So I don't think we've been drugged."

She closed the book. "You still haven't told me why you wanted to follow her or Jake."

"How much do you know about Saveriano?"

"Only as much as I've already told you."

"Have you noticed anything unusual about Lalonde—" He corrected himself and decided to use the familiar, "—about Jake lately?"

She squinted into the dark, trying to decipher his motives, reluctant to have him criticise Jake or accuse him of anything criminal or perverted. "No."

He frowned at her.

"Okay, fine," she admitted, struggling with her emotions. "He's acting strange. And there's this peculiar, earthy smell around him. He's aggressive one minute and timid the next. That's not like him. He's always been impulsive, but never this erratic in his behaviour or his actions, and he won't confide in me. I don't feel close to him anymore, not even when we're in bed. There's something wrong!" She instantly dropped her voice. Oh, God, probably the whole household had heard that.

He patted her arm lightly. "It's okay, Angeline. There's nobody here except Susanne. Mauro, the manservant left to go home around midnight. Our gracious hostess has left the building, and your Jake obviously isn't here either." He took out one of his electronic gizmos and turned it on. A green light appeared and the device made a low humming sound.

"What's that?" she asked.

"An EMF meter. It's an electromagnetic detector. If there's something weird in this house, this device will go off like the fourth of July." Angeline grabbed Chancellor's wrist and swung him to look at her. "Steady, girl. You almost made me drop this thing. Do you know how much these gadgets cost?"

No, she didn't. But she knew how much his ghost-hunting charade was costing her. "Who is the ghost, Tom? Saveriano? And why the hell do you think she's a spook?"

"I never said I thought anything like that."

"You don't have to. You're walking around with all these stupid ghost-hunting devices on you. And you're scaring me."

"Saveriano is not what she seems."

"Is she a murderer?"

"*I* think so."

"Is she human?"

"That depends on how you define human."

"Stop playing games with me. I want the truth. I want to know what *you* know. Jake's life is in danger."

"All right. I think Saveriano is at the head of a cult. I think she's looking for something or someone specific, that's why she's using all of these young men. But so far, none of them are exactly what she's looking for. Don't ask me what this thing or person is. Or what *it* or *they* are supposed to do for her. But I think she's trying these young men out, then discarding them left and right. There's a pattern here, a puzzle, but I haven't figured out what that is yet."

Angeline couldn't believe what she was hearing. The whole thing was becoming more and more bizarre.

CHAPTER SEVENTEEN

The stone bowl in Jake's hands trembled as he wiped away a dribble from the corner of his mouth, his tongue thick, arms and legs numb, cold. His heart hammered. He tried to speak, but his lips resisted all effort. He felt tremulous and loose like his muscles had mutated to liquid. Everything was too bright, hurting his eyes. The colour of Sophia's hair glared like wrought silver. A luminous mist seemed to surround her, and when he looked at the candles littering the tables, they too, shone with a frenzied aura.

The cave itself seemed to swell and breathe, and suddenly he wasn't in a mithraeum in Italy anymore. He could smell the sea, hear the dripping of water, feel the drafts inside the sandstone caves near his West Coast home.

All was black—but for a crack in the cave's ceiling, sending daylight below. So how could that be? It was after midnight when he had slipped away to meet Sophia here. And all mithraea were built underground. There couldn't possibly be a crack in the ceiling without the whole thing crashing down on him.

But this *was* a cave. He had no doubts that he was inside a cave.

And not just any cave.

The crescent moon and stars sparkled out of the stone sky. A raven flew from out of the gloom to perch upon his shoulder, leaving a wake of phosphorescence. His mind flooded with fear, his body trembled as he recognized the scenario, the mind-crippling events that were about to happen.

The cave floor morphed into an elliptical pool scarred by ancient etchings, and no matter how hard he tried to wake up, his mind was trapped. He purposely focused on Sophia, strained to locate her in the blackness, but her image faded, and he finally gave in to the miasma that was consuming his thoughts.

Jake rubbed his numbed lips that dripped with Sophia's foul-tasting brew, and set the stone bowl on the floor at his feet. The pull to act out the disturbing charade was fated because he had no will, no body, no mind to change. There was only need, and a power he could not deny.

The mask was there, hanging on a knob against the stone wall above the petroglyphs, as he knew it would be—*Yehlh's* chosen guise. This, he set on his head without questioning the logic of his actions, turned his back on the petroglyphs, and transmuted into the wraith of his nightmares.

Wings flapped behind him and the raven followed.

"You betrayed me. I would have given all to you, but now I must take what I want. Where is your lover?"

The voice came from his right, and although Jake knew he should run, he didn't. Instead, he turned to face the enemy, drawn by the circle of fire.

The raven screeched, but the warning arrived too late.

Stars burst in his head and his mask tore away, and he found himself facedown on the floor with a warrior threatening a knife at his throat. He rose in the direction the warrior indicated, coughed to clear the dust from his lungs, raising his head. Eyes wide, a spectre lanced his vision, dancing among the flickering stones of fire.

He knew exactly what was about to happen.

The wraith of the Eagle was set to defile the woman of his heart.

Felled to the ground, feet lashed, hands twisted behind his back, he was forced to watch. He was desperate to close his eyes, slice off the horror they were about to commit, because he was powerless to stop what already was.

Jake clawed at the ropes that bound him, but realized he was free. The darkness had given way to brilliant day. The cave over his head was precious blue sky. The vignette that met his sight was a silver paradise. And his heartbeats began to calm.

The woman sat in the rocky crevice of a shelter by a grey lake that rippled from the harsh north wind. A slick-furred marten peered over a ridge of barren earth, and scampered into the dusk. Eight moons she had journeyed by land and sea to seek his homeland, and soon she would reach her destination. Another moon, across the wide strip of sea, and she would be there.

The raven had left her early that morning to join his master in the realm of the spirits. *Yehlh* had brought light to the world, and now returned to the dark.

She put a stick of hemlock to her fire, and brought it into the cave. On the ground lay the raven, his smooth black feathers brushed back by her own loving hand. Beside him a stone glittered, the shadows etching a shallow depression on its worn surface as she touched the stick to the stone, and watched the oil catch and lick into flame. She had spent the day preparing his grave, and with her own hands had scraped away the raw earth.

She laid him now in his bed of dirt and placed the lamp beside him. It flickered and surged and consumed the oil, and died. With each handful of soil she scattered, she prayed for his safe passage; she prayed he would return to the land where he was born. She had faith, and remembered her own words, the conviction that had given her courage to go and seek her own destiny. *Our enemy has taken my body but not my heart. If the forces of your Spirit World are stronger than that of this earth, then the life I carry within me is surely yours.*

Jake's body seemed to move of its own volition, melting from rock to tree to grave. From out of the pit where the raven was laid, his own being, shimmering like nightwaves in moonlight, rose to stand by her side.

Her eyes grew to radiant orbs as Jake reabsorbed the shaman's form.

*   *   *

The face before him rippled like an unearthly thing. The bluffs, the lake, the evergreen trees wavered in and out of his vision. He leaned over to touch her lips, her cheeks, but suddenly they flared up red, and he jumped aside to see that the red had turned to yellow and then to white.

Candlelight ebbed and flowed, and as she moved toward him a shimmering wake seemed to trail her limbs, following her every movement.

"Jake," she whispered, "Wake up. You're coming out of it."

He choked on the thin air of the mithraeum, mouth sandy, the taste left behind by the brew mouldy. He tried to wet his lips but his tongue was dry. The hand touching his shoulder was not the young hand of the shaman's woman. The hand touching him was tanned from working outdoors, and softly wrinkled with middle age.

Sophia slapped his face and he awoke with precision. "What did you see?"

He rubbed his jaw, giving her a myopic stare. He was lying on the floor and now she helped him to his feet.

"I'm sorry I had to slap you, but you were in the transitory phase. It's not a good place for an initiate." She moved back until her hands rested on one of the stone tables and reclined as though she had all the time in the world.

"How long was I out?"

She glanced at the glowing digital watch on her wrist. "Six hours. It's morning now."

"Holy shit, Angeline will be wondering what happened to me."

"She's been wondering that a few days now, Jake. What have you told her?"

Not much. He didn't want to upset her until he understood what was happening to him.

Sophia lightly patted some dust from his sleeve. "It's just as I said. You have powers that you weren't even aware of. What did you see on your journey to the Other Side?"

"That wasn't the Other Side. That was something I've seen before, only I didn't understand what it meant."

"And you understand now?"

Jake exhaled, shook his head. Not quite. But he was more certain than ever that he was the descendent of *Yehlh*, the Raven. He told her this, to which she replied, "How could you ever doubt it?" He stared at her, at the candles around her and the cavernous room they occupied. How could he not? It was absurd, but he felt like he had visited another world.

The world of the past!

"You have all the memories of your ancestors," she informed him.

"No, I don't. I have the memories of *one* ancestor. Why?"

"Because there is something you have yet to do. That *he* has yet to do."

Jake raised his hands hopelessly. And it had to do with this? What did a mithraeum have to do with his Haida heritage? What did the Raven have to do with the Black Goddess?

Sophia smiled. "I told you that if you joined me, your experience would be a journey. I didn't say it would be a short one. Now drink this and clear your mind." She handed him a glass of water. "The potion can be quite dehydrating. You must rehydrate and get some rest." She led him to a bed made of eagle down, covered with a wolf's pelt that sat against the far wall. "Lie down. Try to sleep. I'll return for you when you're rested."

CHAPTER EIGHTEEN

Angeline remained awake all night. Chancellor returned to his hotel after failing to track down Jake or Saveriano. Saveriano never left her room, he'd said. How would he know? He was too busy entertaining Susanne. If he was as smart as he purported to be, he would have waited outside the front doors rather than in the house.

She finished her morning routine and went to Jake's room and looked in. The room was the same as it was last night, only now the nightmarish quality was gone. His bed was neatly made. Where was he? And where was their host? She backtracked to Saveriano's bedroom. Chancellor insisted that she had not left her room, and yet he had also said she was not in the house. How did one do that? There was only one way to find out. Angeline tried to think up some reason why she should be knocking at the professor's door, thought of nothing credible and knocked anyway. No one answered.

"Hello?" She gripped the doorknob, pushed the door impulsively. The room was empty, huge, and painted white. Everything was white and there were no tapestries or oil paintings on the walls. Everything—from the carpet to the furniture to the bedding—was pristine white. It should have been beautiful to look at, but somehow it just seemed creepy.

The king-sized bed was unslept in. So, she was never here. Angeline pinched her brows together. If she had never left and she was never here, where was she? How did she leave without anyone seeing or hearing her? Chancellor said he had been here all night, and that sonorous ringing in her head had awakened her at 1:00 A.M. By the time Chancellor had left and she returned to bed, it was almost four in the morning.

She went downstairs for breakfast. Everyone was out, Mauro told her.

"Even Susanne?"

"Even Signorina—I mean *Mademoiselle* Susanne."

Angeline quaffed a quick mug of coffee and a biscotti. Not the most nutritious breakfast, but who cared? She wasn't about to fuss around in a stranger's kitchen for whole grain toast and poached eggs. She took a second mug with her to the library.

A bird, a cup, a staff, a torch, a diadem and a lamp, what did they mean? She had to find the parchment with the text. The parchment had more written on it than just the strange iconographic cypher.

The door to the library was open and no one was about. She walked in and set her cup on the coffee table where the photographs were. When had Jake dressed up in this raven costume? When and why had Saveriano taken his picture? She pulled out her cell phone and pressed the camera function, focused on the photograph until Jake's shamanic image came into view, then snapped the picture, but just before she did, she could swear she saw a red mist flare up, turn yellow and then white.

She retrieved the photo and stared at the screen. What the—?

Just like in that photo of Vincent in his death throes. A pale aura shaped like a female. She shoved her cell phone into her pocket and went to the desk to pull out the drawer where she had seen the letter last night. She could swear it was signed with Jake's scrawl.

There it was, beneath the expensive pen, typed on the University of Washington's official stationary. She had absolutely no scruples about reading it, and glanced up at the door before adjusting her eyes to the type.

June 2, 2010

Dear Vincent,

I know we've had our differences on your Mithraic theory, but the only way to prove which of us is right is with concrete proof. You say you have that? I say, great. But what's with all the secrecy? Why didn't you want me to email you. It's a lot more efficient. Now I'll have to wait for weeks for the mail to get through. By the way, I am not making a trip to Rome to see it. Whatever it is, you'll have to bring it here. And don't give me any bull about the cost. You can pay for it out of your big fat grant.

Best,
Jake Lalonde

And yet Jake *had* gone to Rome. Not only to Rome, but to Israel. How had Vincent convinced him? Angeline stared at the computer-generated font. Was there something in this correspondence that she was missing? What exactly was Vincent's theory? It had something to do with a Persian origin of a female Raven cult that spawned the Mithraic Mysteries. The mention of the Raven was the only thing she could see about Vincent's theory that would interest Jake, but what was Saveriano's role in all of this? How did she get Vincent's mail and why had she kept it? The letter was brief, all of one paragraph, hardly worth the stamp that was purchased to mail it. The letter said virtually nothing—except that Vincent had found proof that his theory was correct, which meant that he had evidence for a Persian origin of a female Raven cult that had spawned the Mithraic Mysteries.

"Angeline, what are you doing in Sophia's library?" It was Jake standing in the doorway. "What have you got in your hand? Are you snooping in her desk?"

"Since when do you call her Sophia?"

He coloured, moved to take the sheet of paper pinched between her tense fingertips and stared at the letter that he had obviously written.

Did he have an explanation for why Saveriano had a letter addressed to Vincent and signed by himself? *Did* he write it?

"I don't know why she has this, Angel. But there's nothing in it that anyone can't read. I've got no secrets."

She glowered. He looked exhausted, his hair unkempt, clothes rumpled. He had clearly changed to T-shirt and jeans before leaving the house last evening. Where *was* he last night? The memory sent a spicule of fear up her spine—that sibilant screaming inside her head, scarcely awake, tearing at her eyes, unable to see who lay beside her. The weight of an arm across her chest, fingers laced with hers, squeezing so hard she could feel the bones. She shuddered. The body pressed hard against her hip—if it wasn't Jake's, whose was it? Her stomach went cold. And what . . . what *was* that horrible sound, that shrill whine that had her nerves in spikes?

"I went to find you last night and you were gone. Your bed was never slept in. I checked again this morning." She let the silence hang distant between them and she could feel the frigidity of her temper chill him, too. "I checked Saveriano's bedroom. She never went to bed."

Jake's face had guilt painted all over it. He must have arranged a tryst, met the Ghost Lady at one of her dank, creepy mithraea, maybe the one beneath the Basilica of San Clemente.

Did she have a lover's nest in there? Angeline crossed her arms, clamping her hands onto her shoulders, hugging herself, tears strangling her voice so that she couldn't trust it. Was there something going on between them, was he having an affair with her? Why wouldn't he tell her what was going on?

"She's helping me."

"Helping you do what, exactly?"

He tossed the letter back inside the drawer and slammed it shut. He didn't know why she had that letter. She and Vincent were colleagues, rivals. The proof mentioned in that piece of correspondence was something Sophia was interested in, and he presumed it was the statue, the Venus figure they called the Black

Goddess—the triple goddess phenom. But now they would never know for sure, because Vincent was dead.

Angeline narrowed her brow. The puzzle was getting fainter and fuzzier. Was modern day Israel part of ancient Persia? Her thoughts were muddled, but there was a reason why they were headed in this direction, and even though she knew the answer to her own question as well as Jake did, she wanted confirmation from his own lips. If Israel covered the same terrain as Persia, that would link the Black Goddess to the ancient world of Mithras.

Jake frowned, answering her lightly. To some scholars no, Israel was not part of Persia, to others yes, the part of northern Israel where the sculpture was found. He suspected it was originally Vincent's find and not Sophia's.

So, they were cavorting with a murderess. She had killed Vincent for the statue and now they were guests in a killer's home.

Jake looked gravely into Angeline's eyes. "You can't seriously think that Sophia murdered Vincent for a statue?"

Chancellor believed Saveriano killed Vincent, that she was possessed by some kind of a spirit. When Angeline told Jake this, he laughed, tossed his head back and roared. She grabbed his arm. She didn't know if Chancellor was a kook, but he seemed genuinely sincere. "You met him, Jake. *Is* he a loon?"

He shrugged. He didn't trust Chancellor, but the Interpol agent's speculations reeked of crazy. Just because Sophia and Vincent were working on similar topics didn't mean that she killed him. Angeline disagreed. Sure Chancellor was walking around with any number of ghost-hunting gadgets, but he seemed stable. If he were a fruitcake, would he have such a high-profile job?

"Ghost-hunting stuff?" Jake asked. "What do you mean?"

"You know. Night vision goggles, infrared cameras, heat detectors, Geiger counters and a host of other gizmos. I caught him in the act one day, in his hotel room."

"What were you doing in his hotel room?"

Who was he to ask when he had just come from some sordid tryst with the Phantom Queen herself?

She was looking for Chancellor because he had lied to her about Saveriano being missing. Chancellor's door was open and it was pitch black in there and . . . . She stopped to take a quick breath. Now it was his turn. What was *he* doing with Sophia in the middle of the night? This was his last chance because she was done with his disappearing acts and his cryptic relationships with strange women. She flashed the diamond engagement ring at him.

"If this means nothing to you, then just say so. Maybe Chancellor was right after all. You don't want to marry me. You just don't want anyone else to. And that isn't fair. Do you want me to give this back to you for good?" She tore off the ring.

Jake took Angeline's hand and slipped the ring back onto her finger. He sighed and pulled her close to him until her head nestled under his jaw. He raised her chin and turned her face to meet his. "I am so confused."

Well, so am I. Her heart was racing and she knew any minute she would give in to him. She pushed him away. The truth was, he was lying to her, and she couldn't allow that anymore, so she would make it easy for him. They were quits. No confusion there. She tore the ring off for the second time and dropped it into his palm.

He was on his own. She was going home.

She ran out of the library, tears rolling down her cheeks and raced up the stairs to her room to pack.

* * *

The diamond was mesmerising, spun like a raindrop pierced by sunlight. Jake stared at the tiny gem glittering in his hand. It was too small. He should have bought her something bigger, gone into hock for it and purchased her something that was worthy of her.

Go talk to her.

But the memory of the vision clouded his judgement. He couldn't bring her into this; it was too dangerous. He couldn't confide in her without placing her in the middle of something that had an outcome he couldn't foresee.

"*Bonjour*, Jake."

It was Susanne's French accent that broke his daze.

"You look like you just lost your best friend. Surely you and Vincent Carpello were not close?"

He lowered the diamond into his pocket, her eyes following.

She smiled. "Lover's spat?" She spoke as though she enjoyed the fact that he was miserable.

He ignored the incomprehensible gloat in her voice. "What do you want?"

"Dr. Saveriano asked me to find you. You were not supposed to leave the temple so soon after your experience."

So she knew about his spell with the drug-induced visions. "I couldn't stay in that damp cave any longer," he said.

"Ah, well." She tossed a backward glance into the foyer and the stairs leading to the bedrooms. "She does not understand, you know. But *I* understand. I and Sophia. You don't need the ice princess. You were meant for greater things."

"I'm starting to have my doubts."

"Did not the dream convince you?"

Jake exhaled. "It was more like a nightmare."

"You were afraid?"

Not exactly. He was disturbed. The scenes were all too familiar and all too old.

Her hands flew up like he was some kind of an idiot. "She, that woman you think you are in love with, Angeline is her name? She is not enough for you. She can never go where you can go."

The words were eerily familiar. They creeped him out.

"I don't want her to go there. It's because I love her that I want to leave her out of this whole thing."

"Good. Sophia will be pleased. Things are as they should be. We will be rid of her today. I saw her packing as I came down the stairs."

"Where is Sophia?"

"She is resting now. Tonight you and she have much work to do if you want to get to the meaning of your dreams . . . I mean your vision."

Jake glanced over Susanne's shoulder, and saw Angeline come down the stairs with her luggage and head for the door.

CHAPTER NINETEEN

A loud, insistent banging hammered in his ears. What now? Chancellor snapped his eyes open at the dark as he lay in bed, slammed his hand onto his travel alarm but it wasn't buzzing. Realizing it was someone at the door, he threw the covers off his torso and went to answer it dressed in shorts and nothing else. He opened the door, shoving a strand of straggling hair out of his eyes.

Angeline dropped her luggage at the threshold and threw herself into his arms.

"Hey, wait a minute," he said. "What's going on here?"

"Jake and I broke up."

He stroked her hair and led her into his room and sat her on the edge of his unmade bed, then switched on the bedside lamp, but didn't bother to open the curtains to admit the midday sun. "Not for the first time, I'm sure."

"You know everything about us, don't you?" she accused him, sobbing.

"I know a lot," he admitted.

"Well then, you should know this time it's for good. I've had it."

He sat down beside her. "So, your plan is to move in with me?"

She blinked the tears out of her eyes, and he reached across her to the nightstand to remove a tissue from the holder. She blotted her cheeks. "I thought . . . I thought you were attracted to me."

"I am. But I don't want you this way."

"But you want me."

Yeah, he wanted her.

"Tell me what happened," he said.

"We had a fight. He can't—*won't*—commit to me. He's obsessed with his shamanic ancestry. I can't take it anymore."

"Maybe it isn't his fault. Sophia Saveriano seems to be having an enormous influence on him."

Angeline sniffed. "Jake is not a child. He can make his own decisions. He just doesn't want to make *this* one."

Chancellor sighed. "I'm not so sure he's making the decisions anymore." He couldn't let this go any further. "Angeline," he said. "I think Saveriano is using Jake to prove a theory. Only I don't think Saveriano is herself anymore either, I can't seem to pin her down, I can't track her movements, she just appears and disappears at will, but I can track Jake. I have to follow him tonight. Before you completely write him off, let me find out exactly what's happening."

"What *is* happening, Tom? What is Jake involved in?"

He shifted his gaze from hers. Saveriano had her own version of the Mithraic Mysteries. And while she was following the order of the ranks as they were known historically, she had some hidden agenda specifically for Jake. There were parallels between her beliefs and his in Haida shamanism—that much was clear. But Chancellor couldn't tell Angeline what he suspected.

"I know it has to do with the Mithraic cult," she insisted. "There are seven ranks in the Mithras Mysteries. The initiate is 'ceremonially' killed before achieving each of the ranks." She made air quotes with her fingers. "Are you telling me that she is initiating Jake through these ranks? What for? I know Haida shamans ceremonially die and are reborn during rites that allow them to pass into the Spirit World, but why would Jake consent to do this? What has this got to do with his ancestry?"

Chancellor shrugged. "Have you asked him?"

"He won't answer me. He gives me the generic answer, which doesn't explain anything at all."

"Have you ever been to a mithraeum?"

Angeline shook her head.

"I think it's time we went."

He got dressed in the bathroom while Angeline waited outside in his bedroom. *Am I nuts? Here is this gorgeous female sitting on my bed, who is practically throwing herself at me, and I'm taking her to an old temple in some wet, stinking cave instead of making use of that highly resilient mattress.* He shoved a hand into his waistband to tuck in his shirt, opened the door, and saw Angeline rise from the bed to meet him.

When they arrived at the Basilica of San Clemente, they saw no evidence of an excavation inside the buildings or on the grounds. Chancellor asked one of the passing priests where the mithraeum was and the holy man looked at him like he was demented.

"The site has been sealed up," the priest said in a thick Italian accent, "for the time being. There is no public access, nor is there likely to be in the near future."

"But it was open to the public not too long ago?" Angeline prompted.

The priest nodded.

Chancellor showed the priest his Interpol badge.

"After that gruesome discovery outside the basilica," the priest said, "the *polizia* have made most of the buildings off limits."

"So, they are investigating the mithraeum?" Angeline asked.

"Yes. They have finished examining the buildings until further notice."

"I'd like to see the temple," Chancellor requested. "Officially."

The priest stared. "You are working with the local authorities?"

He nodded. "This case may have wide-ranging implications."

The expression on the priest's face barely changed. "All right then," he said in his heavily accented English. "This way."

They followed the wide sweep of the priest's cassock through the main foyer of the basilica, a bold white, three-tiered structure with high ceilings. Chancellor noted that the original entrance was through an axial peristyle surrounded by arcades, which now served as a cloister, and on the ceiling and floor were some mighty impressive mosaics. He tailed the priest to Fontana's chaste facade, which was supported on antique columns.

The basilica church behind it had three naves divided by arcades on old marble columns with inlaid paving and when they reached an unused portion of the church, the priest halted. The silence was complete, and except for a row of small arched windows near the ceiling, there was no light. He noted some buckets and shovels lying about as he crossed to where the floor was dug into a neat, square pit.

"I cannot help you from here," the priest said. "The attending archaeologist unfortunately is not available as far as I know. You will have to find your own way down there if you still insist upon seeing the temple."

Chancellor thanked him, watched Angeline contemplate the pit. A ladder led into the darkness and he lowered himself in behind her. At the bottom they stood quiet, staring. The tunnel was cold and damp and felt like the inside of a coffin—or at least what he imagined one would feel like. He touched the walls of tile and marble slabs, squinted into the entrance of another shaft. "Don't worry. I brought a flashlight."

She leaned back to get her bearings as he switched the beam on, and dragged a hand through her hair, sweeping it into a ponytail and securing it with an elastic band before following his lead.

"Wow," he said as he fumbled his way into the narrow passage. "This is something. Where the blazes are we?"

"A subterranean graveyard," she answered. "A catacomb."

Above her head a lightbulb dangled from a wire, unlit, and Angeline took the flashlight from him and turned to her left. Their shadows played on the wall ahead as she stopped in front of an opening with a frescoed arch above it.

"The mithraeum?" he asked.

"I thought you knew all about this stuff."

"I've never actually been inside a real mithraeum."

She snorted. "This is an arcosolium." It was a burial chamber for an entire family and looked like it used to be sealed by a marble slab that leaned against the north wall. She swept a hand in the direction of the polished stone, moved on past the chamber and through another tunnel that branched into several smaller crypts. "Cubicula, I think." She jerked a foot, her running-shoed toe pointing to the floor of one of the rooms. "Those are called the forma, human tombs dug into the ground."

He quickly walked into another of the crypts. This one held a stone sarcophagus in the centre of the floor, adorned with sculptured reliefs and inscriptions. Beyond it, in the walls, were the vertical tiles marking more tombs.

"This is so odd," she said. "So elaborate." He tripped over a loose stone and nearly fell. "Watch it," she warned. "We're in an archaeological dig. God knows what booby traps were left by the excavators."

The original tunnels had been hand dug and the idea of people toiling away in this sunless environment triggered an admiration, which Chancellor had not expected to feel.

Necropolis, he thought. So this was what they called a city of the dead.

He stopped to have a look inside one of the caverns. "Flash the light over here."

The beam hit a painted fresco on which the colours had faded, but it showed a man leading a pilgrimage. Beside the fresco was an epigraph in Latin. Farther up the tunnel was another chamber where the flashlight struck a row of grinning skulls. Kitty-corner to the ghoulish sight, a pattern of tiles decorated the wall. The tiles marked tombs, called loculi, and were engraved with symbols, but the one that caught his eye was that of a bird. It looked vaguely familiar, with an uncharacteristically heavy skull and thick beak. A raven.

"What is the image of a raven doing here?" Angeline asked.

Yeah, what? And where the devil was the mithraeum?

As if she had read his mind, she turned, pointed. "There—"

He swivelled to look, borrowed the flashlight from her and aimed the light into a vaulted portal, branching off from the crypt. Large fallen stones hid the opening, and as he moved closer to the void, he could see that it led into a shaft. She was right. It was at the end of the shaft.

They stood inside a rectangular chamber with a high, vaulted ceiling. An aisle ran lengthwise down the center with stone benches on either side.

An unexpected threat of claustrophobia teetered on the edge of Chancellor's nerves, but he sucked it down and squashed it. He and Angeline stood at the end of an earthen maze, God knows how many meters below the surface of the ground.

Angeline walked down the aisle to the rear of the cavern where a carved, painted relief hung above a pedestalled altar. The piece was a sharp representation of Mithras killing a sacred bull. His form was that of a young man wearing a Phrygian cap, a short tunic that flared at the bottom, pants and a cloak furling out behind him. He was grasping the bull, forcing it into submission, one knee on its spine, and one hand yanking back its head while he sliced its throat. A serpent and a dog drank from the bull's open wound, while a scorpion attacked the bull's testicles. A raven and a lion watched on the periphery. The celestial twins of light and darkness were the torchbearers and above Mithras were paintings of the sun and moon surrounded by stars.

"Do you know what this is?" Chancellor asked.

"Yes," she said, nodding, her voice coming as an awed whisper from beside him as she stepped back to take in the full view; then she pivoted to face him. "What does the god Mithras have to do with Jake? I see a raven in the relief, but other than that I don't see anything else to concern him."

Her hands panned over the chamber, encompassing all of the elaborate artwork. "Vincent Carpello thought the Tauroctony was a pictorial representation of a Persian—or rather an Iranian—myth. He thought that women figured strongly in the rituals."

"So did Saveriano, but she believed he was wrong about its origins."

"How do you know that?"

"I told you. I've kept up with her research. I've been following her every move. The way she sees it, this—" He waved his hands fluidly in the air. "—is not an Iranian myth but a detailed, illustrated map of the cosmos, with every figure in the standard Tauroctony reflected among a group of constellations located along a continuum in the sky. Look there . . . . Taurus, Canis Minor, Hydra, Corvus, and Scorpio . . . each a known constellation, each represented by an earthly beast."

As he spoke, their eyes roamed the vaulted ceiling of the shrine. He watched her expression change as her imagination took over—and he knew that she, too, saw a great sky, a cosmos.

"If you accept her interpretation, the Tauroctony represents the constellations," Chancellor said. "Does that ring a bell?"

"It does," Angeline replied. "Haida shamans often used caves for their secret rituals because the roof of the cave looked like the night sky." She frowned at him. "Tell me something. You said you've been following her. What's stopping you now? How did you lose track of her? Where is she? I want to know."

"She appears when she feels like it and disappears when she doesn't want to be found."

"That's ridiculous. She has to be somewhere."

"That's why I brought this." He fetched an infrasound detection meter out of his pocket. Infrasound was the frequency lower than the normal limit of human hearing. Animals were the champions of infrasonics, but apparently so were ghosts.

He moved the device around in the air following its signal. It led him out of the temple and back inside the crypt of skulls. Chancellor stared at the row of tiles covering the loculi and noticed something now that he hadn't noticed before. Along with the usual Christian symbols, some of the tombs were tiled with the insignia of the Mithraic ranks. That's why the Raven. There, the Lion. The Nymphus, the Persian, the Sun-courier and the Father.

The meter started beeping and he ran the sensor over the vertical tombs until a shrill, nonstop beeping threatened to break his eardrums.

"Hold this."

She held the ISD meter while he took a trowel from out of his pocket and started to pry away the tile covering the tomb with the symbol of the Soldier. His hands began to sweat, his mind reeling in anticipation. What was he going to dig up?

"Don't look," he told her as the tile fell away. He caught it just before it smashed onto the ground.

Inside was a body, cold now. He didn't pull the body out. He knew what he'd see. Two legs, but only one of them would have a foot.

CHAPTER TWENTY

Before the police hauled the dead man away, Angeline hooked eyes with Chancellor. They had both seen the mark on the corpse's head, and not only was the corpse missing a foot, but on the victim's forehead was a trio of strange symbols, burned into the flesh—a military kitbag, a helmet and a lance. "That mean anything to you?" Chancellor asked her. "They look to be part of the initiation ranks."

Angeline nodded. She had downloaded some of Vincent's private notes just before coming to Rome, and in free moments had studied those sections pertaining to the Mithraic Mysteries. The kitbag, the helmet and the lance were the symbols of the *Miles*, the Soldier, which came third in the Mithraic rites.

She watched in stupefaction when the police came to remove the body from its vertical grave, anxious to vacate this creepy mausoleum and discover the meaning behind the branding of the victim. They both gave statements following some lengthy questioning, and after Chancellor reflashed his ID they were permitted to leave. They returned to his hotel room and she opened her notebook computer to retrieve the description of the symbols.

He was right; the symbols on the frieze that were jammed down Vincent's throat *were* part of the ranking order of initiates. She pulled up a file to display her correlations.

Rank #1 Raven = Corax = light. Symbols are the bird, the cup and the staff. Associated with the planet Mercury.

Rank #2 Nymphus = bridegroom = water. Symbols are the torch, the diadem and the lamp. Associated with the planet Venus.

Rank #3 Miles = soldier = earth. Symbols are the kitbag, the helmet and the lance. Associated with the planet Mars.

Rank #4 Leo = lion = fire. Symbols are the fire shovel, the rattle, and the thunderbolts. Associated with the planet Jupiter.

Rank #5 Perses = Persian = moon. Symbols are the sickle, the scythe and the crescent. Associated with the Moon.

Rank #6 Heliodromus = sun courier = sun. Symbols are the globe, the nimbus, and the whip. Associated with the Sun.

Rank #7 Pater = Father. Symbols are the sickle of Saturn, the Phrygian cap, the staff and the ring. Associated with the planet Saturn.

The symbols on that dead man's forehead were the symbols of the Soldier.

"Interesting," Chancellor said. "So, why do you suppose that frieze found in Carpello's throat had the symbols of the Raven juxtaposed with the symbols of the Nymphus?"

"I don't know, but if it has anything to do with Jake, then I sure as hell am going to find out."

He rose from the bed where they were sitting studying the screen on Angeline's computer. "That's what I thought you'd say." He looked down at her as she closed her computer. "I guess that means you have no plans to go home? And that this—" He indicated the freshly made bed. "Is out of the question?"

She closed her eyes, raised them slowly. "I feel so stupid. I'm sorry, Tom. I just didn't know who else to turn to. I love Jake. I always will."

A muscle twitched in his cheek. That was the only show of emotion he allowed, then he started to pace the room. "Tell me what you know about Jake's affiliation with the Haida Raven. No, let me put that more succinctly. Tell me what you know about the mythical figure."

Angeline didn't have to think too hard about this. Jake had been living with this conflict for as long as she had known him. What did Chancellor know already? Did he know that Jake thought he was the descendent of a prehistoric shaman who was the inspiration for the Raven myths, that he believed the Raven—the mythical Haida figure—was originally a man and that they had found his burial in a cave on an island off the coast of Washington State?

Apparently, he did, because when she finally mustered the courage to divulge this most secret of secrets, he didn't flinch. So it wasn't so secret after all.

They had discovered the bones of a 10,000-year-old man at the bottom of a stone pool inside this cave, but before they could study the remains, a rockslide buried the site.

Jake believed that he was descended from this man, that the man was a shaman. He even had weird dreams about the ancient past where he relived this shaman's actions.

Frustrated, she'd had to live with this, believe what Jake believed because she didn't have proof of things being otherwise. But she only had his word for it, the vividness, the reality of these dreams. They could be anything, couldn't they? And yet he had shared these dreams—what he called inherited memories—with others, because he was sure the events in his nightmares actually happened. He had shared the visions with his father Jimmy Sky before he died, with his worst enemy, the developer, Clifford Radisson and with his equally evil daughter, the art dealer, Celeste. They all experienced these events that happened thousands of years in the past. How could this be?

"Angeline," Chancellor said, waking her out of her trance.

"Sorry." She shook off the thoughts. Somehow all of this had something to do with Saveriano's interest in Jake. "Did you hear what I said?" she asked. "Jake thinks he's descended from the Raven."

"I heard," he said. "So that's where we have to start. Tell me about him."

A knot coiled in her stomach. The Raven had brought Jake to her, but he had also taken him away. She knew almost as much about the mythical bird as Jake did, but of what Jake was doing now, she knew nothing. She turned to face Chancellor.

The Raven was a character of honour and derision among the Haida, who created the earth and humanity, and had the powers of a hero, trickster and transformer. He was also an infamous womanizer, who was restless, curious and easily bored. Constantly in search of exciting adventures, his voracious appetite for food and sex got him into deep trouble. He was a loner, and avoided rules in order to keep himself entertained.

"Does any of this sound like Jake?" Chancellor asked when she finished her description.

Her face crumpled. "You know it does."

She whipped out her laptop again and searched the web for 'Northwest Coast Raven.' Words appeared on the screen:

> Raven plays the role of creator: changing the landscape; liberating the sun, moon, and stars; and making over each animal in their present-day form. As a hero, Raven is responsible for cultural innovations such as teaching humans how to use fire. As a deceiving trickster, however, he is a liar, a thief, a cheat, a pervert, and a murderer. He can be selfish and childlike. He can also be a seducer of some skill or an innovative fop. Sometimes deceptively clever, at other times he is plain stupid. (Krammer 1995)

Angeline's eyes fixed on the line 'As a deceiving trickster, however, he is a liar, a thief, a cheat, a pervert, and a murderer.'

Murderer. Could Jake be a murderer? Oh, shit. What was she thinking? Saveriano was the murderer, not Jake.

She looked up at Chancellor with imploring eyes. "I can't leave him, Tom. I have to get him out of her clutches. Can't you just arrest her?"

"For what, Angeline? What has she done?"

"She's doing something to Jake. I know she is. He isn't himself. He's doing things—I don't know what—but it's changing him."

"That isn't a crime."

"We have to help him."

"We will. But we can't do anything much if he doesn't want our help."

CHAPTER TWENTY-ONE

The initiate swung the long scarlet cloak back from his shoulders. *You have an arid and fiery nature,* she told him, her voice breathy in his mind. *You are the Leo. The Lion.* His symbol was a fire-shovel. She poured honey over his hands to cleanse them. *Only then are the hands kept pure of all evil, all crime and contamination. As becomes an initiate.*

Because fire was purifying, the fitting ablution of honey was administered, rejecting water as hostile to fire. He opened his mouth to receive the cleansing over his tongue and tasted a dark, thick, sweetness. Over his face, she placed the lion's mask.

Now his vision was focused, his hands sticky with honey.

The initiate stood proud. He was one of the chosen. The Lion possessed a special place in the Mithraic Mysteries. Fourth in the procession of the seven ranks, the Miles was to pay him special homage. He walked down the aisle inside the church of Santa Prista. She had promised that he, with his scarlet train, coal-black eyes and proud dignified bearing, would be immortalized in a truly unforgettable manner.

Fiery breath, which for the magi must also be a bath of those sanctified. A relief behind him, carved in very early times showed flaming breath spewing from the Time-god's lion mouth. A statue before him blazed with living fire as kindling and oil was ignited in the stone bowl carved in the back of the lion-sculpture's head.

"Are you ready?" she asked him.

He growled his assent.

"The Soldier awaits you."

The Leo walked toward the flaming lion's head, his hands outspread like a supplicant. His vision was limited, and he only stopped when he almost tripped over something. He looked down, but just as he did, he heard a loud hiss, then a roar like the flood of water. But it wasn't water; it was fire. And the last thing he saw before the flames consumed his screams was a severed foot, the object that had tripped him.

* * *

Emergency vehicles surrounded the Church of Santa Prista. The fire was already doused by the time Angeline and Chancellor parked two blocks away. There was not even a wisp of smoke in the air. Chancellor put a hand over Angeline's eyes as they approached the basilica. "Don't look," he said. "It won't be a pretty sight."

"What happened?"

"Another victim. This time burned to death." He had listened in on the police radio frequencies. Fortunately, he was fluent in Italian. "Stay here while I speak to the beat cop. He was the first to arrive on the scene."

There was a coat over the upper portion of the body while it waited for the CSI unit to arrive with a body bag, and Angeline could see it from where she stood. A shovel lay beside it. Chancellor was asking the cop something, and the officer lifted the coat so that Chancellor could look at the dead man's face. When the officer went to respond to a radio call, Chancellor leaned deeper into the body, plucked something out from between the blackened fist of the corpse, and slid it into his pocket. He caught Angeline's eye and her frown, returned the coat to the body, and made his way back.

"What did you take?" she demanded. "That was evidence."

"Sure, it's evidence. But nothing the local authorities would understand and I didn't want it tied up in red tape before I could get access to it."

"Your methods are unconventional, Mr. Chancellor," Angeline said.

"My methods are necessary. The CSI unit of Rome and Interpol are not investigating the same crime. I doubt that this bit of paper will have any meaning for them at all."

"How do you know? You didn't read it. I saw you pry it out of the victim's hand and hide it in your pocket without reading it."

He turned his back on the church and suggested she do the same. The folded paper crunched in his hand as he lifted it out and straightened it. The letters were computer generated, any printer could have produced it, but what they read could not have been written by just anyone.

"You see, I was right. Any markings on the body were totally fried, but he was found with that shovel and a rattle in his hand, and this message." He jiggled the paper. "The wooden handle of the shovel was reduced to cinders, but the metal blade survived. The rattle was also made of metal, but this—this piece of paper had to be put into his hand after he was burned. As you can see, it isn't charred in the least."

"The Leo," she whispered. "It makes reference to the lion. Does anyone know who the dead guy was? Was he alone?"

"We won't know his identity until dental records are checked. He's too badly maimed and his fingerprints are all burned off. There were no other bodies." Chancellor frowned thoughtfully. "If he was with anyone else, they escaped."

"It's so strange," Angeline said. "The victims seem to be participating in the initiation rites of the Mithras Mysteries, but they aren't accompanied by others. What kind of cult does that? And what kind of cult kills their initiates?" She exhaled. "We have to get inside that church."

"The fire chief says it's not safe to go inside yet. Have to wait until the timbers stabilize and they've had a chance to take down anything that could collapse."

"I need to see the inside of that church," she insisted.

He nodded and refolded the paper, replacing it inside his coat pocket.

Santa Prisca, the Roman basilica church devoted to Saint Prisca the martyr, was built on the Aventine Hill in the 4th

century overtop a temple of Mithras. If a clue to the burnt victim's identity and the motive for his horrible death existed, it would be there. She followed Chancellor around to the rear of the church, examining the ground as they went. Footprints marred the soft sod, but that was all.

Old churches had service doors, and there had to be one that was opened that they could use to gain entry into the nave.

"Was he found inside?" she asked as they slipped, unnoticed, into a side entrance.

Chancellor shrugged, holding the rickety, wooden door open for her. She sniffed the stuffy air, noting that the interior of the church was not as ancient as she had expected. After the Norman sack of Rome, he told her, the church had been restored several times. The current interior was a 17th century restoration and the obtrusive columns were the only visible remains of the original nave.

They moved into the center of the nave and saw that the wooden pews were untouched by fire. The walls were frescoed with saints and angels. Anastasio Fontebuoni's *Saints and Angels with the Instruments of Passion*, Chancellor informed her, a diagnostic piece of work. He paused, gazing about, brows furled.

That was odd, Angeline thought, noticing too.

None of this had been touched by fire.

She shuddered at the idea of fire. It was gruesome. Someone might have lugged the body outside the church, after it was burned. But where had the fire taken place? There were no signs of anything heavy being dragged across the ground outdoors or along the floors inside.

They discovered the sacristy and found it was the same. A painting of *The Immaculate Conception with Angels* glared down at them. Searching the inner sanctums further, they ended up in the church's crypt where an altar housed the preserved remains of the saint.

"How do you know that that's Saint Prisca?" she asked.

"Who else would it be?"

He turned from her and raked his vision over the walls. More frescoes here, but none were marred by smoke or flame.

And yet something felt off. She sniffed. She could smell smoke.

That was why the fire chief wanted no one in the church, but obviously the fire wasn't started inside. Not on this level.

How about the basement? Could there be a trapdoor leading into the subterranean temple? The tourist brochures named Santa Prisca as one of the ancient churches built on top of a mithraeum, so there had to be one here.

They found the basement, but no trapdoor leading into a cavern underground. The basement had several rooms and locked storage spaces. There were old oak casks and wooden crates stacked against the walls, old furniture and unwanted paintings, and although some of those works of art looked like they might be worth something, it was none of her business why the priests would have cached them down here in the damp and mould.

They returned to the main floor and stepped outside again. Chancellor studied the footprints in the sod. The grass was slick, damp, and the tracks looked silvery in the sunlight. People walked around here all the time, didn't they? Those prints could be anyone's.

Angeline looked around the outside of the church. The walls were covered in ivy, but against the vines a couple of shovels leaned up against the exterior doorframe. Was someone doing some extraneous gardening? She moved closer and saw that a trowel and a stack of buckets rested under the eaves of one of the doorways.

She glanced from the digging implements to the churchyard. No garden. So, why all the gardening tools?

Unless they *weren't* gardening tools.

She tried the doorknob and it gave. This door was identical to the one they had entered on the opposite side of the church. The police and other emergency officials were busy at the front of the building, so no one had noticed them snooping around the back.

This way. She crooked a finger without speaking and Chancellor followed silently.

By the left wall, veiled in a niche, a wooden plank lay overtop the dirt floor. She motioned for him to help her lift it and they saw beneath the outer edge that a pit was dug into the ground. The police had not thought to look under it because the police were not looking for a buried shrine. The odour puffing up at them indicated that the lid had been clamped tight on this hole for quite a while.

She wasn't exactly dressed for a spelunking or tunnelling expedition, but this might be their only chance to investigate any subterranean caves below the church.

She went first, sliding down the muddy hole that opened out into a well-scraped tunnel, crawling on hands and knees, conscious of Chancellor behind her. The smell of smoke was stronger here, and unlike the underground labyrinth of tunnels and crypts below the Basilica of San Clemente, this mithraeum had no such maze leading to it. The tunnel was short and led to a large cavernous space with a vaulted ceiling.

This temple seemed to have a single theme. Paintings of horses—*three* horses set ablaze by the fiery breath of a lion—which represented, without a doubt, baptism by fire.

"Flame will spread over the earth at the end of time and strike down evil-doers only. The righteous will be spared, and for them, this will be merely a cleansing bath," Chancellor recited.

"What's that from?"

He pointed to a line of inscription beneath the fiery horse painting that described the relationship between the Lion, Mithras and the cosmic firestorm.

Angeline had more than a rudimentary knowledge of Latin, and could make out the meaning of some of the inscriptions. 'Here the faithful ask that the incense-burning lions be received by Mithras. The Lions, through whom we ourselves offer the incense, through whom we ourselves are consumed . . . .' What did that mean?

Chancellor squinted, mumbling the inscription before looking up. "Okay, I'm just going to go out on a limb here. I'm no classical archaeologist, nor am I a specialist in Mithraism, but I'll tell you what I think." He stared at the painting, then said, "The purifying force of fire used in the cult's mysteries transforms the Lion into a new man, one who is sanctified; and who, like Jupiter, defeats the Titans with lightning and joins Mithras in hunting down the powers of evil."

That was pretty presumptuous. He got that from one inscription?

Chancellor shrugged. "I may not be an academic, but I'm highly trained in cult ideology. It's an interpretation. And based on what we saw upstairs—" he jerked a thumb heavenward, "—and what was typed on that piece of paper I took from the corpse, I think it's pretty safe to say that this was a rite of initiation into the rank of the Lion AKA the Leo. Only the initiate was also a sacrifice."

Angeline took the sheet of paper that Chancellor retrieved from his pocket to further punch home his point. She unfolded it and read:

"The Leo was united with Mithras and the sun through fire, and so also with the Chariot of the Sun. Purified by fire, they would ultimately become immune from its all-consuming power."

She lifted her head, eyes questioning. Who had left this in the victim's fist for the police to find?

Chancellor shook his head; he didn't think it was meant for the police. "I think it was meant for us."

Angeline suddenly frowned. There was no sign of a fire in here, no soot, no charcoal, nothing charred. The frescoes were immaculate, just that smell of smoke.

CHAPTER TWENTY-TWO

It was late afternoon by the time they returned to the hotel. Chancellor sat down on the bed, hoisting his laptop onto his thighs and proceeded to check his email while Angeline went to turn on the small flat-screen TV that stood on a bookcase against the wall. "I don't get what happened in there," she said, removing her sweater and flinging it aside. "There was no sign of fire anywhere in the church or the mithraeum, just that lingering smell of smoke." She settled herself on the bed beside him to watch the news.

"When the authorities know more, I'll find out exactly where the fire took place—" Suddenly he stiffened, eyes glued to the computer screen.

"What is it?"

"Official business." He angled the laptop away to read the email from his forensics expert in Lyons. That midnight tryst with Susanne after Saveriano's gracious dinner party had paid off. He'd managed to get a sample of the French girl's hair as well as lipstick prints that she had left all over his neck and collar. She had acted like she had absolutely nothing to hide, but little did she know, he had couriered the lipstick-stained shirt and strands of hair to Trudy with an ASAP request. If the girl had a record, no amount of acting would hide her. Trudy had come through. Susanne's identity was no longer a mystery. *I know exactly who you are sweetheart*, he thought derogatorily, remembering their luscious night of amour. *Or should I say, I now know exactly who you 'were.'*

A sucking gasp came from beside him and he swung to see what had brought it on. He could barely keep from choking himself when he saw what Angeline was watching. "She's . . . stepping up the pace," Angeline said, coughing at intervals to clear her throat. "How can that woman be so arrogant as to think no one will catch her. Another victim!"

"We don't know for sure that this is Saveriano's work. I'm just guessing." Before Angeline could object, Chancellor raised a hand to silence her, his eyes firmly peeled to the TV set. *Ostia Antica.* He pondered over the words for a second. Where had he heard those words before? *Antica* meant old, didn't it? And *Ostia* . . . . Of course. Ostia was the ancient port of Rome. He slapped down the top on his computer and stood up. "Ostia is about twenty miles from here. It's the site of an archaeological dig." He snatched up his jacket from where he'd tossed it onto a chair earlier, and pushed his arms through the sleeves.

Angeline also got to her feet, grabbing her sweater. "I've heard of Ostia Antica. It's at the mouth of the Tiber River. Is that where the latest murder happened? That means it's got a mithraeum, too." She returned her attention to the screen, arms clasped around her chest, trying to control her agitation long enough to watch the rest of the newscast. The TV camera panned over a scene of stone ruins while a voice-over explained the gruesome circumstances of the execution. The victim was decapitated, and in the hands of the headless body were some odd implements—a sickle and a scythe. Early speculation claimed that the tools were not used to defend the poor man from his attacker, nor were they used to inflict the deathblow.

By now a tarp had been placed over the upper portion of the body and no blood or gore could be seen. The *Polizia di Stato* herded a group of morbid, but decidedly determined looky-loos from the crime scene, one of them busily tapping notes on a Blackberry.

"That looks like Cristine Kletter," Angeline said.

Chancellor studied the woman in question as she was backhanded away by a policeman, nearly dropping her cell phone. A heavy frown creased his forehead. He had got what he'd wanted from her. She had located Lalonde and reported to him, and now she was supposed to go home content with his promise that she'd get an exclusive when the case was closed. He squinted at the screen hoping it was only a doppelganger, a look-alike, but the harder he scrutinized the more certain he became. "Dammit, it is *her*. What the hell is that nosy reporter doing there?"

"A man was decapitated, execution style at an archaeological site. Where else would she be?" Angeline paused, suddenly comprehending his point. "Yeah, you're right. What is she doing in *Rome?*"

He sealed his lips and made for the door, heard Angeline click off the TV and run for the elevator right at his heels.

*   *   *

Ostia was one of Rome's first colonies. Founded in the seventh century by Ancus Marcius, the legendary fourth king of Rome, the settlement had been built and rebuilt as a consequence of the sacking and resacking by Arab pirates. The crumbling walls built by the statesman Marcus Cicero to protect its people from the invaders could still be seen. It didn't take long by car to reach the old port.

They stood staring at the scene with the muddy mouth of the Tiber River in the backdrop, the slimy yellow water swirling sluggishly on its way. The tourists that were witness to the gruesome discovery were still hovering, and in fact had grown tenfold since the live airing of the broadcast. The body had been taken away and Chancellor went to speak to one of the remaining investigating officers, flashing his Interpol badge, while Angeline scouted the ruins for signs of a mithraeum.

She stumbled across the remains of a public *latrinae*, built and organized for collective use as a series of stone toilet seats, wrought in a rectangular chamber that allowed the users of the facility to socialize with each other while performing their bodily functions. There seemed to be a row of six toilets at opposite sides of the chamber, and three at each end: enough for eighteen people.

"Gross," a familiar voice said over her shoulder. "Is that really a public toilet? What did they do here besides poop? Weigh in on the stock market?"

She turned, expecting exactly whom she saw at the edge of the ruins, and smiled at Cristine Kletter. "Yeah, it *is* a public latrine. And what are *you* doing here, in Rome?"

"Same as you. I'm looking for a motive for why that initiate was killed."

"Pardon? How do you know that poor man was an initiate of a cult?"

"Oh, quit giving me the innocent act, Angeline. Didn't your new boyfriend there tell you I was in town? And where's Jake by the way? Thought you two were simpatico. Like married?"

"You know we haven't set the date." She hated the tone of Cristine's voice. She knew the journalist had an eye for Jake, always had, but Jake had never responded to her ever so subtle overtures. She shrugged as if to say 'too bad,' but the glint in her eyes let Angeline know she wasn't sorry in the least.

Angeline was feeling quite defeated by the killing that was going on and her fear that Jake was somehow involved. She did not have the time or the patience for guessing games and decided to lay everything on the table. "Why are you talking to me like this, like somehow *I'm* the enemy? I thought we were friends. Did I say or do something to offend you, Cristine?"

"Shit. I'm sorry. It's just that . . . I like Jake. We've been buddies for a while despite the fact that he probably thinks I stabbed him in the back. You did tell him about the editorial decision? Well, I'm worried about him—"

"He isn't exactly going to go over the deep end because of a magazine story."

"Well, shit. I know what it meant to him." She paused for a second, her face reddening. The wind tossed a stripe of hair across her eyes and she swiped at it. "What the hell are you doing with that Interpol cop when you're supposed to be engaged to Jake?"

Angeline's breath caught. It was her turn to pause. She finally found her voice and said, "I am not 'with' him."

"Why aren't you with Jake? If Chancellor is investigating Jake for murder, why are you here in Ostia with the enemy?"

"Interpol does not suspect Jake. It's Saveriano they're after. And the reason why I'm not with Jake is because . . . ." She didn't finish. It was none of her business. She gazed across the ruins to search for Chancellor. The smell of the river swept up from the muddy bank. "Jake is mixed up in something strange," she said.

Just then, a man's silhouette appeared in the distance and came toward them—just in the nick of time because she sensed Cristine's eyes on her left hand. She did not relish explaining the absence of her diamond engagement ring.

"Get out of here, Ms. Kletter," Chancellor said. "Go write your story or whatever, but stop pestering me."

"No way, Chancellor. I'm sticking with you. You're onto a big story and I want in."

"You're impeding an investigation. Do you want me to call Security to haul you off the site?" He backhanded a thumb toward the crime scene.

He glared at her and she glared back.

Something strange was going on here, Angeline thought. They were both acting a little over the top. If Cristine wanted in, what could it hurt? She might have some insights on the case that neither of them had thought of. "Let her come with us," Angeline said. "I'll vouch for her."

Cristine gave Chancellor a sneery look.

The smell from the river was getting stronger and Angeline turned her head to cover her nose with her sleeve. "You'll behave yourself, won't you, Cristine?"

"Natch," the journalist replied.

The ruins were widespread much of it exposed to the delight of tourists, and the pink and golden stone bricks gleamed in the late afternoon sun. If they didn't find the mithraeum soon, they would have to call it a day. They walked past the remains of a theatre and the public baths.

So far, most of the other mithraea they'd visited were linked to underground tunnels. Was this one like that, too? Angeline searched for clues to an opening that would lead into a subterranean passage, one that hadn't been unearthed by archaeologists yet. The only obvious place was the toilets, and she cringed at the idea of clawing her way through Ostia's ancient sewer system. Back in the day, when this sewer system was in operation, the murkiness of the river came from human sewage being carried out to sea. But whatever sewage remained inside the tunnels would be long since fossilized.

She backtracked to the *latrinae*, one-handed herself down the stone embankment of toilet seats, and landed on the rough marble floor.

"Hey, isn't it a no-no to step all over the ruins?" Cristine queried in a loud voice.

Angeline raised her head from where she was examining the stone toilets, and sheepishly touched a finger to her lips. She gestured for Cristine and Chancellor to hurry and each got down into the latrine behind her. Angeline shifted a block of stone beneath the opening of one of the toilets. If she could remove enough of the brickwork, she could climb inside the shaft. "The archaeologists working here haven't exposed any mithraeum that I can see, so I figure the temple's got to be underground," she explained.

"Why do you think there's one down there?" Cristine asked.

"All of the killings have been associated with mithraea," Chancellor replied. "It has to be somewhere. There are eighteen associated with the ancient port town of Ostia. Most of those have been excavated and the relics removed to museums for further study. What's left remains to be found."

"Wouldn't it just be easier to ask the archaeologists who are digging this site where they are?"

"Most of them are demolished, the evidence just bits and pieces of statuary and paintings."

"You think there's a complete untouched temple somewhere?"

"I know it," Angeline answered for Chancellor.

"Better duck," Cristine said. "Security just looked this way. I'll go distract them. You find the doorway." She hefted herself out of the latrine and went to meet an angry-looking guard.

Chancellor tucked his head down. Angeline was sure she hadn't been seen. All the while they'd been talking she'd been below the level of the embankment containing the toilet seats.

CHAPTER TWENTY-THREE

"Is it true that they didn't find the head with the body?" she asked.

Chancellor nodded. From what the officer had told him, there was only a decapitated torso and they had no idea where the head was. Angeline shuddered. She had a feeling if they found the mithraeum they would find the missing head. "I'm going first," she said, ducking to the level of the opening where they had removed enough of the brickwork under one of the toilet seats to make a hole large enough for a person to crawl through.

It was definitely a tunnel and led down into a black void. "Have you got a light on you?" she whispered over her shoulder.

She felt the handle of a small penlight thrust between her fingers and flicked it on. The sewage tunnels angled into a maze of low, narrow shafts that had long since dried up. There was no moisture, only here and there solid lumps of stone or what *appeared* to be stone. Could these be coprolites, one-thousand-year-old human shit? She steadied the light on the walls ahead of her. The stone was cold, the smell musty, and the walls were beginning to close in on her.

What if this passage didn't lead anywhere? How were they going to get out? There was nowhere to turn around and she didn't relish the idea of crawling the entire way backwards.

"Angeline." Chancellor's voice came as a low, muffled echo from behind her. "You okay? Why did you stop?"

She took a deep breath of the thin, foul air. "Trying to get my bearings," she answered, heart pounding irrationally now.

Focus, she told herself. *Focus*. Don't think about suffocating or being crushed to death in this one-foot tube of a tunnel. Crawl.

Just *crawl*. One inch at a time. And pray there's an opening soon. She opened her eyes, forcing herself not to blink, aimed the beam of the penlight straight in front of her as she snaked on her hands and knees along the long, black passage. "I see something," she called back to Chancellor. "An entranceway to a chamber!" She picked up the pace, bruising her knees and her elbows in her need to get into a more open space.

The tunnel was widening. She could sit up on her haunches. This was not part of the sewage system because someone had been digging here.

The fresh marks of excavation were clear as trowel scrapings. Excavators had opened the wall and removed some of the stonework, leaving a pile of stones scattered on either side of the entrance. This was interesting, a mithraeum side by side with a sewer? Well, that was one way to keep it secret and to deter any undesirables from locating it.

Angeline paused at the end of the passage where the opening dropped into a large chamber. She manoeuvered her legs over a ledge until they dangled into empty space, then shone the light below her feet. Empty space. She spun the light into the void beyond until it struck the vaulted ceiling, bouncing off statuary and friezes and glorious painted frescoes.

"I'm going down."

"Down?" His voice echoed from behind her.

Angeline turned her head to the bulky shadow that was Chancellor, and nodded. "We have to jump from here. I only hope there's something to use for a ladder when we want to leave."

"Better let me go first."

She was about to object, then shrugged.

Chancellor squeezed beside her and eased his legs over the ledge. "Doesn't look too far," he said, boosting himself off with his hands and emitting a grunt after landing with a crushing sound of rubble.

"You okay?" She flashed the light down at him. The drop wasn't that deep and his face came to the level of her knees. Even so, she might have knocked her joints out sticking the landing had she jumped first.

"Let me give you a hand," he said, reaching up to take her by the waist.

She leaped as he lifted her so that she was airborne before he could feel the full brunt of her weight.

They both looked around before moving deeper into the chamber. The layout was the same as every mithraeum that was ever described in scholarly studies, a stone structure mimicking a cave, dark and windowless. There were raised benches along the side and a recess at the far end with a pedestalled altar. The paintings and frescoes on the walls showed a figure in a grey tunic standing under the moon. Angeline racked her brains to recall what she'd learned about the Persian, AKA the Perses, whom this image represented.

Chancellor interrupted her thoughts when he approached the altar.

"What's the matter?" she asked.

An oozy substance glistened at the edge of the altar, and in the weak glow of his penlight showed no colour. He dipped a finger to the substance, sniffed, and touched it to his lips. "Honey."

"Honey?"

"Like the Leo, the hands of the Persian are cleansed with honey."

Honey was the sugar of antiquity and was valued for its preservation qualities. The ancient Persians thought that honey came from the moon, where the semen of the bull slain by Mithras was extracted and purified in order to produce new fruits and plants.

"So the victim's head is here somewhere," Angeline said.

"And I don't relish finding it. I think we should get out while we can. We've confirmed that this murder was the killing of the fifth initiate, the Persian or Perses. That's all I need to know."

"That means the Heliodromus is next. The Sun Courier."

Chancellor had seen enough, rubbed the honey off his fingers onto the thigh of his trousered leg, and turned to exit the mithraeum the same way they had entered.

"Wait," she said.

He shoved a block of stone to the bottom of the ledge, which was at his head level. "I need something else to give me a step up. Help me find another block like this." He glanced over when she failed to respond. "What are you waiting for, Angeline? I have to report this find to the authorities."

"Wait." She put a hand to her nose; there was a strange sweetish, even metallic smell that was making her nauseated. She forced it back. "There's a pattern here. Saveriano is knocking off an initiate from each of the seven ranks. Why?"

Chancellor's eyes gleamed in the dull light. "Haven't you noticed something wrong with the order in which the slayings have occurred?"

"They're all in order. The Sun Courier is next. I'm worried about Jake. Jake's family crest is the Raven. The Raven is associated with the Sun in Haida mythology."

He shook his head. "The Raven was the first initiate. Jake is the Raven. She didn't kill the Raven."

"But this is the Sun Courier. And in Haida mythology, the Raven is often depicted carrying the sun in his beak. There are loads of stories about how the Raven stole the light."

"Don't worry, Jake is not the Sun Courier."

"Then what does he have to do with any of this?"

"I don't think it's Jake we have to worry about next. The person we have to worry about will be a young man, probably a grad student or a research assistant. Or a young scholar like Vincent."

"Hold on a second." Angeline gulped. "Vincent. *Vincent* was the Raven. His hands were clasped to symbolize the Corax."

Chancellor agreed, but shook his head as he explained why. He had no doubt Saveriano was still searching for the Raven. Vincent just wasn't the right one, so she killed him.

Chancellor had given up all pretense that Sophia was not the killer, and yet they had absolutely no concrete evidence against her. It was too late to save Vincent, but they could save the next victim if they could figure out who he was.

"If not Jake, who then? And how can we warn him? Tom. You have to arrest her. You have to stop this, now!" Angeline screamed as she crouched to push a block of stone toward Chancellor to increase the height of the stone steps he was building. It wasn't a stone, but a human head. And she had almost touched it.

"Get a grip," he warned, grabbing her wrists. He let his glance ricochet off the gruesome sight before returning to her. "Don't look at it. Climb up on these blocks and I'll boost you over the ledge." Angeline could not drag her eyes from the sight. As an archaeologist she was accustomed to skeletons and disarticulated skulls. But this . . . this was different. Fortunately, it was too dark to see anything clearly. But on the forehead of the victim was burned the image of a crescent, the symbol of the moon. Angeline pinched her eyes closed, fighting down the nausea. The headless body discovered on the surface, by a tourist, held a sickle in one hand and a scythe in the other. The sickle, the scythe and the crescent were the symbols of the Perses.

She clamped her lips shut in a thin line.

She had to get out of here.

Now!

She swung desperately toward Chancellor and stepped up on the blocks of stone. His strong hands raised her to the ledge where she crawled onto the floor of the tunnel, dragging her legs up behind her. He was close behind, and as soon as she saw his head and shoulders darken the entrance to the mithraeum, she turned and started to creep along the passage back in the direction of the ancient sewer system.

She gasped as she sucked in a breath of fresh air. Cristine was just outside the opening, in the latrine, waiting for them. The sun was setting.

"Oh my god, Angeline. You look like you saw a ghost."

"Worse. We found the missing head."

Cristine reached out to help her out of the sewer system, then stood aside as Chancellor's tousled dun-coloured hair appeared in the wide gap between the brickwork.

*   *   *

They returned to the hotel defeated. They had racked their brains for hours but couldn't come up with any suggestions for the identity of the next victim.

"Saveriano has no more grad students or research assistants. She let them all go when she decided to pursue this avenue of her research. And by that, I mean the Black Goddess. She doesn't want any help with this project," Cristine said. "I did my homework."

"So you talked to all of her colleagues and former assistants?" Chancellor asked.

"I did. All of those that were at the museum anyway."

Which weren't many, Angeline thought. She'd been to the National Museum and they were in a state of chaos because of ongoing restoration of the ancient buildings. Many of the curators had taken offices in outbuildings and alternate campuses.

Regretting, now, her overreaction to Jake this morning, she realized that had she kept a rein on her emotions she could just go back to the villa and look for him, but as it was, no one was going to let her into the house because it was being guarded by that French witch. When they drove over there after leaving Ostia, Susanne had told them in no uncertain terms that they were unwelcome, that Jake did not want to see her, and that her employer was absent from home. So they had backtracked to Chancellor's hotel because neither she nor Cristine had accommodations for the night.

Why couldn't they find this woman? If she was responsible for the killings, how did she disappear so quickly without leaving a trace? And why was there no blood in the sewers leading from the mithraeum under the *latrinae*? The head was there; the body was outside, dragged meters away from the kill site.

Of course, they didn't know for certain that the victim was decapitated inside the temple. Until the authorities finished their investigation, they could only speculate.

But either way, if the body was dragged out of the tunnels or the head was carried into it, blood would have been everywhere and it wasn't.

Chancellor glanced at his watch, noting the date next to the digital time. "When is that public lecture and unveiling she's supposed to do?"

Angeline hated the way he always avoided talking about Saveriano's mysterious disappearing acts, adamantly refusing to offer suggestions as to how she was capable of actions that were simply humanly impossible.

"This weekend," Cristine said. "She will have to show up for her lecture. She's the star of the show after all, and we all know how academics crave the limelight. That's when we'll corner her."

Angeline fished out her cell phone from her bag and punched in Jake's number. The phone rang and rang and rang, and then an automated voice said the party she was trying to reach was unavailable.

Shit. She clenched her eyes tight. Where was he? She should never have left him. What had made her do that?

"It's not your fault," Chancellor said.

What wasn't her fault? She was thoroughly aggravated at his inconvenient and inconsiderate eavesdropping on her private grief.

He lifted her limp wrist, which still held the cell phone, and she stiffened immediately upon his touch.

"Where's your ring?"

"I gave it back."

"You really *were* mad at him."

The pale band on her skin where the diamond had sat for almost a year gleamed in accusation, and as she caught Cristine's quizzical stare, she coloured. She made sure her sentiments were clear on her face. "Where is he, Tom? You seem to know Saveriano better than anyone else. You've been studying her. What has she done to him? Where has she taken him?"

"I don't know, Angeline. But I do know one thing. Cristine is right. She'll show up at her lecture and gala. She'll have to.

She has too big of an ego to pass up the opportunity to let the academic community and the public know her theories on the Black Goddess."

"Why is this Black Goddess so important to her?" Cristine asked.

Chancellor shrugged, loosening his yellow necktie until it lay draped over his shoulders. "I guess we'll find out in a couple of days."

CHAPTER TWENTY-FOUR

Angeline usually slept until her alarm went off, but this morning her brain broke consciousness without help. Oblivious, Cristine rolled over and sighed. They had shared the bed while Chancellor had slept on the armchair, and now as Angeline's eyes took in her surroundings, she noticed that his trench coat, which he had used for a blanket was missing, and so was the yellow necktie he'd left on the dresser last night. She stumbled out of bed and snatched at a scribbled note on hotel stationary taped to the door. It said he had gone to follow a lead and that he thought they could both use a rest so he had resisted waking them.

What lead?

Angeline slapped the note onto the nightstand. How dare he follow up on a lead and not tell her!

"He must have been really quiet," Cristine said. "'Cause I'm a light sleeper."

"Obviously, not that light," Angeline snapped.

In the bathroom, she quickly showered and brushed her teeth, then returned to check any messages on her cell phone but there was nothing from Chancellor or Jake. While Cristine went to have her shower, she made coffee on the hotel's two-cup machine, set a cup aside to cool and shouted through the slightly opened bathroom door, "Where do you think he went?"

Her voice was obliterated by the steady downbeat of the shower. She brushed her hair hard, waiting out the restless minutes until the journalist stepped from the bathroom wrapped in a coarse, white hotel towel. She set down her brush and made a production of lifting her cup and tasting the coffee. Cristine was fresh-faced and rosy from the steam, her hair clinging sexily to her skull, and she could see how Jake might find her attractive.

Not the time to compare physical attributes, she thought as she set down the cup and indicated to the journalist that the rest in the pot was for her, and retrieved her brush. Her hair was almost dry and floated down in a black cloud around her shoulders. Nor was it the time to feel insecure about her looks.

Cristine dressed in yesterday's clothes, while Angeline put on a fresh pair of jeans and a turquoise sweater that showed off her not too shabby attributes.

Chancellor's laptop was still on the table where he'd left it, and Angeline lifted it onto her lap and sat down on the armchair by the window. She opened it, proceeded to go through his search history, and didn't have to dig far before she found what she was looking for. He had purchased an airline ticket to Nice, and the last thing he had consulted before logging off was a road map to Eze.

Angeline raised her head from the computer and showed the results of her search to Cristine. "You think Chancellor went there to find Saveriano?"

Cristine buttoned up her short leather jacket. "If Saveriano intends to put on another show starring the Heliodromus, AKA, the Sun Courier, she'd go to a mithraeum, and probably not one in Rome because I think she knows that Chancellor is on to her."

"But there are tons of mithraea in Italy. Why leave the country? Nice is so far. It's in France. We'll have to fly."

"Do you want to see Jake again?" Cristine asked.

"You think he went with her?"

"I'm almost certain."

Unfortunately, Angeline had no passport. Thanks to the mischief of the local gypsies. Did the European Union allow border-free passage to foreigners within their boundaries?

She would soon find out.

Cristine drove them to the airport where she left the car. Several seats were available on a flight to Nice that was leaving in ten minutes. Angeline had little time to haggle with officials, so after purchasing tickets, they mixed with the locals who needed no passport, and found window seats aboard. As the plane took off, the thick cloud that had gathered overnight broke, revealing sandy white coast and green mountains, while the sea glittered, jade-blue against the white, red-roofed houses terracing the hills.

The flight was short and for a moment it looked like they were going to land on the water, then it became clear that the runway was a manmade promontory jutting into the sea.

When they debarked at the Nice-Côte d'Azur Airport, Cristine rented an old compact Lancia and drove them to a hotel. She seemed to know where she was going, and for that reason they agreed that she would do the driving. Angeline had never driven in Europe, while Cristine was a foreign correspondent that travelled all the time.

The hotel Cristine chose was called the Négresco and was one of the original Grand Hotels of the Riviera. When they pulled up Angeline was awe-struck by the opulent, domed masterpiece of early twentieth century architecture.

They couldn't afford this. Well, she couldn't anyway.

Cristine smiled. It was just for one night and they were leaving tomorrow. They could share a room one more time.

The lobby was amazingly plush without being gaudy. Period pieces and works of art were everywhere. In the Salon Royal, they admired the baccarat crystal chandelier which the bellhop informed them weighed at least a ton. They checked in and had their luggage stowed in a luxurious room, then they returned to the rental car. Hopefully, it would only take a day to find the mithraeum in Eze, explore it, and find Chancellor, if not Jake, in the process.

They drove east toward the coastal highway.

Something didn't feel right about this. The mithraeum in Eze was buried below a castle ruin and was opened to the public. Why a castle ruin? Almost all mithraea were buried beneath churches. And why had Chancellor left before it was light? The wariness Angeline felt refused to abate.

Exotic scenery glided by. Nice, like all other Riviera towns, was originally a winter resort, later used for a summer playground by the rich and famous. The most striking image it offered was a long sea-front view to the west, the world famous Promenade des Anglais which had been financed by the English in the 19th century, and stretched away in a creamy ribbon against the blue of sea and sky. Banking the road were the original Edwardian and Victorian buildings, and now they were leaving Nice to see the local colour on the highway.

The coast was grand and dramatic. Much of it was so steep, so awesome, that the road along it was a major phenomenon. Called the Moyenne Corniche, it hugged the shoreline climbing and dropping in rhythm to the landscape. Above it was the Grande Corniche, the road carved into the mountain passes; and below was the Inférieure Corniche, the route closest to the water. At the foot of the steepest stretch nestled the beautiful resorts of Beaulieu and Villefranche, and behind them high villages clung to crags. Two peninsulas broke the coastline: Cap Ferrat and Cap Martin.

Sheer cliff faces abounded as they swept by, and as Angeline felt the wind bite her face and the sea fill her lungs, she glimpsed elegant villas perched among trees and gardens. The cape extended some three kilometers south of Beaulieu with an arm off the east where the little port town of St-Jean-Cap-Ferrat was situated.

They arrived in town so that Cristine could take a break from driving, and parked near a seaside walk to stretch their legs. After the exhilarating drive, not only was Angeline focused enough to appreciate the rich scenery, but her other senses were heightened, too.

Maybe she had made a mistake, she thought. Had she dialled the wrong number yesterday? Maybe Jake *wasn't* with Saveriano. She fished out her phone and called his number again and got the same message.

She joined Cristine on the boardwalk. Late wild roses—dusty and shrivelled but still fragrant—and silvery-grey bay trees perfumed the air. A clean, cool wind whisked in from the sea.

Overlooking the waterfront was the Baroness Ephrussi de Rothschild's pink palace with its Moorish collections, which was now a public art museum.

"What's the matter?" Cristine asked, slowing down to keep pace. "You seem so preoccupied."

Angeline made an irritated gesture.

Cristine pinned her with an accusatory look, then glanced away. "All right, be that way. But we're going to be spending the whole day together, so the least you can do is be civil. After all, I'm only trying to help. Besides, you owe me. Remember?"

"I'm sorry," Angeline said. "I just don't understand why Jake doesn't answer his phone."

"Well, if that road map we found on Chancellor's laptop is any indication—and he's as super a sleuth as he thinks he is—maybe we'll find them both at Eze. It's an ancient town, built as a retreat from Saracen raids and is a pretty cluster of houses on a hill with a castle ruin on top."

They returned to their rental and headed back onto the highway. The time passed in silence—more grey road and vivid scenery whizzing by—until Cristine raised a hand from the steering wheel, rousing Angeline from her semi-slumber.

Coming up was the village of Eze.

From this distance it looked like a wasp's nest, grey and powdery, clinging to its crag above the sea. The cone on which Eze was built rose from the Moyenne Corniche, twelve kilometers from Nice. They were actually closer to Monte Carlo, now, than they were to Nice according to the GPS on the dashboard.

It was past peak tourist season so they wouldn't see many visitors. Ordinarily thronging crowds spilling out of buses and cars packed the base of the cone, but only three or four other vehicles stood in the lot as they rolled up. Cristine braked, swung the car door open and pointed to a handsome 14th century gateway that led into the tiny, immaculately restored town.

They walked up a set of stone steps, then through a narrow pink alley and up yet another stone staircase, directly below a pair of spectacularly situated but smallish hotels with restaurants that had open-air patios roosting on the hillside.

"Are you hungry?" Cristine asked.

Famished. They hadn't stopped for breakfast. But from the looks of the empty tables with their chairs tilted inward, the restaurants weren't open. She'd have to lump it.

They climbed higher through the stone village between the ancient stonework—comprising all of the structures—including the tourist shops and artists' studios that were closed for the season. Angeline stopped for a minute to catch her breath and to admire some pretty terrace houses of pink stone with red Spanish tile roofs. Straggling vines of pink bougainvillea crawled up the house walls to meet geranium-filled window boxes, the blooms well past their prime. Directly in front of her was a stone drinking fountain in the shape of a cherub's face with water trickling out of its mouth.

How could such an enchanting scene seem creepy? A crippling sense of unease turned her knees to rubber. The quietness was too much, and the farther they scaled uphill, the more uneasy she became. She almost did an about-face and backpedalled down the steps. If only more people were around. A body or two made an appearance before being swallowed by the stonework alleys.

It was a long climb uphill; she was exhausted. Cristine reached down to jokingly haul her up the last few steps. On the summit were castle ruins: masonry levelled everywhere, with the tallest part of the hill rising just a bit higher than the spire of a church, protruding from a lower site on the steep slope. Angeline squinted as the sun sliced through a cloud. There was something strange about the spire. It seemed almost to be alive. Black against the orange sunshine, she blinked at the tricks the sun was playing on her vision. She was seeing things, had to be. There wasn't something strapped to that steeple.

"Well, what do you think?" Cristine shot a glance behind them. "The castle was destroyed in 1706. I don't know how old the mithraeum is or where the entrance could be."

The scene was breathtaking—the ruins, the clusters of pink houses along the slope mimicking the staircases leading to the summit. The hill was rocky and sharp, and now that they were at the top, she could see they had accomplished a precarious climb. One slip, and she might have broken something.

Cristine tapped her arm to gain her attention. She turned and smiled. Someone had planted exotic cactuses among the fallen masonry; the idea of a person doing that brought back a sense of normalcy. A few of the cactuses were familiar: barrel cactuses, brain cactuses and tall spiny cactuses with fleshy trunks and dangerous spikes. Some were in full colour just like the Christmas cactus she had at home—which blossomed in October and not December—with showy white and scarlet flowers.

Cristine pulled out her Blackberry and pressed the camera function. "Go over there. I'll take your picture." She pointed to a tall cactus. In the sunlight the dusty, green stalk against the pink stone looked striking.

Picture taken, she moved and snapped a shot from a different angle, got down on one knee and aimed the camera up into Angeline's face. "Act like you just made an incredible discovery in this rubble. If I break the story here, I can use some of these pictures for local colour."

Cristine inched backward, still aiming the Blackberry. "I can't go any farther, you'll have to move back. I want to get a broad shot with you poking among the ruins." She was already very near the cliff drop. "Just a bit more. These camera phones don't focus well up close."

Angeline's left foot prodded behind, rubble grating under her leather shoe. Despite the fact that it was late October, the air was moist, oppressive. It was going to be another warm day.

Suddenly she slipped. Her shoe worked loose and fishtailed down the slope. She grabbed the cactus as her knees gave out. Heart hammering like a steel band, her stockinged toes caught on a crag of rock. She held her breath, tried to heave herself up, but with poor results. She glanced over the ridge for help, but then the crag supporting her toehold broke loose and she was hanging by the cactus.

"Cristine!"

Footsteps raced, and the journalist appeared over the edge and seized Angeline's wrist.

"Hurry!" she shouted hysterically, grabbing frantically with her free hand.

Cristine tightened her grip, but didn't pull. *Don't just sit there; pull me up!* Hands slippery with sweat, the memory of the block falling at the Colosseum flashed across her mind. Rubble scuttled down the slope and the cactus snapped off. Now she was clinging to the edge of the cliff by the mercy of Cristine's right hand.

CHAPTER TWENTY-FIVE

She probably weighed no more than Angeline did, and it was costing her to hold on. Angeline threw an arm up to grab a projecting rock, her foot hooking a toehold while the journalist shouted down, "Are you stable?"

She nodded as Cristine rearranged her grip to grasp both of Angeline's arms and, with their combine effort, managed to haul her up and over the precipice.

Cristine rose to her knees and stared at Angeline. They were face-to-face, eye-to-eye.

"What are you staring at?" Cristine asked.

"Nothing," Angeline said icily.

Cristine frowned, crowed with spontaneous laughter and for a minute there, she did look kind of birdlike with her skinny nose and pointy chin and too round eyes. "So that's what you're thinking. Don't be crazy. Why would I want to get rid of you? I don't relish the idea of spending the rest of my life in prison for your murder."

The journalist's eyes, so dark and unblinking, pierced her. The gaze, despite being masked behind superficial good humour, was emotionless. Shrugging, she eyed the steep drop past Angeline's head. "Yes, that *would* be quite a fall."

"Are you in love with Jake?" Angeline demanded.

"Oh, come on. Get a grip. This whole thing with the murders and Jake's disappearance and all the strange incidences surrounding Saveriano have got you spooked. You're not making sense. Think about it. Even if I did have the hots for your boyfriend, do you think I'd be crazy enough to kill for him? It's not like I could *make* him love me."

Her emphasis on the word 'make' reminded Angeline that Jake was likely with Saveriano.

Clear of the ledge now, she crawled to her feet and straightened completely. She stared at the broken cactus, the bits of stalk scattered on the ground and the slimy juices running from it. She was warm, keyed up from fear and frustration.

"I won't quit helping you and Chancellor just because you're accusing me of something insane," Cristine said scornfully. She rose from where she had been squatting in the rubble.

Angeline swallowed, brushed the dirt from her clothing. What did she know about this journalist anyway? The woman had known Jake since he discovered the Raven's Pool. She had covered that story when it broke. What else did she know about her?

She was ambitious. Ambitious enough to make the trip to Italy, out of her own pocket, in the hopes of covering the most sensational find of the decade.

Cristine glanced past Angeline's shoulder at the precipice again, then back, her expression resplendent with humour. It wasn't a sheer drop. She would have been battered up somewhat, but not killed. "If I wanted to murder you, I would have found a more effective way to do it."

"Like pushing a boulder off the attic story of the Colosseum?"

A laugh erupted out of the journalist's tightly pursed mouth, and she wiggled her slim fingers in the air. "And I suppose I did that with my bare hands?" She fumbled in her jacket pocket to make sure her Blackberry was still there. "The truth is, Angeline, you're kind of clumsy. Look at all of the accidents you've had since you arrived in Italy."

"How did you know about the Colosseum?"

"How do you think?"

Chancellor. "He brought you here, didn't he?"

"He thought I could help to find Jake. When we made that pact, he didn't know it was going to be so easy to get you to go.

He called me after he left the lab and I was already on a plane before you guys left."

"You were going to trade Jake for a story?"

"'Course not. But it was one way I could be in on the ground floor."

Angeline twisted away. She was coated in dust and had only one shoe, and she was going to have to hobble down those stone steps and back to the car. God, how could she ever have trusted that conniving journalist?

She started for the steps, brushing ferociously at the bits of dirt and gravel in her hair. Cristine chased her, blocked her departure because they hadn't found the mithraeum yet.

After what just happened, did that self-obsessed power monger actually think Angeline had any intention of searching this mound of cracked masonry for an underground shrine?

Cristine slipped past and climbed the castle ruins, tossed bricks aside and kicked at rubble and earth. Hardly anyone came up here ever since the mithraeum was discovered by looters a century ago and then was reburied when the Archaeology Society of Southern France failed to acquire the funds to excavate it. She dropped to her knees frowning and slowly got to her feet.

"Chancellor's been here."

Angeline glowered. If Chancellor was here, he was buried alive in all this mess. The low-lying ruins allowed a severe view of the site. Cristine waved something yellow in the air, and at first Angeline thought it was a strip of ribbon, but when she realized it was a necktie, she raced to join the journalist among the debris. "It's Chancellor's," she said, taking it from her. "I'd know it anywhere."

"I pried it out from those rocks, but why did he take it off?" Cristine retrieved the tie from her, stroking it.

Angeline shaded her eyes. The woman had an agenda. Was it as simple as getting an exclusive on a stupid story?

She turned away to investigate deeper among the larger structures of the ruin, lost her footing and screamed.

She went sliding down a debris-filled chute.

The journalist was right behind her. The slip had caused an avalanche of rubble covering a sinkhole, and the two landed on a pile of dirt and gravel.

"What the hell—?" Cristine broke off before she could get more colourful in her expletives. She groaned while Angeline looked up. Oh great. Her heart started to bang against her ribcage to the point where she was so frightened that she couldn't tell if she was injured. Her breath rasped.

The opening to this chamber was at least two people's height. They could never reach it to get out. She massaged a sore wrist. Nothing broken.

"I think we found it," Cristine said, feeling her own bones for damage.

The calmness in her voice was unsettling. They both looked around. Other than some serious bruises and scrapes, they had both survived the fall relatively unscathed. Neither of them was limping and Angeline peeled her eyes upward. The cavernous ceiling resembled the night sky, except for the squarish opening above their heads. One large fresco caught her eye, a representation of a Heliodromus, the sun crossing the heavens in his chariot, whipping his horses into action. Below it was an inscription in Latin.

"Can you read it?" Cristine asked.

Since embarking on this project with Chancellor, Angeline's Latin had improved and only rarely did she have to consult a dictionary. Roughly, it said: "through the agency of the Raven, the Sun Courier communicated to Mithras the order for the bull-slaying. He—meaning the Sun Courier or Heliodromus—made a pact with Mithras. From Mithras he received the accolade." Her voice dropped slightly. "With Mithras he enjoyed the sacred meal before ascending into heaven." She stopped there. It was possible that the events depicted in this fresco were imitated during ceremonies inside this shrine.

Cristine pulled out her Blackberry, tapped a few buttons to search the Internet. Suddenly, her eyes jerked up at the fresco. "Look how that figure is dressed and what he's carrying."

The figure of the Sun Courier wore a red robe with a yellow belt that strangely reminded Angeline of Chancellor's yellow necktie. Around the figure's head was a halo and in his left hand was blue globe, while between his curled fingers was a whip. He was approaching a tree with low-hanging, leafy branches.

She swallowed nervously. "So what does it mean?" Angeline's voice cracked. She was pretty certain what Cristine was going to say before she said it.

"The Heliodromus or Sun Courier is a member of the mystic community."

It was an idea that made Angeline even more nervous because Chancellor believed in the supernatural.

"What's the matter with you? Worried I'm going to bury you alive? Don't forget, I'm stuck down here, too. And I have no intention of spending any longer in this stinkin' hole than I have to."

If Angeline wasn't so terrified she might have relished the look on Cristine's face when she said, "I don't know any more about secret temple passages than you do. If we're going to get out of here, it's going to have to be a joint effort."

"Look, let's get something straight before we go any further ... I'm sorry I scared you on the cliff. To tell you the truth, I *did* hesitate to pull you up. But it wasn't because I wanted Jake for myself." Cristine looked away, clearly conflicted, and paused for an agonizing ten seconds. "I was afraid you might pull me down with you. Beneath this swaggering exterior, I'm basically a coward."

In Cristine's place, Angeline would have instinctively grabbed her and tried to haul her up even if it meant they both went tumbling to their deaths. In hindsight, that really wasn't so smart from a self-preservation point of view.

"I know. Narcissistic, lame-ass coward: that's me. I'm not proud of it."

"Is that why you always strut around so fearless and full of bravado?"

"Rub it in, why don't you? I told you it was. But you have to understand. I have to be like that. My job requires it. I have to do dangerous things, put myself in dangerous situations. All the time my first inclination is toward self-preservation." Cristine grabbed her arm. "Promise me, you won't tell anyone. Please."

*   *   *

The thirst was unbearable. Chancellor regretted not telling Angeline about Susanne. He regretted not telling her where he was going. When he'd learned the assistant's true identity, he should have revealed the information straight away, but the threat of a new victim in Saveriano's killing spree had taken precedence. He had made the mistake of leaving Susanne a cryptic email, suggesting knowledge of her secret, and although he hadn't threatened her, his hope was for information in exchange for non-exposure.

He'd keep her secret if she provided evidence on her employer.

Big mistake. Underestimating a pretty woman was always a mistake, especially underestimating a *spiteful*, pretty woman. She could not be swayed and she had proved it.

Who would have thought, the snippy Frenchwoman knew how to handle a gun or climb a steeple for that matter? They had met for coffee and somehow she had spiked it. She had lured him with the promise of what she had given him before, and had drugged him with some kind of poison, rendering him weak. Now, he was here, and Angeline and Cristine were nowhere in sight. But they were both smart women; they would find him. Certainly, if he didn't show up at the lecture and gala in two days, they'd return to look for him. He had been watching them from his forced vantage point, muzzled, paralysed. The sun had appeared at exactly the wrong time, blinding them and masking his contours. The horrible thing was that he could see them, hear their voices, unable to answer them. They had stared right at him and didn't know it.

How long did it take for a man to die of thirst? He knew a human body could go for weeks without food, but no water?

Chancellor shut his eyelids. The wind at this altitude was drying out his eyes as well as his entire respiratory system. How had she done it? How had she trapped him?

He remembered climbing the ladder on the side of the church, a gun to his spine, his stomach queasy from the poison. It was enough to weaken him, not to kill, just enough to make him passive. Saveriano had used her pawn, once again, to deliberately steer him out of her way. She wanted the night of her lecture free from any interference. Surely she must know that eventually someone would see him. A man strapped to a church spire was not your average tourist sight. But tourist season at Eze was pretty much over. Hardly anyone made the pilgrimage this time of year.

Why did she want him out of the way? What was going to happen on November 1st?

He stared across the rooftops to the cliff that held the castle ruins. Where had those two disappeared? For one breath-stopping moment he had thought they were going to climb down the slope to the church, and find him.

CHAPTER TWENTY-SIX

A dripping sound echoed through the aqueducts, thunderous because of the quiet. Jake dragged his feet, his legs leaden, fighting the pull, a force like that of a gigantic magnet drawing him between the tapering walls. The stone steps tumbled down and down as they wended their way beneath the Baths of Diocletian, the headquarters of the National Museum of Rome. An eerie sensation of familiarity sent adrenalin flooding his corpse. *Yeah, corpse*, he thought. Because that was how he felt—like he was dead. Like he had no will. Like he was buried under the earth awaiting exhumation. But the vibrations of his breathing told him otherwise, as did the damp and the strong odour of mould, an odour not unlike that of the drink Sophia had given him before they left her villa.

Agitated, he shoved his hand into his pant's pocket to squash its shaking, and his fingers jabbed something small, sharp—Angeline's ring.

Sophia took him by the hand, murmuring reassurances. It was fine; it wouldn't be long now. She needed him to visit a cavern, a mithraeum like the others. Only this one was special.

At the end of their pilgrimage the shaft opened out into a cavernous chamber and she stepped inside while he followed. It was the shrine of another mithraeum as she had promised. It had the same painted fresco walls and cavelike ceiling, where the torchbearers—the celestial twins of light and darkness—rose above a figure of Mithras amidst a mass of stars.

On his right, was the Father—Sophia spread her arms to encompass the scene—also known as the Pater. She encouraged him to examine the depictions of the Pater.

Jake opened his mouth to respond, but he emitted no sound. He was spellbound, awestruck. The Father was highest of the ranks in the Mithraic cult. This initiate was the deputy on earth of the god himself. He was the teacher, whose wisdom was symbolised by a ring and a staff. He was astute in astrology, and now Jake realized just how deeply Mithraism was steeped in astrological concepts from which stemmed the doctrine of the seven ranks, each placed under the protection of the seven planets. Saturn, as far as he knew, was the guardian of the Father.

"Hail all Fathers from East to West under the protection of Saturn," Sophia recited. She laughed, a horrible satirical laugh, and the sound of it bursting the silence made him tremble.

She pointed to the fresco where the Pater was surrounded by his symbols: the sickle of Saturn, the Phrygian cap of Mithras and the staff and ring.

"I think you're the *one*, Jake."

He raised the flashlight that he was holding into Sophia's face. "The one? The one for what?"

"Shush," she said, her voice resonating. "And lower that; you're blinding me. How do you feel?"

"I . . . ." He gulped, hesitated, exhaled. The potion was taking effect. He couldn't breathe, his head spun. He closed his eyes then opened them and saw a shimmer of mist where Sophia should have been. A shiver chased up his spine inducing panic, then a strange sensation overwhelmed him, like he was being watched. *Sophia!* He tried to shout, but nothing came out. He should be used to these frightening sensations by now, but how did one habituate to the knowledge of certain death? He sensed eyes straining all around, watching him. It was familiar. Frescoes . . . no . . . carvings. *Petroglyphs.* Everything was dark, unwieldy. His mind was frantic, but in one crushing instant, recognition shot like a lance through his brain.

Ovoid eyes stared down, and at the far end, dancing on the wall the tales of the Raven mocked him. Jake froze in horror, breath catching in his throat, every muscle in his body rigid as wood.

All he had to do was find Sophia and he would be all right. He cried out, spinning around to search for her but she was gone.

He flailed his arms like a blind man. He shook, feeling the freezing sweat film his face. He stumbled, tripping over the uneven floor and frowned. Nodules of stone everywhere: stalagmites and stalactites. *Mites go up, tights go down*, he muttered incoherently, trying to ground his thoughts. But the shaft of this stalagmite was as hard and as stippled as the goosebumps on his arm. *Is this an hallucination? Or am I really back in this place?* He stood rooted where he was, gazed at the etchings in stone. His mind began to repeat a fearful litany. He had entered something forbidden. These images belonged to another time, another place: a time when the will of nature took precedence over that of men. Fresh air blew from somewhere inside the cave. Desperately, he reminded himself that he was inside the shrine, the temple of Mithras, and that all of the rest of it was a drug-induced hallucination—or a memory.

His flashlight lapped, moving in a ghostly dance. The shadows of a man in a Raven costume played on the walls and the ceiling. Jake forced himself to relax, to accept the truth—he was no longer inside the mithraeum.

The light poured onto the ground. They were there! The cobbles, those damn cobbles were there. Five of them. Dark spaces, glittering round stones. The shadow of a manlike bird. Jake crouched down and touched one of the granite cobbles that was rolled up against the wall. He dipped his finger into the bowl-like depression to taste the remnants of the potion that he knew the shaman had prepared. The hell of it was that he *could* taste it. The remains of the potion in the bowl tasted like cedar. Light spilled catching sparks of fool's gold in the stone.

Jake released the cobble to the ground and walked to the nearest wall. On its surface was a petroglyph, grotesque, eerie—and familiar. The claws of a large hook-beaked bird dug into the breast of a smaller one, the wings arced behind. A horrid feeling of repetition overwhelmed him: The Eagle battling it out with the Raven, the prize, the Salmon Princess.

He stiffened as a rattle and boom shook the ground. Something knocked him off balance and his head whiplashed as a crash jarred the cave, and a grating sound came from above. His heart leaped into his throat, and things rumbled and slid and shook. The walls threatened to topple down, a surge of adrenalin coursed from his gut, and he gripped his chest as he folded to his knees.

Thunder pealed and things fell and then there was silence.

Jake probed the dark with nervous fingers, but his flashlight had rolled out of reach. Blind, he staggered to his feet and struck a fist into solid night. He had to wake up, break the spell, get out of here. But only a hard, invisible wall met his fists.

At the far end from where he stood, an ethereal shimmering pooled over the floor and slowly tilted upward making shadows loom. Jake gulped, clamped his eyes shut. *I'm hallucinating*, he reminded himself. This isn't, *can't* be, real. He was led to the flashlight by the shimmering, which was as nebulous as gas but as fluid as liquid, and he gaped like an idiot. He made his way back to the wall where he aimed it at the darkness but nothing happened. The scene in front of him remained a solid, black wall. He clawed, using both hands, until his arms ached. The wall didn't change. He thrust his hands in, trowelling at emptiness until his knuckles burned, then he tried to walk right through the blackness but his body was stopped.

The shimmering stayed where it was, watching him. It touched his shoulder, glided away leaving an ethereal wake.

It was like someone had taken his hand and was leading him back through the cave to where the stone ceiling vaulted over his head. In here, the flashlight seemed to work, destroying the obsidian night. A yellow glow washed the dome in welcome warmth. The chamber emerged looking smaller, now that he knew he couldn't wake up. The arch above his head felt lower, the walls closer. The etchings seemed sharper, and he noticed a familiar stone pillar rising sharply from the ground.

The petroglyphs fluttered in the shimmering stream, straining his sight, compelling him to search the void beyond the pillar. He forced his feet to move first, followed by his hands, and lowered himself onto his stomach to snake through a tunnel into deeper hell.

On the other side he stood upright, weaving. Having risen too quickly, he had to coach himself not to lose his sanity in the biting quiet. He crammed his eyes tight, dragged them open, knowing what he would see.

The space was a large vaulted chamber, larger than the one he had just left. In the centre, a cavernous void gaped and a tingling assailed his fingertips, travelling up his arms. Inhaling, he clenched his free fist and looked down. A whistling came from somewhere beyond. The smooth stone basin ran about seventeen feet over the length of the floor and eight feet wide. When he moved to look more closely, the flashlight hit water, and he remembered the depth to be about six feet.

His light poured over and across the ground, moving this way and that. Almost two feet down from the rim he found the circular frieze of petroglyphs. He dropped to his belly, resting awkwardly, and saw thin stripes in the sides, left by retreating water. At the top of the stone basin, high above the top rim of the frieze, was a darkened band, which formed when spring runoff filled the pool, completely submerging the etchings. Later in the year when rainfall lessened, the water was as it was now, only about a foot deep with the petroglyphs high and dry. The winter band of striations was directly at the lower rim of the pictures. The shaman had worked here in the dead of winter, up to his knees in cold water.

Jake felt the panic return. Was any of this even real? Of course not . . . and yet, he could feel the rough texture of stone.

Another deep breath and he waited, listened to the silence. He stretched his arm, tilting the light. On the floor all around the rim, hard globular objects, rocks that had stuck in his abdomen as he had leaned over to examine the watermarks, lined the pool.

Cobbles. Cobbles flecked with fool's gold. They twinkled all around the edge. He touched a cobble, lifted it to cradle in his hand, brushed the black smudge in the center. The shaman had built little fires in these and had fed them with oil.

He put the cobble on the ground, and raised the light, circling the walls inside the pool. There were five figures etched into the stone. According to the northern tribes, the world began in black chaos, but *Yehlh* created men and stole light, fresh water, and fire from the other spirits to give to humanity.

That spiral. That's where sunlight comes from. And that—he fixed his eyes on the shape of a thick-beaked bird—*is the Raven.* The petroglyph showed *Yehlh* in his bird form.

That stick thing is fire, the burning branch he stole from the sun. Linked with the Raven was a symbol made of three concentric circles, which represented the earth. *And there*—Jake moved the light unsteadily around the *pool*—*is Hoon, the North Wind.* The figure beside him, the wolf, was Kun-nook, the guardian of freshwater. The Raven stole freshwater from him.

This was the same stone pool that he had visited in an earlier hallucination, depicting the Raven creating the world.

Jake passed his arm over the edge of the pool to a carving of the Raven stealing the sun. The Raven had a star-shaped object in his beak, and was shooting, wings taut, upward at the sky. Behind him was the curved beak and hooked talons of the Eagle.

That should be east, he thought. The direction the sun rose and where the Eagle made the Raven drop the sun. He doused the light. Blackness descended, then the whole cavern sparkled like a million diamonds.

The domed ceiling over his head looked like the night sky, like the Milky Way in a universe of endless velvet. He could swear there were constellations up there . . . .

But he was no longer inside the Raven's cave. The celestial bodies of Mithras stared down at him, and Sophia caught his hands as he crashed to the floor.

* * *

"Are you all right, Jake?"

The garbled sounds of Sophia's voice recalled him to consciousness. Lights filtered through his inebriated brain. She spoke again, and this time the sounds made words. His head was fuzzy, mouth crusty, cheeks swollen. He felt like he had fallen out of a cement mixer. Except that he wasn't dead.

He blinked, felt the muscles of his legs flex weakly as he sat up. Sophia was cradling him in her arms and gently released him. He didn't trust his tongue to speak, but still he tried. "What happen?"

"You transported again."

Jake licked his dry lips, attempted to swallow with difficulty. His throat felt like it had forced down a baseball. He put a hand to his head. Had he heard her right? Had she actually said he had transported? The saliva was beginning to flow again, but just barely. He glanced up at her, his eyes hardly focusing. The only light in the temple was Sophia's flashlight that stood upended on the floor a few feet away from them. His own had rolled out of sight.

He tried to get up, but she pushed him down and told him to sit until the disorientation was fully past. She smiled sympathetically. "Transporting has a way of disorienting the senses."

Why did she call it that? He was uncomfortable with her choice of words. "I know I have inherited memories," he said. "My father had them, but they're more like visions of the past."

"Except that you felt disembodied. You felt like you were physically there. That's why you fainted."

Okay. He was not ready to accept this. Disembodied? Transported? He knew that Haida shamans claimed to have this ability. But he had seen the dances, the rituals, joined in the Secret Societies, which were not so secret these days. Sure, they claimed to be able to enter the world of spirits with the aid of entheogens, but no matter his Native heritage, he was a scientist first. Shamans did not travel bodily into a Spirit World. Shamans drugged themselves so that their brains would provide them with illusions.

"It was not a vision, Jake, you were there. Tell me what you saw."

How did she know? She had given him some psychoactive substance to drink, which made him hallucinate, made him think he was somewhere he wasn't! His rage was irrational, but it was real. She had sent his mind to a place that he didn't want to be.

He realized he was trembling; his anger was so great. Sweat left an icy film on the palms of his hands as he tried to get up only to fail miserably. He hit the ground on his backside, breaking the impact with his hands while Sophia stood watching. "I never wanted to go there again. I promised Angeline."

"Why?"

Why? Because that cave was where the Eagle had taken the Raven's beloved. Where a psychopathic developer had tried to rape Angeline.

"You learned something while you were there. I can see it on your face. What was it?"

Jake swallowed. There was something.

It had to do with the Raven, with *Yehlh* and his travels.

He looked up at Sophia. "The Raven travelled from the Old World to the New."

She walked thoughtfully to where her flashlight was and lifted it, then returned and helped him to his feet, brushing dirt from his shoulder. She swung him around and pointed to the floor with the light. A few paces away sat one of the gold-flecked cobbles that he had seen inside the shaman's cave.

"I knew you were the one."

The transportation of the human consciousness through time and space was not a concept Jake could fathom at this moment. He only knew that the evidence was staring him in the face. He stooped to lift the cobble from the temple floor and noted the slight, bowl-like groove where a smudge of soot indicated that the cobble had been used as a lamp. He did *not* just transport . . . . The flecks of fool's gold in the stone contradicted him as they glinted in the beam of Sophia's flashlight.

"Do you believe me now?" She took the stone from him and gauged the weight of it in her hand. "Where else did this come from? It wasn't here before."

No. Jake shook his head. He *didn't* believe it. It was impossible. His experience might have been hallucination, yes, even inherited memory, but teleportation? No. And it couldn't be an ancient memory either. This scene was real, but it had not taken place during the shaman's time. Not all of the etchings on the cave wall were old. That petroglyph of the Eagle—the claws of the hooked-beaked bird gouged into the breast of the smaller one, that petroglyph had been a fake.

Jake looked up.

"You went into the past?"

He nodded.

"How far into the past?"

"Not far. Five, maybe six years into my own past."

"What did you see? Where did you transport to?"

He ignored Sophia's choice of words. "I went back to the cave in the San Juan Islands where Angeline and I found the Raven's pool."

"Perfect. And how do you know this was the recent past and not the prehistoric past?"

"I know because the fake petroglyph that we exposed was there." He described it to her, eerie, grotesque, because it meant something to both him and Angeline. What he didn't understand was why he had returned there.

"You just told me why you returned there, Jake. Because you misread the petroglyphs the first time around. Didn't you just say so? You learned something you didn't notice before. *Yehlh* travelled from the Old World to the New." She took his hand, massaged the chill out of it with the tips of her fingers. "You look better now. How do you feel?"

Not so good. He needed a drink of water. Sophia noticed him swallowing ineffectively and took a bottle of water out of a satchel that she had slung over her shoulder, instructing him to drink, but not too quickly or he'd feel worse.

Jake took the bottle, twisted off the cap and slugged down a mouthful.

"You're getting better at this," she said. "Soon you will be master of your own powers."

"I have no powers."

"How can you still not believe after what you've just experienced?"

Well, that was just it, he thought, kneading his throbbing temples. He didn't really know what he had experienced. He couldn't describe it. It was inconceivable to him that the human consciousness could be transported through time and space.

"Come with me. Maybe you will see what I see now."

* * *

Sophia waited outside the bold, white, three-tiered structure of the Basilica of San Clemente waiting for Jake to join her. He was still a bit unsteady and lacked her enthusiasm. His feet lagged like they had a persona of their own.

They entered through the side entrance and walked beneath the tiled ceiling, past the arcades that made up the cloister. Their sneakered feet padded over the mosaic floor in the wake of some tourists who had come to see Fontana's chaste facade. They reached the basilica church behind it where the three naves were divided by arcades on ancient marble columns. In the unused portion of the church at the rear, it was quiet and dark except for the small arched windows below the ceiling. The same old buckets and shovels lay scattered about. When Jake's eyes reconciled to the lower light level he followed Sophia to the pit—the same entrance to the mithraeum that he had used the day he met her.

At Sophia's urging, he climbed down the ladder into what he had nicknamed 'the abyss.' Like the previous time, the shaft was cold and silent, and filled with shadows. His hands slid over the tile and marble slabs of the walls as he stepped aside to wait. When she reached him, perspiration gleamed on her forehead and she rubbed it away. She gave him a half smile, saying nothing, merely beckoning with a finger. A shiver travelled up his shoulder as she took him by the arm. Her cool touch on his skin was magnetic, her fingers holding him possessively.

Her flashlight diluted the glare from the overhanging lightbulb. In the tunnel, their shadows played tag on the walls ahead. When Sophia slowed her pace, Jake recognized the arcosolium, the burial chamber for an entire family. They bypassed it, onward to another tunnel that branched into smaller rooms where he recognized the cubicula. She waved her hand, grazing his arm as she pointed to the floor where the forma—human tombs—were set in the ground.

"Do you know where we are?" she asked.

He nodded. This room held a stone sarcophagus, adorned with sculptured reliefs and inscriptions. Beyond it, in the walls, he knew there were vertical tiles marking more loculi.

They were following the same route she had led him before. Shudders of recognition coursed up his spine. If he believed in ghosts he would say the place was haunted.

Through the entrance, across the dirt floor, light flooded onto the wall at the far right. A row of grim skulls burst into his vision. Like instant replay on a DVD that was stuck in a loop, he couldn't get out. As he moved past to the tiles on the loculi at the adjacent wall, images emerged from the shadows: the Dove holding an olive branch, the Alpha and Omega, the Phoenix, the mythical Arabian bird. Some of the tiles were even decorated with symbols from the Mithraic ranks.

"Sophia . . . ." A strange dizziness assailed him. His breath shortened. Dark images, a figure in a Raven mask circling a ring of burning stones. A stone cup filled with a foul liquid. Jake's hands went to grasp it, hold it to his lips, but his body passed through the vision, and he hit the wall. He tottered, fell to his knees and crawled. Why was he having a vision, the *same* vision! Oh, God was he going to transport? He held his breath, clutched his hands to his heart.

He followed the edge of the wall toward a pale shimmering in the distance. Something burned at the end of this tunnel. He lowered his arms, shot forward and emerged into a crypt that seemed to burst with light. He looked around, startled when the familiar row of skulls reappeared on the wall in front of him.

Scuff marks on the dirt floor. Tread marks leading to the tiles mounted on the wall. The tiles decorated with symbols arranged in a checkerboard pattern, the sign of the Raven.

He dropped to his knees behind a tomb, still dizzy. He dared not move, dared not shift a muscle except to let his eyes dart about in the semi darkness. There was no movement, no sound. He waited a few more seconds, got to his feet. Something shimmered before everything went black.

"Jake? What's wrong?" The beam of Sophia's flashlight shot into his eyes as she emerged from the shadows.

"I'm fine," he said, mortified by his confusion.

He pointed to a fallen tile and some splinters of glass on the floor. A broken strip of yellow police tape was dangling from the wall.

"Why is that there?"

Sophia frowned, then a euphoric expression spread over her face. "Tell me what just happened to you."

He felt like he was repeating that day when he met her, when the lightbulb exploded.

She smiled at him gently, studied his face and body, the tenseness of his muscles beneath his denim jacket and jeans. His shadow cast an eerie image against the earthen wall. "Your power grows stronger. The shaman in you is bursting to get out."

"Why are we here, Sophia? Before we go another step, I want an explanation."

"You know the explanation, Jake. You simply refuse to accept it . . . ."

Was he crazy to follow this woman around like she held some kind of profound secret to his existence? Why was he so drawn to her? Two weeks ago he wouldn't have given her the time of day. After all, she was the lunatic that had made the absurd declaration that God had a wife.

Then something she had said inside this very catacomb returned to haunt him.

It was the day he accused her of murdering Vincent. She had baited him then by mentioning the Raven. The Raven was his obsession. How did she know that?

How did she know his Haida name, He-Whose-Voice-Is-Obeyed.

I know many things about you, she had said. I know that you are sometimes called *Yehlh*.

Yehlh was the name of the ancient shaman who possessed his dreams. *Yehlh* was the name of the Raven, the old and mythical figure depicted on the walls of the Raven's pool.

"What are you thinking?" he asked.

"As I told you the first time we were here, words will not suffice. I must show you. Maybe this time you will understand."

They came to the faded fresco depicting a man leading a pilgrimage with its Latin epigraph. Jake exhaled in a failed effort to curb his frustration. "Follow me to the sleep of death," he translated the line aloud. "I've seen this epigraph before. I've even seen it in a dream."

"Do you know what it means?"

He ran his finger lightly over the familiar letters. His stomach went cold as he realized he knew her thoughts. "Yahweh has a wife."

After a lengthy silence, he looked up at her and said, "Her name is Asherah."

Eyes wide, glazed, she wet her lips and smiled triumphantly at him.

Asherah was sometimes known as the Black Goddess.

Yehlh had striking similarities with Yahweh.

CHAPTER TWENTY-SEVEN

The Sun Courier was a member of the mystic community. Chancellor believed in the supernatural, and Angeline found that against all reason she was beginning to believe in it, too. *Are you here, Tom?* Her eyes flittered from wall to ceiling to wall, taking in all the painted frescoes of the shrine, then stopped on the Sun Courier.

She grabbed the wide end of Chancellor's yellow tie that Cristine had fastened around her neck just before they went sliding into the sinkhole, and stared at it.

"Hey!" Cristine tugged the tie out of her hands before she could choke her. "You got my attention. What gives?"

She pointed to the Sun Courier.

The fresco was brightly coloured, and, with no light below ground to fade the pigments, the image was almost as sharp as the day it was painted. The central character wore a red robe with a yellow belt, and that was what had reminded her of Chancellor's necktie. She swallowed as she followed the elaborate details with her eyes. Around the figure's head was a halo and in his left hand was a blue globe while his right hand held a whip. He was approaching a tree, painted in muted browns and greens, with low-hanging, leafy branches.

It was a fine, though stark scene, and undisturbing except for one thing. And this thing, this idea, kept looping relentlessly in her mind.

The Heliodromus or Sun Courier was a member of the mystic community.

"Chancellor isn't here," Cristine said, totally oblivious to Angeline's line of thought. The chamber was cavernous, but other than the recess where the altar stood, there were no other nooks and crannies where one could hide a body. "Oh, come on, he's not dead," she insisted, openly scoffing as she realized why Angeline was searching the chamber so thoroughly. "He's Interpol, a trained agent. I don't think they kill that easily. Especially not by some feeble old woman."

"Saveriano is no ordinary woman. And I wouldn't call her old."

"Still, she's no match for Chancellor. He's close to twice her weight."

"I don't think she's normal." Angeline didn't know how to explain what she meant except that the renowned archaeologist was impossible to trace.

"Well, I think we'd better stop worrying about Chancellor and start worrying about ourselves. He's probably up there somewhere." Cristine gestured upward, indicating outside the temple. "We're stuck down here. How are we going to get out? I'm serious, Angeline. I don't relish staying here any longer, no matter how many epiphanies you seem to be having." Her voice sounded genuinely frightened. In another time, another place, Angeline would have been terrified too, but she knew that as long as Jake was in danger, nothing was going to stop her from escaping this tomblike shrine to find him.

"There's air down here," Angeline said. "It's not as musty as it should be if we were the first to open it up. There must be another opening somewhere."

"More tunnels?" Cristine asked, hopelessly.

"Yeah, I think more tunnels."

Angeline sized up the fresco of the Sun Courier traversing the heavens in his chariot, whip in hand, urging on his horses. The figures were pointing west, the direction that the sun set.

"Let's try that way," she said, indicating the same direction. "I remember there was a church steeple in sight of the bluff. I remember because the sun was behind it, moving west. That means the village is there, if I'm interpreting the fresco correctly. The other direction would put us deeper into the hill."

"I hope you know what you're doing," Cristine said.

I do, too, Angeline thought.

Along the west wall, she found the usual raised benches where initiates would have their communal meal before any ceremony, and wandered alongside one until she came to a change in the pattern of the seats. The wall above was uniform; no evidence of a doorway, but the stone bench here was cracked in two places. The bench was about two feet deep and between the cracks, the slab of rock looked like it would move. She motioned for the journalist to follow her lead. She squatted and placed both hands under the slab at one end while Cristine did the same at the other. The slab was about three feet long from crack to crack, but when they shoved, it refused to budge.

"Try again. Remember how we got into the mithraeum at Ostia? I went through a gap in the brickwork under the toilet seats."

"It's too heavy," Cristine complained. "We need a crowbar."

They had no crowbar.

Angeline studied the slab of rock. Wait a minute. She was mistaken. There weren't just two cracks here; there were multiple hairline fractures in the stone. She got to her feet and hopped onto the bench, landing as hard as she could without damaging her joints. "Help me. Jump up here."

Cristine sighed. "This is nuts. You can't expect to get out the same way we got in—"

As Cristine landed with a thud and Angeline joined her impact with another hard jump, the web of cracks broke and the stone bench crashed down into another void. But this time it didn't go far. Their heads and shoulders were still above the level of the bench and they could still get back into the mithraeum if they had to. "Maybe we should have just stood under that sinkhole and yelled," Cristine said, rubbing her sore knees. "Surely someone would have heard us."

"You saw it out there. There was no one around. We could've been yelling for hours."

Besides, Angeline believed in irony. Sometimes the least likely option was the right choice. Sometimes the solution to a problem was right before your eyes and all the analysing and strategizing wouldn't solve diddly when all you had to do was step up, and jump up and down.

The journalist ducked into the opening beneath the stone bench behind Angeline. This was indeed a tunnel and, although it was low at this end—more like a ventilation shaft than a passageway—it seemed to widen further on. Fortunately, Angeline had kept Chancellor's penlight, and it gleamed from between her clenched teeth as she crawled on hands and knees toward the broadening end of the passage.

"So, this was an escape way?" Cristine asked from behind her. "Like an emergency exit?"

"Something like that. Because they were subterranean, these shrines usually had more than one entrance in case one of them got blocked."

"Smart."

The shaft had expanded into a corridor high enough for them to stand up. Angeline started walking along it, the flashlight now in her right fist. She extended her free hand to help the journalist avoid stumbling on some fallen rubble.

"Oh, I so hope this doesn't take long," Cristine grumbled, teeth chattering from the subterranean cold.

"Not too much farther, I think. We're heading downhill."

A good sign.

But on the other hand, it could mean they were forging deeper under the earth.

* * *

The thing about tunnels was that they were quite disorienting because they all looked the same. This one was no different. Never having been in this particular tunnel before, she had no way to recognize any pattern or changes in the walls, floor or ceiling. Which was the preferred method that archaeologists used to reason themselves out of a tight spot. Recognizing the tiniest difference in a floor or a wall could be the difference between freedom and permanent entombment. That was why professionals made maps everywhere they went, whether it was in the desert, the woods, up a mountain, inside a cave or underwater.

Maps showed the way in and the way out.

Angeline didn't know whether her snap decision to enter this shaft was the right one. So far, the path made for a linear trek but it could be one piece of a complex maze—like the labyrinths she'd experienced beneath some of the churches in Rome. Despite the absence of a map or a compass to show her they were on the right course, the main reason she retained her confidence was the fact that this shaft *seemed* to be headed in a single direction.

At least they hadn't yet hit any branching passageways to confuse them.

"I think I see a way out," Cristine said, pushing ahead.

"Wait." She stopped the journalist from rushing headlong through the black tunnel toward a crescent of light by grabbing Chancellor's yellow tie that was still wound around her neck.

Cristine jerked free. "Look, if you're so in love with this thing, you take it, and stop dragging me around like a dog on a leash." She unlaced the tie and whipped it toward Angeline. Ahead of them a gap of light appeared. "It looks like there's an opening behind that block of stone."

Angeline put her fingers to her lips. The gap darkened suddenly, then materialized again.

"People walking by," Cristine whispered excitedly. "We've found the way outside to the village!" She cleared her throat and spoke in a low but more normal tone. "Why are we whispering? Oh, I get it. Looters. Don't worry; I'll be very discreet. I know you don't want people to find this site before archaeologists have a chance to study it."

That wasn't it. Maybe she had spent too much time with Jake and his research into shamanistic powers, inherited memories, sixth senses and other supernatural nonsense, but the nape of Angeline's neck crawled. What she felt was an undeniably malignant sensation.

"I'm getting out of here," Cristine said.

Angeline moved to grab the journalist's arm, but she twisted away and disappeared through the crescent into the sunshine, leaving Chancellor's necktie dangling in her hand.

* * *

"*Bonjour,*" Susanne said, studying the journalist who had appeared from behind a large boulder. Her eyes twitched to the slope leading to the castle ruins, but when she realized what she was doing, she immediately withdrew them. *Alors, she knows who I am.* The nosy reporter had come to the villa asking about her employer before she was sent away on a wild goose chase to Ostia. It seems the goose was not so wild after all. She had misjudged the woman's determination . . . but why was she covered in dust?

"What are you doing in France?" Cristine asked her.

"I could ask you the same question. *Je suis Française n'est-ce pas?* Why should I not visit my home country? Whereas you . . . you are filthy; did you have a fall?"

Cristine shrugged insouciantly, brushing herself off. "A minor tumble while exploring the town. The stairs and alleyways are steep, you know."

"Oh? And what could possibly be of interest to you here in Eze, Mademoiselle Kletter? Were there not enough dead bodies for you in Ostia?"

"How did you know about that body?"

"I saw it on the news, just as I saw *you* on the television harassing the police officers. Now it is your turn to answer some questions. You are looking for information regarding Dr. Saveriano's research. I understand your interest in Ostia as that is an old archaeological site with many ruins pertaining to the professor's good research. But here? In Eze? What makes you think Dr. Saveriano would be here?"

"Is she? Is she in Eze?"

"Alas, no," Susanne said. "Only I. I had the day off so I came to visit an old aunt who is ill. I must return immediately to help the professor prepare for her big night . . . . And you? I would think that you would like to be present at the unveiling of the Black Goddess? You are, are you not, covering a story for your magazine?" Her face was smooth, but her voice held a hint of velvety malice.

"I'm interested in the castle ruins," Cristine said, nodding at the stone remains up the hill.

"Then what were you doing behind that rock?"

Susanne smiled. She had her now. What sort of an excuse did she intend to make up?

"I couldn't find a bathroom," Cristine said, coolly. "I really had to pee."

Eh, *bien*. She was not about to go behind that rock to find out. "I would not loiter. The sun sets soon. They close the gates at four P.M." She barely restrained herself from sending her sight to the sun behind the church spire.

Susanne turned to go. Her job was done. She must return to the villa. She walked away from the reporter, her wandering gaze glancing off a shoe in the rubble at the base of the hill.

*   *   *

Angeline waited in the dark, absentmindedly stuffing the yellow necktie deep into the pocket of her jeans. She would recognize that voice anywhere. For a hair-raising instant, she was paralysed by a blast from the past. The image she conjured was not of a dark, red-lipped brunette, but a long-faced, sneery-mouthed blonde with a golden braid that hung down to her waist. She shook off the disturbing memory, confused, then risked a peek and saw that the voice belonged to Saveriano's assistant Susanne. What was that French witch doing here? Not for one second was the story about the old aunt credible. Inside her pocket she touched the coolness of silk. Did Susanne have something to do with this? She scrunched Chancellor's necktie into a ball.

The Heliodromus or Sun Courier was a member of the mystic community. She resisted a shudder. They had to find him and get back to Rome.

Her breathing was steadier now and her heart had stopped its racing car speed, settling down to a simple drumbeat against her ribcage. At the sound of Susanne's mocking adieu, she hissed a sigh of relief and stepped outside until she was directly behind the masking boulder.

Cristine was staring downhill toward the gates of the village.

"Is she gone?" Angeline whispered loudly.

The journalist moved out of the shadow of rock to a position within Angeline's line of vision, glanced up at the church spire in the distance, and nodded.

Angeline slipped into the sunshine. "Public urination?" she jeered. "That's all you could think of?"

"Well, you didn't want me to let her know about that subterranean whatzit, did you?"

She stooped to pick up something from the rubble.

Her shoe! Angeline quickly snatched it and slapped it onto her foot, stepping hard into the heel of the leather loafer. Thank God. She didn't relish the idea of hobbling into that ritzy hotel in Nice half-shod like a hobo. But that was the least of their problems, she realized, as she followed the journalist's gaze backwards, and up the church steeple.

"Oh, shit." Cristine's voice was barely audible.

Whatever it was, it was capable of tiny, scarcely perceptible movement. Was somebody up there? The sun was so bright, they could barely make out the figure, but as Angeline squinted and the sun dipped for a split second behind a cloud, she was certain a person was strapped to the spire.

Their eyes met in simultaneous agreement. Cristine had seen it, too. It was Chancellor. She knew it was. How had Susanne managed to get him up there against his will? Because it could be no one else but Susanne. Why else was she here? No coincidence, that. And no time to speculate either. They had better go and see how to get him down.

The village was quite deserted now. Angeline glanced at her watch. They had less than an hour before the gates closed and they'd be locked inside the village until morning.

The sun was low, the shadows black against the orange light, and as they got nearer, they saw that someone was definitely strapped up there. Why didn't anyone in these houses see that? Maybe they weren't looking. If you weren't looking, you wouldn't see it. He stayed motionless, unmoving, hands tied behind his back; legs stiff together like a tree trunk.

The church was halfway up the hill with nothing around it. No houses, just the rocky road, which levelled onto a scrub and stone terrace where the church was situated. The church was not large, but it was tall and built on an angle against the hill. The tallest thing about it was the steeple. Angeline scoured the landscape surrounding the building. This church, clearly, had not been used in a very long time. It was totally abandoned.

She looked up and gasped as Chancellor's image came into full view. *The Sun Courier.* "Recognize the costume?" she asked Cristine.

"Why did she do that?" It was obvious that Susanne had somehow lured Chancellor to Eze and strapped him to the church spire, but how?

"Because he is the Heliodromus, the next sacrifice," she said, eyes travelling over the colourful costume in which the Interpol agent was adorned.

How had Susanne convinced him to don the garments? How had she gotten him up there? Her eyes lowered from the steeple to the shingles at his feet. She studied the lines of the edifice, trying to come up with a solution to reaching the roof. A sound, like a cracking twig, came from above, and her eyes shot up to see the sun highlighting Chancellor's head like a halo.

He was worldly, hence the globe.

He thought he was above the law, hence the halo.

He thought he was all-powerful, hence the whip, which apparently was the rope tying him to the steeple.

She prayed he was still alive, that that witch hadn't physically branded him with any of the rank's symbols. Hopefully, she had not had time.

A nudge to her arm brought her back to face Cristine, who pointed to a ladder at the base of the church, lying sideways against the stonework in the shade. Angeline told Cristine to help her to right it. It would get them onto the roof.

CHAPTER TWENTY-EIGHT

It had not been hard to lure Vincent Carpello. He was gullible to her charms as all men were. She hadn't done it for the pay, but for the chance at vindication. She had been sorely wronged, and Sophia had offered her a second chance. She had been on the brink of taking her own life. After the accident, what did she have to lose? Looking at herself now in the rearview mirror of her Maserati, she found it hard to believe she had ever considered suicide. All evidence of the burns was gone. She was beautiful. Her jet-black hair was cut in a short, fringed bob. She had soft mahogany eyes and full red lips. She was not new to cosmetic surgery.

"*Alors*," she said aloud. A year ago today, Sophia had saved Susanne from herself. After her release from the hospital, Susanne had left for Europe, hoping to disappear. She didn't have the money she needed for the required corrective surgery and she had gone to the catacomb to lose herself. It was all gone, her looks, her job, her meal ticket—her life. So the catacomb had seemed a good option.

Her mind spun back the months. Not here, she remembered thinking. It was too close to the entrance and the archaeologists working in the catacomb might see her. Walk farther down the passage . . . . Her head was heavy. She'd had too much to drink and was still on Tylenol 3 for the phantom pain. The mix had given her palpitations, then a calm, easy feeling, as though she were walking on mist, all feeling drifting away. Actually, it felt good. She hadn't felt this carefree in a long time.

Something gleamed inside the tunnel; a pick struck rock, ringing in the distance. It was black at her end, but somewhere in the shadows she glimpsed a pale glow. The path was roped off; NO TRESPASSING the sign said, but the post holding the barrier gave way, and overhead, a massive hole in the ceiling poured dusk below. Through the fog of her inebriated mind, she wandered blindly.

The passages were deep, black and empty, the rough walls cold. This was not a place to be lost. Her heart pulsed; her mouth went dry. She was trapped in a maze of tombs, and inside one of the darkly lit caverns hung a painted fresco. The colours had faded with time, but it showed a man—or what she thought was a man—leading a pilgrimage. Farther up was another opening where dirty light showed the path. Through the entrance, over the earthen floor she followed to where more light shone to the far right. Straight ahead, a row of skulls jutted out from the wall. Susanne had almost screamed, but stopped herself. Adjacent to the skulls, ceramic tiles formed a pattern on the wall, decorated with symbols.

She recognized one of the symbols, the Raven.

Every fibre of her being shrieked with rage. She ran into a dark passage, then stopped, one foot poised over a gaping hole.

A voice startled her. "What are you doing here?" It occurred to Susanne that the words were simply her own thoughts, but when she jerked up her head she saw a woman's face. A fist appeared and aimed a flashlight at her. "This is an archaeological site. There are deep, open pits, and walls that could cave in. Do you really want to die?"

That was the moment she met Sophia. She hadn't the will to utter a word. The archaeologist had stared at her, eyes picking out the deformation of the face and the hideously scarred skin on the skeleton-of-a-woman that dodged her scrutiny. Susanne cringed, backstepped out of the condemning light to cower in the shadows while the woman followed with her accursed flashlight, eyes glinting in comprehension. "I know you," she said. "The archaeology grapevine is very small. We are in the same business, you and I. I heard about your tragic accident."

Susanne gazed hopelessly down into the hole.

Sophia's voice came soft and slow. "To be . . . or not to be . . . ?"

Susanne laughed at what was now a dim memory, tossed her half-smoked cigarette out the side of her Maserati, and drove down the highway leaving behind the tiny village of Eze. Her hair whipped out behind her; she was happy. As she pulled away farther, the village shrank to the size of a wasp's nest, grey and powdery, clinging to its precipice above the sea. The cone that was Eze rose from the Moyenne Corniche, twelve kilometers from Nice. She still had a ways to go and had to hurry. Dealing with Chancellor had been harder than dealing with Carpello, and she was needed back in Rome. The day of the Black Goddess was approaching and Susanne must be available to ensure her success.

The top was down on the convertible and she raced along the road, humming to herself. Much of it was so steep that the gut-wrenching climbs and vertigo-inducing drops exhilarated her no end. The sensation literally radiated from the tip of her tongue to the base of her navel. It was as good, better than sex.

The highway hugged the shoreline escalating and dipping in harmony with the landscape. Above her the Grande Corniche bit into the mountain passes, and below, the Inférieure Corniche traced a winding path at the edge of the sea. Her eyes barely glimpsed the resorts of Villefranche and Beaulieu at the foot of the steepest stretch as she sang at the top of her lungs. Sheer cliff facades fenced her in on one side of the road. As she embraced the wind on her face and the sea in her lungs, she glimpsed in her peripheral vision elegant villas among colourful trees and gardens. The thought of seeing Jake Lalonde wrenched from that frightful girl Angeline fed her insatiable lust. Foot to gas pedal, she left in her wake the high crag-clinging villages, and sped to the Nice airport.

The flight home was as commonplace as driving to the National Museum in Rome. That was the wonder of working for Sophia. She had money, loads of it, and where it came from,

Susanne never asked. But she could come and go anywhere, anytime, just as she pleased.

Home again in the villa, she went to her room. The house was empty, as she knew it would be. The first thing she did on entering her bedchamber was to fumble beneath her mattress for the passport she had hidden there. She lifted it by her fingertips like it stung, and took it to the kitchen and checked to see that Mauro had left for the market before she ignited the gas stove. Fire flared up orange and blue from the front burner. She lit the corner of the passport and watched the laminated cover melt. Eyes glazed, she held the very edge of the passport until it was almost consumed, until her fingers flinched from the scorching heat, then she dropped the fiery remains into the stainless steel sink. *Burn Angelica, like you made me burn.* The pet name sizzled on her tongue.

The ice princess would not need this anymore.

*   *   *

Chancellor could hardly speak, he failed to express the relief he felt at the sight of those two women crawling up the church wall to rescue him. Angeline reached him first, balancing on the sloped roof in brown loafers, trying not to fall as she untied his feet. Cristine met up on the other side of him and unfastened the ropes around his hands while Angeline held him upright and kept him from falling. His legs felt like raw meat, his hands like wet clams. He grabbed at the steeple to keep from losing his balance completely. If he didn't get off this roof pretty soon he'd lose it to the fluctuating vertigo.

He did not speak.

Couldn't.

The strength of these two women amazed him. Or maybe he was dreaming. He thought he had habituated to the power of the psychoactive funguses, but apparently Susanne had known something he hadn't.

Water was pressed to his lips from a plastic bottle and he drank ravenously. He was sitting on the sloped shingles with the women on either side of him. After a short rest and a chance to rehydrate, the journalist plunged her empty bottle into a small satchel that was crossed over her shoulder, and looked down at the surrounding scrub and stone terrace. "Ready?"

He wasn't sure if she was speaking to him.

Somehow they managed to get him to the ground and to their car. Cristine drove back to Nice where they insisted he stay in their hotel overnight, but he refused. He had to return to Rome at once, and when they saw that he couldn't be swayed, they submitted and returned with him.

"What's the hurry?" Cristine asked when they were finally ensconced in his hotel room.

They tried to make him take it easy, but he had work to do. He was feeling much better, though still not one hundred percent, and his voice had returned.

He had to get away from these women.

He showered and changed, and when he came out Angeline handed him his yellow silk tie. It was a bit dusty, but undamaged, and he left it on the dresser and decided to do without one. Where he was going, no dress code would be in force. He grabbed some granola bars that he had stashed away in his suitcase and passed them around, wolfing his down like he hadn't eaten in a week. He drank water straight from the tap even though he knew rehydrating so quickly might make him sick, determined to purge his system of the poison Susanne had forced on him.

She was clever, skilled and well taught. She knew the dosage that would disable him without killing him. That wasn't the kind of death Saveriano had in mind for him. He was the Heliodromus and she wanted him to play out his role.

"Tom," Angeline said. "I don't think you should go anywhere. You've just been through a tremendous physical ordeal."

When he thought about Susanne's ambush of him, the urge to take the final step was irresistible. His body's ability to process the toxins had grown, and if he was to stop Lalonde from doing what he suspected, he had to cross the plane to where the man would be. Saveriano would do everything in her power to keep the two of them apart. Angeline could not sway him, so it was unlikely anything Chancellor said would make a difference. Just how much of the toxin had Lalonde habituated himself to? Whatever the amount, he was still human, even if he *was* the descendant of a shaman.

Only one way to find out; he had to take the chance. He glanced at the annoyed and irritated frowns on the women's faces, but there was no time to explain. It was better if he kept them out of it. Safer.

He drew a Colt Single Action Army .45 calibre revolver from a locked briefcase, loading it with a full cartridge before placing it on the nightstand by the bed. He glared at the colourful robes lying on the floor that Susanne had costumed him in, and cursed himself for his stupidity, imprudence and arrogance. He should have known better than to let down his guard. Susanne was dangerous, and she had a lot at stake.

Angeline grabbed his arm. "You're not going anywhere until you explain some things to me."

He wrenched his captured limb out of her grasp. She fell backwards with the force of his rebuttal, and he lunged to keep her from hitting the floor. "Sorry," he said, hauling her up by the wrists. This was no way to treat his rescuers, and he knew it, but he was furious and humiliated by his own idiocy.

Angeline stood up, stable now, swept the .45 Colt off the nightstand and aimed it at him.

He stared. "Are you out of your mind?"

In the corner, near the bathroom door, Cristine's eyes bulged out of her head as Angeline glared at him. "I mean it," she said, clenching the butt with both fists. The smooth metal of the cylinder gleamed like river water. "I want some answers."

"All right. But put that down before you hurt somebody."

Angeline was shaking, but she lowered the gun to her side. "You know more about this, about Saveriano and Susanne than you've told me. I want the truth. All of it. And until you tell me all of it, you aren't going anywhere." She raised the weapon again.

"You don't know how to use that, do you?"

"Do you really want to find out?"

He laughed. "I'm not the enemy, Angeline."

"You know, I'm not even sure about that anymore. I'm tired of you giving me the run around. Where were you planning to go before I stopped you? What were you planning to do?"

That was none of her business—because it would sound insane. "Look Angeline. Give me the gun. I'll tell you what I can. But put down the gun."

Cristine nodded from the periphery. "Yes, please, Angeline. You're making me nervous. He hasn't done anything to hurt you. Why are you acting so irrational?"

"I'm irrational? We just rescued this ingrate from certain death by dehydration or mycetism or both and he wants to ditch us? To do what?" She paused to grab a breath. "Are you going after Susanne? Because if you are, I'm coming with you."

"The gun, Angeline." His voice was grim. He stuck out his hand, palm up.

"Oh, all right." She slapped it into his hand, and he hoped the slight wince didn't show. She clenched her fists. "You realize I would never have used it."

He grinned. "I know. I was more worried about you firing it off by accident, and breaking something I'd have to pay for."

"How did Susanne get you up there on that steeple? What were you doing with her anyway? Was she the lead you mentioned in that note you left us this morning?"

He nodded, glanced at the digital alarm clock. It was late now, past the dinner hour, and dark outside. He had to get out of here, but how was he going to do this without answering any of her questions?

"Well?" She was insistent.

Chancellor struggled to stay conscious when all he really wanted to do was collapse on that bed. He glanced at Cristine. Could he trust her? "If you don't let me go right now, I won't be able to tell you any more about Saveriano than I've told you already. I won't be able to help Jake. Do you want me to help Jake?"

Angeline nodded, her objections crushed.

"Good. I'm leaving now. You two stay here where you're safe. I'll be back before dawn."

He gathered up the red robe and yellow belt belonging to the Sun Courier and tucked the costume under his arm, opened the door and went out, slamming it behind him.

* * *

Angeline glowered at the closed door, went to it, opened it defiantly and stepped out, straining her vision down the hall. He was gone, the elevator door fully shut.

She re-entered Chancellor's room to find Cristine still standing, dazed, where she had stood during the entire confrontation. She looked grey and more than a little exhausted. If she felt anything like Angeline did, there was nothing she could want more than a good meal and a solid night's sleep, but there was no time for that. She munched one of the granola bars Chancellor had left them and marched over to the laptop, which he had left on his bed and opened it. Stupid man. She knew his password—she had caught a glimpse of it that day when he checked his messages right in front of her, on this very bed, before they'd made the trip to Ostia—and she could access his email easily.

He knew something about Susanne that he was hiding. What was it? There were several messages from someone called Tru@ forensics, at the Interpol headquarters in Lyons. She knew she could be imprisoned for this if caught, but she had to know, and glanced up to see Cristine's expression of stark horror. What was *she* so uppity about all of a sudden? She was a reporter. They did stuff like this all the time.

Angeline's look questioned her, and Cristine's facial muscles relaxed, then she shrugged. Her attitude said what her voice failed to. *Hell, may as well get it over with. They were in it too deep now.*

The journalist came and sat down beside her on the bed. "Okay. Partners in crime. Open it."

Angeline clicked OPEN and read the forensics report on Susanne—a woman whose last name was a blank.

Apparently, Interpol was aware of who she was. Her name was Susanne Clouteau, but her real name was Celeste Beaulieu. Angeline choked on the air in her lungs; her face froze as she read the rest. Beaulieu was an art dealer who'd had some shady dealings, and Interpol had collected information on her and kept her DNA on file. The samples of Susanne's hair and lip prints that Chancellor had sent to their lab matched the art dealer.

The memory of her visit to Tonga a year earlier flashed violently across her brain. She and Jake were investigating the Ravenstone, a stone of execution with a cryptic emblem that was exactly replicated motif by motif on a rocky cliff in the territory of the Queen Charlotte Haida, off the coast of British Columbia. Susanne AKA Celeste had meant to use the stone to punish Angeline by performing an ancient Tongan rite, whereby one of her fingers would be chopped off. Jake, whom Celeste coveted herself, had come to the rescue, but too late to stop the murderous art dealer from killing her father. The agony of that bloody day replayed in Angeline's mind like a ghostly video, and what transpired after Celeste axed her own father to death was too dreadful to remember. But she forced herself to remember . . . .

The night was moist, hot, and strange, and Celeste was drunk on Kava. Stumbling backward in horror at her own act of murder, she knocked over a Tiki torch, which fell, catching her hair. What happened next was obvious. Flame shot up her long, golden hair like a wick, engulfing her—and Celeste was burned out of recognition before anyone could stop it. But somehow she had survived, and Celeste Beaulieu became Susanne Clouteau. And now the art dealer-turned-archaeological assistant was alive, here, in Rome, working for Sophia Saveriano.

Celeste despised Angeline and Jake. If not for them, she would never have known her father, would never have learned how he had abandoned her pregnant mother and then used her to trap Jake and Angeline before committing the final outrage of incest. She would have had a brilliant career and more money than she could dream of had things gone otherwise; she would still have her long, golden braid and her cocky attitude.

It was unimaginable the pain Celeste must have endured, and the cost for the plastic surgery must have broken her. Where had she gotten the funds to do it? How had she ended up here? And how did she play into this scheme with Saveriano.

Chancellor, you bastard, why didn't you tell me?

"What's the matter, Angeline?" Cristine asked. "You look like you're about to have a seizure."

Angeline forced her breathing to slow, and her heartrate to settle to a normal rhythm.

"Nothing," she said, deciding not to go into the details. "It's just that I knew this woman, that witch, Susanne, before she became Saveriano's assistant. She's undergone extensive reconstructive surgery, that's why I didn't recognize her."

The journalist read over her shoulder, and when she was finished absorbing the report she said, "Frenchie is one scary lady.

The fire had burned Celeste's face and body, scorched her skin and marred her features, but it had not incinerated her brain. Nothing frightened Angeline more than the idea that Celeste's mind was still intact. Oh, she was crazy, but it wasn't her craziness that was a threat; and if Celeste AKA Susanne still had the ability to access her inherited memories, then she could reach Jake in a way that Angeline could not.

She already felt disconnected from him because he refused to confide in her. Susanne's father and Jake were mortal enemies. The father was dead. But that left Susanne to carry out a 10,000-year-old feud. The past did not die. The Raven of legend still tormented them, and they would never be free of its legacy. What was this all leading to? In some way, she now understood why Jake had to probe the final depths of his inheritance. And that was to find what it meant to be the descendent of a notorious shaman. But this epiphany frightened her more than anything else they had ever experienced together. Jake wanted to know what it meant to be a shaman, *the* shaman. The Raven.

To what extent would he go?

What trials would he take?

She shivered. She had never been more terrified in her life. She spoke, hoping the pallor of her thoughts didn't show on her face, "Come on. We have to find Jake."

CHAPTER TWENTY-NINE

The only way he could confront her was in her own medium. In person, in her human form, she denied anything unnatural, and that meant he'd have to take the chance that the Destroying Angel wouldn't kill him.

Chancellor chose the Basilica of San Clemente. It was the closest mithraeum that he knew of. On his arrival, he nodded to one of the priests and marched on into the church like he knew exactly where he was headed. The archaeological site was sealed off, there was no public access, but that didn't deter him. Another priest stopped to question him and Chancellor flashed his Interpol badge.

"I have official business inside the Mithraic shrine," he explained. The priest stared, and didn't try to stop him.

He watched the wide sweep of the priest's cassock disappear into the main foyer of the basilica, then he strolled past the cloister, the axial peristyle surrounded by arcades, listening to his footsteps clatter over the mosaics on the floor. He passed another priest on his way to Fontana's chaste facade and its antique columns. His memory of this place was acute, and he knew that ahead were three naves divided by arcades on ancient marble columns with inlaid paving.

He finally arrived in the unused portion of the church where it was quiet and unlit except for the row of tiny windows near the ceiling. Sidestepping the PRIVATE sign blocking the entrance, he saw that the same archaeological tools lay about. When his eyes adjusted to the darker light he located the pit at the rear.

He lowered himself down the ladder until he stood at the bottom. The tunnel was damp and cold, and filled with shadows.

He memorized the arrangement of tile and marble to collect his bearings, and found the shaft that he knew would lead him to the mithraeum.

He retrieved a flashlight from his pocket, turned left. His shadow danced on the wall ahead, quickening as he passed the loculi and the arcosolium. He ran his hand over the polished stone slab that used to seal the crypt and through another tunnel that branched into the small rooms containing the cubicula.

At a crypt containing a stone sarcophagus, he paused. Why had he not noticed this before? Footsteps, running-shoe marks in the dirt, seeming to backtrack on themselves—not his own, for his shoes did not have such deep treads. Someone had been here before—he crouched to look more closely—recently, maybe even within the hour. A smaller pair of footprints coincided with the larger. Lalonde and Sophia. Were they still here? He listened, but only his breathing responded to his vigilance. He let his gaze wander from the footprints to the reliefs and inscriptions on the sides of the sarcophagus. Beyond the sarcophagus, in the walls, were vertical tiles.

Rising, he left the crypt, travelled deeper into the tunnel until his flashlight hit a wall with a painted fresco. The colours had faded with time, but a figure leading a pilgrimage remained legible. Legible, too, was the epigraph beside it. He understood now what the writing meant, a sign that he had come to the right location, a sign that the time was right to contact her.

Farther up the passage was another opening where the flashlight sent a smoky glow through the entrance. Straight ahead, a row of skulls, and adjacent to them an array of tiles engraved with religious and military insignia. His vision skipped over the symbols, landing on the heavy skull and thick beak of the Raven.

Angeline's words reverberated in his mind. *Why a raven?*

He was near the temple.

He turned, aimed the flashlight, and followed the ray into a vaulted portal, branching off from the crypt where he was standing. Large fallen stones hid the shrine, but as he moved closer, he could see the familiar shaft.

Entering, he saw the linear, rectangular chamber with its vaulted ceiling. An aisle ran lengthwise down the center with a stone bench on either side. He walked to the rear of the cavern where the painted relief of the Tauroctony hung above a pedestalled altar. The cavernous chamber loomed ominous, and the sculptures and paintings decorating it brought to mind his conversation with Angeline. She had said that Vincent Carpello thought this to be a pictorial representation of a Persian myth, and that women were somehow involved in the mysteries. Carpello was correct about women being part of the cult, but he was wrong about its origins. He was certain now that this was neither a Persian nor an Iranian myth, but an astronomical star map. Every figure depicted here was a constellation along a continuous band in the sky.

He moved to the focus of the temple, the carved, painted relief above the altar. The piece was a sharp representation of Mithras killing a sacred bull. He was a young man wearing a Phrygian cap, a short tunic that flared at the bottom, pants and a cloak furling out behind him; and he was grasping the bull, forcing it into submission, one knee between its shoulder blades, and one hand jerking up its head while he sliced its throat. A serpent and a dog drank from the bull's open wound, while a scorpion attacked the bull's testicles. A raven and a lion watched on the periphery. The celestial twins of light and darkness were the torchbearers and above Mithras, were the symbols of the sun and moon amidst a mass of stars.

"The constellations," Chancellor murmured to himself.

He stared and as his gaze roved down from the ceiling, something else captured his vision. Was there an opening behind the altar? He moved until he stood under the overhang of the relief. Yes, there was another shaft! He went into the shaft and arrived at an arched doorway where a huge slab rested against the wall beside it. That slab used to cover the entrance to the mithraeum. How had she moved it? She would have needed a bulldozer.

His eye roamed above the arch to a spot on the flat rock, and he silently mouthed the letters that were scored into the stone over his head until the image was burned into his mind:

MITHRAEVM

His hands began to tingle, his heartrate to increase. He grabbed a deep breath and retraced the letters, contour by contour, irises twitching up and down, side to side.

MITHRAEVM

MYTH RAVEN

RAVEN MYTH.

Was Lalonde the messenger of Mithras? Was he willing to find out where that journey would lead him?

Chancellor stood at the entrance below the inscription and gazed at the space that widened before him. This was an antechamber, and it was smaller than the outer temple. Inside were stone blocks that served as tables. On the tables were between thirty and fifty tall candles. What went on in here? He meandered in, noting every feature of the cavelike room, jerking his flashlight into every crook and recess. His search took him to a stone table where he found a cardboard box of matches, and where he lit a dozen candles until one corner of the chamber burst into light like a pagan shrine. He wandered over to where he saw what appeared to be a crude apothecary, and singled out a few species of dried funguses in labelled ceramic jars. He located a pottery bowl with a clay pestle, and a large bottle of cool water, a stainless steel pot and a portable propane hotplate.

His breath was exceedingly short, his hands and forehead broke out in a frigid sweat.

What are you, madam? A witch, a phantasm, or both?

He snapped off his flashlight, shook out the red robe and yellow sash of the Sun Courier and studied them before putting the guise on over his street clothes. He picked up the ceramic jar containing the most deadly poisonous mushroom available among the eclectic collection, and began preparations for the ritual that he knew would admit him into her world.

"Sophia," he whispered. "You have the wrong man."

It took no time to mix the brew on the propane cooker. Had the raw mushroom been available he would have popped off its seemingly innocuous, smooth, white cap, and consumed it whole. He knew he was taking a chance. He'd read up on everything he could find on the Destroying Angel.

If his hunch was wrong, the amatoxins of the *Amanita virosa* would shut down first his liver and then his kidneys—and he would die.

His already cold hands felt icy now; his rapidly beating heart was speeding. When he lifted his hand to his mouth and cheeks, no sensation met them; his blood pressure was rising, and every muscle in his normally strong limbs turned as though to liquid. He gazed into the polished, curvature of the stainless steel pot in which he had mixed the powdered mushroom with water, and saw his reflection deflected at him, a miasma of deformed flesh and hair, and horrible, hollow, black eyes.

The trick is in accepting your own death.

Chancellor raised his eyelids. The antechamber swam. The stone tables seemed to move, shifting, one moment here, the next moment somewhere else. The candles glowed as a single mass, like the burning sun. The pot dropped from his hands, and crashed to the floor. It rolled over and over, as though it had a power all to itself. A diaphanous stream, mistlike spiralled in its wake, seeming red, then yellow, then white, and finally blue. The mist lay low on the ground, flowed across the floor avoiding his touch as he crawled after it, trying to seize its nebulous structure.

It had no shape or form, no physical mass by which he could hang on.

Chancellor rose to his feet. He tried to call out, but no sound left his lips. The room was now amorphous, it had no recognizable shape, everything that was in it, the stone tables, the apothecary, the candles were gone. He saw only the sun blazing like a yellow, haloed ball in one corner, and the elusive mist creeping along the floor.

He knew he had but one chance. Speaking to her would not work. He had to reach her at her baser, preternatural level.

He started to hum in order to focus his mind and blank out the unreality of what his eyes were seeing. He turned in on himself, forcing his mind to attenuate into a single tunnelled point. He became only his consciousness, no body, no voice. Nothing existed except his thoughts and hers.

Commune with me, lady, hear my thoughts.

They were two souls: hers older than anything he had ever imagined. His older than he knew. He reached for her with every ounce of his being.

My very presence here, in your realm, proves it. Lalonde is not the one. Let him be.

A flaming red light exploded in his brain, knocking him down.

Chancellor awoke, weak, gagging. The undigested brew spilled out of his stomach and onto the earthen floor of the antechamber.

* * *

Angeline found him stumbling out of the mithraeum beneath the Basilica of San Clemente with the robe of the Sun Courier tucked under his arm. He was running like a ghost was after him, teetering like he was drunk, down the honeycombed tunnels of the catacomb. She slammed into him in the dark as he tried to push past her to reach the ladder at the end of the passage.

"Chancellor!" she shouted. "Stop right there."

Chancellor froze in his tracks, raised gritty eyes to her.

She grabbed him by the arm and dragged him toward the ladder, to where the soft light of daybreak filtered down from the hole above. She glared at him, her anger suddenly dissipating, melting to fear. "Your eyes, your face! What happened to you?"

And the smell. He smelled awful, a combination of mould and vomit.

Despite her revulsion, she ran a hand down his normally angular jaw, which was puffy. His pupils were so huge they turned his irises into solid balls of black. His lips were a dead shade of blue.

"Can't talk now," he mumbled. "Have to find Lalonde."

"Well, I want to find him too, but you aren't going anywhere in that condition except back to the hotel. Tom, you look like walking death!"

Cristine, who had been hidden by the shadows, covered her nose with her sleeve and grabbed his other arm. "She's right, Chancellor. If you don't get some rest now, you'll die."

They helped him manoeuver the short length of tunnel, then up the ladder and through the church, where they met no one in their retreat from the basilica. When they got to the car, he was ready to give in and let them take care of him. Angeline was really scared now. What had he done to himself? His appearance reminded her of that day she'd gone to the villa to find Jake, and they had ended up in bed. On that day, Jake had done something to himself; his cold hands and dilated pupils were no side effects of experiencing an inherited memory. She was no idiot. She'd seen him experience them before, and they had never caused physical changes or extremes in behaviour. Whatever it was those two were experimenting with, they both managed to recover quickly, so it couldn't be poison. Could it?

At the hotel, Chancellor went to take a shower and brush his teeth. Cristine went out to get them some food, and Angeline waited patiently by the bed for him to finish with the bathroom. His laptop was where she had left it before she and the journalist had gotten the notion to shadow him. She opened it; the image of his distorted features sharp in her mind, and searched the Internet for the symptoms. Rows and rows of links appeared and she selected a likely medical explanation, clicking onto the website. The fool. No illness this. He had been toying with entheogens. His were the distinct features of a specific type of poisoning.

She looked up, slamming the lid down on the laptop when she heard the shower stop, and slid the computer off her lap to the bed. She rose and traced a groove into the hotel carpeting, pacing back and forth in front of the window. When he stepped out of the bathroom in grey slacks, shirtless, she took one look at him and gasped.

His features *and* his eyes had returned normal.

His seeming wellbeing left her no compulsion to handle him with kid gloves. Instead, she realized that all along her suspicions of him were justified. His revolver sat on the nightstand where he had left it before going to have a shower, and she grabbed it now and held it on him once more. "All right. I've had it with your lies. Why didn't you tell me about Susanne? And how could you go running off when you knew who she was and that she would stop at nothing to get at Jake?"

"She can't hurt Jake."

"Oh yeah? Look at what she did to you. If we hadn't found you, you'd be dead."

"Someone would have found me."

"Yes, you would like to think so."

"Susanne is a woman."

"No kidding."

Chancellor paused. "What's with the gun, Angeline? Just what are you thinking? How is it that I've suddenly become the enemy again?" This time he didn't try to talk her out of shooting him. He watched her, and turned to retrieve a clean shirt from out of his suitcase. He drew it on while Angeline shook her head thoroughly enraged and flustered.

"That's no answer. Of course she's a woman. What did you think? That she was a man in disguise? Pretty damn good disguise if that were the case, but it's not. Susanne is Celeste Beaulieu. She has a private vendetta against Jake and me. She'll stop at nothing to destroy him and drag me down in the process. Is that what you want? Is this what it's about? You think Jake is responsible for Vincent Carpello's death and you're willing to let Susanne punish him for it? What kind of a cop are you? What's in it for you?"

"Listen to yourself, Angeline. Does what you're saying even make any sense? Susanne tried to kill me, remember?"

She slumped to her knees, banged her head on the carpet, while clasping the revolver in both of her hands. She was at her wits end. She raised her head and left the gun on the floor. "What am I supposed to think?" she asked desperately.

He finished tucking in his shirt and moved over to her, accepted the gun, slipping it into his back pocket, and raised her by her hands, standing her up until they were face to face.

"I told you to go home. Why didn't you do it?"

"Because I love Jake and I won't let you or Susanne or Saveriano hurt him."

"You're a very brave woman," he said.

She sighed. "Help me, Tom."

"I'm trying to. I'm also trying to keep you out of trouble. You should go home and let me take care of it."

"Didn't you hear one word I said?"

He smiled. "I heard you."

She sat down, hard, on the bed while he watched her. "Tell me why you don't think I have to worry about Susanne. What did you mean when you said, 'she's a woman'?"

Frenchie was devoted to her employer, Chancellor told her. Saveriano needed Jake and she wasn't about to let her minion kill him. But Susanne's vendetta meant she would do everything in her power to keep Angeline away from him. "She might kill you if you try to keep Saveriano from fulfilling her purpose. That's why I want you to go home."

"I can't," she whispered.

He nodded. "I know."

She glanced over at the ball of red and yellow clothing that Chancellor had tossed to the armchair when they returned from the basilica. "Can you at least tell me what that's all about?"

When he remained mute, she shoved herself off the bed and planted her feet in front of him, blocking his path to the door. "Who the blazes are you? Or should I say *what* are you?"

His blank face offered no explanation. Angeline had experienced some strange things during her acquaintanceship with Chancellor—coloured mists, cold spots, invisible forces, apparitions that held a female form, plus that surreal escapade in Eze, the hostage situation atop the church steeple, or was that meant to be a human sacrifice? Whatever it was meant to be, Chancellor had survived. Furthermore, whatever it was he had done in the mithraeum beneath the Basilica of San Clemente, he had emerged looking like the devil himself. He had taken poison. Those were the visible symptoms of acute mycetism; his swollen face, his engorged eyes, his clammy skin, the vomiting and the obvious weakness were all characteristics of severe mushroom poisoning. God knew what was happening inside his body. Apparently the organs shut down one by one, starting with the liver. The toxins passed through the liver first. He wasn't normal like her or Cristine or even Jake. Jake's lips were not blue like that when he had experimented with whatever hallucinogen it was that had made his pupils dilate and his hands like ice. The blueness indicated a toxic drop in oxygen levels in the blood, a sign of organ failure. The man should be dead, but he wasn't, he was a super human. And now each and every one of the symptoms had vanished.

She snatched at the balled up robe of the Sun Courier. "You believe you're an initiate, don't you? You think you are the Heliodromus and that you passed the test."

"No," Chancellor said.

"Then what the hell is this? Why were you wearing this?"

He didn't answer at first. Angeline threw the robe at him and he caught it and fingered the colourful fabric as though it had the answers.

"I don't believe that I am the Sun Courier," he said.

"The Pater, then? The Father of this whole ridiculous cult that Saveriano has reinvented?"

The Pater was the highest rank in the Mithraic cult, the deputy on earth of the god himself. He was father to the other initiates, the teacher whose symbols were a ring and a staff. Angeline found herself staring wildly at him, searching his body for the absurd accoutrements.

"No, Angeline. I am not the Pater, but I will probably approach the goddess that way, since she did not accept me as the Heliodromus."

"The goddess?" Her eyes stretched wide until she thought her eyelashes would scrape her eyebrows. She swallowed. Now he was getting scary.

"Sophia Saveriano is no longer a woman—if she ever was."

"What are you talking about?"

"Haven't you wondered why we never see her unless she wants to be seen?"

"Of course, but I thought she just didn't *want* to be seen."

"She can come and go on a whim right under your eyes and you wouldn't see her. But you might see signs of her or feel her presence."

Angeline wondered if the poison was still active, affecting Chancellor's logic. She decided it was best to stay alert and silent, and let him talk.

"She isn't looking for God's wife," he said. "She's looking for God. *Yehlh* is the same as Yahweh is the same as Mithras is the same as God. She is looking for her mate, her equal."

Angeline gulped. Was he crazy? He didn't seem to be. She knew he had studied the paranormal, that he was an expert on the subject and that officials used him as a consultant on inexplicable cases like X-Files, like TV's Scully and Muldur. Oh God, really? He wasn't just pulling her leg? This was for real? She hadn't quite believed him when he first told her of his suspicions, but now . . . but now, the look on his face was frighteningly serious, in fact she had never seen him more dangerous . . . which meant Saveriano was crazy, if she believed what he believed. She shook her head in horrified amazement. His explanation was insane, his pronouncement that Saveriano was not human.

"Tom, she *is* a woman. I saw her. *You* saw her. I shook hands with her, touched her skin, her flesh. She is made of flesh and blood and bone—like the rest of us."

He looked at her, but his eyes seemed not to see her. They were looking deeper into hers like they were searching for something that should be there but was hidden. "Do you believe that Jake has inherited memories?" he asked.

She shut her eyes for a second. From the moment she had met Jake, his inherited memories had ruled their lives. "Yes," she answered.

"Then why is it so hard for you to believe that Saveriano is not a woman?"

"Then what is she, Tom? A witch? A spirit? A *ghost?*"

"All of those, and more."

Oh my god, she thought. He believes what he said. He thinks she's a goddess.

"I can't fathom this," she said, wringing the hem of her shirt.

"You don't have to. But I do—if I'm to stop her hunting spree."

"She's got Jake."

He nodded.

"She thinks Jake is the Raven, *Yehlh,* the god figure of Haida cosmology."

His head bobbed again. "She sees his inherited memories as evidence of his consciousness being passed down through the ages."

"Like reincarnation? She thinks Jake is the reincarnation of the Raven?" Her own question didn't seem absurd to her anymore. She had accepted what Chancellor had said. It didn't matter what she believed, because goddess or not, Saveriano had Jake, and she planned to do something unspeakable to him.

Chancellor shook his head. "Not reincarnation. There is no reincarnation, not the way the books explain it."

"How do you know?"

"The consciousness is not reincarnated because it never dies. There is continuity to life, Angeline. We are all part of that continuum, all matter on this earth never dies, only changes."

"Then why don't I have these genetic . . . these inherited memories? I don't know of a single other person who does." She clapped a hand to her lips. That was wrong, she knew three others who had those memories, two of whom were dead—Jake's father, Jimmy Sky, and Susanne's or should she say Celeste's father, Jake's mortal enemy, the developer Clifford Radisson.

"We aren't all born into the world remembering. Only a few privileged people are granted that gift. Jake is the descendent and the manifestation of *Yehlh.*"

"I see." His own people, the Haida, believed that when a member of the tribe died, the soul returned in the body of a newborn baby of the same family.

Chancellor grabbed his jacket. "I'm leaving now, Angeline. I must find her."

Angeline took hold of his sleeve, her voice austere. "You're going to use the mushrooms again, aren't you?"

He nodded. "It's the only way I can reach her. I have to meet her in her own realm before she'll believe that Jake is not the man she wants."

"And *you* are?"

"We'll have to see."

"Don't do it, Tom. I'm grateful to you for putting yourself in danger to save Jake. But I could never forgive myself if you died saving him. There's got to be another way. We should call the police." But even as she said these words she knew no policeman would believe her. Saveriano: the spirit of a goddess? Set to wreak havoc in the world until she found her mate? They'd laugh her right to the immigration office to sign her deportation papers.

Chancellor did not reply, but the look on his face was almost as expressive as if he had said, *I am not doing it for Jake.*

"Please don't do it for me, either."

"I'm not." He pulled his sleeve away.

"Tom." She hesitated. How was she going to keep him from sacrificing himself? "Aren't you afraid of dying?" She swallowed. She had never faced this question before. People in their twenties generally didn't. She did not know how to think about the subject of death. Did she believe in heaven or hell? In God? Her parents had raised her as a liberal Christian. Her mother had exposed her to church but wasn't tyrannical about her attending. In her second year of high school she quit going out of sheer boredom. Her parents divorced, and church was never an issue again. "It's the great unknown," she said helplessly. "I'm terrified of the idea."

Chancellor patted her paternally on the shoulder, his eyes softening in compassion. "You already know what it's like to be dead, Angeline. Before you were born, you did not exist—and not existing is the same thing as being dead."

"But I don't remember anything," she whined. She couldn't believe she was having this conversation, and yet, his explanation made perfect sense.

"Of course you don't remember. If we remembered our entire spiritual journey on this planet, we would be totally confused." He went to the nightstand and yanked the telephone cord out of the wall, emptied her purse onto the bed, and slipped her cell phone into his pocket. "I promise you'll get this back when it's all over." He turned to the door.

"Wait, where are you going? What are you planning to do?"

"I am going to meet with Asherah."

"The goddess? Tom, Asherah and Mithras did not coexist in the same time period."

"It doesn't matter. Don't you get it yet? They are all the same. One God, different names."

"Then answer me this. Who are you? Who do you think it is that you've reincarnated into?"

"I told you, Angeline. I don't believe in reincarnation. Reincarnation implies that you die. I don't believe in death. What I am about to engage in is the next step in the continuity of the spirit."

"But isn't that the same thing as the Indo-European reincarnation of the soul?" She didn't know why she insisted on engaging in a philosophical discussion right now, but it was one way of detaining him long enough to figure out how to get him to make her his accomplice.

"No."

She stuck out her hand to physically block him. "There's no way to prove it."

"There is *one* way to prove it."

Angeline was aghast. "That means you would have to die. Aren't you afraid you might be wrong? That Saveriano is merely psychotic and not the spirit of an ancient goddess—and that death is just death?"

"There is only one way to find out."

"Tom, no!"

It was too late; he was out the door, slamming it behind him. And when she tried to force the door open, she found that it was blocked.

CHAPTER THIRTY

A low tone bonged from the grandfather clock. Sophia slammed the top drawer to her desk, twirling the swivel chair in multiple gyrations before marching around to face her assistant who dared not approach. She stood by the coffee table in front of the leather sofa, trembling in anticipation. She had failed. Oh how she had failed. *Please don't punish me; I'll do better next time.* The words never came out. In all the time of her employment, she had never spoken to Sophia until she was asked to.

Sophia stopped behind the sofa, placing her hands on the back of the black leather, her eyes dipping at the photographs of Jake Lalonde that she always kept scattered on the coffee table like a taunt. He will die, she thought. He *must* die. Where Sophia wished to take him, she dared not travel. She hadn't been asked to.

Sophia sighed, impatiently. "Well, my dear," she said. "Chancellor is still alive. Why is this?"

"You asked me not to kill him quickly. You asked that he perform the rights of the Heliodromus . . . . Sophia, I do not think he is the Sun Courier. Even if that lame excuse for an archaeologist, Angeline, and that brat from the magazine had not found him, he would have lasted too long for my liking. Someone eventually would have seen him and rescued him."

"True." Sophia paused to study her options.

Susanne had a better idea. "He is the Pater," she said. "At least that's what he believes himself to be. That's why he would not die. He thinks he is the Father of all initiates. He wants to grab your power. But I will give him a trial of proof that he cannot pass."

"No." Sophia shook her head. She wasn't angry and Susanne was grateful for that, but she wasn't pleased either. "No," she repeated, reflectively. "Let him be."

She noticed Sophia's gaze dart to the doorway. She turned to look and saw Jake standing on the threshold.

"Busy?" he asked, shooting a glance back.

Her eyes travelled up Jake's body, from his tight hips to his broad chest and shoulders. His face hard and angular, with high cheekbones and oddly grey eyes, which appeared incongruous and cold against his warm, sun-darkened skin. His hair straggled to just below his jawline.

She knew what his body felt like, had sampled it herself, once, while he was sleeping. She smiled to herself. Too bad he didn't know the truth. His face crinkled into puzzlement as she continued to assess his physical endowments. No. He did not have a clue as to who she really was. Oh well, it didn't matter. This was not between him and her, it was between him and Sophia, and in the process Susanne would get the justice she deserved. Sophia did not know that Susanne also had inherited memories, that her memories were linked to his. If she knew, would she use her in a different way? Susanne wasn't sure. She wasn't sure how long she wanted to be used now that she was whole and beautiful again, now that her past had been erased and was known only to herself. She snickered silently. That was the funny thing. Her trauma, her ordeal by fire, had given her another gift, the ability to experience her dreams at will. She could see what Jake was seeing, without the need of hallucinogens, but she didn't dare enter that world now that his powers had grown. She would wait to see if Sophia succeeded.

"Susanne," Sophia said sharply, waking her out of her reverie. "Tonight is my night. Go prepare my things. See that my gown has returned from the cleaners. Pack my lecture notes and my laptop."

She nodded and left her employer alone with Jake.

*   *   *

225

Sophia's eyes trailed her assistant's back. When she was gone, she gestured to Jake to enter and close the door to her library. He did as she wished and walked past several bookcases until he reached the place where Susanne had been standing in front of the coffee table. He glanced down at the photos, the costumed pictures of himself dressed like the Raven. Why did she keep these here, in the open, for everyone to see? Then it occurred to him that Angeline must have seen them that morning when they'd had their final argument, when she had left him and run to Chancellor, and he hadn't stopped her. Why didn't he stop her? She was precious to him. That's why. And he was being forced—Sophia was forcing him—to choose between the woman he loved and wanted to spend the rest of his life with, and a life of surreal metaphysics, preternaturalism—a shaman's existence.

He had forced himself to put Angeline out of his mind. Each step that Sophia led him into the world of the shaman brought him closer to taking control of the process. He could feel it. Was it wrong to want to know how far he could go? The last trip he experienced was so real that he could feel the texture of the stones around the Raven's pool, the fiery cobbles—in fact, he had brought one of them back with him, unknowingly. It sat on Sophia's library desk now, like a glittering monument to an impossible quest.

She didn't have to say a word. He knew her mind. She had given him until the night of the gala—tonight—to decide if he wanted to take the final step, to unite with her spiritually and see who he as *Yehlh*—the Raven—really was.

Every fibre of his muscles trembled with lust, terror and anticipation. He could barely resist. She knew this—he could tell—but still she didn't speak.

"Why aren't you dressed, Jake?" she asked. "The event is formal. Black tie. Or business attire if you prefer."

His eyes lowered to his blue-jeans and T-shirt. "It's hours yet."

"Then take a hot bath. It will relax your nerves."

Certain his nerves would never relax again, Jake shook his head. "I need to talk to you, Sophia. I .... I'm ...." This was so hard to say. He'd never thought of himself as a coward; after all, he had fought every obstacle in his path from the time he was born, and he had single-handedly removed them. No mother, no father, only a series of foster parents. No money, no opportunity, no privilege. Everything he possessed he had acquired by himself—his education, his job, his home, his wife .... He swallowed as he reiterated his last thought. His wife? Angeline was not his wife. Not yet.

"You're torn, Jake," she said.

He raised his eyes from the pictures of himself.

"You're having doubts."

"I'm afraid, Sophia. I'm afraid that if you're not right about me, I could lose it all, not the least of it being my life."

She smiled. "Fear is natural. Embrace it. Fear is only a prelude to something better—an impediment to be crossed." She leaned forward, took his hand and drew him around to the other side of the sofa where they could stand face to face. "Asherah is the Black Goddess, *Yehlh* is Yahweh. You saw it yourself how true it must be. Both are embodied in the cult of Mithras."

"How?" Jake demanded, sliding his hand away. He didn't dare offend her; he didn't want to. She was more powerful and more frightening than anyone he had ever encountered. But at the moment he could not endure her touch. "I can't see the connection."

"You will see. If you perform the final rite with me, it will all come clear."

This was the part of her plan that had him shaking in his Reebok's. She hadn't lied; she swore she always told the truth. This time was no exception. What she was asking him to do was unheard of. No one in his right mind would willingly perform such an act. But he wasn't in his right mind. In the final ritual, she would ask him to drink a brew made from the Death Cap. This potion would kill him, but he would enter the Spirit World and, like her, would be able to cross the two metaphysical planes—that of the living and that of the dead.

I will exist in both worlds, conscious of both realms.

And Angeline? What part would she play in his life after that, providing it worked? And what if it didn't? What if it didn't work? What if he died and didn't come back? *Am I willing to sacrifice my love for her to find out?* He desperately wanted, needed, to learn what it meant to be Raven, to be able to cross planes at will. But if he just died and death was just death, then that death would have no meaning. It would become a pointless death, a death for nothing, for no good reason, because who did this whole experiment benefit except him? Angeline would reap nothing from it. The academic world—archaeology—would reap nothing from it. And if his *death* had no meaning, then what did that say about his *life*?

"The choice remains yours, Jake. I cannot force your hand. But I think you already know what choice you will make."

Silent, the air felt trapped in his lungs as he tried to exhale. Sophia gazed knowingly at him. "Is not all death meaningless? Why do you think I want to do this for you? If you follow me you'll have the opportunity to transcend death."

"I have trouble believing," he said, bluntly.

"Yes. That's a problem."

"You haven't guaranteed me that I won't just die." He knew his plea sounded like a whine, but he had no will to stop it.

"I have no guarantee. There is a very real possibility that you will die and remain in the unconscious world of the dead. On the other hand, if you believe—and I have never met a man more likely to succeed than you—then you will follow me to the other side."

The idea of eternal life versus everything he would lose. That was his dilemma. He had experienced things under the influence of psychoactive substances that seemed completely real. He had been transported back in time; he was physically there in the cave of the Raven's pool. He had brought back a souvenir, the cobble lamp flecked with fool's gold. But was this for real? *Did I really have some sort of power, not only to tap my ancestor's memories but also to physically visit their time?* Why did it all seem so real? More real than the dreams ever had. The dreams drawn from his genetic memories were recognizably conjurings of the brain, similar to hallucinations except that they actually occurred in the past—his past. The dreams were not real in the sense that his body did not move to become part of the scene, nor could he touch or feel anything solid. All he could do was watch—watch what was happening to other people, presumably his ancestors. He could not interfere in their actions. But his latest experiences under Sophia's guidance were not like that. Those experiences were real. And they were happening to him, physically.

Can I take the chance that I'm not just hallucinating?

Can I take the chance of dying a meaningless death?

What had he done that anyone would remember him for? What had he contributed to human knowledge, society or humanity in general? Whose lives had he touched, improved, inspired? What kind of a boyfriend had he been to Angeline? What kind of a husband would he make? What did she fundamentally want out of life, and was his existence essential to her acquiring it?

Sophia tapped his arm lightly to return his attention to her. "Tell me, exactly, what you mean by a meaningful death. *Is* there such a thing?"

Jake looked at her. "Of course, there is. A soldier who dies in battle defending his country dies a meaningful death. A mother who dies trying to rescue her baby from a fire dies a meaningful death, a man who dies protecting his family from a burglar dies a meaningful death, an astronaut who dies in a shuttle explosion while exploring the universe dies a meaningful death. A terminally ill person who agrees to clinical trials with experimental therapy dies a meaningful death in aid of medical research . . . . But me? I will just be dead for no reason at all, except my selfish desire to transcend death; to discover if there is something more, and whether I can return at will to the living. How is that meaningful—to anyone but myself?"

Her eyes lifted, glassy, round. "How can you doubt yourself, Jake? You have already seen what you're capable of. Whether you face it or not, admit it to yourself or not, you already believe . . . . I didn't send you into the past. You sent yourself there. If you can believe that you actually visited the shaman's sacred pool on the San Juan Islands, then why is it so hard for you to believe this? That death is transitional for men of your power." Her voice went quiet. "You will not die."

CHAPTER THIRTY-ONE

"Chancellor!" she yelled. "Tom, open this door!"

Angeline yanked, but it stuck. Sounds came from the hallway, a scratching noise. How could he lock it from the outside? The knob gave and turned easily, and she could feel the latch release, but the door refused to budge.

She searched the door's sides, giving special attention to the edge opposite the hinges. Something was wedged between the door and the jamb. The unusual humidity in the air had swollen the wood of the door, adding pressure to the jamb. Smart man. But not that smart. What was it? A credit card, a folded up sheet of paper? She must have something thin enough to fit inside the tight gap with which to force out the obstruction.

The contents of her purse were still strewn across Chancellor's bed.

A nail file should do it. She found one among her belongings and brought it to the door. With a little elbow grease she was able to jam the tapered end into the gap, but the actual work of teasing out the obstruction was delicate and she broke into a sweat.

No luck. She returned to the room and lifted the wire that used to attach the telephone to the wall. She was no technician and had no idea how to reattach the cord. This hotel was archaic and the telephones were ancient—like something out of the 1950's—they did not use modern phone jacks. She dropped the end of the wire. No cell phone either. She went back to the door, prepared to try extracting the impediment again, when she heard footsteps approach.

"Cristine! Is that you?"

Silence, then a familiar voice said, "Yeah? What's the matter?"

"I'm trapped in here. I need you to help me push the door open. There's something stuck between the jamb and the door. Can you see it?"

A shuffling sound followed, then a scratching like fingernails on stone.

"Got it," she said. "You can open the door."

The latch gave and the door swung wide, and Angeline sucked air into her lungs like she'd been trapped for days. The staleness from the hallway flooded the inert space, and although the hall air was hardly fresh, to Angeline it seemed as sharp as an autumn gale. She felt suffocated inside the muggy hotel room where steam from the shower lingered, having nowhere to escape.

Cristine laughed when she caught sight of Angeline stripped to a camisole and jeans. "What on earth have you been doing? Where's Chancellor? I'm assuming he's the one that barricaded you in here? What did he do, pull a gun on you?"

She refused to respond. She went to the bathroom and snapped up a face cloth to wipe the moisture from her face. Her hair hung limp around her neck like overcooked spaghetti. When she returned, Cristine emptied a paper grocery bag of Italian loaves, sausage and cheese, plus three bottles of spring water onto the dresser by the wall.

"What did he block the door with?" Angeline asked, fastening her damp hair back with a clip.

"This—" The journalist raised a folded square of thin cardboard and handed it over.

Angeline unfolded it and studied the picture that was printed on one surface. It was a card, like a playing card, but embossed with an unfamiliar symbol—a starlike emblem in solid black on a white background. The points to the star were shaped like arrows. There were eight of them.

A chill replaced the earlier heat of frustration and exhaustion. Just how deep was Chancellor involved in the occult? Furthermore, how could such a thin piece of cardboard obstruct the door? Was this some sort of sigil magic?

Sigil magic used the concept of 'belief' as a tool. It drew on science fiction, scientific theories, traditional ritual magic, Neo-shamanism, and individual experimentation. Some practitioners used psychoactive drugs in practices such as psychedelic semenancy and chemognosticism. They had unique symbols, which were used for different purposes. Was Chancellor into this stuff?

A shiver forced its way along Angeline's spine and into her lungs, despite her best effort to suppress it. She looked up to seek Cristine, and found her gorging unceremoniously on bread and cheese. Mimicry is often a reflex action, and as if on cue, the acid in Angeline's stomach surged, painfully reminding her that she had eaten nothing but a granola bar all day. She shot one final glance at the strange black symbol and tucked the card into her purse. Joining the journalist at the dresser where the feast was laid out, she tore off the heel of a loaf and swallowed it before she had chewed three times, then informed Cristine that Chancellor was crazy.

He was about to trade his life for Jake's. She quickly summarised the gist of their argument before Chancellor had locked her inside his room. He thought Sophia was some kind of goddess, the incarnation of Asherah for God's sake! Then she realized the levity of her outburst. She was careful to omit the word 'reincarnation' because Chancellor did not believe in that particular ideology. But what then? What *did* he believe? Did he actually believe in gods and goddesses? Oh hell, why not? What was Christianity except the same thing: all-encompassing, invisible God or stone god idol, it was the same thing. A belief system that was totally unprovable.

It was mind-boggling that an intelligent, educated person could so thoroughly embrace such a belief . . . and yet, she had no choice but to accept it because he was damned serious . . . he had all these ghost-hunting gadgets . . . and then there was that sigil card—haunting evidence of, if not a corrupted mind, then a confused one. To him the occult was not a joke.

Her eyes scouted over his furniture. They needed a gun. For the first time Cristine seemed open to the absurd, she did not laugh, she simply stopped Angeline's search with one question: how did the Mithraic raven and *Yehlh* have anything to do with each other? Angeline raised both hands helplessly because she wasn't quite clear on that. One god, different names—that was what Chancellor had espoused.

They still needed a gun if they were to follow him into the realm of the goddess. She told Cristine to help her search for one. He must have another weapon stashed somewhere. In his luggage? They turned the Interpol agent's gear inside out, but found nothing.

Finally Angeline returned to Chancellor's briefcase. She'd already searched it thoroughly once; she'd do it again. He had returned most of his ghost-hunting gadgets to the briefcase, but there was one device that still waited on the dresser. It was an EMF meter. So what did this thing do? EMF stood for Electro-magnetic field meter. This particular device was called a K-2 meter and it used flashing lights to signal an increase in electromagnetic energy. Electromagnetic fields were generated by AC or DC currents and were encountered everyday in household or industrial appliances. Did ghosts affect electromagnetic fields? She pressed some buttons and nothing happened. She returned to where the journalist was now examining Chancellor's briefcase.

"What are you looking at?" Angeline asked. "It's empty."

"Yeah, but doesn't the interior space look really small for the size of the briefcase?"

She bent down to have a look. Yes, it did.

She ran her finger over the inside lining which felt like silk. "Pretty strange lining for a briefcase come to think of it."

Cristine banged her knuckles against one side that appeared thicker than the remaining sides of the briefcase. "You know, I think there's something here, a secret compartment."

Typical of Chancellor. Well, that wasn't very bright of him. She picked up the briefcase and brought it to the window so that she could see it better. The journalist was not mistaken. There was a hidden space there, but how did it open? She pressed all around the lining, searched for buttons and latches and hidden touch-sensitive locks, but found nothing. She dropped the briefcase on the bed, discouraged, and Cristine took up the search, while Angeline walked back to the window and absentmindedly fingered the EMF meter that she had left on the sill.

Agitated, she pressed the button repeatedly. The digital readout began to fluctuate and a series of numbers flashed in sequence, then a squeal came from the bed and Angeline raced over to see what had triggered the squealing.

"Whatever you did, it worked," Cristine said.

"I didn't do anything." Angeline glanced down at the K-2 meter. Was this some sort of remote control? The point was moot. The compartment had opened, and inside was the self-contained, digitized, environmentally-controlled container that housed the missing text.

Her eyes lifted to meet Cristine's. So, Chancellor had had it all the time.

The tubular box weighed next to nothing and she sat it on her lap. If she opened the box, she would allow air in to attack the integrity of the parchment. But she had no choice. The text on this parchment was the key to what the deranged archaeologist intended to do with Jake, and more importantly—where. Chancellor believed that Saveriano planned some sort of ritual with Jake, and that the ritual was scheduled for tonight.

Angeline's mind muttered a repetitive litany: PNR, PNR, PNR. She had to find him before it was too late, before he passed the point of no return.

She knew the lock sequence and tapped in the numbers. The lock registered the combination and clicked open.

The figures of a bird, a cup, a staff, a torch, a diadem and a lamp were inked in spare, linear detail across the parchment. Below the drawings was a line of Latin. She could read the ancient writing and recognized the symbols, but what did the whole thing mean?

She studied the parchment scrupulously. The bird, the cup and the staff belonged to the raven. As far as Saveriano was concerned, did Jake still represent the Raven? The torch, the diadem and the lamp belonged to the Nymphus.

Who was the Nymphus?

She was struck by the juxtaposition of the symbols for the Mithraic Nymphus (bride) with the icons of the raven, Corax. Angeline mumbled aloud one line "*ide Nymphus*" which meant Behold Nymphus or Hail Nymphus. Then a thought occurred to her. If she translated it as "*aide Nymphus*" then the meaning was completely different. It would read Sing Nymphus—as in sing the *marriage* hymn.

A booming started in the middle of her chest. Her pulse began to race; her mouth went dry. Vincent's postulation was dead on. Women did have a role in the Mithraic Mysteries.

Was that why he was murdered? Saveriano was the icon of a secret branch of the cult that feminized the Nymphus and worshipped the Raven—and she wanted Jake's power.

The next ritual would be the last and it had nothing to do with the Pater.

The next ritual would be a wedding.

Angeline went for her cell phone and quickly realized that Chancellor had it. She asked Cristine for her Blackberry, and frantically punched in Jake's number. Please answer, she begged.

No response.

She texted three letters.

PNR

CHAPTER THIRTY-TWO

Chancellor hit the expressway heading into the countryside. Even driving at top speed, twenty minutes were gone before he swerved up the serpentine drive bordered by fading grass, wildflowers, and pines. He careened past marble fountains and statues, flower gardens and cypresses, braking at the foot of the villa.

He shifted into park and stepped out of the Fiat staring up at the three-storied, pillared palace with its ochre-coloured walls and iron-railed terraces: a magnificent house for a magnificent being.

Now that he was here, he was having second thoughts about invading her home. It wasn't that he was afraid, fear did not enter the equation at all because a man dealing with an unknown entity such as the mysterious professor would be stupid to dismiss fear. Fear made one sharp, quick, and smart. He would need all the smartness, quickness and sharpness he could muster if he wasn't to lose Lalonde to Sophia tonight. He studied the windows. No movement behind the curtains or blinds. No lights either, but then it was still daytime, and would be for hours yet.

He mounted the short flight of steps and lifted the doorknocker, paused.

Why hadn't he noticed that before? The instrument was made of solid iron, burnished to a polished gunmetal grey, moulded into the form of a raven perched on what looked like some sort of ring. Or diadem. For some reason, the word diadem came to mind.

What was a diadem again?

A band or a crown that held a veil in place.

The front door opened before he had even knocked, and the French assistant, Susanne, stood at the threshold in a white satin gown, evidently carefully preened for the night's event. Her spiteful brown eyes questioned his audacity to be here, to even be alive.

"After all we've meant to each other, I don't even get a '*Bonsoir*. How are you?' You are a hasty and ungrateful lover. I am surprised you had the courage to come here," she said, her full red lips smiling.

Any lust he had ever felt for her was forever and terminally vanquished. She was a being of the living and the natural and the ordinary. His concern now was with the dead, the preternatural and the extraordinary. She had nothing to offer him and unbeknownst to her she had triggered this chain of events herself. Had she not tested him, had he not survived, he wouldn't have had the wherewithal or the strength to test himself. To him she was nothing, only a servant, Saveriano's assistant.

"Where is he?" he demanded. "I need to talk to him."

Annoyance was obvious in her eyes but the tight line of her smile did not waver as she feigned ignorance. "Where is who? And how, *Cherie*, is that any of my business even if I knew who you were talking about?"

No time for this. She'd had the chance to kill him in Eze and hadn't. A quick death was not the plan for him. Susanne was not a threat.

He pulled out his Colt Single Action Army .45 calibre revolver and barged past her into the opulent lobby, skating over the polished black and white marble, and made for the circular staircase beneath the ostentatious crystal chandelier. While she whirled to follow him with sardonic eyes, the white statues and columns inside the foyer's niches glared at his intrusion into their museum-like peace.

A cold change in the air stopped him mid-climb. He shivered involuntarily.

"*C'est froid*," Susanne said from the foyer, staring up, her expression smug. "She is watching you."

"Where is she?" Chancellor demanded.

Susanne raised her hands, palms up. "She is here and she is there. I believe she can be anywhere."

"Gimme a break," he muttered and started up the steps.

She stalked up behind him and placed a slender hand on his arm. He shrugged her off, conscious that her hands felt icy. He two-stepped the remainder of the marble staircase and made straight for Lalonde's room. The door was open, but the man wasn't there. He ignored the mess of dirt and leaves he was tracking onto the carpet, and manoeuvred farther into the room.

There was a large bed and armoire and two armchairs, and the wardrobe in the corner was partly opened, revealing some hanging clothes. The walls were hung with gaudy tapestries and religious oil paintings, and the window on the far side opened out onto a terrace overlooking the river, the sun glaring down on random boats. Chancellor turned back to the room. Nothing to tell him what Lalonde planned to do. The room had been cleaned up since that night he and Angeline had snuck in here and saw all of those shaman's paraphernalia.

He left the room and searched several others. All empty. Only the bathroom was left and it was vacant. Through the partially opened door he glimpsed travertine marble floors, a gleaming white porcelain tub with gold-clawed feet, and fuzzy wine-coloured bath sheets on gold towel racks. Chancellor closed the door quietly and walked down the hall until he found the master bedroom.

Pristine, white, and empty like the others. No indication of what she planned for tonight.

He slid his .45 Colt into his waistband and removed an infrasound detection meter from his pocket. It had located her once before, and now he raised it into the air, moving his hand in a figure eight. The device remained silent, and the cold he had felt earlier did not return. He should have used it earlier, but if Sophia wished to remain hidden, his efforts, then as now, were probably pointless.

"She is not here," Susanne said from behind him. "And I am certain that she would disapprove of your snooping in her room."

Chancellor turned to look at the assistant. He enjoyed sparring with her. She was flesh and blood, a mere woman, and he was reminded once more of the night they had spent together in her room downstairs. The surgeons had performed wonders on her; there was not a scar or a blemish left on her smooth, satiny skin.

"You hate him that much?" he asked, holding the ISD meter toward her. It remained silent.

She shrugged. "Who? Lalonde? He's nothing to me now."

He returned the device to his pocket and admired the smooth flat angles of her hair, black as a raven's wing. She was beautiful, but beauty had its own agenda. It always did. "Where will the marriage take place?"

"You think I'm going to tell you anything?"

He raised his gun to her face. "I could kill you."

"But you won't. If you were going to, you would have done so earlier." She paused. "Why did you follow me up to the roof of that church, Monsieur Chancellor? It was not like you to be such a fool." When her question went unanswered, she nodded. "I think I see. You wished to prove something to her didn't you? That you could survive? But you didn't prove that, did you? You had to be rescued by two women . . . . Did you really think she would come to you? Do you think you are *the* one?"

"I don't know what I think," Chancellor said, using his favourite ambiguous response. "I only know that *he* is not *the* one."

"And who is?"

He was silent, at first, and then he smiled at her. "You don't think he is either."

Her eyes rolled to the ceiling. "And what does it matter what I think?"

Enough time had been wasted sparring. What he needed now was her cooperation. The question was: would she cooperate? Or was she still set on taking him down?

*   *   *

Angeline swallowed as she returned the journalist her Blackberry, and a prickle crept over her scalp. Jake wasn't answering, but hopefully he would see the text and think twice before he acted. She captured Cristine's eye; they both had the same thought. Whatever was going down was going to happen tonight at the lecture and gala, and Jake would be there with Saveriano.

"We need dresses," Cristine said. "These things are formal."

She agreed. She would have to dress to the nines to get Jake's attention. He must have eyes only for her—if it wasn't too late.

They left the hotel and found a taxi to take them to the fashionable district of town.

Fortunately, this was not too far away. The driver dropped them off in front of a boutique and a stylish young shop woman smiled as they entered. Angeline tried to smile, but her lips stiffened. *Focus*, she thought. Focus on finding a dress.

She caressed the smooth lines and filmy fabrics, her thoughts askew. So worried was she about Jake and Chancellor that she was having difficulty concentrating. The hot sexy secretary look was in, elegant in predominantly pinks and silver. The fashion suited her body type with their fitted waists and fluid fabrics, but none were formal enough for her purposes.

"Nothing appropriate here," Cristine said.

They left the shop and wandered down the street, browsed several other stores. Cristine found a beautiful black gown, but none of the designers had created what Angeline was looking for, and she was not going to let the journalist choose a gown for her, even though the self-proclaimed narcissist was generous enough to compliment every single one she tried.

On the other side of the road, next to a trendy café, Angeline noticed a boutique selling Manolo Blahnik shoes. She crossed the street, ignoring Cristine's nagging whine about getting a dress before her own went out of fashion, and scanned the window display. The selection of shoes ranged in price from five hundred dollars to several thousand a pair. The scope of colours and styles was phenomenal, from bright green and hot pink to basic black and muted copper. They came in pumps, mules and slings. They were beaded, embroidered, laced, bejewelled, floral, eyelet and cutout. Each shoe was a work of art. Each shoe made the female foot easily the sexiest part of the body, and with those towering spiked heels, the most dangerous.

Inside the shop, a middle-aged gentleman approached them. "You need help?" he asked in a thick Italian accent.

"Yes, I'd like to try on that pearl-beaded shoe I saw in the window," Angeline said.

"An excellent choice. They are Signor Blahnik's latest creation. He calls them Scorpion."

"I can see why."

The gentleman clerk smiled and went to the back room, brought her the proper size and sat opposite her to help her with the fit. They were exquisite, beaded with copper pink pearls, slung high over the heel with the same delicate beadwork, the heels tapering to a blunt point.

"You could put an eye out with that," Cristine joked.

Angeline turned her ankle to look. The man adjusting her shoe moved his hand just as she shifted position and the sharp heel scraped his palm. Mortified, she rose. "Oh, I'm so sorry."

"It is nothing. An accident."

"Oh no, you're bleeding. I feel terrible."

"Don't worry yourself." The clerk rose and pulled a handkerchief out of his pocket and wrapped it around his hand.

"Is there something I can do? Do you need to see a doctor?"

"No, no. It is only a scratch."

It was more than a scratch, but he wouldn't need stitches. Cristine twitched her eyebrows as if to say: 'Now, you have to buy the shoes, and screw the price.' If she didn't she'd be known as the scorpion shopper.

* * *

242

The bustle of final preparations clattered around him as Jake waited for Sophia in the lobby of the Baths of Diocletian, the headquarters of The National Museum. He sought the theatre where the lecture would take place, but the signage hadn't yet been posted at the front doors. He was very early, unable to take Sophia's suggestion of a hot bath to calm his nerves, so instead he had taken a cab here. He wanted to see the statue of Asherah, the Black Goddess.

Like a lost tourist, Jake meandered through the museum. No one questioned him because he looked official in his rented black suit, white shirt and black tie. He peeked into what was formerly a *natatio* or *frigidarium*—a large open-air swimming pool which no longer held water, then into some meeting rooms, libraries, nymphiums, dressing rooms, concert rooms and gymnasiums. The place was a maze and except for the odd museum worker and wait staff, flitting in and out between rooms, the outer wings to the building seemed abandoned. He went through an exhibition of funerary materials that housed sarcophagi, statues and urns. The Masterpiece Rooms, now the Epigraphical Department, contained 10,000 inscriptions, and he was tempted to make a visit, but he knew he would not find what he needed in that part of the museum. He moved through the Michelangelo cloister, past a display on the protohistory of Rome, then into the Octagonal Hall, which stood at the southwest corner of the complex where he admired the Lyceum Apollo and the Aphrodite of Cyrene.

Clearly, they planned to hold the reception here. White-clothed tables were laden with silver servers and stemware. A bar at the far end held bottles of wine in tidy rows of red and white. The luscious smell of hors d'oeuvres ranged in the air, while black and white costumed wait staff hurried from one room to another, arms filled with trays.

Completely ignored, Jake wandered through a doorway, into an exhibition gallery with a single statue in the centre of the floor covered by a black tarp. No one was around, and the longer he was left alone, the more desperate his need to see the goddess.

When the last waiter disappeared behind the far door, he crept closer to the covered idol.

Not until you are ready. Not until you consent to the trial.

Sophia's voice echoed in his mind.

His heart throbbed; his hands tingled. One peek could not possibly hurt. But then her words came at him again. *If you look upon the face of the crone, you are bound.*

A consistent *thump thump thump* had started in his chest. His hands felt moist. His tongue stuck in the dryness of his mouth; he swallowed, squashed his nervousness, and glanced quickly at the door.

Sophia was not here, nor was anyone else. No one would know, no one could tell her. A step stool stood to one side of the statue, and Jake fingered the tarp uneasily. Then on impulse, he placed a foot on the second step and boosted himself up.

At first glance, the statue looked like an ordinary Venus figurine except that it was twelve feet tall with pendulous breasts, a swollen belly and bulging hips. But something about it sent prickles of ice up his spine. She was unlike anything he had ever seen before. On her head was a diadem holding a veil; in her hands were a torch and a lamp.

"Magnificent, is she not?"

Jake dropped the tarp at the sound of the voice and whirled, nearly toppling off the step stool.

"What are you doing here?" he demanded, correcting his footing and leaping down.

Susanne stood in the doorway, dressed in a white satin gown that set off her sleek black hair shining in the recessed lighting. "What am *I* doing here?" She snorted. "This gallery is off-limits until the unveiling." She smiled spontaneously. "But it is a little late now, isn't it?"

She looked incredibly beautiful, and that only made him dislike her more. There was something familiar about her confidence, and her air of belonging where he didn't that flustered him. And yet, why should she feel like that? She was a nobody, just Sophia's assistant. He had as much right to be here as she did. Sophia had promised him a private showing of the goddess. But still there was something disconcertingly unnerving about her attitude.

"The door was opened, so I just wandered in," he said lamely.

She moistened her red lips, tossed her shiny bob of black hair as if she knew exactly what her presence did to his body. *Shit*, he thought. *Who is this bitch?*

"This is a very unusual piece. I don't blame you for giving in to curiosity. Well, now that you've seen it, I guess it won't make any difference if you see the rest." She pushed the stool to the other side and beckoned him to follow. She hiked up her gown, which had a slit down the side, showing more leg then he wanted to see, and stepped to the top of the stool to raise the tarp, grinning as his jaw dropped.

"*Magnifique*, no?" she asked. "The Black Goddess, the triple goddess. The Nymph, the Mother, the Crone. I see you recognize the facade of the Mother, which represents fertility."

His eyes tore away from Susanne's shapely thighs and latched onto the statue like some sort of force involuntarily drew him to it. When he first saw the statue in the cave it was encrusted with dirt. Now he realized it constituted three images. On the other two sides were the Nymph and the Crone. The Nymph, hips draped in a skirtlike garment, was a more gracile version of the Mother minus the diadem and the torch.

The Crone was the most startling of the three. This facet of the goddess was ugly, withered and stooped. "The creator and destroyer of all life," Susanne said.

Why did his entire body suddenly feel like jelly? Why did Susanne's voice suddenly sound so familiar?

"She is at the heart of all creative process. She is also wisdom and death." She flipped the tarp wide so that he could see the Crone in all her awful splendour. "A woman who outlives her husband has used up his life force."

Susanne's smile was unnerving, her last comment profoundly unsettling. Jake found himself shuddering. Of the three images, the Crone was the true rendition of power.

A bird, a cup, a staff, a torch, a diadem and a lamp were the symbols on Vincent's missing text. Vincent had protected the text's meaning, but now Jake's mind reeled to the letter that Sophia kept in her library desk, the letter written in his very own hand and addressed to Vincent. He had spoken of a magnificent find, something that would turn the archaeological world on its head. This was the secret.

He traced the Black Goddess's triple forms with his eyes. She had something to do with the missing text. What did the symbols have to do with this statue? But somehow now, that issue wasn't uppermost in his thoughts.

Seeing the triple goddess had made up his mind.

Awed by its size, Jake circled the statue. He stopped in front of the Mother aspect of the goddess, eyes affixed to the diadem, the band that held the veil in place.

His cell phone suddenly chimed. A text. He thought he had shut the thing off, and went to do it now, but his eye caught the message before he could switch off the phone. It could only be from Angeline and it was made up of three letters: PNR

Susanne raised a hand as he clicked off the phone. "Help me get down from here."

Acting automatically, Jake seized the assistant's hand before he remembered his disgust with her. She stepped down from the stool and he dropped his grip at the very same instant that a wall of cold air struck him in the face.

CHAPTER THIRTY-THREE

Cold air. But it wasn't Sophia. Sophia often brought with her a wave of cold air. Jake hadn't ascertained what that was all about. People often brought the outdoors with them when they came in from outside, but Sophia seemed to do it whether it was cold outside or not. She was still somewhere inside the museum preparing for her lecture and he had been left to explore on his own.

The woman dressed in the long black gown standing in the doorway was the journalist, Cristine Kletter. He noted Susanne's nod in her direction and Cristine's mutual recognition. Apparently no introductions were necessary.

"This room is off-limits until the unveiling," Susanne said, this time pointedly at Cristine. Jake watched her sweep the canvas over the statue before ushering them away. "The lecture theatre is past the Octagonal Hall."

"I came to see Jake," the journalist said.

Susanne shrugged. "Fine. But not in here."

Her hand indicated the door and Jake led the journalist into the reception area. "What are *you* doing here? Where's Angeline?"

"So, you've decided you want to see her?"

Determined to reveal no emotion, he relaxed his facial muscles. "What are you doing here?" he repeated.

"I came to find you. And *without* Angeline. She's still at the hotel waiting for Chancellor. She pretty much arrived at the conclusion that Saveriano won't allow him near her, so she figures he has to return to dress for the event tonight."

"Where did he go?"

"I assumed, failing to find her, he came to see you. Did he find you?"

"Obviously not or I wouldn't have asked you where he was, now would I? What I want to know is: what are *you* doing here in Rome?"

"Keeping tabs on you. I am so excited for you, Jake! I've been here pretty much as long as Angeline and Chancellor. I know you're trying to avoid them, that's why I came here alone. Are you really going to go through with it?"

Cristine swished her gown like wearing anything so fancy was novel, but that was probably untrue since an ambitious, self-centred gal like Kletter would make sure she got invited to all the posh events of the season. That was why she was here.

A piece of jewellery circling her neck caught his eye. A pendant of some sort, it was carved from black stone and was fastened to a fake gold chain at the base of her throat. He raised it by his fingertips, sweeping her lightly freckled chest, and was surprised when she graciously lowered her mascaraed lashes to inspect it with him.

A Chaos star.

It had eight solid arrows radiating from a black-filled circle.

One of the sigils of Neo-shamanism.

Jake knew enough about Chaos magic, through an anthropological perspective, to mistrust its use among the layperson. It was a modern term and a modern practice with its roots in the 1970s. Though it denied any links to traditional forms of magic, it obviously borrowed from many societies and cultures. Its main concept was to bring the practitioner to a state of gnosis—an altered state of consciousness—in order to manipulate reality. The purpose of achieving gnosis was to force out negative thoughts and, through a single idea or direction experienced during the altered state, to instantly forget. In other words, to eradicate all doubt by bypassing the 'Psychic Censor'—the faculties of the mind adverse to the magical manipulation of reality.

Changing belief systems at will was at the center of Chaos magic and the whole purpose of the user was to accept an altered reality. None of this was new to Jake. Ever since he began to research traditional shamanism, he recognized that modern practices had adopted the methods of the aboriginal. Ritual involving the use of meditation, dance, music (especially drums), costumes and psychoactive drugs, all contributed to the gnostic state. The point of all the ritual was to have the practitioner believe in a different reality. The end result of this belief was that he or she would live in the alternate reality with great influence. Chaos practitioners also engaged in retrochronal magic—the changing of past events. This was a skill peculiar to Chaos magicians, requiring a deep understanding of the nature of memory and belief, and was the proposed mechanism through which all magic worked. It required the practitioner to replace their memory of how things used to be with a belief that things were in constant flux, that change would occur and that the resulting change was real.

The tenets of Chaos magic—this level of belief—were what Jake had strived for all along in his experiments with the shamanistic practices of the Haida. He had no idea that anyone other than Sophia saw the connection.

"It's dangerous to tinker with things that you don't understand," he said. "Since when did you start tampering with Chaos magic?"

Cristine's brows arced. "I don't tamper. I liked this necklace. I bought it from a street vendor after I saw a card that Chancellor had embossed with this symbol. But if you're so concerned, and clearly you are, then enlighten me. It's obvious this pendant means something to you. What does it mean? Why all the secrecy? Why are you hiding from Angeline? She's frantic about you, you know. And then of course, there's Chancellor. He's probably here by now."

Jake lowered his gaze as she turned to search for the Interpol agent. That was the last man he wanted to see. He sighed. The Black Goddess, Chaos magic, Vincent, himself . . . . What was any of this to her? A story? What kind of story? What did she think he was about to do?

He looked up to see her gorging on the expression on his face. He nudged her to a corner of the room where several glasses of red wine had been poured and set on a tray, pilfered a glass and swallowed some before he broke control and had to speak.

If she knew anything about what Sophia intended to happen tonight, it was apparent that she had no details. Yet her eyes continued to blaze with excitement and she couldn't or wouldn't stop babbling. She had news for him, she said. Important news.

And if he didn't know it yet, he had better know it now. Chancellor was crazy, or so Angeline insisted.

"He's about to trade his life for yours." That was his exact phrasing according to Angeline. She quickly outlined Chancellor's reasoning; how the man thought Sophia was some kind of goddess, the incarnation of Asherah! Was it true? When he stood spellbound and voiceless, she recounted the rest, careful to omit the word 'reincarnation' because Chancellor, apparently, did not concur with that specific doctrine. He believed in the continuity of life and that death was only a temporary, but still dynamic stage in the process. So what about Asherah, the Black Goddess? *Yehlh,* Yahweh, Mithras, etcetera, etcetera? Did Chancellor actually believe in gods and goddesses? Did Jake? Oh hell, why not? What was Christianity, Hinduism, Judaism, Buddhism, Islam, except the same thing. All-seeing, invisible God or stone idol—wasn't it the same thing? A religion that was quite impossible . . . unless someone took the step to prove it.

"Is that what you're about to do?" Her eyes rolled with excitement, leaving him flabbergasted. So, that was her story. Pulitzer screamed all over her face.

At one time it had been inconceivable to him that an intelligent, educated person could so completely adopt the belief in an existential death. But why not? He had. Susanne believed. And so, apparently, did Chancellor.

"All right," she said. "I didn't exactly tell you the truth. I *have* been dabbling in Neo-shamanism, thanks to you. I've experienced some awesome things. Jake, I think maybe Chancellor is on to something. I can't get close enough to Saveriano to interview her, that witch of an assistant of hers won't let me near. But you're tight with her, and from what Chancellor's told me she's offering you a once in a lifetime chance to find out what happens after you die! I know it all sounds crazy, but . . . I've been talking to Susanne too, and she's let some things slip. And besides, I've done some digging on both her and Chancellor; they're both into this Neo-shamanism thing deep. They just won't call it that. Susanne thinks she's some kind of modern witch and Chancellor, well, he's really just all about gadgets and spooks and stuff." She frowned for an instant as though some memory had crossed her mind. "Well, he might be more than that, I don't know. It may be that he's just hardier than the rest of us. But you . . . you're the only true shaman among the bunch. You are an hereditary shaman. It will only work if *you* do it."

He swallowed nervously. What was she saying? That she believed in Sophia's doctrines, that he should take the Death Cap, come what may?

How did she even know about that?

"I've known you a while now, Jake. I've seen you in operation. I know what you're searching for and I also know that Angeline is probably the only thing that's keeping you from it. You owe it to yourself to find out." She paused again, breathless. She had been talking almost nonstop since she arrived.

He swallowed the last of the wine and set the glass down, leaving a bright scarlet ring on the white tablecloth. "Let me get this straight. You believe that I am *Yehlh* the Raven, and that I am destined to join with the Black Goddess."

She nodded vigorously. "Don't you want to find out?"

Jake took a deep breath. "Where's Angeline?" he asked again. "What time is she planning to come?

"Soon, I think." She looked down at her silk purse as a chime went off inside it. "Hold on a sec. It's my cell."

CHAPTER THIRTY-FOUR

Angeline was standing by the window staring outside when she heard him walk in. She looked down. Could he tell that she was seething? From out of the corner of her eye, she saw him snap off his cell phone, drop it onto the nightstand and dig out hers—which looked identical except for the logo—setting them side-by-side. She swung around. He'd promised she'd get her cell back when he returned.

Still no explanation from him but at least now he noticed her. As a matter of fact his eyes were shifting from the designer shopping bags on the bed to her face.

That's right, I went shopping.

She grabbed her cell phone from the nightstand, and he went to the group of bags on the bed and pulled out a gown from the largest one, a stunning deep copper, with thin beaded straps. Looping horizontal threads of matching pearls formed the V-shaped neckline, which dropped to the navel, and swung seductively when the dress moved. It was stitched from fine chiffon netting, ensnared with strings of tiny beads and pearls, and interlaced in a tortoiseshell pattern of black satin and velvet. With two slits, one on either side, the gown was perfect for showcasing long shapely legs. If this didn't catch Jake's eye she didn't know what would.

"Very nice. Is this what you were planning to wear tonight?"

"And what's that to you?" She shook out the dress and laid it flat on the bed. "Shouldn't you be preening about now?"

He stared at her. "Look. I'm sorry I had to lock you in here. I couldn't have you following me, but it seems I shouldn't have bothered since you managed to find your way out."

Angeline held the creased card in his face that she had been fiddling with when he entered the room. The Chaos star embossed on it glared evilly. "What does this mean?" she demanded.

He went to take it, but she jerked away her hand. "What kind of hocus-pocus are you into, Tom?"

"I have to get dressed," he said wearily. "Are you just going to stand there and watch me?"

"I want to know where you went after you trapped me in here."

At the closet, he started digging out a black formal suit, white shirt and silver tie. "I want you to go home, Angeline."

"We've been over that. I thought it was clear. I'm not going anywhere without Jake."

A hard look descended over his features. "I've changed my mind. I want you out of here. Tonight."

She planted her feet firmly on the floor. "Why?"

"You don't understand, Angeline. You have no idea what's going to happen tonight."

She sucked in her lower lip, let her tongue linger over it a while. Her breathing was erratic but she masked it as well as she could. "I think I understand more than you know."

"Then leave. Let me do my job."

"Not until I know exactly what your job is. Sophia wants to marry Jake, isn't that right? I deciphered the text, but I guess I don't have to tell you that. You know what that cypher says, you've known it all along. That's why you wanted to find Jake, that's why you didn't arrest him. You deliberately let him escape to Italy so that you could follow him, so that I would follow him and lead you straight to him, which would lead you to Sophia." She stopped for a breath. "Well? Am I right?"

When Chancellor didn't answer, Angeline lit into him. "What kind of marriage ceremony is this?"

Silence. She was starting to get really pissed off. And the anger was diluting the fear. It all made sense now. The inconsistencies. The lies. Sometimes he seemed to know too much about the Mithraic Mysteries, Saveriano's work, and even Vincent's, and other times he pretended to know nothing. Everything had become twisted now and he was starting to lose the threads of his own lies.

She grabbed the ECS box that held the parchment and carefully withdrew it. The papyrus on which the cypher was written was going to suffer, but Jake's life was worth more to her than a piece of ancient paper. She slowly unrolled it to Chancellor's unbelieving eyes and traced the only line that mattered to her. *Aide Nymphus.*

The female deity was critical to the Mithraic Mysteries. A bird, a cup, a staff, a torch, a diadem and a lamp. The bird, the cup and the staff belonged to the raven. To Saveriano Jake was the Raven. The torch, the diadem and the lamp belonged to the Nymphus. In the new ideology, the Black Goddess fulfilled that role. And the juxtaposition of the symbols for the Nymphus (bride) with the icons of the Raven meant only one thing. *Aide Nymphus.* Sing Nymphus. Sing the *marriage* hymn.

"Vincent was one of the initiates. That's why he was murdered."

"I wouldn't exactly call it a murder," Chancellor said.

"Then what would you call it? A ritual killing? It's the same thing to me and it will be the same thing to any law enforcement agency in the world."

"I told you, you didn't understand."

"Then enlighten me."

"These men were not forced to do anything. And *She* did not kill them."

Angeline wanted to grab her hair and yank it out of her head. Or at the very least, grab his and shake some measure of sanity back into his handsome face. "Tom." Her voice was quiet, as though speaking to a child. It reminded her of the way she'd heard Saveriano talk to Jake. "These young men didn't die by their own hands."

Deep, reverberating silence. She could hear herself swallow and her own heartbeats, a soft *boom, boom* against her ribs. "What are you saying?" she demanded, voice reaching a deadly pitch.

The truth was, he had said nothing, but it was the way his silence ricocheted in her head that triggered the insight to her brain.

Ritual suicide?

"Think what you like, Angeline," Chancellor said. "I don't have time for this. I want you to go home. In fact, I've got a taxi coming in fifteen minutes to take you to the airport."

"I am not going to the airport, Tom. And you can't make me. You'll have to shoot me first." Her eye glanced around for his gun.

He sighed. "Fine. Get dressed." He went to the bed and threw her the gown. "Change in there." He kicked wide the door of the bathroom with his heel. "I'll dress out here."

She took the gown and the bag containing her new Manolo Blahniks and disappeared behind the closed door. Was he planning to trap her in the bathroom? No. He'd already tried locking her inside the room earlier and if he was going to stop her from going to the lecture, he'd have to do something more drastic. She hung the dress on the hook behind the door and set the shoes on the floor, then pulled out her assemblage of makeup and arranged it on the vanity.

The next ritual would be the last and it had nothing to do with the Pater.

The next ritual would be a wedding.

Angeline was not taking any chances. She was going to the lecture and she wasn't leaving until she had Jake in tow. Chancellor could do whatever the hell he wanted. Jake was not marrying Sophia.

Time was everything now. She had to hurry. A quick nap after her shopping trip had left her hair tangled like a rat's nest. She brushed it out, then sprayed, teased and combed her ponytail into a loose coil and pinned it above her nape. With a Kleenex, she eradicated a smudge under her left eye and applied fresh mascara, shadow and blush. She really should have skipped that nap. As a kid reluctant to rise for school, her nanny used to shout at her: *Wake up, Angeline. Plenty of time for sleeping when you're dead.*

Now it looked like she was faced with looking death straight in the eye. Not for an iota did she trust Chancellor. It was unlike him to give in so easily.

"Better get a move on," he shouted through the door. "I'm leaving in five minutes if you want a ride."

Where was his gun? In his belt? She hadn't seen it anywhere in the room. She zipped up the gown and slid the stilettoes on her feet, her first pair of Manolo Blahniks and she was wearing them to a murder.

"Angeline?"

Her last thought was *murder*. Just who did she think was going to be murdered? Not Jake if she could help it. And not Chancellor either. He might be a twit on occasion and even a jerk, but his intentions were decent. He only wanted her out of the way because he wanted her safe. He had a slight crush on her, wasn't that it? But now, another nagging feeling trembled on the edge of her nerves. Who was he talking to just before he entered the room? She'd heard his voice in the hallway, presumably talking on the phone. The words were mostly mumbled but she'd distinctly heard him say that he wanted to make a deal, a truce. A deal with whom? About what? What kind of truce? His last words were: *We have to keep her out of the way. Can you do that?*

She had the distinct impression that he was speaking to a woman.

He banged at the door.

"I'm coming."

She stepped out of the bathroom and saw his eyes brighten with pleasure. But just for a second. No way was he going to display an inch of weakness.

Her phone chimed and she looked down as she untangled it from the array of cosmetics in her beaded purse. *Please be Jake.* The handset felt odd. As she raised it to her face, she realized it wasn't her phone. A text bled across the screen:

ALRIGHT. I'LL TAKE CARE OF ANGELINE.

Chancellor recognized the mix-up a second after she did and his hand went for the phone. She bolted for the door, yanked it open and lunged down the corridor—smack into Susanne.

She turned to run back the other way, but Chancellor was waiting for her, fondling his revolver, so she made to dodge Susanne instead, but the Manolos hindered her reflexes. Her hands shot out, a foot tripped her, felling her flat on her face.

"*Alors*, If only Jake could see you now. Get up."

Her dress wasn't torn, only her dignity, and she stumbled into the room while Chancellor held the door for her, a look of mixed apology and defeat on his features.

No, this couldn't be. Chancellor wasn't the enemy . . . he couldn't possibly be mixed up with the she-witch. Susanne pulled something out of her silk purse and as Angeline turned to see what it was, a needle jabbed her arm.

* * *

Groggy. Achy. Mouth dry, sticky. Eyes bleary. Her first thought was that she had died and gone to hell. She was supposed to be at the lecture at the National Museum. Then a smidgen of relief reached her as she realized she was still in Rome and not in the trunk of a car on the way to the airport. No time to celebrate yet. She was still in the hotel room, but Chancellor and Susanne were gone. What time was it? Thank God, she hadn't missed the lecture or the reception. The lecture was at eight; the unveiling was due to happen at nine o'clock. It was 7:46 P.M. She could make it if she hurried. She grabbed a taxi outside the hotel and asked to be taken to the Baths of Diocletian, the headquarters of the National Museum of Rome.

When she arrived everyone was already inside, no activity was happening on the grounds. She paid the fare and manoeuvred herself from the cab to the doors of the museum, stepped inside, and noticed that the lobby was empty. She walked through the corridors to where she knew the Octagonal Hall was located, following the signage and the roar of voices. But before she could search for Jake, the scent of tobacco invaded her senses and a French-accented voice taunted from behind her. "Would you care to experience a full dose of the happy juice? If not, do what I say. Do not turn around. Go into that vacant hallway."

She couldn't take any chances, could not risk being drugged again. A cigarette landed on the marble floor next to her foot, its glowing orange ash vanquished as a black stilettoed sandal followed.

"Where are you taking me?"

A flashlight lit a stone stairwell and she was poked forward. "Somewhere to keep you out of sight until Sophia has what she wants."

"She will never have Jake. He won't marry her."

The voice laughed. "You'd be surprised what a man will do for the promise of immortality."

A hollow dripping sound echoed through the aqueducts, somewhere over their heads as she was pushed roughly down the smooth, worn steps. They were in a catacomb and all of the lights were out, except for a single dull lightbulb dangling from the ceiling. Did her kidnapper really have another drug-filled hypodermic in her pocket as promised?

"I am going to make sure that you miss the party my sweet Angeline. Chancellor wouldn't allow me to give you the full dose earlier. He yanked the needle out of your arm before the hypo emptied, otherwise you'd still be in dreamland."

Her stomach went cold, and as Susanne grabbed her arm, she dodged the needle, but not fast enough. The point shot home.

Angeline darted into the next lightless tunnel, and ducked inside a crevice in the wall to her left, expecting any minute to keel over. Caught off guard by her escape, Susanne shouted, "In a few minutes *Cherie* you will not feel much like running."

The needle had struck her handbag, sinking into the soft quilted fabric of her beaded purse, missing her flesh.

Susanne dashed past her hiding place, yelling at the top of her lungs and the smell of fragrant tobacco passed with her.

"You might as well come back! You won't be running for much longer!"

Footsteps pounded down the tunnel, then quietly returned. The flashlight swung, a curse sounded as metal bumped against rock and hit the ground. A band of light spun at Angeline's feet, flickered and went out, then fumbling sounds ranged close as the search for the fallen flashlight commenced. A hand groped toward Angeline's crevice, the faint scent of tobacco grew stronger and the raw light from the top of the stairs sent a diaphanous orange rainbow.

A whisper of movement brushed Angeline's ankle, her breath caught, tension strangling her throat like she'd swallowed a rock. The shadow rose, swept past, and paused just before turning toward the stairs. There was no escape that way. She had to find another tunnel, another exit, or wait until her pursuer gave up.

Harsh, laboured breathing. The lightbulb swinging frantically from bare wires across the walls and floor of the passage, trying to illuminate the tunnel. Soon, the crazy woman would be after her and if the light struck this crevice, her position would be exposed. She shrank against the wall; almost fell backwards when she realized part of the wall was missing. Her foot moved to adjust her balance, and a tiny metallic *clink* stopped her heart. *The flashlight!*

A draft blew in from somewhere and the light from the bulb began moving again as footsteps approached. On her haunches now, she flailed her hands on the floor, touched cold metal and rose. She had the flashlight. She realized, too, that where she stood wasn't a mere crevice. It was the entrance to another tunnel—hopefully, one of which Susanne was unaware. Her hands felt the edge of the dirt walls as she inched her way back, and her body easily slipped into a small opening, partly filled with dirt. A landslide had collapsed a section of the wall.

Crawling on all fours, she felt her way with one hand into the abyss.

The archaeologists had not been here. The floor was uneven and the walls partially buried, loose earth and rubble everywhere. She could barely walk in her stiletto heels, so she took off the shoes and carried them, letting her beautiful beaded chiffon gown drag in the dirt.

"What is that game your American children like to play?" The voice came to her in a distant taunt. "Ring around the rosy, a pocket full of posies . . . ."

I am not American, she swore under her breath. The irritating French-accented sing-songy voice trailed down the passage. The madwoman had found her tunnel. Time to move, fast.

"Angelica, my sweet Angelica. Come out. Soon you will not be able to crawl out on your own."

The nickname haunted her. Susanne was Celeste. She was reverting to her former ego.

Angeline ran, climbing over mounds of fallen earth, but she wasn't making much progress. This tunnel had to lead to somewhere. *Please, it didn't just end in a wall of dirt.*

"Husha, husha, we all fall *down* . . . ."

She flashed on the light for a second, had to see where she was, had to find another tunnel, a clearer one to make her getaway. There it was—to her right. She snapped off the light, scrambled over another mountain of dirt, hiking her gown up to her hips to give her the necessary stride. Susanne was gaining on her, moving swiftly and dexterously because she knew these tunnels inside out and backward, while Angeline was as blind as a cave mouse.

She slowed, grappled the stones and earth wall until her hand shot into a gap. A swift backward reconnoitre revealed nothing but blackness. She plunged through the gap, feeling solid ground on her feet, but no walls. It was like tar in here, and except for the white stars she saw behind her tight lids, there was nothing even remotely resembling light.

A thud sounded and a curse as Susanne tripped.

* * *

The Octagonal Hall was suffocating, the air thick with the mingled odours of food, alcohol, perfume and sweat. The noise level of the chattering guests had risen to a steady roar. Glasses tinkled.

No one was supposed to have drinks until after the lecture, but the delay was causing restlessness, and restlessness fed impatience. The wait staff was ordered to open several more bottles of wine.

Jake held a glass in his hand and sipped slowly. The contrast of Sophia's red velvet gown against the white cloth-covered tables was stunning. The black and white uniformed wait staff circling her as they went about serving guests gave the vignette a surreal aspect. Red, black and white—sharp, primary colours, the colours of Chaos. Sophia slipped past the director, searching for her assistant. Tonight, she looked radiant and shockingly young. It was as though she were a different person.

He could make out Chancellor and Cristine engaged in separate conversations with various experts from the archaeological community. He frowned, recalling his earlier conversation with the journalist. As Chancellor turned, Jake stepped behind a pillar. Instinct had made him do that. Why? He felt his heartrate inch up ever so slightly. Obviously, if the Interpol agent intended to arrest him for killing Vincent, he would have done it by now. He had no intention of arresting him for murder. Instead, his eyes were on Sophia. Jake's pulse began to beat a little faster. He had counted on the Interpol agent to protect Angeline. But after what Cristine had divulged . . . . Adrenalin shot to his heart.

Where *was* Angeline? He dug into his jacket pocket for his cell phone and punched in the number to hers.

No answer. He flipped the phone closed.

"So where is she?" a man asked, stepping up to him.

He slipped the phone into his jacket pocket and glanced around. "Where is who?"

Marco Delvecchio was a reporter from the Italian press. He was known to be a headline chaser and a sensationalist when it came to reporting on events. "The Black Goddess of course. Where are they hiding her? What are they waiting for? I am anxious to see the star attraction."

A blur of red flew into Jake's peripheral vision. A few seconds later Sophia approached from his right, smiling. "Marco," she said, extending a hand and kissing him on each cheek. "I'm so happy you have come."

Delvecchio obliged her with the custom, lingering a little longer on her left cheek. When he raised his head, his eyes were mocking. "Where is this mysterious statue, Sophia? You're known for having tricks up your sleeve, but this is pushing it. Is this some kind of publicity stunt? Does the triple goddess really exist?"

Jake knew that Sophia was thoroughly frustrated, explaining to people that she was waiting on her assistant who had her lecture notes and PowerPoint presentation, and while most of the guests were sympathetic, some, especially the older academics, were sceptical. The reporter however was merely teasing. He and Sophia had a long history. She returned his teasing smile and said, "Any minute now. Go into the lecture theatre and sit down."

CHAPTER THIRTY-FIVE

It was too quiet. Angeline stumbled in the dark, down a narrow shaft, grappling the wall of the catacomb. Oh God, she thought. *Someone, please come and save me.* But no one knew she was here, and to top it off she didn't even have her cell phone.

The footsteps had stopped. She switched the flashlight on to get her bearings, clutched her breath, panicky, totally disoriented, and twitched the light around the tunnel. A labyrinth. Just like the Greek Labyrinth built to house the Minotaur. Had the beast ever escaped? It didn't matter. This was Rome and there was no Minotaur, only a phantom archaeologist and a vicious crazy from her past.

Nothing looked familiar; all of the passageways looked exactly alike. How would she find the entrance? She had never been inside this catacomb before, and although she had read up on them, taken some courses, and knew that the largest of them could cover fifteen hectares and have galleries spread through multiple levels, some were twenty kilometers long, containing half a million tombs. *God help me if this catacomb is one of those.*

She slipped on her shoes. Dammit if they weren't ruined. The floor was level here. She plunged deeper into the tunnels. She backtracked, once, attempting to retrace her steps to find the stone staircase where she had been forced to enter, and now she was more lost than ever.

The passage narrowed until it opened out to a vaulted chamber where the cool smell of clay and stone greeted her. After the oppressiveness of the tunnels, this was an oasis of space and air. Her light hit the ground, rolled over mounds of excavated dirt, struck a solitary bucket and a trowel lying beside it. She stepped over and knelt, scrutinizing the contents of the bucket which was half filled with dirt, then raised her eyes and followed the ray of light up the walls to a series of vertical loculi.

Her light nicked a coil of rope on the ground. Thank heaven for the archaeologists. That rope might come in handy. She left the cavern with the emptied bucket and rope looped over her shoulder.

* * *

"Susanne, where have you been?" Sophia scolded.

Susanne apologized vociferously and produced the lecture notes and PowerPoint on Sophia's laptop. "I'll have everything set up straight away. I am so sorry, but there was a last minute detail to attend to." She hoped her voice sounded as sincere as her feelings, and that her gown and shoes exhibited minimal damage from their foray into the tunnels.

"When you have done that," Sophia said. "I want you to report to the kitchen. The staff is shorthanded. We will need you to serve."

Susanne stared at her in utter disbelief.

"Are you questioning me?"

She shook her head, immediately went to the lecture hall and presented the materials to the media technician who was waiting to set up. It was all Chancellor's fault. If he'd let her drug the ice princess fully, dear sweet Angelica would be sound asleep in his hotel bed. Well maybe this was better. She'd much prefer to hunt Angeline a little longer. And now—she glared at the skimpy uniform that the caterer had handed to her—she had even more reason to torture her.

She stopped at the makeshift dressing room that was set up for the wait staff. What the hell was this? A short black dress and white apron. Were they insane? This wasn't some Playboy event at the Hugh Heffner estate. All she needed now were bunny ears and a pompom tail.

Susanne stripped out of her satin gown and donned the stupid uniform. This dress was meant for someone much shorter than her and rose well above her knees. She knew she looked ridiculous and it was just as well that there was no mirror in here. Otherwise, she would have had a fit. So, Sophia did not want her at the lecture? Fine. She walked out of the kitchen, arms laden with cold finger foods and set down the tray.

* * *

Another breath of wind stole down the passage ahead of her. There was fresh air coming in from somewhere. If only someone could hear her shouts.

Something felt familiar about this passage, and Angeline resumed her trek. She was close to a crypt, could tell by the way the air pressure seemed to release, not so close and suffocating. As she approached, her heart beat faster, and she walked into the crypt, smelling the fresh air. How did they decide which caverns and passageways to light? She raised the flashlight and passed it over the walls. And yet there *was* light. She smiled grimly, had no idea where she was. It was obvious that she was no longer beneath the museum buildings because over her head was a huge hole with moonlight filtering below.

The earth flaked around the edge of the floor and Angeline glanced down. At her feet the moon haloed a familiar engraving. A Chaos star.

* * *

In the public passage, Susanne shone the penlight she'd pilfered from the museum onto the ground. So much for being a serving wench. Sophia wouldn't miss her. She needed half an hour tops to make sure that Angeline was incapacitated, and then she would return to her duties. Hell, if events went according to plan, Sophia intended to be engaged elsewhere anyway.

Nothing must go wrong. She had already botched up once, and she must not fail the goddess again.

What had happened to that little bitch? She must have collapsed around here somewhere. How far could she get with so much dope in her? Even so, no telling how far Angeline had run before the drug had taken effect. Susanne did not trust her. She was too smart, and if she saw the sigils on the floor, she might guess what they meant.

* * *

From a dark tunnel, Angeline watched Susanne, the doused flashlight raised like a weapon. Who was she kidding? She could no longer buy into the pretense. That French cream puff was Celeste; even her voice when she forgot to pour on the thick accent betrayed her.

The penlight ejected a thin ray of light like a laser, slicing the walls, and disappeared down a dark shaft. The wait was agonizing but it looked like Susanne had abandoned the hunt.

Angeline glanced nervously around, knowing that any moment the crazy bitch could change her mind. Her only chance was to locate the stairwell she'd come in from, but where was it? She stepped out of the black recess and backed her way into the crypt, raised her head, seeking the circular ventilation hole pouring moonlight onto the Chaos star. The sight of it startled her again, sent her heart racing. Why did Chancellor have a card with that same symbol printed on it? What did it mean? She clasped her cold hands together and focused her thoughts. First things first. She had to get out of here.

Could she use the bucket and rope to get out through the ceiling? She lowered the equipment to the ground, switched off the flashlight, and looked up at what appeared to be a ten-meter climb to the surface.

Overturning the bucket, she stepped up, hefting the coil of rope with her. Was there something up there she could snag the rope to? She tottered on her stilettoes, almost fell then regained her balance, draped the rope over her shoulder, hitching up her gown to her hips, and stretched. The bucket began to wobble. She grabbed at the wall, leaned forward to try to balance her weight. Then toppled and landed on her rear in the dust.

"So, I missed with the injection," a voice mocked from above her. "You are not even a tiny bit dizzy." Susanne stooped and plucked at the beaded evening bag that was slung across Angeline's chest, hanging open at her hip, contents spilling onto the floor, gleaming wet. In her intense concentration to get out of this place, she missed hearing the enemy tiptoe down the tunnel.

Susanne stuck out a finger, tasted the moisture on Angeline's compact, before spitting it out. Angeline tried to rise, but her gown encumbered her. She hiked it up to get to her feet and bolted toward a passage, Susanne after her. The damned stiletto heels made escape impossible, and if she hadn't been dunked, she would have tripped anyway. Susanne butted her head into Angeline's spine, hooked an arm around her waist and dragged her down into her lap. They made a comical pair. Two grown women in a catfight.

"Get up. Slowly. If you try to escape, I will shoot you."

Angeline struggled to her feet. Susanne wasn't kidding. She was standing now, holding a revolver.

"I despise you, Angelica. Do you know why?"

"I have an idea."

The gun backhanded her face. She ducked instinctively, the attempt missed, and her hand went to her lips.

"That is for being a smartass." The gun motioned in the direction of a black shaft. "Pick up your things and put them back into your purse. We mustn't leave any evidence."

Evidence? Evidence of what? Now Angeline's heart really sped into overdrive. Was Celeste so twisted that she really believed she was this Frenchwoman, Susanne? Would she actually pull that trigger? As the memory of Celeste in Tonga, with the axe in her hand, reared its ugly head, she no longer had any doubt.

"Pick up that flashlight you dropped on the ground. Switch it on and walk down that passage. I'll be right behind you."

They walked in silence, the revolver poking her in the spine, indicating she turn left into a passage leading to a crypt before the beam swung erratically and Angeline turned to face her persecutor.

Susanne stared her straight in the eye. "You cannot stop the ceremony. I won't let you."

Susanne went to a large plastic box that stood in the middle of the crypt. The lid was off and inside was a large camera case that she hoisted and placed on the floor. One eye on Angeline, gun still firmly targeting her, she withdrew a key that she wore on a chain around her neck and unlocked the case to reveal a digital camera, a digital video camcorder—standard archaeological equipment—then a handful of prints which she carefully laid in a single line on the ground. Angeline glanced down but resisted moving to examine the photos more closely.

The gun pointed to them, pictures of dead men, all dressed in Raven costumes like Jake's. To her horror, she recognized one of the faces.

Vincent's.

"Celeste, I know who you are. Do you realize what Saveriano did to these men? They're all dead."

Celeste's eyes widened at her name, then she shrugged. "Don't call me that. I am Susanne."

* * *

"The Black Goddess is at the heart of all creative processes," Saveriano said. She aimed her laser pointer at the image on the large screen facing the audience, drawing all eyes from the dazzling, red velvet gown that she wore.

"As women we are confronted throughout our lives with unavoidable body messages regarding the uniqueness of our form and the inevitable changes that characterize aging and the passage of time. Although aging presents difficult challenges for both men and women, women face some specific difficulties because of their gender. In traditional narratives, the end of biological fertility has relegated females to the status of 'old women' who are viewed as poor, powerless and pitiful in a sexist, youth-oriented culture. The Black Goddess is intrinsic to the psyche of girls and women because she reveals to us how the illusion of form can hide wonderful qualities."

Chancellor let his eyes skim over the audience. He was seated near the back of the large semi-elliptical lecture theatre with its worn red leather seats, where he could get a bird's eye view of the presentation. He spotted Cristine at the front, near the podium, mixed in with other guests from the press. Lalonde was also in the front rows, eyes peeled to the speaker. As long as he had him in sight, he needn't worry. There were four exits: two at the front and two at the rear. The seats were graduated, sloping down toward the dais and podium. The theatre was newish compared to the rest of the museum buildings, an extension built in the 1970s.

He settled back to listen. She was speaking on female symbolism, on how conscious femininity was a cyclical process involving an awakened awareness of the triple form of the Goddess—Mother, Virgin and Crone—and how she existed simultaneously and continuously in the human psyche, each taking ascendancy at different stages of the life cycle. These archetypal patterns were considered intra-psychic modes of consciousness. But a centuries-long indoctrination had limited the imagination, encouraging a negative perception of the ancient feminine. Her image was one of decay, loss of beauty, fertility, and usefulness, and eventually death. The fear of nonexistence or the unconscious made the Crone one of the most frightening images of evil. Hence, natural death was to be feared, hidden away, certainly not recognized as part of the natural cycle of life. Death was a monster to be feared. It was this concept that the Mithraic cult adopted, to vanquish fear from its initiates. The denial that women were engaged in the mysteries was a lie. The soldiers hid the fact, by not recording it, because images of women often preceded death. In order to control the fear, the monster was tamed by its capture and subjugation, its entrapment in the form of solid stone.

The talk ended with a picture of the enshrouded statue, yet to be unveiled.

Lalonde was on the edge of his seat, muscles tense, alert, as he absorbed her final words. Cristine, too, was fixated on the eloquent speaker, enslaved by mindless ambition.

Suddenly, an exchange of glances crossed between Sophia and Lalonde.

Chancellor clapped as the audience lauded her with fierce applause. He rose as they elevated themselves in a single wave, determined to keep her in sight. She descended the dais, the red velvet of her gown luffing, and went to meet her admirers. Why red? Did it have some symbolism he didn't foresee? And how did she plan to perform the ritual, tonight of all nights?

Bravo, Sophia, he thought. She had not disappointed. Neither had she revealed the entire truth. Perhaps that was to come with the unveiling.

It looked like she was going to be a while, answering questions. He went to the exit, stepped out into the hallway, and watched the audience fracture into small groups as they made their way in excited conversation to the Octagonal Hall. Servers dressed in black and white passed out drinks. Chancellor accepted a glass of red wine and joined the crowd that was gathering around the tarped statue. The Black Goddess had been moved to the center of the room, all other statuary removed.

Cristine ran up to him and grabbed his arm. "When is it going to happen?"

"I don't know. Did you happen to see where the assistant, Susanne, went to?"

"I saw her earlier, dressed like one of the caterers. I guess she really is Saveriano's Girl Friday."

Not likely, he thought.

"Actually, I saw her leave the hall. Maybe she went outside for a smoke. She smokes, you know."

He nodded and took his leave, went to the front doors and poked his head outside but didn't see anyone except a couple of men dressed in formal wear enjoying cigars. In the distance, a dog howled.

Someone was about to die.

He ducked inside to join the reception where the statue would be unveiled. The press were crowded as close to the sculpture as they were allowed to be. Cristine joined him on the periphery. Several officials began fidgeting and the director, whom Chancellor had seen earlier fussing with arrangements, was starting to look worried.

"Something's wrong," Cristine said.

"Where is she?"

"I don't know. She was still inside the lecture hall last time I saw her."

The director kept looking at his watch. Another man, a curator, Chancellor thought, approached and spoke rapidly and angrily to him. They sent one of the female servers to the restrooms to search for Saveriano. As Chancellor waited outside the washroom doors, he noticed the server exit alone; so clearly, the elusive professor was not in there.

He re-joined the reception and saw that the man whom he had assumed was one of the museum's curators was testing a microphone. The director apologized for the delay. Fifty-five minutes had passed and she was nowhere in sight.

"I am Professor Leo Nunzo," the man said, introducing himself. "It seems that Dr. Saveriano is indisposed, so I will be unveiling the statue myself."

He gave a few more words praising the remarkable discovery, before signalling to two uniformed men to raise the tarp.

The entire room gasped. The statue was missing. In its place was a solid, uncarved block of stone.

CHAPTER THIRTY-SIX

The tunnel was deserted, silent except for water dripping in the aqueducts. Jake dragged his half-reluctant body, fighting his indecision while at the same time drawn by a curiosity and wonder unlike anything he had experienced in his entire academic career. The stone steps tumbled down, broken in places, coiling beneath the museum. A powerful sense of familiarity sent shockwaves up his spine. Whatever this power was that she had over him, it was strong. Like he had no will. Like he was already consumed by her being and as though it remained only for his body to be interred after his mind was freed. The vibrations of his breathing told him he still had a choice, so why was he following her?

The damp, claylike smell of the tunnels sharpened his senses. Agitated, he shoved his hand into the pocket of his formal trousers, and his finger was pricked by something sharp. He lifted it out and stared at Angeline's ring. When had he placed it there?

Sophia took him by the hand, murmuring reassurances. Relax; it won't be long now. While the guests engaged in their revelry upstairs, the ritual would take place below them.

The shaft ended in the cavernous chamber of the temple. She stepped inside while he followed. The familiar cavelike ceiling with the painted frescoes on the walls met his upturned eyes, and overhead, the torchbearers, the celestial twins of light and darkness flanked Mithras in a blanket of stars.

Sophia spread her arms toward the Pater.

Jake opened his mouth to speak, but no sound came out. It was like he was spellbound, bewitched by her presence, by the entirety of this shrine. She wanted him to supersede the role of the Father, the highest of the ranks in the Mithraic cult, the deputy on earth and become the god himself.

"I want you to change out of that suit," Sophia said, and now her voice sounded horrible, taunting, and the ring of it cracked the silence making him break out in a sweat.

She pointed to the fresco where the Pater was surrounded by his symbols: the sickle of Saturn, the Phrygian cap of Mithras and the staff and ring.

"I think you're the *One*, Jake."

He raised the flashlight that he was holding into her face. For a second nothing came out as he tried to speak, then his voice returned with a slight croak. "I haven't made up my mind, Sophia. I told you I'd come down here with you, but I didn't agree to participate."

"Shush," she said, her voice echoing. "You are still afraid. You must believe, Jake."

He closed his eyes, gulped, and exhaled. He had refused any drink she had offered him upstairs, and yet his breathing was wretched and his head spun. Neither could she have spiked his drink earlier, for she didn't know he was there. Opening his eyes, he saw a shimmer of mist where Sophia should have been. A shiver chased up his spine inducing panic, then a strange sensation overwhelmed him. He *really* did not believe.

She came back into focus and frowned. "You refuse me?"

"You said yourself that if I don't believe, it won't work."

"And so you must. Change into this." She passed him a stack of folded clothing, which served as a pillow for a hooked sickle with a fiercely sharp-looking blade; a strange cap; a long, thin staff and a jewelled ring. "You are at the last stage of the initiation, having skipped all others. From here you will begin the final journey, and you will either be or not be."

The wooziness in Jake's head was muddling his thoughts. All he could think of was Shakespeare's famous line: To be or not to be.

It repeated over and over in his head like a chant. He nodded at Sophia, hugged the bundle she had handed to him and proceeded to change into the billowing robe and adorn it with the paraphernalia.

She removed a flask that she had hidden behind the altar and poured a foul-smelling liquid into a stone bowl. He recognized the bowl; it was the gold-flecked cobble that he had denied absconding from the past.

A warning voice in his head now replaced Shakespeare's litany.

PNR. PNR. PNR.

Point of No Return.

Before his brain could register the motions of his hands and his lips, the bowl was at his mouth and a bitter taste nipped at his tongue. He forced every bit of will into preventing the reflex of swallowing, even to the extent of shouting *no, no, no, no, no.* But no sound came out; liquid went in and a sinking feeling engulfed him.

Death Cap.

Jake recognized the taste, the smell. The fear.

The clatter of metal hitting the floor resounded throughout the shrine as the sickle left his hand. It was followed by the thud of the wooden staff and a shout of, "Be careful!"

The words of warning weren't his, the voice unfamiliar. But that didn't matter. The sickle had missed his foot and even had it struck it, he doubted that he would have felt its cut. His mind was locked, trapped, vividly reacting to the potion, and because he wanted to believe, he had downed every drop.

He opened his eyes to an aura, a scintillating stream waxing out of the temple's shadows and wallowed in the rainbow mist that enveloped him. His mind was numb, the taste of her poison and the odour of mould tingling all of his senses. There was no turning back. He must follow her to the sleep of death if he wanted to know. But he *didn't* want to know. He did *not* want to know! He wanted to wake up, reverse his actions, *change the past!*

He gazed up at the goddess, her rock-solid form miming a virgin, a womb and the secret of the everlasting.

The shimmering stream circled his throat and he opened his mouth to protest, hands blocking it from consuming him. Hallucinating, his eyes made familiar symbols with the strange splashes of light his retinas were receiving. A bird, a cup, a staff, a torch, a diadem and a lamp. Compelled by a force not his own, his mouth opened wider, his expression convulsed with terror, and his objections rang in silence.

Heart hammering against his chest, sweat flowing down his neck and spine, the aura swarmed around him. His vision dimmed, hearing gone. Arms numb, tongue thick, legs stiff as frozen meat. Only one thought remained clear, a magnetic link to his former life—*I love Angeline*. Nausea buffeted in his gut and an incredible pain burst in his ribcage.

This was shock.

Horror.

Realization of what he had done.

Then he fell.

*   *   *

Unconscious, he lay on the ground. Blackness folded his vision, but in his semi-blindness he could see. The grey light of the Mithraic shrine had morphed into the pale luminosity of a cave.

Cold, shivering, Jake lay silent.

"Sit up."

The voice speaking to him was familiar. It came from the shadows, and the figure that had spoken cast a silhouette shaped like a giant bird. Jake shuddered as fear swept through him, but memory told him if he failed to obey, he would never get out of here. His arms and legs were bound somehow.

The shadow drew nearer, urging him. "Sit up. You are not paralysed. She can't reach you here."

"Who are you?" Jake demanded, struggling to his knees.

"I am your father's father's father and all of their fathers before them."

Drums beat in the background and fires twisted in the distance, and the shadow of the shaman lowered itself to sit cross-legged opposite him. A flicker of recognition began to make its way into his clouded mind. This cave. It was the same cave he had found himself in, twenty odd years ago when he'd broken his legs.

"You are *Yehlh*?"

"I am what you call Raven."

"Where am I?"

"Where do you want to be?"

"Am I dead? Am I like her?" Jake's eyes darted frantically around to search for Sophia, but she was not here, nor was the shimmering mist—and he was glad.

The shadow behind the shaman heaved, its back puffed out like folded wings. Jake tried to look into the shaman's face but found he could discern no features. There was only long, silver-black hair framing a murky hole.

"She cannot enter my world—yet," the shaman said.

"What world is that?"

"The world of your past."

"But she will?"

"Not until you let her."

"I can't let her," Jake said.

"Why not? You wanted to be like her. Able to move between worlds."

"I've changed my mind. I love Angeline. I want to marry her. I want to have babies with her. How do I get out of here?"

"You can't."

"But I must. I have to!" Jake realized, suddenly, that he wasn't speaking aloud because his objection had risen to a hysterical pitch inside his head. All of this was taking place *inside* his head!

There had to be a way. There was always a way. When he was a boy, the shaman had given him an antidote to drink, which had returned him from the world of the spirits to that of his own. He demanded it now.

"You remember?" the shaman asked. "Then you will remember that I did not actually give you anything to drink."

Jake was frantic now. He had to wake up. He wasn't dead. He couldn't be. He had to find Angeline and tell her how he felt.

The scent of mushroom filled his nostrils, his eyes swam. Jake tore off the jewelled ring, ripped the robes of the Pater from his body. "I'm leaving. NOW!"

CHAPTER THIRTY-SEVEN

Chancellor shot out of the hall and into the passageway. She'd given him the slip. Again. His head jerked left and right, but there was no sign of Lalonde either. *Shit.* Was he too late? He tried to piece together what he'd cobbled of their plans, and came up with a single idea. The ritual would take place inside a mithraeum. But which one? He exhaled, forcing his heart to quieten. Asking Museum Security if one existed here was too great a risk. He must avoid interference at all cost.

But there must be one and he knew how to find it. He removed the ISD meter from his pocket and started to search every stairwell that led below the museum.

* * *

No sign of Saveriano. Was it possible she'd gone the wrong way? What was she thinking? It was highly likely that she'd made a wrong turn. She was no expert. Her hands patted the cold, damp walls; she nervously turned around. *What was that?* Cristine paused to listen, caught her breath; the shaft was deadly quiet, there were at least three tunnels radiating out from this spot, and nothing to tell her which direction to go. She had no flashlight, and the tight evening gown hugging her thighs and the high heels she sported were inappropriate for the situation in which she found herself now.

Something metallic pinged off her shoe as she walked into it blindly. With only the light from her Blackberry, she fumbled to increase the brightness. The bluish light left what turned out to be a bucket, dancing crazily like a nightclub strobe when she straightened to search for more clues. Light hit the floor and glanced off something shiny, opalescent, and she crouched to lift the object from where it lay in a damp spot—a string of beads ripped from Angeline's dress. Oh shit, she thought. What had happened? Her cowardly impulses threatened to stop her from moving on. Get a grip. *Get a grip!*

Her eyes wandered down. How odd. The shaft was not pitch dark as she had expected, and moonlight poured from a hole in the ceiling, pooling the floor with silver. How far had she wandered away from the museum core? If that was a ventilation hole and that was open sky up there, these passageways were much deeper and farther ranging than she had imagined.

Of course, that was a ventilation hole; fresh air was necessary for anyone who worked down here and for those who had dug the tunnels. As she approached, she tripped over something that looked like a snake, nearly screamed, squashed the urge, and then backed away to see a coil of rope on the floor. She laughed. She was getting hysterical, and was beginning to think that coming down here was more than a serious mistake.

Blinking to adjust to the dimness, she surveyed the blind gaps radiating out from where she stood. All of the openings were black and she walked cautiously, decided to take a chance by turning right. This passageway was blind too, but there was just a glimmer of orange light coming from around the next bend. She stopped to listen as sounds floated, muted, toward her ears.

Voices? She slipped quietly around the corner and saw where they were coming from, then flattened herself against the wall and melded into the shadows.

* * *

Celeste's eyes, in the dim light of the crypt, were brilliant. She raised one hand and snapped a digital image of Angeline's startled face, then she perched the camera on the thick corner of the plastic box and motioned with the revolver. "A little memento of this evening. Now, we are going to switch dresses."

279

She unbuttoned the front of her blouse, slid it to her waist and down past her hips. Under the skimpy waitress uniform she was wearing a white strapless bra. Not once did she let the gun slip as she tossed the black and white outfit at Angeline, saturating the tepid air with the scent of perfume and tobacco. Angeline threw it to the ground in disgust.

"Now you. Give me the gown."

She was beginning to see Celeste's recent life in sharp focus, how Saveriano must have paid for her surgery, which was why she was a waitress or an assistant or whatever else Saveriano wanted her to be. She owed her big-time.

"The dress. Give me that beautiful gown!"

"It's covered in dirt. And it won't fit you. It's too short." Angeline gritted her teeth, knowing her next remark might just make the psycho witch squeeze the trigger. "You're too big."

The gun moved up several inches in the direction of Angeline's head, and Celeste's left hand joined her right, clasping together while her finger jumped to the trigger. "You are nothing but a spoiled bitch."

Ignoring the insult, Angeline struggled with the zipper. "All right, you want to know what it feels like to be me? Why should I deny you that? You've spent your entire life envying women like me."

Celeste glared at her. "Stop talking and take off the dress!"

She was trying to, but the zipper was awkward. Finally, in frustration, Celeste stepped over, spun Angeline by the forearm and undid the gown for her, forcing the shapely beaded net chiffon to slither off Angeline's shoulders to the ground.

"Put on the waitress uniform."

As Angeline did so, Celeste took the gown and stepped into it, drawing it up over her hips and glided one arm after the other through the straps, keeping the gun and her eyes trained on her captive while struggling to fasten the dress one-handed.

God, look at her in this ridiculous waitress thing. It looked like something out of the 1950s. The blouse had puffy sleeves with buttons down the front and the smell of cigarette smoke intermingled with sharp perfume permeated the entire ensemble. Angeline held her breath, then released it, and watched her nemesis struggling with the gown. By some miracle it zipped, but fitted way too tight, causing some of the pearls and beads to pop off.

"Toss me your purse."

"Chancellor didn't put you up to this, did he?" Angeline said, tossing the beaded handbag. "You're even more insane than he is." Her eyes dropped to the waitress uniform. "Why are you doing this?"

Celeste unclasped Angeline's purse and ordered her to hold her hands out while she flipped the beaded bag inside out, expelling a compact, eyeliner, mascara, lipstick, and comb. She was ordered to sit on an overturned bucket, and then holding the gun to Angeline's temple with one hand, Celeste proceeded with the other to draw on Angeline's face with the black liquid eyeliner.

What was the demented witch up to? The sensation half-tickled, half hurt. She covered the tip of Angeline's nose in black, then drew whiskers radiating out over her cheeks. She tossed the liner away and took up the lipstick, but it was a pale coppery pink to match the black and copper beaded net chiffon, not what the witch had in mind.

Celeste shoved her hand into the apron pocket of the waitress uniform and withdrew a bright red tube of lipstick—her own shade—then painted it over Angeline's lips in bold, thick strokes before stepping back to admire her handiwork.

Angeline writhed from behind the painted mask. Celeste strutted about, waving the revolver slightly from side to side, then stopped, stared hard for a moment before one by one withdrawing the pins holding Angeline's hair in its classy roll, allowing the sleek waves to tumble to her shoulders.

"What's the point in doing this, if there's no one to see it? Jake isn't here."

"This isn't about Jake. This is about you and me. Jake is with Sophia. He's going someplace you can't follow. Well, you can, but . . . ." She laughed. "I prefer you take the long way there."

"What do you mean?"

A smirk returned to Celeste's face.

Witch. Demented, perverted, psycho witch. What was she planning to do to her? Only now did Angeline notice that there were tiles patched against the walls of this crypt, and only now did their significance strike her because she knew exactly what was behind those tiles.

Tombs.

Angeline plucked the silver compact from where Celeste had dropped it and with swift and malicious desperation pitched it fiercely at her face and ran. She left the crypt and scooted down the first tunnel, not stopping to see if she was followed. The compact was hard—made of solid silver, an heirloom from her grandmother—but not hard enough to knock the bitch senseless. Her only hope was to hide in the dark and remain perfectly silent, then hopefully . . . .

A shriek almost left her mouth as someone grabbed her arm.

"It's okay, Angeline. It's only me."

Angeline jerked her eyes up to see Cristine's face illuminated by the light of her Blackberry. "Thank God. How did you find me?"

"I followed Chancellor down here. He's looking for Saveriano and Jake. Then I heard voices. Susanne's and yours. And Susanne did not sound nice, so I kept quiet until I could figure out how to help you. Guess you didn't need me."

"She's insane, Cristine. We've got to get out of here. She threatened to wall me up in one of those vertical tombs. And she painted me up like some kind of freak."

The journalist aimed the light of her Blackberry on Angeline's face, shook her head in wonder, and then handed her a wet wipe from her purse to scrub off the makeup. Dark or not, it was humiliating to be painted up like a sex kitten.

"What about Jake? And Saveriano?"

"We can't do anything without help."

Cristine fiddled with her cell phone. "I'll call the police." She started to punch in 911 but an icon indicating no service appeared. "Shit. Must be because we're in a tunnel."

Footsteps were running down a side passage, and Angeline grabbed the journalist by the arm and started to run the opposite way. They ducked into a crypt and to her horror she saw that it was the crypt with the ventilation hole. No way out, except up. Or back the way they came—and probably smack into Celeste.

"Let's go," Angeline whispered.

"Wait."

"No time." Angeline's voice was a desperate wail. Celeste had a loaded gun.

"What's that on the floor?" Cristine stared at the etching on the ground, shone the light from her Blackberry onto the pendant around her neck. "Does it look like this?"

It looked exactly like the Chaos star around her neck. "What are you doing with that?"

Celeste appeared at the door of the crypt and fired. The shot went wide and Cristine seized Angeline by the wrist and hauled her onto the center of the star.

"What are you doing?" she whispered. "We're sitting targets now."

"No. Trust me. We're not."

Celeste walked up to them and fired at point blank range, all the while the journalist mumbled some strange incantation, making certain that she and Angeline were solidly inside the dark-filled circle, clear of the eight radiating arrows. The bullet ricocheted as though it had hit Kevlar or bulletproof glass. Enraged, she fired again and again, but each time the bullets went flying as they struck the invisible barricade. Eventually, the clip emptied and Celeste was out of ammunition. She had to reload.

Two against one, Angeline thought. Celeste might be strong, crazed by adrenalin and rage, but if even one of them escaped, they had a chance. Taking advantage of the break in the gunfire, she edged to the rear of the star and slid her right hand along her calf to her ankle. As Celeste slammed in the fresh clip, Angeline shucked the stiletto from her foot, and with one sharp swing, lunging forward at a dead run, she slammed the spike heel at

Celeste's eye. Attuned to the intent, Celeste ducked, and the heel drove into her brow, knocking her senseless.

Stripping off the other shoe, Angeline clasped it by the strap and ran, Cristine close behind her. Down the dark passage until she thought her heart would give out, she ducked into a recess, stood perfectly still, listening to the rasp of her own breathing, then silence. The hiss of breathing came again, but this time she knew it wasn't her own. *That had better be Cristine*, she thought, *'cause I'm just about done.* She had no weapon. Except a single shoe. She held her breath, arm raised, heel pointed into the air.

A scent drifted toward her. Something familiar. But not cigarette smoke. *Mushrooms!*

Her heart started racing, she had to get out of here; she couldn't stand it anymore. She had to run. She bolted down the first turn she could feel with her hands, but someone grabbed her around the waist from behind. Angeline opened her mouth to scream and a hand cupped it.

"Angeline. It's me. Jake."

Angeline swung around and collapsed into his arms. His hands ran over her body, feeling the crepe of the maid uniform. "Why are you wearing this? I thought you were Celeste at first. That's why I had to sneak up on you."

"Long story. It has to wait. So you know? You know that Susanne is Celeste?"

He nodded, took her hand and pulled her back into his arms. "Cristine told me earlier today." He kissed her until she thought she would melt, and even though his face was a blank in the darkness, everything about him was familiar to her touch. She ran her fingers along the side of his face, reached up to kiss him again and again.

"Speaking of the devil. Where is she? She was right behind me." Angeline turned to look.

"I'm here," the journalist said out of the dark.

Angeline thrust out a hand to find her shoulder. "Thank God. And thanks again for showing up when you did. You have yet to explain what happened back there, but it'll have to wait. We've got to get out of here."

"Where's Chancellor? Have you seen him?" Cristine asked.

"He went after Saveriano."

Jake was silent. It was like the gravity of his actions only hit him now, at the mention of Chancellor's name. Angeline wanted an explanation but he started walking rapidly and they followed. His gait was faster than she liked. "Not so fast . . . . I've got no shoes on . . . can't keep up."

Her objection was cut short. His footsteps were inaudible now. Oh, God, she thought. *Don't leave us!* She ran as quickly as her bare feet would let her.

* * *

The success of Neo-shamanism depended upon using belief as a tool to create an alternate reality, one that benefited the practitioner, then to convince those around them that the invented reality was the true one. Different forms of Neo-shamanism adopted different sigils like the Chaos star or idols like the Black Goddess. Those precepts were adopted from traditional shamanism, and that was how Jake was able to break the bond that held him in the Spirit World. His desire to leave was so strong, and his belief in his future so tangible that Sophia could not keep him.

Jake slowed his pace as Angeline's desperation caught up to him. He reached backward and seized her hand and drew her close. The journalist was not far behind and bumped into Angeline's back. "All accounted for?" he asked in a low voice.

He felt Angeline's body move as she nodded. He wanted her and Cristine out of this maze and back upstairs in the safety of the museum, but he had no time to be their guide and if he knew Angeline, she would never let him return to the mithraeum alone. But if he didn't return, all hell could break loose.

It suddenly dawned on Jake what Sophia was planning. If Chancellor participated in the marriage rite, Sophia could still get what she wanted. And she wanted him—Jake Lalonde, not Thomas Chancellor. No wonder she hadn't raised a fuss when he'd broken her spell and made a quick exit. He would rather live a life of limited mortality with Angeline, than a life everlasting with a creature whose sole purpose was to alter people's beliefs. Besides, the truth was, he didn't believe and without absolute belief, what Sophia proposed had failed.

"Jake," Angeline said. "What are you waiting for? Let's get out of here."

"I can't. Not yet. Can you two find your way out of here alone?"

"No. Or I would have left this deathtrap of a maze a long time ago."

"Then you'll have to come with me. Both of you."

"Where are we going?"

He turned to face her, though he couldn't really see her in the thick darkness until the journalist's Blackberry flashed on and its light illuminated their faces just enough for him to see their eyes. "I have to stop Sophia from performing the ritual with Chancellor."

"Why? He believes in that crap. Those two deserve each other."

Jake reached past Angeline to Cristine and lifted the pendant of the Chaos star from her chest. "Have you ever seen this symbol anywhere else?" he asked.

"Twice," Angeline said. "On the floor in that crypt back there, and on a card that belonged to Chancellor. Why?"

He turned to Cristine, eyes asking the same question, wondering what her role in this was.

"I swear to God, Jake. To me, this stuff is just meat for a story."

He frowned suspiciously at her, but he had no time to mistrust her. "Either of you ever heard of retrochronal magic?"

The journalist shook her head, and Jake believed her. He glanced at Angeline's silhouette and she gulped, nodding. Her voice came out in a soft whisper. "I saw a mention of it in one of your books."

"It's a form of Chaos magic that can change past events. Sophia was not happy that I chose you, Angeline, over her. She does not have the power to change my mind, but she does have the power to change the events of the past. To punish me, she'll perform the marriage ritual using Chancellor and make it so that you and I never meet."

CHAPTER THIRTY-EIGHT

Her head ached fiercely. She opened her eyes, blinking up at the hole in the ceiling of the crypt above her head. That much she had gotten right. She was inside a cavern, a crypt of some sort. Her vision blurred, and something hot, wet, trickled down her brow and into her eye, dripping off her lashes as she snapped them shut, and then open.

Blood. It came away on her fingertips glistening. The copper scent of it disturbed her. She stared at her strange surroundings, the moon pouring in from the opening overhead and down onto a starlike symbol. Off to the side was the gleam of gunmetal, and oddly, a single, beaded, stiletto shoe.

A shot of adrenalin kick-started her body into action and she rose from where she lay propped on her elbows on the dusty floor. Had she shot someone?

She ran her hands over her throbbing head to check for more injuries and was surprised to find that her hair was short, chin length in fact, and when she pulled it toward her eyes she saw that it was quite dark in the moonlight. Wasn't her hair golden blonde? When had she coloured it?

Her mind was racing now. She struggled to her feet, briefly aware that she was dressed in a beaded gown that was way too tight. Was she in hell?

She picked up the gun and stared at it, a Smith and Wesson LadySmith .38. How did she know that? She raised her eyes and stared at the strange eight-arrowed star carved into the ground, stared at the stiletto shoe that clearly wasn't her own. She was already wearing black high-heeled sandals.

None of this tweaked a memory.

She walked out of the crypt and into a tunnel, saw that there were multiple openings radiating out from where she stood. A maze.

Now, that rang a bell.

Her arms and legs moved at will. She licked her dry lips and knew if there had been someone to speak to she would most certainly be able to talk. What was her name? She frowned.

Who am I?

She patted herself physically, with her hands, to reassure herself that she was alive. She could feel her fingertips; hear the sound of her heels clicking on the floor. And then there was that .38 LadySmith that she still clasped in her right hand. Who was she going to use it on? Had she succeeded?

Suddenly it came to her. She had come here to kill herself. This was a catacomb.

Oh God, am I dead?

Her skin burned. She dropped the gun and listened to the metallic clatter that in the silence would have woken the dead. She was among the dead. That's why she had opened her eyes to a crypt: a crypt with no bodies, but a Chaos star.

How did she know that?

Her breathing strained against the tight dress and a few beads popped off as she inhaled deeply. The maze was familiar; she had seen it the last time she had died.

Where was she?

Purgatory?

Trapped, unable to find her way out, she threw her hands up to her face only to find that there were no bandages. Not a nightmare then, not a memory—and maybe, not dead.

She ran her hands over the walls. The passages seemed familiar even though she had no light. But when she first entered this place, she did have a light. Where was it? A few things were coming back to her now.

This was a maze of tunnels. It was familiar because she had died once before—in a hospital. She was burned from head to foot. Ten minutes she was gone. And this was what she saw—tunnels, black tunnels and lights burning at the end of every passage she took. But she was trapped, unable to return to the living or escape to the Afterworld. She did not see anyone that she knew. All the stories about meeting dead friends and relatives—all lies. Heaven was not open to just anyone. The newly arrived had to find their way through the maze first.

Her chest heaved. Blackness engulfed her. The souls could not be seen—only felt—but not like normal touch. It was more like having a sixth sense. Intuition. She could feel their presence, but not see them or touch them. Oddly enough she could hear them. Right now, she could feel them in her chest, punching in and out trying to use her body as a pathway back to life. So, she *wasn't* dead or she wouldn't be able to feel this. She knew because she had experienced this before. *She* had been the soul punching her way back through the body of one of the living. Someone in the operating room, a face vivid to her now. Dark hair streaked with attractive highlights of grey. The OR swirling in shades of red, white and black.

One single name came to her—Sophia.

And she knew the name wasn't her own. Everything was returning to her now. Jake Lalonde, Angeline Lisbon, Thomas Chancellor, that meddling journalist, Cristine Kletter: she had to stop them.

She doubled over in an agony of pain as something inside her tried to punch its way out of her chest. She held her breath, tucked in her muscles and straightened her torso, rigid and firm. Vertigo assailed her—a sensation of falling like a car had just tipped over the summit of a roller coaster ride—sending her heart into her mouth.

Then she dropped straight down.

Anger, despair, sorrow overwhelmed her, but these were not *her* emotions. They belonged to the Others. She had long since demolished any semblance of emotion.

This time, it was *they* who were trapped—asking, begging for her help to get them out—stuck between dimensions, neither here nor there.

She had no desire to re-enter that world. She possessed none of the power that Sophia had to walk the two planes. If she died again, she would be trapped just like the pitiful beings now cursing her for abandoning them.

CHAPTER THIRTY-NINE

They entered the shaft where a strange light burned. Jake picked up the pace with Angeline and Cristine behind him, and stepped into the temple. The place was ablaze with candles. Nothing inside the mithraeum seemed to matter except for the two people at the far end where the altar had been obscured by the statue of the Black Goddess. How had it come to be here? How could it possibly have been transported from its display site inside the Octagonal Hall to the depths of this subterranean shrine in a matter of minutes?

Stay where you are. You cannot enter. Not until you consent to the trial.

Sophia's voice echoed in his mind. Her terrible beauty was inestimable.

His head throbbed; his hands tingled. A painful thumping escalated inside his chest. His hands perspired, tongue thick in the vacuity of his mouth; he swallowed, squashed his terror, and shot a glance at Angeline, whose eyes were peeled to the scene before them.

In this surreal context, the statue stood almost the height of the vaulted ceiling, dwarfing the couple that stood beneath it. Prickles of ice rolled up his spine. The figure's pendulous breasts, swollen belly and bulging hips seemed to morph from fertile woman, to ambiguous youth, to obvious hag. A rainbowed shimmering in the air oscillated between the statue and the shadows of Chancellor and Sophia.

"Holy mother of—" Cristine suddenly saw the couple in their strange costumes, and Jake cut her off as he whirled, accidentally cuffing her with his shoulder.

She touched a hand to her cheek where his jacket had scraped the skin and demanded to know what the hell Chancellor and Saveriano were doing.

Angeline pushed through the doorway. "We have to stop this, Jake." She shoved past him but when she made a step down the aisle something unseen struck her in the face, knocking her backwards.

Chancellor turned around at the commotion behind him. "Don't come any closer," he said. "You can't or you'll be hurt. That is an invisible electric field. She won't speak to you now."

She was Sophia, and she looked incredibly beautiful, but that didn't bring Jake any closer to changing his mind.

Sophia moistened her lips, tossed her silver streaked hair as if she knew exactly what her presence did to him.

Look at what you have refused, Jake. The Black Goddess, the triple goddess. The Nymph, the Mother, the Crone. You see her in all her splendour now.

He realized with a jerk, that she had not spoken aloud. That the only one who could hear her was himself. Not even Chancellor was aware that she had sent this missive to him; his face had re-settled into its serious demeanour as though no one else mattered. A force beyond his control was drawing him to her and Jake was helpless against her will.

The nebulous morphing of shapes continued, as the Mother became the Crone, then once more transmuted into the Nymph. Sophia's red gown had transformed, her whole being had changed and she was young and firm, topless with hips draped in a diaphanous wrapped skirt, and on her head was a diadem and a veil. Beneath the veil and the skirt, her hair and skin gleamed like they were wet, and in her hands were a flaming torch and lamp.

"The creator and destroyer of all life," a voice said from behind them.

Jake's entire body suddenly felt like jelly. Celeste appeared at the temple door. "She is at the heart of all creative process. She is wisdom and death." She stepped between him and Angeline in a torn, beaded gown, and forced a finger out in front of her, snapping it back as the electric field repelled it.

"How do we shut down this barrier?" Jake demanded, grabbing Celeste by the arm. Celeste raised her gun to Jake's head. "We don't."

Angeline, still holding her single stiletto in her right hand, slammed the spike heel into Celeste's wrist causing her to drop the gun, even as a shot fired and ricocheted off the floor, then the walls, before bouncing off the electric barrier and tumbling to the ground.

"That was supposed to be you," Celeste said, angrily pointing to Chancellor.

Angeline retrieved the gun and removed the clip and shoved both into the apron of the waitress uniform she wore.

Celeste's scowl smoothed into a smile when she fixed her gaze to the scene in front of them. "There is nothing you can do. Even I can't stop it now."

All eyes bent to the stage as they watched helplessly unable to shatter the barrier, but able to see and hear every aspect of the ceremony. Chancellor was garbed in the costume of the Pater. On his head was the Phrygian cap, in his left hand was the sickle of Saturn and in the right were the staff and the ring. He stood before the seminude goddess, the globes of her white breasts reflecting the light from the torch and lamp. She set these down on the ground by the goddess's feet and began to speak. He recited after her:

"I come to you under the protection of the planet Venus. I offer you the sacred promise *iunctio dextrarum.*" Chancellor rammed the sharp base of the staff into the ground and offered his right hand as a pledge of fidelity and alliance. "Behold Nymphus, hail Nymphus. *Aide Nymphus.*"

Sophia began to sing.

When she was done, she went to the feet of the sculpture and raised a stone bowl. Every muscle in Jake's body trembled, strained to find a way to break through the charged field in order to stop Chancellor from killing himself. He had no doubt that the bowl was filled with a potion, and that the potion was brewed from the Death Cap. He recognized the smell.

Angeline's hand went to his arm and he could feel her nails dig into the cloth of his jacket.

"She's going to kill him."

"Chancellor!" Jake shouted. "Don't do it. If you drink that, you will die!"

The Interpol agent's eyes remained fixed on the bowl. He had an almost maniacal expression on his face. He took the bowl in his right hand, the jewelled ring of the Pater gleaming on his finger as the brew touched his lips and he swallowed it all. Jake lunged through the electrified barrier but the pain was so intense that he was thrown backwards into Angeline, Cristine and Celeste. He got up, reaching for the women to help them to their feet, mumbling apologies, but still frantic to stop Chancellor.

"It's too late," Celeste said, crawling to her feet. "Now, see the Crone in all her awful splendour. A woman who outlives her husband has used up his life force."

Jake realized that Celeste, or Susanne, if that was what she was calling herself now, had witnessed this ritual before, had helped Sophia search for her mate, watched her kill them one at a time when they failed to survive the test. What would happen to Chancellor? Was Chancellor the one? He shut his eyes in horror as Sophia's youthful beauty deteriorated before their eyes; her shoulders stooped and her spine twisted like a crooked tree, her face sagged, her skin withered like a dried prune, her nails grew yellow and curled, just like her teeth.

"He's making a mistake," Angeline whispered, trembling by his side.

Jake inhaled slowly. "No. He's making a choice."

Chancellor's body lay cloaked in the folds of the Pater's robes. He didn't move. The staff and the sickle of Saturn lay fallen nearby, the Phrygian cap askew. The ring had slipped off his finger. The Crone knelt by the body. She lifted the staff and drew a Chaosphere around the body. The sigil was similar to the Chaos star, but it lacked the black center and the direction of the arrows was reversed. The center of Chaos was Chancellor's body, now shaped like an X, with eight arrows radiating toward his core.

Jake turned and saw Celeste still smiling. Her last comment was profoundly unsettling. Of the three images, the Crone was the true rendition of power. And if she had her way, his life would be changed forever.

Angeline was the first one to run. She charged down the aisle between the benches leading to the altar, the space, which now served as the seat of the Black Goddess.

The electrified field was down. A shimmering mist swirled, enveloping the feet of the statue and the body of Chancellor.

"Tom!" Angeline shouted, tears coursing down her cheeks.

The rest of them reached the body around the same time. Sophia was gone and so was the multicoloured mist.

"Chancellor!" Jake shook him.

"He's dead," Celeste said. "Just like Vincent Carpello."

* * *

Angeline glanced around the shrine, head spinning. The stone statue had stopped its preternatural, nebulous transfigurations. She did not believe a single thing that had happened here tonight. It was all incredibly insane.

Jake had a strange look on his face. He came to her, no longer concerned about Celeste or Cristine or even Chancellor. The look on his face was not concern over the whereabouts of Sophia either. She recognized that look. It was the look of utter peril he had when something life-changing was about to happen.

Angeline clasped her hands to her mouth and slowly breathed. "I know," she said. "We're gong to have a hell of a time explaining what just happened here. The authorities are going to come after you Jake. They'll think you killed Chancellor. And maybe even Sophia. And God only knows what happened to Sophia—or even what she is. I don't like the way this feels. Like we've done this before."

Jake took Angeline by both hands and lifted her until she stood with him, face to face. "I love you. Don't ever forget that," he said.

"I know you do." She paused. The look on his face was indescribable. It was the kind of look you saw on the face of someone who was terminally ill. "What's the matter, Jake?"

"Nothing. I want to marry you. Now."

"Now?"

"Yes, now. As soon as we get out of here and all of this is cleaned up."

"But Chancellor's body. What will we do with it? What will we tell the police?"

Angeline felt someone pinch her arm. "What body?" Cristine said.

Everyone who remained in the temple turned to look. Where Chancellor had been lying, there was now just a puddle of folded clothing. She lifted the robe and tossed it aside, revealing a dark circle in the middle of the inverted arrows.

"Let's get out of here," Jake said. He motioned for Cristine to head for the entrance, and then looked for Celeste. "Where is that split-brained witch?"

Angeline whirled to face the entrance. It was a wide gap, but no Celeste. She wasn't anywhere in the mithraeum for they had searched every possible crack and crevice.

"She stole the body?" Angeline asked. "Why would she do that?"

Jake shrugged. "Didn't you see anything, Cristine?"

The journalist shrugged. "Sorry, I was busy making notes for my article."

Of course, back to that.

Angeline's eyes raked in the walls of the temple, finally landing on the floor at the foot of one of the benches. Something gleamed there, shiny and plastic.

"What's that?" he asked, following the direction of her stare.

She recognized it, went over and lifted it from the ground, and switched it on. An ISD meter. Chancellor must have brought it with him to search for Saveriano. Well, he had found her. Was he happy? Was this what he had expected?

She raised the infrasound device to chest-level and waved it in the air in the sign of a figure eight. It began to beep out a high-pitched shrill. She shot a brief look at Jake and Cristine but their foreheads were a mess of frowns.

Cristine's voice oscillated to a squeak, head flashing from side to side to see. "Oh my god, that's one of Chancellor's ghost-tracking gadgets, isn't it? He's here. Oh shit. He's here! She ran to the exit of the temple, shouting, "Come on, let's get out of this graveyard. This place is really beginning to creep me out!"

Angeline watched the journalist's back disappear through the gap. "She'll be back. She doesn't know her way out of here, and all she's got to light her way is that Blackberry."

Jake nodded and rose, although Angeline could see that something weighed heavily on his mind.

"Jake, what is it?" She seized his wrist and clasped both of her hands around his. "None of this was your fault."

"Promise me you won't forget me. Promise me."

"Why will I forget you? I'm not ever letting you out of my sight again."

He let out a pained laugh, shrugged. "Dammit, Angel. Why am I so impulsive? I should have never left Seattle. I should have ignored Vincent's invitation. None of this would have happened if I had stayed put. And now . . . now I have to think of a way to keep us connected. So we don't forget each other."

"I'll never forget you, Jake. Even when I'm dead. That I can promise. As for the rest of it, all of it would have happened. Vincent would have died; Interpol would have suspected you of his murder. Saveriano would have found a way to get to you. You can't alter the past."

His face suddenly changed. Fear, sadness, longing, regret, all reflected in a look of—of farewell?

"Jake, where are you going? Haven't you learned anything? You can't run away. We'll get out of this the regular way."

"There is nothing remotely regular or even rational about what happened here tonight." His head arched to take in the empty shrine.

"That's right," Angeline said, suddenly excited. "No bodies, no evidence. Let's get out of here and go home. We'll get married tomorrow. In a gondola in Venice. Do you still want to marry me?"

"More than anything in this universe."

"Then what are we waiting for?" She grabbed his hand and ran toward the exit, but the invisible electrified barrier had somehow been reset and as she struck it, the impact twisted her body, snapped her onto her side, causing her head to hit the ground, hard.

The last words she heard were: "Angel! Are you all right?"

*   *   *

Down on his knees at once, Jake leaned over Angeline, frantic. She wasn't moving, but a strong beat at her throat told him she was alive. Her head was turned to the side and when he raised her slightly, he could see blood. But not too much, thank God.

He raced down the aisle to the concealed cavity behind the altar where he knew there was an ewer of water. He unravelled his bowtie from around his throat and soaked it well, then returned to bathe the wound.

The abrasion was on her right temple, near the hairline. He washed it and saw that the injury was superficial. The odd thing, though, was its shape. When it healed, it would leave a slight scar.

Shaped like a raven.

Jake turned his eyes to the Chaosphere, the only proof of what had happened tonight. He racked his brains, but came up with nothing to reverse the ancient words. He was a neophyte. The years of knowing that his inherited memories were a doorway into the metaphysical had not prepared him for the reality or the skill of actual practice. He had no idea what to do. All he knew as he stared helplessly at the sigil—the reversed array of arrows piercing the open disc—was that they did not call this form of shamanic magic Chaos for nothing.

So, Sophia's will would come to pass. It was going to happen and he was powerless to change it. Jake tore the engagement ring out of his trouser pocket where he'd been carrying it for days, and shoved the diamond onto Angeline's third, lefthand finger.

"I love you, Angeline," he whispered. "More than life itself." He took the sickle that lay on the ground and cut a lock of her hair and shoved it into his pocket. Then he lifted her in his arms and walked to the exit, stuck a foot into the electrified field and saw that it was down. The hysterical beeping continued from the ISD meter where Angeline had dropped it to the floor when she fell, but Jake kept walking.

CHAPTER FORTY

The high pitched beeping of the ISD meter eventually brought Security down into the mithraeum beneath the Baths of Diocletian at the National Museum of Rome.

He could see them, but they could not see him. He tried to touch one of the officers, to explain that he was one of them, that he'd made a mistake—but his hand went through the man's uniform like magic dust. So this was it. His body and soul, enslaved. Desperate to know the truth, he had swallowed every last drop. Now what was to be? Was he hallucinating? Would they take him out of here? He stretched his eyes, but the shimmering stream that had wept out of the statue in a multicoloured, multicourse chaos was gone. His mind was numb and yet his desire was strong. The taste of poison persisted on his tongue and the smell of mould lingered. He had followed her to the sleep of death. And she had abandoned him.

He gazed up at the goddess, opened his mouth to scream but it was like a vice circled his throat. His hands flew up trying to force the attention of the museum personnel, but they heard nothing, saw nothing, only fiddled with the infrasound meter in agitated frustration, until one of the officers ejected its batteries.

The beeping ceased.

Desperation shrieked inside him. His thoughts remained lucid, a pointless link to an unreachable reality. He watched the officers exit the shrine, tried to follow, but an invisible barrier prevented his passing.

New men, workmen arrived in the doorway and began sealing the entrance with mortar and stone. He opened his mouth, a cry of frustration erupting to awaken the dead, his objections remaining unheard. One of the workers doubled up, nausea rose and a seemingly insurmountable pain forced him to vomit in front of his friends.

More pain, even as it exploded in the workman's gut.

Still he could not get out.

Panic, horror, a sudden acute dread . . . .

Then, he faded, staring, until nothing remained in his consciousness but the stars of Mithras.

EPILOGUE

June 14, 2004
San Juan Islands, WA

Jake shivered, though he was not cold, and released the clutch on his Bronco. Josie Davies, his passenger, turned to the sunny, sea swept beaches of Cedar Island outside her window.

What was the matter with him? It was only a nightmare. In the brilliant turquoise day, he could see that. But the memory raised the hackles on the nape of his neck.

"Dreams don't tell us anything," she said, measuring her words carefully. "They are manifestations of our fears and anxieties. You're anticipating seeing the petroglyphs; it's as simple as that."

"Do you believe in inherited memories?" he asked her.

Josie smiled, her mischievous eyes tilting at the corners like a tiger's. "I don't think so."

Her hair twisted in the breeze from the open window. She was the kind of woman you didn't dare cross. She did not forgive.

Jake was a professor from the University of Washington and Josie was a colleague who had joined his archaeology crew in the San Juan Islands for the summer. The crew had been working almost a month, not bothering the locals much. Then, yesterday, a New York developer had heard about the Raven's Pool and wanted to turn the islands into a theme park.

A windstorm last night had scattered twigs and leaves all over the road, and as Jake drove over a branch, it cracked and shot out the side. He swerved along the shoreline, passing a gnarly arbutus tree with thinly peeling orange bark that reminded him of onion skin. A grove of hemlock took its place, and left of him

303

a tongue of land jutted out into the sea. Above the tumble of sandstone, a lighthouse, red and white, chrome fixtures flashing in the sunlight, stood nestled in deep yellow grass.

A long ramp led from a twist in the road down to a wooden dock, and beneath it ferns, salal, and tall grass dwindled to yellow rock. The tide was out and wet sandstone textured with seaweed glistened in the sun. In the shallow bay, another ramp joined the dock to floating planks where colourful boats bobbed. Beyond that, the craggy peak of Lookout Island loomed sharp and green.

They rented a boat and rowed to the island. When they arrived, they climbed the steep hill to the cave, clicked on their flashlights and went inside.

Ovoid eyes stared down, and at the far end, dancing on the cave wall the tales of the Raven mocked him.

Rooted where he stood, Jake gazed at the etchings in stone. He had entered something forbidden. These images belonged to another time, another place: a time when the will of nature took precedence over that of men. Fresh air gusted from somewhere deep inside the hollows, and he reminded himself that this was just a cave.

His flashlight lapped, moving in a shaded dance. The shadows of a man in a Raven costume twisted on the walls, the ceiling, and the floor. Imagination? Perhaps. Or perhaps it was something more. Jake quivered, forced himself to relax, to accept the truth.

There was something wrong with him.

He had known it the moment he stepped inside the cave.

The beam poured onto the ground. They were there! The cobbles, those damn cobbles from his dreams, they were there. Five of them. Dark spaces, glittering round stones, the shadow of a manlike bird. Jake crouched down and touched one of the granite cobbles that had rolled up against the wall. He dipped his finger into the bowl-like depression to taste the remnants of the poison that he knew the shaman had prepared. The hell of it was that he *could* taste it. It tasted like cedar. Light spilled downward catching sparks of fool's gold in the bowl.

Letting the cobble glide to the ground, he rose.

The petroglyph on the wall where he now stood was familiar: the claws of a large hook-beaked bird digging into the breast of a smaller one, wings arced behind. A horrid feeling of repetition overwhelmed him as he studied the carving warily: the Eagle battling it out with the Raven, the prize, the Salmon Princess.

Jake thrust his hands inside his pockets to still their trembling. He pulled out a handful of silky black hair that he kept inside a plastic Ziploc bag.

He had found this strange artifact among his equipment, and for the life of him could not remember putting it there.

Josie said, "Okay, we've recorded everything we can today. It'll get dark soon. We'd better head back."

Jake nodded and they left the cave and rowed across the strait to their camp.

That night he sat alone in his tent with a Coleman lamp illuminating the papers that were scattered all about him. Paper work and more paper work. He stacked the sheets into a messy pile and returned them to his briefcase, before he opened his laptop to check his email.

He had been waiting to hear if the grad students he'd accepted were taking the department's offers. Two Yeses, one No. He was curious. Not that he cared if some highbrow Toronto girl turned him down, but still, he was curious as to her reasons.

Was accepted into Cambridge University in England, it said. *Well la-de-da*, he thought. *Too good for me, are you?* He looked at her name. Angeline Lisbon.

And the name sent a tremor of pain to his heart.

Acknowledgements

In the Mithraic Mysteries of ancient Rome, the Raven was a messenger of the god Mithras. Modern theories suggest that this cult, which was once thought to be exclusive to men, may have included women. When I conceived of the Black Goddess, the fourth novel in my Raven series became something of a ghost story.

The inspiration for the Black Goddess is a ghostly tale in itself. A character in fairytales, fables and mythologies, I adopted the triple form of the goddess from an anonymous essay I found online. Entitled *Baba Yaga—The Black Goddess*, the essay appears on a website created by Dr. Kathleen Jenks. She originally read the essay on a Slavic Pagan list, asked permission to link to it, and learned that the man who posted it obtained it from someone who took it from a site called the Dark Goddess list. When Dr. Jenks contacted her, she was put in touch with someone else who was thought to be the author. This person, too, turned out to be a false lead. Someone had copied the essay into an email and sent it to her. The trail stops there. Dr. Jenks could not track down the identity of the author. It was published on *Crones and Sages* on March 9, 2000, and to date, no one has come forward to claim authorship. But I would like to thank "Anonymous" for her inspiring essay.

The saga of archaeologists Jake Lalonde and Angeline Lisbon was originally a trilogy, but because of requests for more stories I wrote *Raven's Blood*. This novel would not exist without the dedication of my readers and so I would like to express my appreciation to them. As always, I am grateful to my husband as my first reader, my technical support, and my most honest critic.

About the Author

Deborah Cannon's love of the Pacific landscape, her work as an archaeologist and her fascination with mythology are what shapes her fiction. She is author of The Raven Chronicles, a series of anthropological thrillers with a supernatural bent, which began with THE RAVEN'S POOL, followed by WHITE RAVEN, then RAVENSTONE. RAVEN'S BLOOD is the fourth in the series. She has also written a young adult adventure, THE PIRATE VORTEX. Deborah lives in Ontario with her archaeologist husband and two Shih-poos.

Visit her pages on Facebook:
www.facebook.com/pages/Ravensworld/212730442126853
www.facebook.com/pages/The-Pirate-Vortex/171764512855

Novels by Deborah Cannon:

The Raven Chronicles Series:

Raven's Blood (Book 4)

When a colleague of Jake Lalonde and Angeline Lisbon is found dead amidst ghostly sightings and murderous cult activity, the clues lead to a Raven-worshipping goddess cult in the subterranean Mithraic temples of Rome.

Ravenstone (Book 3)

On the island kingdom of Tonga, a carving of a Raven replicated on Canada's west coast leads Jake Lalonde and Angeline Lisbon to his daughter, a pawn used to exact revenge for an insult committed by his ancestors.

White Raven (Book 2)

When Jake Lalonde and Angeline Lisbon visit a remote logging community of the Queen Charlotte Islands, the alleged home of his birth parents, they find people mysteriously missing, wildlife brutally butchered, and a village with something to hide.

The Raven's Pool (Book 1)

The serenity of the San Juan Islands is disrupted when a developer threatens to build a theme park atop a sacred Native burial, turning archaeologists Jake Lalonde and Angeline Lisbon into the targets of a 10,000-year-old feud between a Haida shaman and his chief.

www.facebook.com/pages/Ravensworld/212730442126853

Young Adult Adventure:
Elizabeth Latimer, Pirate Hunter Series

The Pirate Vortex (Book 1)

When teen fencing champ Elizabeth Latimer's mother mysteriously disappears during an underwater salvage operation, she finds herself in the pirate past, forced to rescue her pirate ancestors Jack Rackham and Anne Bonny from the clutches of the governor.

www.facebook.com/pages/The-Pirate-Vortex/171764512855